# PLAYING WITH FIRE

## KATE MEADER

Pocket Books

New York   London   Toronto   Sydney   New Delhi

Pocket Books
An Imprint of Simon & Schuster, Inc.
1230 Avenue of the Americas
New York, NY 10020

This book is a work of fiction. Any references to historical events, real people, or real places are used fictitiously. Other names, characters, places, and events are products of the author's imagination, and any resemblance to actual events or places or persons, living or dead, is entirely coincidental.

First Pocket Books paperback edition October 2015

POCKET and colophon are registered trademarks of Simon & Schuster, Inc.

For information about special discounts for bulk purchases, please contact Simon & Schuster Special Sales at 1-866-506-1949 or business@simonandschuster.com.

The Simon & Schuster Speakers Bureau can bring authors to your live event. For more information or to book an event contact the Simon & Schuster Speakers Bureau at 1-866-248-3049 or visit our website at www.simonspeakers.com.

Manufactured in the United States of America

10  9  8  7  6  5  4  3  2  1

ISBN 978-1-4767-8592-9
ISBN 978-1-4767-8595-0 (ebook)

*To the 3.4 percent.*

*Women of the Chicago Fire Department, rock on!*

# ACKNOWLEDGMENTS

Thanks to Captain Jerry Hughes of the Chicago Fire Department for answering all my questions; Julie James for her legal expertise; and Nicole Resciniti for helping me plot this bad boy. To my editors at Pocket Books, Elana Cohen and Lauren McKenna, your input and wisdom was incalculable, as always. And finally, to Jimmie, my sounding board and oh-so-patient hero, I couldn't do any of this without you.

# CHAPTER ONE

"So, America's Favorite Firefighter?"

Across the table in the farmer-chic restaurant Smith & Jones, Alex Dempsey blinked at her thirty-fourth date in ten months and pondered a suitable response. Perhaps the smartass retort, which she could manage in her sleep. Or the bitch-slap, which would be eminently more satisfying.

"I have good people on my PR payroll," she finally said with a deferential smile.

Ah, ye olde classic, the minimizer.

So it didn't feel like her, Alex Dempsey, kick-ass firefighter. *That* Alex could blitz a fifty-foot ladder propped against a burning building and haul a metric asston hose bundle up multiple flights of stairs. But that Alex's love life was less breathtaking fireworks and more damp squib. She had officially earned the title of Chicago's most successful serial first dater.

Something had to give.

Tonight she was unveiling Alex Dempsey 2.0 with a test-drive of a few new tools. A slinky dress that left little to the imagination. Smoky eyes that were more emo panda than sex kitten, along with a pair of inadvisable heels—inadvisable because she was already too tall at five ten. On the plus side, courtesy of an uncharacteristically successful bout with a hair iron, her usual rumpus of chocolate curls now knew who was boss.

She didn't crave excitement—she got that in her line of work. She just wanted someone who wasn't a complete dick and could stand up to her occasionally abrasive personality. All the men she had dated in the last year enjoyed the novelty of breaking bread with a female firefighter, but once the honeymoon was over—usually by dessert—doubts scudded like petulant storm clouds across their faces, the forecast always the same.

*How can I be the man if you're being the man?*

Tonight's ~~victim~~ opportunity was a Chicago police detective who she hoped had enough self-confidence to handle hers. In his off-time, he bashed a hockey puck around a rink with her brother Gage, which was what had led to this setup in the first place.

*Detective Michael Martinez, are you the one?*

"Remind me not to get on your bad side," date number thirty-four was saying, still stuck on the America's Favorite Firefighter thing. "Plenty of nights on the sofa in my future, right?"

No nights, if he didn't quit being such a jackass. But then, wasn't she a magnet for jackasses?

Five months ago, she had made headlines all over the country when she took the firefighter's equivalent of a chainsaw to the Lamborghini of one of Chicago's wealthiest and most influential men. Mega mogul and Trump wannabe Sam Cochrane had drunkenly crashed his car and miraculously not injured himself or others. When he wasn't extracted quickly enough, he leveled a chauvinistic, racist, and homophobic rant against Alex and her family.

Oh, she had extracted Cochrane from that car all right—through the large opening left by the sawed-off door. There was also the two-foot gash she'd carved (unnecessarily) into the roof.

Pretty.

Also pretty stupid. So not her finest moment, but anyone who messed with her family risked her wrath. Growing up Dempsey meant all other considerations fell by the wayside.

"Good thing someone filmed it," Michael continued. "Got the women and the gays on your side. Put the mayor in a difficult spot."

Yeah, yeah. Alex had escaped with her job, a rap on the wrist, and damp toes from her dip in the fifteen-minutes-of-fame pool. Now she saw no reason why that unfortunate incident should have any effect on her professional or love life.

Except that everyone kept bringing it up.

"You know how the news blows stuff out of proportion," she said, adding the half shrug Alex Dempsey 2.0 would use. That Alex was more dateable. More lovable. Less likely to use the Jaws of Life on the personal property of anyone who pissed her off.

She leaned in, a tip she had read today on HuffPo's Love & Sex section. Boobs out, smile wide, voice low. Being sexy was exhausting.

His gaze fell to her cleavage. Spectacular stuff, she knew, but rarely did the girls get this much air.

"Do you like the squash blossoms?" Alex asked with a drop to bedroom-husky as she tried to redirect the date.

"The what?" *Eyes still at nipple level. Possibly thinks* squash blossoms *is a euphemism for tits.*

She gestured to the dish of tempura-fried goodness between them. Chef Brady Smith, who was currently groping Gage on a regular basis, had sent it over with his compliments.

"Oh yeah, they're good." He shrugged, looking a little embarrassed. "These flashy places don't really do it for me. Overpriced food, undersized portions. Gimme a burger any day."

She laughed, feeling at ease for the first time tonight. New and improved Alex would have let her date choose where to eat, but Michael had told her to pick a place, and Brady was an awesome chef. "I know. Gage is a big foodie, so he's always dragging me to restaurants with stuff like veal cheeks and charred orange and—"

"Seaweed and shit."

"Yes!"

He chuckled and she joined in. Three days before the New Year and the restaurant was cheerfully festive with beautiful wreaths adorning the antique mirrors. It was also packed with Prius-driving, cigarette-pants-wearing, Wilco-ticket-stubs-in-the-pockets-of-their-ironic-bowling-shirts hipsters.

"Gage is all loved up with the chef," she whispered, to keep her traitor talk out of the hearing range of Brady's server spies, "so I thought it might be a good place, but . . ."

"Next time, we'll get a burger."

Next time? *Score!* But she needed to rein in her runaway thoughts. It ain't over till the gingerbread pudding has made an appearance.

His phone pinged—again—and his expression morphed to cop-serious. "Got to take this, sweets, back in a sec. You choose whatever you want off the menu."

*Gee, thanks, mister.*

He headed off toward the restrooms, and her heart sank a little. Had he designated a buddy to dial in for rescue at a certain point into the date? Like "call a friend," but in reverse?

Time for her own check-in. She conference texted her posse: Gage, who was on shift at Engine Company 6, where they both worked, and her friends/future sisters-in-law Darcy and Kinsey. Otherwise known as Team Get Alex Laid.

*He's left the table 2X in 10 mins. Either his gun's digging into his tiny bladder or he's on a "coke" break in the can.*

Five seconds later from her brother: *stop looking for faults.*

*He keeps staring at my tits.*

Darcy chimed in with: *That's what they're fucking for!*

Touché.

Next up on deck was Kinsey, who could usually be relied upon for a healthy jolt of common sense. *Bring out your inner sexpot. Suck on a straw.*

*Real subtle,* Alex texted back.

*Subtle does not lead to man-made orgasms!* Gage again.

Alex found it rather priceless how people channeled the love child of Yoda and Oprah the second they bagged a regular sex partner. But after twenty-six years on this planet, she wanted what they had with a heady desperation that sometimes left her breathless.

She wanted to be smugly in love.

The next buzz had a smile tugging her lips at the prospect of more oh-so-sage advice. But the new message wasn't from her best peeps.

Her pulse rate skyrocketed as it always did when she heard his name or saw him on TV or spent a single moment in his presence. Of course he had no idea how much he affected her. She planned to keep it that way.

*Try the quail,* the text said. *It's excellent.*

He was here. In the restaurant. Either that or he had surveillance trained on her, which, given her past behavior tainting the good name of the CFD, might not be so far-fetched. Another message came in.

*Check your six.*

If she ignored him, it would look like she cared, and yet the idea of turning her head because he issued an order was equally galling.

Deciding that following his "suggestion" sat with her better than letting him think his presence bothered her, she twisted her shoulders and met the raw blue gaze of Mayor Eli Cooper. He was seated alone in a booth near the back, paperwork and an iPad laid out before him, long fingers curled around a tumbler of scotch.

He didn't smile. She wouldn't have believed it if he did. There was something silkily predatory about him, like a lazy python lying in the sun ready to uncoil and strike at any moment. Before he straightened to his full six two, she just knew he would come to her table.

Hell and damn.

Watching him walk over, Alex mused that Eli Cooper was the sort of man who knew how to use his physicality. Beneath his handmade shirts and tailored suits, a street fighter hummed through every loose-limbed motion. But that impression did not extend to his face, which was structurally perfect. Skyscraper-high cheekbones. Superhero jaw. A mouth that should have a government warning. There were no signs of past trouble with a jealous husband or an abandoned girlfriend. No one had ever broken his nose. No one had busted his lip.

Strange, because her first instinct on seeing him was to roundhouse kick him into the next millennium.

"Alexandra," he drawled. It was never Alex with him, which everybody and their aunt called her, but her full name. Just another dig that ensured her XX chromosomes would not be forgotten.

"Mr. Mayor."

He sat without invitation. "How's your date going?"

"Fabulous. Probably won't appreciate a three-some, though."

The words were barely spoken, and she longed to bite them back. That well-worn smirk, like a stray comma at the corner of his full-lipped mouth, activated.

"No one would like to share you, I imagine, Alexandra. However, you're so difficult you'd probably need several CPD officers to handle you."

Passing over the fact he knew her date was Chicago blue, she gusted a bored sigh.

"Slow night on the campaign trail? I would think you'd want to get out there if your latest approval numbers are anything to go by." She tsked. "Less than two months to the election and you're hovering under forty percent."

"All that matters are the numbers on the night."

"Still, I'm sure you have babies to kiss, MILFs to ogle." Donor dicks to suck. "Don't let me stop you."

"Given your recent popularity, I should have you stump for me, but there's no telling what might come out of your mouth from one second to the next."

Alex raised her fruity Cab to her unpredictable mouth and took a ladylike sip instead of her usual gulp. Now would be a fabulous time for her date to reappear.

"You never fail to bring out the worst in me, Mr. Mayor."

"Oh, it doesn't take much to get you riled, Alexandra. All that passion looking for an outlet."

There he went again. *Alexandra.* But this time, it didn't feel like a dig. It felt like . . . a caress. She lowered her glass of wine to the distressed mahogany table and stared at it accusingly because that was just, well, *loco.*

Done blaming the alcohol for that ludicrous flight of fancy, she lifted her chin and thought she saw his gaze snap up as if he'd been looking at her chest. Not likely. Except to disapprove. Every fiber of Eli Cooper's exalted being disapproved of her, from his perfectly pedicured feet to his overly produced hair.

So the man was an exceptionally good-looking son of a bitch. The gods had been generous, giving him a strong brow beneath that wavy black hair. Ice-blue eyes that hinted at secrets and numerous ways of uncovering hers. A dimple, too. Not that she'd ever seen it up close because he had never smiled at her, not a real smile, anyway. But she'd seen it on TV, a sunshine pop in the hard plane of his cheek. Practically every woman in Chicago had a lady boner for him, even the ones who hated his politics. Put her in the latter camp—not the lady boner part, just the politics-hating.

"Feel free to call me Firefighter Dempsey or plain Dempsey. That seems more appropriate for a boss-employee relationship."

His brows rose. "You consider me your boss?"

"I consider you an asshole."

He laughed, a deep, rich bass that corkscrewed down her spine with a pleasurable thrill she resented. Fascinating how an essentially nice person like herself could turn nasty so suddenly, but then she always felt slightly unhinged around him.

"Ah, but you put it so much more colorfully before when you called me a *patriarchal woman-hating* asshole. In this very restaurant. Over there." He pointed to the booth where he'd been sitting. His regular table, she supposed.

Twice in the last six months she had crossed swords with Mayor Eli Cooper. The first time, he had made it clear that firefighting and breasts were incompatible. The second time he was pissed to all hell at her and she was woman enough to admit he might have had good reason. That foul-mouthed big shot with the Lamborghini? Only Mayor Cooper's preeminent donor, another guy who thought his dick had its own zip code. After her luxury car slice and dice, the mayor had summoned her to his townhouse in Lincoln Park—by text, which is why he now had her number—and proceeded to ream her ass. For a long time. The guy did not like Alex or her family or the CFD.

Goes both ways, Mr. Mayor. Alex did not like a man who had no respect for what she devoted her life to, day in, day out.

"My opinion of you hasn't changed," she gritted out. "Putting aside your caveman pronouncements about what women can and cannot do, during your reign of terror, you've managed to cut funding to libraries, drive city pensions to the brink of bankruptcy, and reduce social services to a fraction of what they were before. All so we can beautify the tourist traps of our fair city and fete George Lucas for the Star Wars museum."

Because a man like Eli Cooper was undoubtedly used to the blows from the opposition, her words had no discernible effect on his ice-compacted heart. "Hard decisions are made by people in charge every day. Someone in your profession should know that."

She imagined she heard a compliment in there, but her passion rolled right over it. "And don't think I've forgotten how you fired your press secretary for taking my side and almost ruined everything between her and my brother." Thank God Kinsey had come to her senses and returned to Chicago, though Luke had been ready to up sticks and move to California to be with her. Eli Cooper's megalomania had almost lost Alex a future sister-in-law *and* her brother.

"The course of true love never did run smooth," the mayor said quietly. "Firing Kinsey was the best thing I could have done. Made them face what's important. And I *still* haven't received that thank-you card."

"Is there anything you won't claim credit for?"

Eying her speculatively, he took a sip of his scotch, likely something expensive and triple-distilled from the tears of Scottish virgins. Everything about him screamed privilege, from his monogrammed cuff links to his Wall Street suspenders.

"I even paired off Gage with Brady. Perhaps I should add that to my campaign ads." He swiped a hand across an imaginary billboard. "Vote for Cooper, the Matchmaking Mayor."

She snorted. "Well, you can forget the Dempsey vote."

His steely stare penetrated to the blood boiling beneath her skin. "Oh, I know," he murmured. "In fact, you and your family seem to take great pleasure in doing what you can to make me look bad."

"Believe me, when I was cutting up Cochrane's car, you were the last thing on my mind."

"Exactly. You don't think."

She tamped down the growl fighting to escape her throat. *Do not engage.*

He flicked a glance over his shoulder. "I must say your date is taking an awfully long time. Perhaps he's a little intimidated by all this passion of yours and he'd rather risk a twisted ankle by escaping through the restroom window. Getting on your wrong side could be costly for any man."

Unavoidably, her gaze traveled toward the restrooms just as Detective Martinez appeared, ankles none the worse for wear. Praise Jesus.

"Looks like this one is brave enough to stick around and take me on, Eli."

*Shit.* She had called him by his first name.

The dimple did a jig.

"Beware of men who claim to be able to handle you, Alexandra. While I've always found our exchanges extremely provocative, I doubt others will be as entertained by you as I am."

"I'm not here for your entertainment." Covering a fake yawn with her hand, she picked up her phone. "I'm going to delete you from my contacts list. If you text me again because you're bored, I won't know who you are. As I was raised to never speak to strangers, it's unlikely we'll be chatting again."

The dimple quickstepped into a samba. "I'm in your contacts list?"

*Double shit,* another damning admission. So what if she'd kept his number from when he'd called to chew her out all those months ago and had even gone to the trouble of completing an entry in her contacts? Forewarned is forearmed.

Discombobulated by that dumb dimple, she turned the phone to him, grasping for the upper hand in this unnerving conversation. "There you are. BFT."

As he leaned in, the smokiness of the whiskey and something indefinably male struck her nostrils. Her stomach gave a treacherous flutter.

"Best Friend *Totes*?"

"Big. Fucking. Tool." Plastering on a saccharine grin, she added, "But I don't need a contacts list entry to remember that." She went ahead and deleted it, each tap more indignant—and gratifying—than the last.

"Want to know what I've called you in mine?"

Her heart rate spiked at the notion he had worked up an entry for her as well. "*Dying* over here."

He tipped the screen toward her to reveal "Splinter" in the contact name field.

*Splinter?*

"Short for Splinter in My Side. I was going to call you Thorn, but you're not worthy of being a thorn, Alexandra. You're a minor annoyance."

"Glad to hear it. Would hate to think you're wasting valuable mental real estate thinking about me and my family and all we do to make you look bad."

The detective arrived at the table, his expression curious. Eli—*no, Mr. Mayor*—uncoiled to a stand. Just running her eyes over all that slickness made her shiver, but neither could she help comparing his physique to that of her date. Eli Cooper had a couple inches in height on Michael and maybe, just maybe, slightly more girth on those biceps. She would think with all his fancy tailoring he could find a shirt that fit him properly instead of one that outlined his bull-like shoulder muscles so obscenely.

"Enjoy your meal, Alexandra. As I said, the quail is excellent." He nodded curtly at her date. "Detective Martinez."

As he walked off toward the restroom, three things stuck with her.

One, the jerk's personality did *not* improve on acquaintance.

Two, in under five minutes, he'd managed to sour the most promising date she'd had in months.

Three—and how she hated herself for even going there—those gray pinstripe pants shaped his ass really, really well.

• • •

In the mirror of the restroom at Smith & Jones, Eli Cooper took a long, assessing look. At thirty-six years old—the last four as leader of this great city— he should be seeing telltale streaks of gray by now, but his jet-black strands refused to show any sign of surrendering to the stress.

If only he could say the same thing for his sputtering reelection campaign.

Gripping the sink, he hauled in a deep breath. Was he ready for four more years? Chicago was buckling under crippling debt. Gang violence was at an all-time high. The municipal pension system was close to bankruptcy. Solutions were hard to come by—not even Caroline Jenkins, his most dogged opponent in the election, had a good answer to appease the police and firefighter unions on that.

Everyone felt they were entitled to something. A piece of the city. A piece of him.

Opponents and allies alike accused him of being overly passionate. Better that than apathetic. Eli couldn't stand apathy. And as someone who was passionate and disdainful of the apathetic, he really shouldn't be giving Alexandra Dempsey such a hard time.

He did enjoy getting her riled, though. But that did not mean he approved of her in any way. Eli's passion was always tempered by reason, unlike Alexandra, who had allowed a few drunken insults from that bigot Sam Cochrane to tip her from professionalism to certifiable insanity. But the citizenry had rallied to her, and Eli risked jeopardizing the upcoming election if he fired a woman for defending her gender, her family, and her fellow firefighters. So he'd let her stay.

Number-one lesson learned in his time as mayor: listen to the fucking voters.

But how he had longed to punish her and rein in that dangerous impulsivity of hers. A firm hand, splaying her across his knee, might teach her a thing or two about humility. He suppressed a groan. Keeping her in line would be a pleasure, but Christ Almighty, what a dangerous path for his mind to travel. Control was his watchword, and it was constantly tested in her presence. She was a singular woman who continually exhibited poor judgment.

Nowhere was it more obvious than with that form-fitting dress, her perfect olive-skinned breasts barely contained, the cleavage an announcement that she was on the market. Next, that pert mouth, just as saucy at rest as when she spoke. And don't get him started on those shamrock-green eyes, flashing her quick temper. The only domesticated part of her tonight was that long, sleek hair. Not her usual unkempt chestnut with those flame-red streaks like Christmas gift ribbons—this evening it looked like hair that took work. She had clearly primped and preened for this date with Michael Martinez, a man who was not worthy of her efforts.

Last year, the detective had applied to be on the mayor's security detail and, unsure as to why, Eli had taken an instant dislike to him. Eli's instincts were usually spot-on. Of course, it didn't hurt that his gut was currently being vindicated by Detective Martinez's exceptionally big mouth.

This was at least the third time the detective had left his date alone at the table. Very bad manners. Now he was on the phone in the hallway outside the restroom, loudly advising a colleague to follow up on a suspect interview before the night was through. The former lawyer in Eli winced as the name of the person of interest was bandied about with no care for privacy. Good Christ. Looked like Eli would be chatting with the police commissioner tomorrow.

With a shake of his head, Eli reached for the door, then pulled up short at the detective's next topic of conversation.

Alexandra Dempsey.

"Yeah, I thought she was a dyke, too." A pause as Martinez listened to whoever was on the other end of the line. "She was on TV last summer for cuttin' up that big shot's car. Got a temper on her for sure. You know what that means?"

Martinez's buddy must have answered correctly, because he laughed, the sound grating on Eli's last nerve.

"Aw, yeah. Probably scratches, as well. And, Jesus, her tits. She's poured into this dress. Great fucking body."

Eli watched as his knuckles popped chalk-white on the handle of the door. He had been right about that dress. He was invariably right about a lot of things.

"Dyke or not, she's up for it tonight. Keeps leaning

in to give me a good view, y'know. She's a bit chunky, but they're usually the most grateful ones."

More laughter. More volcanic heat making Eli dizzy with fury.

And still the man would not shut up. "Yeah, I'm already fantasizing about Alex Dempsey on her knees."

Eli threw open the door and stepped outside. Martinez looked up, colored, and ended the call with a muffled "Later."

"Mr. Mayor," he said with a nod as he edged with tentative steps back toward the dining room.

At the far end of the hallway, Tom Kincaid, the head of Eli's security detail, made eye contact, ready to intervene if necessary. Eli shook his head almost imperceptibly and turned his attention to Martinez once more.

"Detective Martinez, it's been far too long. Step into my office." He gave the restroom door a gentle push.

"I'm kind of busy," the detective said, rather churlishly.

Eli had a smile for every occasion and every little prick who got his goat. Now he dialed up his I-*know*-you-don't-want-to-fuck-with-me one. "Won't take more than a few minutes."

It took less. Moments later, Eli watched from a shaded position near the kitchen as Martinez trudged back to the table where the entrées he would be paying for—but not eating—had just been set down by a server. Typically contrary, Alexandra Dempsey had gone with the steak instead of Eli's recommendation of the quail.

Out of the corner of his eye, he saw a multimuscled

thug with ink-saturated skin settle in for the show. His snowy chef's jacket gleamed in sharp contrast to all those tattoos, fitting companions to the angry scar tissue on the right side of his face.

Brady Smith, chef/owner of Smith & Jones, a Marine brother, and Eli's sometime conscience, asked, "Whatcha doin'?"

"Just taking out the trash."

As much as Eli enjoyed being right, he didn't always enjoy the fruits of his accuracy. Even from his distant vantage point, he could intuit that Alexandra's melted moss green eyes had grown wide at whatever the detective was saying. Her shoulders drooped in disappointment. She fidgeted with her napkin. Quickly she stood, five feet ten inches of total irresponsibility, and holy shit, she had killer legs to complement those gorgeous breasts. Well shaped, golden brown, a mile past eternity.

She placed her hand on Martinez's arm, clearly expecting a signal that the date had gone well but its premature termination couldn't be helped. So when he practically recoiled in horror at the slight incline of her head, her shock was palpable. It rippled through the room, hitting Eli like a toxic wave.

Brady grunted his disapproval beside him.

"Trust me when I say this was for the best," Eli muttered. "And not a word to your boyfriend."

"Ain't mah bo-friend." When Brady got agitated, or uttered anything close to an untruth, his accent tended to revert to its Bayou origins. He would make a terrible politician.

"Whatever gets you through the night. Oh, wait, that would be your boyfriend."

"Fuck you," was Eli's reward, but he had already checked out of the conversation because Martinez was hightailing it to the exit like he really did have an urgent crime to solve. Bravo, Detective.

Eli stilled, his heart poised on a cliff, wondering what would come next. A trip to the restroom to compose herself? A sixty-second wait for her dud date to be on his way before she made a similar move? Maybe she would seek Eli out, ask if she could join him.

*Not.* Of all the possibilities, that was the least likely, but strangely the most pleasurable result that could occur here. She was entertaining, he'd give her that.

The impossible-to-predict Alexandra Dempsey did none of those things. Instead, she shook her head ruefully and . . . laughed. A joyous, passionate, *inappropriate* laugh that drew all eyes in the vicinity and a look of concern from her server.

Then she sat, filled her glass of Cabernet to the rim, and chugged.

All the way down.

Just as he thought. This maddening woman couldn't help but attract the attention of every person in her magnetic orbit. If it wasn't her second-skin dress or her troublesome breasts, it was her terrible taste in men. She was a woman of incredibly poor judgment.

And she needed saving from herself.

# CHAPTER TWO

Damn, she was one hot, hungry bitch.

Ten o'clock on New Year's Day, and the fire gave off enough heat to make Alex forget it was negative freeze-her-nipples on the thermometer. Perched on the balls of her feet, she bunched her calf muscles and tightened her fingers on the mask she had yet to don. Do it too early and you risk claustrophobia. Too late and you waste precious seconds, not to mention pissing off your platoon. All men who were looking for any excuse to label her as weak. Inadequate.

Female.

From the second-floor windows of the Drake Hotel on Walton, a few gilded steps from Michigan Avenue, greedy flames licked the glass-jagged edges. Nine engines and trucks from firehouses far and wide were already on site. Well-heeled guests and revelers stood around, most appearing dazed, several receiving attention for smoke inhalation from EMTs. Alex's crew, Engine Company 6, ancestral seat of the Firefightin' Dempseys, had been last to arrive, a supplementary measure, because hotel fires could get out of control quickly.

But probably not this one. Three of the engines were involved in fire suppression, putting wet stuff on the red stuff, which meant rescue was done and dusted. The water generally only came out after the grabs were complete. Disappointment chilled her gut. Coming up on her one-year anniversary as a candidate firefighter, a rookie, and still no rescues to call her own. Pulling Sam Cochrane from that car last summer didn't count.

Not that a certain quota of rescues was a requirement to pass from candidate to full-fledged firefighter. No, Goal No. 1 on every shift was to do her job the best she could and bring herself and her platoon home safe. (Goal No. 2 was to not end up on YouTube.) But all her foster brothers were in the service, filling her dad's giant work boots—Wyatt, Luke, and Beck older, Gage her baby bro by fourteen months— and each of them had numerous grabs from infernos and mangled car wrecks on their heroic résumés. As an adoptee instead of a foster kid, Alex was the only one of her sibs with "Dempsey" as her legal last name. A double-edged sword perhaps, as she acutely felt both a special sense of belonging and the burden of carrying on the Dempsey family legacy of service and heroism. To say she felt competitive might have been the under-freaking-statement of the century.

Her captain, Matt "Venti" Ventimiglia, strode back from Incident Command, a big truck parked in the middle of the street.

"Fox, Dempsey, they need another round of civilian checks on the first floor. Meet the lieutenant from fifty-nine at the southeast entrance."

Alex squinted at the sight over Venti's shoulder. Battalion chief Lonny Morgan was over at IC talking to CFD's Commissioner Laurence Freeman, better known to the Dempseys as Uncle Larry, her dad's best pal and godfather to them all. Big fire, sure, but what the hell was Larry doing here?

"Dempsey, you waitin' on a special invitation from the Commish?" Venti barked, because her curiosity had frozen her to the spot.

"No, Cap. On it."

She caught up with her eldest brother, Wyatt Fox, who was already moving to the hotel's entrance.

"Hey, you see Larry over at IC?"

Wy nodded. "Cooper's here."

Her heart thudded at the mention of his name. Nothing new there. "But he's out, right?"

Her brother grumbled his disdain for that ridiculous question. "There was some charity shindig hosted by Cooper for the Wounded Warrior Project. Fire started in the kitchen, but didn't reach the grand ballroom. One percenters probably trampled the minimum wagers on their way out."

Not so far off the mark, she imagined. She could see it as clearly as if she'd been there. He would have been seated at one of those five-zillion-dollar-a-plate tables, hand resting casually on the back of his date's chair, showing just enough of his bespoke tailored shirt to reveal gold—no, platinum—cuff links. His other hand would have been midrake through his dark, wavy, overproduced hair that could do with some serious mussing. A member of his security detail would have leaned over and whispered in his ear. *We have a situation, Mr. Mayor.* Then full throttle to get the most powerful man in the city to safety.

Wy pushed through the main door of the hotel. The extravagantly furnished lobby was empty and

unscarred except for muddied carpets and a few gab-
bing firemen. The smell of smoke scented the air. The
smell of death to most people, but not to a firefighter.
This was what they trained, lived, breathed for.

After checking in with the 59 LT, Wy and Alex
headed to their assigned sweep area: staff offices on
the first floor. Looking in, calling out, closing doors,
assuring themselves that no one remained on site.

No doubt the mayor was chin wagging with Uncle
Larry at Incident Command right about now, getting
an update on the situation. The commissioner would
assure him they had it under control, but Mr. Mayor
would probably insist on staying so he could project
his much-vaunted "leadership qualities" and preference for "the buck stops here." Whatever looked good
for the cameras with the election just six weeks off.

"So what's goin' on with you lately?" Wy asked.

"Whatcha mean?"

"You seem a bit less—" He stopped and did the
Wy Fox patented sniff 'n' squint. "Alex than usual."

"Nothing's going on." In truth, she was still reeling from Michael Martinez's unceremonious dump-
ing three days ago in the middle of dinner at Smith
& Jones, using of all things the work excuse. She
knew all about the work excuse to slip out middate.
She had invented it. But she'd thought it was going
reasonably well until he practically ran from that
restaurant like his nut sac was on fire.

"Just can't find a decent date."

Wy huffed out a laugh. "Yeah, I heard Martinez
was a blowout. What are we going to do with you?"

"You'd think having two brothers who are former
Marines, another who's the best boxer in the CFD,

and one more who's intimately familiar with all of the gay and most of the straight men in Chicago, I'd be covered. But, *oh no,* my own family of he-men are useless."

"I introduced you to someone." He pushed open a door, scanned the room, and pulled it shut again. She mirrored his actions on the opposite side of the corridor.

"You mean the former Navy SEAL who kept insisting there would always be secrets between us because"—she gave it air quotes, the effect somewhat lost in her thick CFD-issue gloves—"*'that's the way I roll, babe'*?"

"He was a solid guy."

"Brother mine, I would like to meet someone who doesn't sleep with a knife under his pillow in case his loose lips force him to make a choice between *his* duty and *my* need to know. I'd have to wear earplugs in case he blurts out old mission details in his sleep!"

"Damn, you're fussy."

Maybe she was. Maybe she gave off a vibe of "not worth the trouble" that condemned every date from the outset. But surely there was someone out there for her. After the Sam Cochrane "rescue" incident, she had spent months fending off weasels propositioning her on Facebook to come rescue them, or more particularly their dicks from the confines of their pants. And those were the A pile.

Then she'd made the classic mistake of falling for the smooth talk of a bona fide charmer, a customer at her family's bar in Wicker Park, Dempsey's on Damen. One of those Board of Trade suits who got his kicks slumming it with firefighters and cops on the

weekends. Three—okay, five—shots of tequila later
and she'd dropped her panties faster than a hooker's
on payday at the mine. She hadn't even gotten dinner
out of it (or an orgasm). The shame of what happened
later . . . the hot flush that stole over her body was a
heart-sickening reminder of just how hard it was on
the dating battlefield.

Yet she persevered because she truly believed that
in a city of millions there had to be a guy who could
see all she had to offer. Putting herself out there would
eventually reap its reward.

"We done here?"

"All good." Wy closed the last door in the staff
offices area just as his radio crackled to life. Venti's
voice echoed in the empty hallway.

"Fox, reports of a civilian trapped on level two,
southeast corner. You and Dempsey are closest to the
stairwell."

"Copy that," Wy said. "You hear that, sis? Time
to earn your rescue merit badge."

The heat hit them as soon as they exited the stairwell
on the second level.

"I thought suppression was clear on this side of
the building," Alex said.

"Someone fucked up on comm. Mask on,
Dempsey."

Shit, this was serious. Wy only used her last name
when he was in business mode. She was already tightening the strap and turning the air regulator up on
her bottle.

Wy called in an update to the cap. "Remember

everything you've learned," he said to Alex, his voice calm and purposeful. Of all her brothers, he was the one she'd trust most to lead in any messed-up situation. "Don't suck on it; even draws."

Alex nodded, drew a deep breath. The self-contained breathing apparatus, aka SCBA, could last a half hour. No firefighter expected to run out, but with rookie status, adrenaline, and itchy panic, all bets were off. Thirty minutes of air could be depleted in ten.

They turned a corner into a smoke-filled corridor, past a sign pointing to meeting rooms with names like the Lincoln, the Jefferson, the Washington.

"Fire department, call out!" Wy yelled.

Nothing but the telltale crackle of burning paint. Distant, but too close for comfort. They moved toward the sound, with a purposeful awareness of every step. The smoke thickened to a muddy charcoal haze and then, for the briefest moment, cleared.

Alex could barely make out a shape coming toward them. A tall, dark streak carrying something.

Someone.

The shape lurched forward, stumbled, but remained upright. In three seconds, Alex and Wy had closed the gap.

"I've got her," came a smoke-roughened voice. Not Wy.

Both firefighters' gazes fell to the package, a woman in a cream cocktail dress that no dry cleaner would ever again make pristine. She was unconscious, limp in black-suited arms with snow-white cuffs. A glint of metal flashed through Alex's mind before her attention was ripped back to the woman. That sharp black bob, that jutting jaw . . . Alex recognized her immediately. Madison Maitland, head honcho at the PR firm M Squared.

Who happened to be Kinsey's boss.

And who also happened to be the mayor's election campaign manager. Not to mention his ex-wife.

Alex's eyes shot up and clashed with an ice-pick-blue gaze.

"What the fuck are you doing here?"

*Etiquette on greeting victims in a working fire? Zero points, Alex.*

"Lovely to see you, too, Firefighter Dempsey," Eli Cooper replied smoothly.

"You're not supposed to be in here," Alex said, indignant at his offhand response, and herself for letting him provoke her. Of all the times. "We had a report that you were out."

He blinked away a trickle of blood dripping from a cut over his eye.

Then he swayed. Damn, he was going to . . . .

Wy grabbed Madison. The wall grabbed Cooper.

"She's been out for about ninety seconds," the mayor said to Wy, who had set Madison down and was trying to rouse her. "Got locked in a restroom during the commotion."

Cooper hunkered, his hand outstretched on the wall to steady his crouch, his face a mask of concern. A drop of blood fell on the bodice of Madison's dress. "Mads, can you hear me?"

Nothing. Wy pulled off his glove and fingered her neck.

"Pulse is thready. Time to go," he said, one eye on the smoke soup from which Cooper had made his dramatic entrance.

Pushing her irritation with him down deep, Alex called on her professionalism. The cut over his eye still dribbled blood, some of which had fallen to the immaculate white collar above his tuxedo. He had come perilously close to passing out back there. "Mr. Mayor, can you walk?"

He nodded, his eyes never leaving Madison. "I can take her."

"Let's leave the CFD to do their jobs, Mr. Mayor," Wy said, scooping up Madison and turning back toward the stairwell. "Dempsey, take the rear." No hesitation, he moved forward with his charge. Looked like this grab would go in Wy's column.

"After you, Mr. Mayor."

"Ladies first, Alexandra."

She growled, annoyed that her mask suppressed it. He smirked, guessing at her reaction anyway.

"Really? You're going to pull the female-firefighter-can't-do-the-job card now?"

Ahead, Wy had already turned the corner with Madison. Behind, the smoke was creeping outward like tentacles, blanketing death over the corridor.

Pulling his big body upright, Cooper coughed hard against the back of his hand. "As much as I'd love to debate the subtleties of the gender equality debate with you, Alexandra, I think we should probably use these lovely moments to haul our asses to safety."

"That's what I'm—"

"C'mon." He dragged her by the arm toward where Wy had gone. She let him lead because he was going in the right direction and she was a big fan of choosing her battles.

They had just turned the corner, heading for the

exit-signed stairwell, when it all turned to shit. Eli's grip on her arm, previously firm and dominant, softened and slipped. No more than fifteen feet out, he slumped against the wall. His hand flew to his forehead, over the bloody wound.

"Come on," she urged, "we're almost there."

He didn't respond, just cradled his head.

"How did you come by that injury, Mr. Mayor?"

"Macho shit, trying to get a door open. Looks much easier in the movies." He huffed out a smoky laugh. "And call me Eli."

"You haven't made me angry enough."

At least he was lucid enough to speak. Granted, it was his usual BS and—*fuck*, the situation turned to double shit when his tuxedoed body slithered down the wall.

"C'mon, Cooper. No napping till we're out."

He said nothing. No smartass comeback, not even a grunt. Shit, he was losing consciousness before her eyes. The gases in the hallway were noxious and she had no idea how long he had been inhaling them. He needed clean air. Fast.

Her mind tripped through the options: drag, revive, wait.

*Drag* . . .

Eli Cooper was 220 pounds of rock-solid muscle. Limp, but upright would work for her because, despite the fact that she was trained in dragging bodies from her days back in the academy, hauling this man's deadweight, even with a hasty webbing harness, was another story entirely. Getting him conscious was her first job, because if that didn't work, this might be her last.

*Revive* . . .

As gratifying as a nice slap across one of those gorgeous cheekbones would be, it wouldn't change his respiratory situation, which was up shit creek, paddle MIA. But here was the rub: sharing your air with a civilian was a no-no. As much as it was a firefighter's job to save lives, her own life was paramount—and handing over her mask to someone else placed hers in jeopardy.

*Wait* . . .

If she waited for however long it took for the cavalry to arrive, Eli might suffer from lung damage or airway collapse. Next stop, cell death. Last stop, one dead mayor and bye-bye to her career in CFD.

Decided, she hauled a lungful of precious air, then ripped off her mask and placed it over his face, holding it tight and steady to form a makeshift seal around the edges.

*One, one thousand. Two, one thousand. Three* . . .

Life returned to his body, but as was always the case with this man, consciousness came with its own set of problems. With hands raised, he fought her, pushing the mask away. As if the guy wasn't already difficult enough to deal with.

"Don't need . . ."

"Cooper, let me do my job!"

And that outburst cost her the breath she'd been holding. Got to move.

Everything she had ever learned kicked into gear. She reaffixed the mask to his face. Turned up the air. Felt the pulse on his neck. Strong, but then she knew it would be. Eli Cooper was too much of an asshole to let a little hiccup like smoke inhalation keep him down.

While she waited for the SCBA to do its job, she hit the button on her radio.

"This is Dempsey," she coughed out into the lethal air, using up more precious oxygen stored in her lungs. "I'm on level two near the southeast stairwell with an unconscious male civilian."

*Crackle, crackle,* no response. She should say it was the mayor, but maybe they knew, because Wy had to have made it out with Madison by now. A threat to Chicago's First Citizen would produce quicker results. Depressing, but reality.

She hit her radio button again. "This is Dempsey. I've got the—"

"Dempsey, hold your position," Venti said. "Crews are on the way."

"Copy that."

Alex coughed, the effects of the smoke now a challenge to fully drawn breaths. Her lungs did not like the poisonous concoction. They were certainly not going to like any prolonged exposure to it.

Cooper roused as the air did its job, then tried to yank the mask off again.

"Eli, don't! Just take a breath."

His fingers fisted the jaw of the mask and pulled at it weakly. "Can't . . . breathe."

"It's okay. You're going to be okay. You just need to relax and breathe normally." She ripped off her glove and curled her hand in his big, surprisingly coarse one. "I'm here. I'm not leaving."

"Trapped," he muttered, but more important, his shoulders had softened by degrees, and as his grip tightened on her hand, she could feel him taking steadier breaths. Getting stronger.

He coughed. "Did he call you?"

"What?"

"Did . . . did he call you?"

"Who, Eli?"

He husked out a short, bitter laugh. "I told him if he called you, I'd . . ." He trailed off, hauling another life-affirming lungful of air. "Knew I could get you to say my name."

Yay, the douchebag returns! But now she had another pesky problem: at least a minute had passed with no sign of backup. Worse for Alex, mental hypoxia and nausea had started to set in. They needed to get out.

Now.

"Mr. Mayor, can you stand?" On legs like swaying reeds, she pulled herself up while still holding his hand, hoping that was enough. Needing his strength as much as her own. Using the wall as support, he righted himself.

"We need to get to the exit." She hunched under his arm and took his weight. Her blood was filling with poison, her cells turning black, her life force shriveling.

Eight feet. Seven. Only six more feet.

Christ, he was so fucking heavy.

The smoke wrapped around them. Encased her heart and lungs. Death had come calling. She had expected that when the time arrived, she would be more afraid.

Her mind fogged over. Two steps. Two more. Two . . .

Everything went black.

# ⚡ CHAPTER THREE

Darkness pressed in, a two-ton weight on his chest, forcing his eyes closed, his mouth sealed. They were moving around, the sound distant but close enough to set his heart racing.

*Go away.*

His lungs were unfillable, the air nonexistent. No space to move, no escape possible. Voices wavered in and out, then one clearer tone filtered through the noise.

"Eli, I'm here. You need to wake up now."

A hand in his, unexpectedly supple. Surprisingly strong, too.

He didn't want to wake. Better to stay in the in-between where there were no questions, only the answers he wanted to hear.

Only her.

"Eli . . ."

Even in his dreams, she was difficult. But he liked her that way because it would make the moment he tamed her all the sweeter.

"Wake up, Eli."

"Dammit, woman." He roused, opened his eyes, and met the concerned gaze of . . . his ex-wife.

*Fuck.*

Moments passed as he reckoned with his surroundings. White, sterile walls. A woman in scrubs futzing with equipment. His tuxedo jacket draped over a chair. Slow blinks gave him time to assess and rewind to what secrets he might have been divulging in his semiconscious state.

Finally, he met his ex's gaze head on. "Mads, how are you?" The words croaked out, in the voice of someone else.

"I'm out one Marc Jacobs cocktail dress and some very expensive Laboutins. And before you ask, you heathen, those are shoes." She sounded hoarse and pissy, but at least she was alive.

"Shouldn't you be resting?"

"My room, your room. What's the difference? Someone has to keep you awake, Mr. Mayor."

He sat up in the bed of a hospital exam room, memories resurfacing like a head breaking water. Dragging fingers through his hair tossed up a gritty grime. The spoils of war.

"Mr. Cooper," the nurse said, seeming to appear out of nowhere. She was built like a tank and he was immediately suspicious of her bedside manner. "Can you tell me today's date?"

He'd suffered enough brain-rattling concussions in his lifetime to already be bored with the questions. No harm in having a little fun. "July third, no, fourth, 1998." He turned his attention back to his ex. "Seriously, Mads, how are you feeling?"

She shrugged her slender shoulders—she was dressed in scrubs like the nurse—and let him in for just a moment. "You saved my life, Eli. How do you think I feel?"

"Annoyed, because now I can hold this over you."
Her smile crumbled around the edges. "Exactly, you rotten bastard."

He dropped his gaze, because she was a tough girl who hated showing weakness. Divorced from her for twelve years, he still cared and would hate to see her hurt in any way.

Tank Nurse consulted her clipboard and started in on the dumb shit again. "Who's the president of the United States, Mr. Cooper?"

"Is that a trick question, Nurse? Pretty sure *I'm* the commander-in-chief."

Madison rolled her eyes indulgently. "Wishing it won't make it so."

His probably concussed head was pounding. And stinging. Feeling like they belonged to someone else, his fingers tentatively touched the stitches crisscrossed over his brow.

The night's events came back to him in chunks. The evacuation once the fire alarm sounded. The realization that Madison had not made the exit with the group. Her frantic call to tell him she was locked in a restroom on the second floor. The CFD showing up . . .

Alexandra.

Alexandra saving his life.

"How's Dempsey doing?"

"Oh, fine!" She made a face. "She's part of the most famous firefighting family in Chicago. The country. No doubt she's already lining up her interviews. Should she go with Katie or Diane? Will Oprah make herself available for America's Favorite Firefighter?"

"Don't be catty, Mads."

On a weary sigh, she slumped in her chair. "Five months ago, she almost sank your mayoralty. In fact, that incident made it clear how much the unions hate you. But what happened tonight is a godsend. Not that I'd ever wish a building to be burned down with hundreds of lives placed in danger, but this . . . this is going to win you the election. We can—"

"Let's not get ahead of ourselves." Eli didn't have time for a strategy session. Talking to Alexandra was paramount. He had no idea what he was going to say, but he had a feeling she had her speech all worked out.

*Still think females shouldn't be in the fire department, Mr. Mayor?*

*Still think women are a distraction in life-threatening situations?*

*Still think my lady hormones are a liability?*

Yes, yes, and hell, yes. Just because she happened to save his life did not change that.

"I need to see her."

"Sure. Give me a few minutes to wake the news crews up. No doubt they'll be cage matching it to film your visit—"

"No." He rubbed his forehead. That bathroom door had been a worthy opponent. "No cameras. I need to see her without all that noise."

Mads's usually smooth-as-wax brow knitted. "We have a chance to reverse some of the losses over the last few months. It's been dropped into our laps and we have to use it to get as much leverage as possible."

The woman had a point: pension problems, resource allocation, rivalry with the CPD, which generally had it better come budget time—all were very valid reasons why the CFD would happily beat his ass with a hose if he made an impromptu visit to any of the ninety firehouses within the city limits. A public scene with him practically handing his balls to Alexandra in gratitude could go a long way toward securing that endorsement from the firefighters' union.

But not now. As much as he admired Madison's driven nature, right this minute, he needed her to turn off her campaign manager switch and shut the hell up.

"Me and Dempsey. Alone."

Her eyebrow hitch was more resigned than annoyed. "That might be difficult."

Outside his room, he encountered Obstacle No. 1: his chief of security and good friend, Tom Kincaid.

"Goin' for a little walkabout, Mr. Mayor?"

Shit. When Tom called him that, it meant he was pissed. So he might have had good reason. After exiting the grand ballroom at the Drake with Tom's pincer grip on his shoulder, Eli had slipped past him to go back inside. Rather stupid behavior, he knew now. But the CFD hadn't made it on site yet and Mads was scared. Tom would have demanded he leave the heroics to the first responders, so he made an executive decision.

He was the fucking mayor, after all.

"Tom, I'm sorry. I acted on impulse and I probably should have run it by you."

Incredulity strained the tough guy's expression. "So I could demand you stay put? You knew exactly what my reaction would be, Eli, so let's not pretend otherwise."

"Okay. Glad we sorted that out. Now I need to see Dempsey—where is she?"

"Still gettin' checked out in the ER as far as I know." Tom looked past him to Mads. "Shouldn't he be seeing a doctor about the fact he's an ornery pain in the ass?"

"No cure for that," Mads offered.

"I dunno," Tom muttered mutinously. "I could think of a few things."

Eli tamped down a nascent growl. "I'd love to chat, but I have places to be. Now."

With a sneering lip curl of this-ain't-over, Tom led him to the ER, where he encountered Obstacle No. 2: the Firefightin' Fucking Dempseys.

The entire pride was out in force, a pack of feral beasts standing sentry outside one of the exam rooms. As far as Eli knew, none of Sean Dempsey's foster sons were genetically Irish except for the second old-est, Luke Almeida, who was half. But they all bled green and acted as if they had a dispensation from Pope Bono to behave any damn way they pleased.

Luke straightened from his slump against the wall. De facto leader of the Dempseys, Almeida dis-liked Eli the most. Last summer, the mayor's office had crashed down hard on the Cuban Irish hothead when he played fast and loose with his fists in a video-taped brawl in the Dempsey family's bar. Eli's firing of Luke's girlfriend, Kinsey, the mayor's press secretary at the time, hadn't exactly contributed to the kiss and make up.

"How is she?" Eli asked.

On hearing his voice, Darcy Cochrane jumped up from a chair and hugged Eli. The Cochrane and

Cooper families had been in each other's pockets for years, and Darcy was like an annoying little sister to him. Lately, she was estranged from her father, Sam, Eli's former mentor and campaign backer, due to her questionable life choices. Questionable life choice number one, Beck Rivera—another damn Dempsey— stood off to the side.

"Eli, are you okay?" Darcy asked.

He clung to her, accepting her affection more for her peace of mind than for his own. "I'm fine, monkey. How's Alexandra?"

"She'll live." Luke was usually the spokesperson. "Smoke inhalation, but she'll be okay."

"I'd like to see her."

"She needs to rest," Luke said sternly.

Wyatt Fox, Madison's savior and oldest of the clan, moved several inches to his left, close enough to the exam room's door to make his point clear: None shall pass.

"I just need a minute."

Luke stepped into Eli's space, using every inch of his six-four frame to intimidate. A muscle in his jaw ticked dangerously in case Eli was slow on the uptake. He mentally sighed. Getting into a shoving match with the Dempseys wouldn't have been his first choice, but damn if Eli didn't want to lay down the law here and exercise mayoral privilege.

"Listen, Almeida—"

Eli felt his hand drawn to Luke's grip. Warm, callused, and, surprisingly, not trying to crush him to within an inch of his life.

"We've had our differences, Cooper, but what you did tonight wipes the slate clean."

"It does?"

Luke's smile was wry. "Be a dick about it if you want, but anyone who saves my sister's life is okay in my book."

Anyone who—*what now?*

His head still pounded and Luke's words were not helping. Short-term memory loss was typical of a concussion, but what the man was saying made no sense.

In that corridor, he had lost consciousness and Dempsey had . . . what had she done? His mind reached for the details. The mask. She had taken off her mask and put it on him to help him breathe. She had dragged him out of the smoke to a place where the air was clear and then . . .

"Details are kind of fuzzy," he muttered.

"You pulled her out of that stairwell," Beck said. "Sure gonna look good for your crappy approval ratings."

"Beck!" Darcy snapped at her fiancé.

"Well, it will. *Mayor saves firefighter.* Can't make that shit up."

Luke held up a hand of STFU. "She's safe, that's all that matters."

So this was what Madison had meant about it being a godsend for his election campaign. Not that Alexandra had saved him, but that apparently he had saved *her?*

"I have to see her," Eli insisted. He needed to get to the bottom of this before he talked to anyone else.

Beck parted his lips to engage, but the exam room door opening behind him cut him short. Out came Gage Simpson, looking tired and worn, but on seeing Eli, his face lifted in a grin. The Dempseys were an

Irish pain in Eli's ass, but Gage was the least bothersome, mainly because he was doing a pretty fine job of healing his friend Brady.

Eli had chosen him for that very reason.

"Hey, Mr. Mayor," Gage said. "Come to reap your reward?"

"My what?"

"Save a life, you're owed a life debt." His brow crinkled. "Or maybe it's the other way around. Save a life, then you're responsible for the life you saved. Shit, Wy, that means you're responsible for a lot of freakin' people." Gage smiled easily and jerked a thumb in Wyatt's direction. "He's got the house record for saves."

"I'd love to chat, but I really need to see your sister. Now." How many more times could he say this and not actually have it happen?

"Later," Luke said as he made a move to block.

"No, Luke, it's okay."

All eyes whipped to the source of the voice: Alexandra.

She stood at the exam room door, holding on to the frame like she needed it for support. With her hair in an unruly mess, that fantasy body draped in a hospital gown, and a hint of a pink bra strap, she projected a bewildering combination of fragility, strength, and womanhood.

Bold and resolute, she held his gaze.

"I'd like to talk to the mayor."

The door shut with a soft snick. Eli stood back on his heels, staring at her, a pillar of stock-still energy.

His gaze traveled over her face, seeming to scan for injuries, blemishes, God knew what. Her own gaze matched his in intensity.

She couldn't *not* look at him.

Tiredness should have ruled his handsome face, but he wore the brute demeanor of a man who could haul rocks from a quarry or throw boulders over bridges and still have energy to spare. Streaks of dirt on his face and dots of blood on his shirt collar only added to the impression of undiluted virility. He was a former Marine who had been captured in Afghanistan, and she'd often wondered how someone so adamantly metrosexual could have survived in that Taliban dungeon. Now she knew. Tonight she had seen a different side to him, and her life was forever changed.

It must be the drugs talking—except she wasn't on any.

"How are you? Your head?" Her voice sounded raw, the ravaging aftereffects of the smoke still present.

His fingers flew to the stitches. "I'm sure people will say it can only help." His voice had a grate similar to hers, further confirmation that they had entered some crucible together and emerged changed.

Her first save and it had to be *him*.

The first time she needed saving and . . . *God*.

"You should sit down." He moved forward, to guide her, so she took a seat on the bed before he could make physical contact. If he touched her, she might break down or, worse, fall into the inviting cage of his arms. In her flimsy hospital gown, she felt curiously exposed. Her nail-varnished toes winked at her beneath the garish lights. A little chipped since she'd applied it for her date from hell a few days ago, the last time she had seen the man before her.

If she'd thought that sitting would keep him at a safe distance, she was sorely mistaken. In a couple of ground-eating strides, he was towering over her and had taken her face between his hands, his eyes searching hers intensely. The intimacy of it shocked her.

"Alexandra, are you hurt?"

"J-just my throat. My breathing is back to normal." Or it had been until Eli walked in looking like James Bond on steroids. She fought to restore her lungs to their regular rhythm.

He drew his thumb in a sensuous line along her cheekbone, across her jaw, and it came to rest at the corner of her mouth. She wanted to jerk away, but in her weakened state, she was helpless to defy him.

Brows veed in dark, broody slashes, he dropped his hands. Surely she imagined the brush of his knuckles across the tattoos that adorned her biceps, the same ink that could be found on the arms of all her family members: her father, *Sean* and a pulsing green shamrock on the left, her brother, *Logan* and the intertwined letters of CFD on the right. The Dempseys' fallen.

"Why the hell are you sitting here half naked? You must be freezing."

"I'm okay—" But he was already wrapping his tuxedo jacket around her shoulders.

Well, then.

She foolishly enjoyed how feminine it made her feel. Silly, she knew, but Eli was built, a warrior in Armani, and his jacket felt like a protective cape. Like the next best thing to his arms around her.

*Hold up there, missy.* Maybe the mayor wasn't the only one who'd suffered a brain injury tonight.

"You saved my life, Alexandra, for which I'm very grateful. However, people seem to be under the impression that it's the other way around."

"You don't remember?"

He shrugged his broad shoulders. Thick muscles bulged at the sleeves of his white shirt, the effect delicious. She struggled to focus on what he was saying.

". . . the corridor. The smoke was thick, heavy." His eyes met hers. The discomfort lurking there was not her imagination. "You gave me your air and then you helped me out, though I'm pretty sure I was walking under my own steam by then."

She growled. It hurt her throat, but the physical reminder that he was a tool was most welcome. "Yes, please underplay any part I might have had in this."

"Oh, hush. I suppose you'll be wanting a medal," he said, without any heat; and she managed to suppress a manic giggle. Oh, God, this sexy-hate thing between them was crazy. She felt an overwhelming urge to both punch him and hug him.

"I'm trying to fathom what came next," he said.

That part was still a haze of broken images, ragged sounds, and acrid smells. "Without my mask, I inhaled smoke. Next thing I remember is waking up in the back of the ambulance, fighting for air. Wy told me what happened later."

He arched an eyebrow. "You mean it wasn't captured on camera like every other dramatic moment in your life?"

"No, but don't fret, you've emerged from this looking like an all-American hero. Apparently you appeared in the Drake's lobby, shouting for medical help." She added in a smaller voice, "for me. You don't remember that?"

He scratched his forehead, near his stitches, making her wince at the possibility of reopening the wound. "Vaguely. I must have passed out again just after. But—" Bafflement clouded his brow. "This is just the epilogue. What happened in the corridor between you and me is the real story."

"Well, Mr. Mayor, perception is reality, and plenty of witnesses in that lobby perceived the reality of *you* saving *me*. That's what will make national headlines." Just her dumb luck. She saved the bastard only to have him save her right back—and of course he had witnesses to his heroics. By the time the spin doctors got through with this, Eli would have rescued a gaggle of nuns, a litter of puppies, and half of Engine Company 6.

Eli shook his head. "The truth will be told and your efforts will be recognized. Tomorrow you'll be standing next to me in a press conference when I make a statement about tonight's events."

Getting credit should have pleased her, but the idea of facing the press after all the craziness of several months ago reared a rush of panic in her chest. "Can't you just release the statement now? A press conference seems unnecessary."

Eyes alight, his mouth curved into a snake's smile. "And miss an opportunity to cement your status as America's Favorite Firefighter? Oh no, I wouldn't want to deny you your moment in the sun. Now, there's something else. My memory might be cloudy on some of tonight's events, but I do recall that I fought you when you tried to put on the mask. I'm sorry about that. My delay placed your life in danger."

Caught off guard at his surprise flip of the conversation, not to mention his unadorned apology, she inhaled a sharp breath. "You were panicked and it was my job to calm you down."

"You shouldn't have had to."

She slid to a stand and placed a hand on his arm. Heat fired through her. "Eli, no one knows how they're going to react in that type of situation."

The dimple awoke from its slumber. "You called me Eli."

She made a sound, low in her throat. Still hurt.

"And you're not even angry with me," he added.

"I'm permanently angry with you, Cooper. Even when I'm saving your life."

His smile was grim and shockingly potent. "I've been in worse situations than tonight, Alexandra. I've been shot, stabbed, and held captive by terrorists. I've endured city council meetings where I wanted to murder every alderman in the room. I once dated a woman who made me sit through four-hour operas with only one ten-minute intermission. They really need more intermissions than that, don't you think?" His perturbed frown at the memory drew her reluctant smile. "Not once did I lose my head, but that mask . . . I've been slightly claustrophobic since I was a kid and I've managed to control it all my life until tonight."

Everything softened in her at that, but then she remembered that she felt that way about abused puppies and solo shoes on the highway. She settled for a charitable pat of his arm. His hot-blooded, muscle-corded, oh-my-God arm.

"If you're worried I'm going to tell anyone, then don't be."

His frown deepened. "Tell the world for all I care. I'm more concerned with how I placed you in jeopardy. It's a man's job to take care of—"

"Be careful, Mr. Mayor."

"A woman. So it's a good thing I made up for it by saving your ass."

Mother of Sorrows, give her strength. Knowing that if she let her hand remain on his arm, she would start to squeeze the life clean from it, she took a step back. For her sanity and for his safety.

*Mayor saved from fire; later dies from bedpan-inflicted head wound.*

Pushing up his link-studded cuff, he checked his watch. "Get some sleep and I'll see you at city hall at 9:30. Don't be late." With a twist of that hard, muscled body she should have left to rot in that hotel corridor, he walked toward the door.

"And Alexandra?"

"What?" she snapped.

He smiled over his shoulder, all wolf. "Happy New Year."

# CHAPTER FOUR

Needing one more minute of the pulsing hot spray over his tired muscles, Eli fisted his hands against the tile in his shower and let the water do its holy work. Usually he used shower time to psych himself up for the rest of the day. But this morning, in the wake of last night's misadventure, he had more than the usual crowding his packed-to-capacity brain. Coming close to taking a dirt nap will do that.

He hadn't found God, or suddenly realized that his workaholic ways were standing in the way of a satisfying personal life—a brush with death wasn't *that* revelatory—but it did clarify one thing.

Eli had to break Sam Cochrane's hold over him.

As mayor of Chicago, it went without saying that he was beholden to a number of competing interests. A man in his position did not get *to be* in his position without making a Faustian bargain or two. He wanted to rule. Someone else inevitably wanted something that only the ruler could give: a favorable decision, a ringing endorsement, the chance to bask by association. The quid pro quo was the foundation of the political system.

Sam Cochrane had been a close friend of Eli's father, their families' connection solidified throughout the years of Eli's idyllic childhood. Vacations at the Cooper cabin at Lake Culver in Indiana, barbecues at the Cochrane mansion in the Gold Coast. That all changed with his parents' senseless murders when Eli was twelve years old. Targeted by a mob boss he was prosecuting, Weston Cooper and his wife, Sara, were brutally gunned down by an assassin's .44 in their living room.

One floor below where Eli stood now. While his parents' lifeblood ebbed away, Eli had pissed his pants in a closet.

Almost twenty years later, Sam Cochrane—media mogul, real estate baron, and kingmaker—had bankrolled Eli's first election campaign. Once in power, Eli was careful to pay homage by making sure some of Cochrane's real estate proposals were approved without fuss, but he refused to cave to corporate interests on tax rates and property development incentives. So began the push-pull, with Cochrane calling the mayor out in his newspapers whenever something went wrong at city hall. Such as a brawl between CFD and CPD in a firefighter-owned bar. Or a spat between a female firefighter and a raving, drunken lunatic. In the last three years, Cochrane had been a frenemy and, increasingly, a liability. Eli's preference was to cut him loose, but he had a problem. Cochrane had leverage, an ace in his back pocket that he could produce at will. He could tank Eli's campaign, but worse than that, a reputation would be destroyed. A legacy would be ground into dust.

Eli couldn't let that happen, so for now he had to work with Cochrane and figure out a way to undermine his influence. Standing up to the man who pulled the strings would take guts, bravery Eli was unsure he possessed.

Bravery he was unsure he even wanted to possess—until last night, when he'd been faced with the pulse-pounding heroism of one Alexandra Dempsey. Who had also, coincidentally, stood up to Sam last summer and put her career on the line to defend her family and everything she stood for. If she could be brave, he sure as hell could—and should—be.

*And that, children, is an example of what we call irony.* Was he seriously considering taking life lessons from Ms. Impetuosity herself?

He turned up the temperature of the shower spray, needing the exorcising burn.

He had almost kissed her.

*Almost.*

Holding on to that precious word, the one that kept him on the right side of a sexual harassment suit, his brain rewound to the hospital room at Northwestern Memorial. She had looked so vulnerable in that gown, like she might collapse at any moment. Instinctually, he had held her face in his hands, let himself enjoy the softness of her skin. Inappropriate behavior on his part, he knew, but they had passed through something together. A connection forged in fire.

*A connection he could use,* the cynic in him latched on to. He'd milk the publicity for all it was worth and return to normal, or what passed for normal in his crazy life.

But . . .

She wore pink underwear.

How ridiculous that a sliver of satiny fabric could get him so jacked up. But it wasn't just that he'd seen a glimpse of Alexandra Dempsey's sexy underwear. It was what that bra strap told him about I-can-do-any-man's-job, look-at-my-tough-girl-tattoos, call-me-Dempsey-Mr.-Mayor.

This woman had a feminine, sensual side under that armored exterior. He'd caught a hint of naughty pink that night in the restaurant, as well, the night Detective Martinez had dared to think those sweet lips of hers were his for the taking.

The water crashed over his aching shoulders, sluicing down his chest and falling away in miniwaves over his now very stiff cock.

*Well, hello there.*

He gripped it with a teasing stroke, let his imagination run riot. He liked it gentle to start with, and it might take her time to learn that, but the lesson would be worth teaching.

Alexandra Dempsey on her knees. That's what her dud date had wanted. That's what he couldn't have because that pleasure, at least in Eli's filthy fantasies, belonged to him.

She was a city employee, his subordinate. Off-limits. Which made the idea of dominating her all the more sweet. Commanding her to take him in her mouth, swirl her tongue around the fat, bulging head swollen and primed to please her. In the shower's heat, rougher strokes followed as his hand mimicked what Alexandra's would do. She would enjoy taking a firm grip. She'd enjoy making him beg for that erotic friction, thinking she had some power over him.

But he wouldn't give it to her. Just as he was her boss, he was the boss of this fantasy. He controlled his release. All of it.

His balls tightened and heat built at the base of his spine. Alexandra's mouth increased its suction, sucking the head back to graze her throat, and she hummed her pleasure. Those sage-green eyes, insolent as the day is long, met his, begged, and . . . he let go in ropy spurts against the tile, his reward for a hard night and months of pent-up sexual frustration.

Amazing how a fantasy orgasm with Alexandra Dempsey was better than any actual release he'd had inside a woman.

Stepping out of the shower a few minutes later, Eli was pruned, half-sated, and still clueless about how to move forward on the Cochrane question. He threw on sweats and socks and headed downstairs, checking his messages as he went. Twelve from Madison—wonder what *those* were about. A couple from Kenneth Dubois, his chief of staff. Setting them aside until later, he scrolled through his contacts until he found one particular entry.

*Splinter.*

With a few taps, he upgraded her to *Thorn*. Smiled to himself like a fool.

The smells assaulted him first, followed closely by the sound of clanking pots. Fucker did it to annoy him, no doubt. He'd seen Brady Smith in action in his kitchen at Smith & Jones and he never made as much noise there as he did when cooking breakfast at Eli's house.

Shadow, his Lab-collie mix, ambushed Eli with a full-on lick attack before he'd made it to the kitchen island. His shiny black coat felt comforting under

Eli's hands, and he spent a few moments on extra ear rubs because Shadow liked it and Eli needed it.

"Hey, fella, would you even care if I was gone?" Shadow raised those sad puppy eyes that got him out of trouble constantly. If only Eli could use that one to appeal to the voters.

"Yeah, you'd care about where your next meal would come from."

With what looked like an eye roll at Eli's cynical assessment of the situation, Shadow abandoned him to rub against Brady's leg. His brownnosing was rewarded when Brady dropped a piece of bacon to the floor. Eli poured a cup of coffee neat. Took a seat at the island.

Brady still hadn't said a word, but then this was par for the course, and why the hell should the fact Eli almost died less than twelve hours ago change the habit of a lifetime? It had started two summers ago when Brady moved to Chicago from Paris, where he had apprenticed at a Michelin-starred restaurant. Each Wednesday and Saturday, Brady hit the Green City farmers' market in Lincoln Park a few steps from Eli's door. Afterward, he would amble over to Eli's brownstone, let himself in, and start on breakfast. Now, even when there was no market in the winter and no reason why Brady should be up so early on the opposite side of town from where he lived, he still stopped by.

The two men went way back to their Marine Corps training nearly fifteen years ago, both of them having enlisted on 9/12. As part of an elite team, they had lived in each other's space and knew when to give each other that same space when needed. For the majority of their military careers, Brady had been

Eli's CO, but it had been closer to joint rule. With Brady's taciturnity, Eli was often the backboard-slash-translator for their squad. They had worked well together and remained good friends.

There was also the little matter of Eli saving Brady's life in a desert dungeon.

Within minutes of Eli taking a seat, Brady set the plates down—omelets laced with tomatoes, caramelized onions, and herbs, and a side of apple-smoked bacon and chicken sausage—and took a seat himself. In comfortable silence, they ate and drank. Shadow turned on the eyes. Eli fed him a sausage.

Brady finally spoke. "Alex Dempsey is fuckin' pissed."

"You have personal knowledge of this?"

"Gage was able to convey her outrage pretty well. Thinks you're going to scoop up all the glory. Per usual."

Eli couldn't help his smile. The perennially entertaining Alexandra Dempsey.

"I've no intention of holding back the kudos. She did me a solid." More than that, she had calmed him through his panic at feeling entombed in that mask, a phobia that went back to his parents' deaths. And as if it wasn't bad enough he had shown weakness, he had to make it worse by admitting it to her in that hospital room.

"None of them like you," Brady commented. "Though Alex knows barely half the reasons she don't like you."

"If you're referring to my disposal of her date last week, that was merely me protecting her from yet another bad decision."

Brady hitched an eyebrow, which served to smooth his skin near his scarred temple. They were the scars Eli could see, but he knew there were more. Under his clothes, etched on his psyche. But he seemed to be coming to terms with all that shit he'd endured, with Gage's help.

"Gage says she's looking for somethin' real but she has a hard time on dates. Scares them dickless."

*Quelle surprise.* "Of course she does. She's a menace."

"You want to do her so bad it's not even funny."

Eli let that go without a response, his brain snagged on something else Brady had said. "What do you mean she's looking for something real?"

"She wants to find someone who gets her. Respects her." At that, Brady offered a smartass squint. "Her OTL."

"OTL?"

"One true love."

Jesus. "Well, she won't find it with the likes of Detective Martinez." Eli sipped his coffee, choosing to refocus on his political problems instead of Alexandra Dempsey's search for love in all the wrong places. "I could ride the wave of saving her, but—"

"That would be despicable, even for a black-hearted politico like you."

"Right." Contrary to the urging of his campaign manager, he had no intention of spinning this so Alexandra was cut out and made to look like the damsel in distress. But he needed to work it to his advantage all the same. "Madison thinks she might be of some benefit to the campaign. Get me closer to the unions, the people. Which means I need to get her on board."

"You're gonna have to grovel."

"That's not a good look for me."

Brady's mouth contorted into a grin. "Lots of guys I know would disagree. You on your knees is probably fantasy number one in every bar on Halsted. Good thing you're not my type."

"Yeah, I'm not twenty-five and blond and up for anything." He rolled his neck, working out a kink. "So how's that going?"

Brady slid off the stool and took the plates to the sink. For a moment, Eli thought he wouldn't speak, but he knew that giving his friend time was the way to go.

"Okay, I s'pose." He rinsed the plate and racked it in the dishwasher. "Better than okay. Really good, to be honest."

Eli's heart squeezed. He hadn't dared to hope when he brought Gage into Brady's kitchen at Smith & Jones six months ago. Brady's darkness needed a spotlight and there was none bigger than Gage Simpson.

"Glad to hear it. Rather you than me with that family, though."

"They're good people. Look out for each other." Brady rubbed his chin, a rare smile breaking wide. "You could just ask her out, y'know."

"I could also jump in the lake or put my head in the oven or set my hair on fire." Realizing that none of those things sounded like an adequate rebuttal to Brady's proposition, he regrouped. "I'm not interested. She pushes my buttons, that's all." Bands of muscles tightened across his stomach as he remembered exactly which buttons were pushed during this morning's steamy shower.

Grinning like he knew all Eli's secrets, which wasn't so far from the truth, Brady headed to the door. This happy, shiny version of his friend was most disconcerting.

"Anytime you want to double date with Gage and me, you just let us know. We're always up for helping the course of OTL."

"Oh, fuck off," Eli called out, but Brady was already gone, the ghost of his unfamiliar laugh lingering in the air.

In the restroom of city hall's fifth floor, Alex peered at her reflection in the dull-lustered mirror. Her stupid mane of curls refused to cooperate and she was trying to bobby-pin it into submission so her cap wouldn't just sit at a jaunty angle on top. All her brothers managed to look like gods in the Chicago Fire Department dress uniform, but on Alex, it looked like she was back in St. Jude's, hoping to avoid a beatdown from the nuns.

The tie choked her airway. The navy buttoned-up jacket pressed in like a band of steel around her breasts, which right now felt like half her body weight. Could they have grown since she wore it last at her academy graduation? She kept herself in shape, but Lord knew what was going on between all the stress of the last few months and the fact that she was mainlining her weight in squash blossoms on her weekly dates. Now that food had replaced sex in her life, she could barely get into her *own* pants, which were currently cinching her waist and sitting far too snugly over her butt.

In three minutes, she had to go out and smile for reporters and cameras and look boundlessly grateful to the mayor because he saved her life. He claimed he'd tell the truth, but she didn't believe him. This morning's front page of the *Chicago Tribune* said it all:

## Mr. Mayor Saves Ms. Firefighter

Op-ed encapsulated in a five-word headline. Sam Cochrane, owner of the *Trib*, the mayor's largest donor, and the Dempseys' biggest hater, was having a field day over at his paper.

It had made national, too. *Today* did a piece, casting Eli in a heroic light. And yes, Alex knew he had saved her, but damn, it was so unfair. His junkyard dog, Madison Maitland, had already pulled Alex aside this morning to impress on her the urgency of "getting the story right."

*We love that you saved the mayor. So, so great! But when asked, keep the conversation to the part where he carried you out. That's the focus we want here.*

As if that wasn't bad enough, Madison had hinted at plans for the campaign, nonsense about how Alex would be expected to fall into line with appearances to make the mayor look good. Some bullshit about ball games and "maximizing the story's potential."

The idea of spending time with Eli Cooper turned her inside out with a flapping panic. A strangely sickening, yet pleasurable feeling.

"Hey, babe."

In the mirror, Alex saw Kinsey step inside, wearing a snappy red suit that clung to her petite-framed curves. Out in Chiberia, it was four inches of filthy snow mush, but as always, Cali girl Kinsey looked like the shit in heels.

"What are you doing here?"

With a flick of her blond hair, she grinned. "Couldn't leave you alone with M Squared and the Snake."

Alex giggled, the release blanketing her nerves somewhat. "That sounds like an eighties rap duo." Her levity fled as she caught her reflection in the mirror once more. "I can't do anything with my hair."

"Here, let me." Kinsey, efficient to her bones, took charge and managed to get it under her cap. "So, has Madison tried to bully you? Working with her every day, I know how difficult she can be."

"I'm to ensure the story reflects well on the boss."

Kinsey held her gaze in the mirror, Mama Bear ferocity in her expression. "Now, listen to me. You saved his life, and no matter what happened afterward, that is the take-home here. If either of them tries to minimize your contribution, I'll get up on that podium and unleash my wrath."

"And I'll be right behind her."

Darcy walked in, looking like a rock 'n' roll Snow White in leather, lace, and *fuck-yeah* ink. The woman was well known as one of the best tattoo artists in Chicagoland, and the intricate swirls and patterns on her forearms were a testament to her amazing skills. "This doesn't look like much of a party, ladies. Should I break out my vodka stash?"

"God, I wish I could be drunk while I do this." Alex hugged Darcy.

"Beck thought you might need some support, but to be honest, Eli's not going to screw you over. I've known him all my life. He's a really decent guy." She saw the look Kinsey and Alex exchanged. "Okay, so you've both had different dealings with him, but I know he's fair. And if he isn't, we've got your back."

Warmth spread like molasses across Alex's chest. She'd always had a hard time making girlfriends, but since her brothers hooked up with these two awesome women, she'd felt truly blessed. Her mom used to say, *Surround yourself with people who love and support you, then love and support them right back*. And Alex was a fully paid-up subscriber.

"I'm just so nervous. I hate public speaking, all this crap."

Kinsey straightened Alex's tie. "For someone who despises being the center of attention, you sure do manage to attract it."

"I can't help it. Trouble seems to find me."

"So said every felon in Cook County Correctional Center," Darcy said drily.

A flash of light buzzed Alex's eyes, forcing her to grab Kinsey's hand, the one with the new addition the size of Jupiter. "*Ohmahgerd*, Luke popped the question?"

"At dinner last night. I thought you'd never notice."

The three of them screamed so loudly the mayor's cut crystal decanters probably shattered in his office.

"Why didn't you say anything at the hospital?"

"We had something else on our minds." Kinsey squeezed Alex's arm. "You scared everyone half to death, especially Luke. You know how he is."

Luke had taken on the role of Dempsey dad when Sean and Logan died, and had always been the most protective of her older siblings. The episode with Alex and Cochrane had almost ended things between Kinsey and Luke, and now here she went again, up-staging the happy couple with her shenanigans.

"Took him long enough to do the deed," Darcy said, fingertips on her chin, unsubtly showcasing her own hand complete with the beautiful sapphire Beck had given her last September. "Four whole months together and about to buy a house. You even have a puppy!"

Kinsey's eyes twinkled with emotion and pride. "I told him that I'd have said yes the day I came back to Chicago to be with him, but he wanted to save up for the ring. Do it old school." She'd been engaged before to some hotshot surgeon, which Alex suspected left Luke feeling competitive when it came to the bling.

They all gazed at the ring again and exhaled a chorus of happy, girly sighs. Then Kinsey cleared her throat in a back-to-business fashion. "Now you're the hero, babe, and make sure no one forgets it. But with that said, just try to stay cool in there, 'kay?"

"You mean, don't pull a Luke?"

Kinsey chuckled. "You two might not be related by blood, but you are very, very alike."

Eli strode toward the media room on the fifth floor of city hall where the reporters were waiting to grill him.

"Mr. Mayor," he heard Mads call behind him. "Your jacket."

He stopped and thrust out his hand, while his assistant, Whitney, handed over his gray Armani suit coat. As he drew it on, he took a moment to pull on his cuffs. Dial up his game face. Ignore Alexandra Dempsey, who was standing a few feet off to the side, shuffling from one foot to the other.

The low hum of the reporters hushed as he walked into the media room.

"Good morning"—*vultures and vulturesses*—"ladies and gentlemen."

Murmurs of "Mr. Mayor" waved over the room, as gentle as the Lake Michigan surf in summer, but he knew better. He'd take a gym hall of disgruntled voters or a city council chamber of drunken aldermen before he'd choose to spend a moment with this barrel full of snakes. The media room was like a bad comedy club with a three-drink minimum.

"How many proposals today, Mr. Mayor?" someone called out, the *Sun-Times*'s Kenny Fiedler from the sounds of that two-packs-a-day wheeze. It was a running joke with the press that he received a steady stream of marriage proposals from his female, and occasionally male, fan base.

"Slow day. Only three in my in-box this morning." He raised a hand. "Please hold your questions until I've made a statement."

He hadn't looked, but he could sense Alexandra's presence off to the side. Only sheer willpower kept him from indulging a near uncontrollable impulse to stare at her.

"Last night, a fire broke out at the Drake Hotel, the cause of which is still under investigation. Due to the Chicago Fire Department's perfect execution of their duties, no one was seriously hurt. At one point, I found myself overcome by a minor head injury and smoke inhalation that resulted in me losing consciousness. Firefighter Alexandra Dempsey of Engine Company 6 gave me her air and pulled me to the safety of a nearby stairwell."

Finally, he allowed himself the luxury of glancing in her direction. Color tagged her cheekbones and springy curls had escaped from the prison of her cap. She gnawed on her lip, a move that was as brazenly erotic as it was innocent.

Awe at what she had done for him bloomed in his chest. She was so damn brave. "Without Firefighter Dempsey's quick thinking, I would not be here. She saved my life, and I am immensely grateful."

She raised her gaze to his, and the fragility he saw there struck him all kinds of hard. He wanted to hug her—then take unscrupulous advantage.

"Firefighter Dempsey, would you mind?"

She took a few steps. Once within a couple of feet, he closed the gap. "For the cameras, honey," he murmured.

The sizzle between his shoulder blades as he shook her hand conjured the memory of her curling those fingers around his last night in that hotel corridor. *I'm here*, she had said. *I'm not leaving*. The soft clicks of the reporters' cameras sounded, and still, he held on to her hand.

She frowned, dipped her gaze to their joined hands. Blinking back to the present, he released her and addressed the crowd. "Questions?" With a nod, he gestured to Mac Devlin from NBC 5.

"Our understanding is that you had already been evacuated but went back into the hotel. Can you confirm that?"

"One of my staff was still inside and I went back in before CFD arrived. Probably not the wisest decision, but I have no regrets. Next."

Jillian Malone, Sam Cochrane's favorite flunky over at the *Trib*, spoke next.

"Initial reports stated that you carried Firefighter Dempsey to safety," Malone said, "and not the other way around."

"Yes, it would seem your paper jumped the gun today with that headline, Miss Malone. If you had checked your facts—"

"We had a confirmed source inside CFD," she interrupted.

He glared at her. He was the mayor and he hated interruptions unless he was doing the interrupting.

"Once in the stairwell after Firefighter Dempsey saved me, we traveled down one flight and exited into the lobby. There was a lot of confusion when we emerged. We both needed medical attention, but the facts are as I stated. Alexandra saved my life. End of report."

They were no longer touching, but he felt her stiffen beside him all the same, likely at his overly familiar use of her first name. The slight shift in the room told him the vultures had picked up on it, too.

"Several eyewitness accounts cast you in a more heroic light, Mr. Mayor," Jillian continued, a dog with the proverbial. "You've also made it clear in previous statements your disapproval of women in the fire department."

It might have sounded like a non sequitur, but Eli had learned long ago that there was nothing random about a reporter's questions. He turned on his mega-wattage smile, the one that put him in *People*. The Sexiest Man Alive issue. "Yes, I have. Guess I look pretty dumb now, huh?"

The reporters laughed heartily at his *mea culpa*, but the noise wasn't quite enough to mask what sounded like—a growl?—from the woman to his immediate right. His blood stirred.

"Firefighter Dempsey," John Suarez from the local affiliate at CBS chimed in, "your family isn't afraid of the spotlight and you have a fractious history with the mayor's office."

She cocked an eyebrow beneath a wayward curl. "Is there a question in there?"

Soft chuckles washed over the room. Before Suarez could continue, Alexandra spoke again. "Maybe you mean to ask, given my family's history with the mayor, if I was tempted to leave Mr. Cooper so he could find his own way out?"

The shocked faces of the most jaded and dark souls in Chicago stared back, on tenterhooks for the punch line.

"Sure. I mean we've all wanted to kill him at one point or another."

Jesus, that saucy mouth. He would really enjoy punishing her. "Please, Firefighter Dempsey. Tell the esteemed members of the press how you really feel."

She met his gaze with her usual insolent directness. Humor, and possibly mischief, flashed in those fiery eyes. "Well, I'd be remiss if I didn't use this opportunity to address the concerns of my union. The mayor has made it clear that the needs of the Chicago Fire Department, from resource allocation to our underfunded pensions, are low on his list of priorities. I think if he's reelected he won't make any improvements—"

"So you're voting for Caroline Jenkins?" some wag near the back tossed out.

"Still undecided. She's not impressing me a whole lot, either, but at least she hasn't declared a war on the working class."

Enough. He'd let her have her fun. "Well, it's a good thing your professionalism overrode your dislike, Alexandra. I'm incredibly grateful that you could put that aside when you did your job."

An impudent grin stretched those luscious lips he'd imagined wrapped around his cock this morning. "It was a tough call, but yeah, I'm not sure I was prepared for the womankind backlash I'd face if I didn't haul you out of there. Gnashing of teeth, gouging of hair, deflation of breasts. Just doing my part for the sisterhood."

The toughest room in Chicago went wild over that. Time to call this game for darkness.

"Thank you all for coming and—"

Too late. The vultures had carrion between their beaks. "Alex, do you feel as though the mayor really respects you and the rest of the female firefighters in CFD now that you've proven yourself?"

"I've no idea. You'd have to ask him."

All heads swiveled six inches to the right.

*Tread carefully, Mr. Mayor.* "I've never not respected our female firefighters. I've had reservations about their capability to endure the physicality of the job." He drew in a breath and sealed his fate. "That hasn't changed."

"There's your answer," Alexandra said with unmistakable cheer.

Damn her. She had set him up, knowing he would look like a flip-flopper if he softened his previous stance.

"On that note"—he recognized the need to quit while *she* was ahead—"I think it's time to wrap this up. Ladies. Gentlemen." Alexandra was already bouncing toward the exit. Practically skipping.

As Eli passed Madison, she murmured, "Can't you just lie like a regular politician?" while Tom thumbed over his shoulder to a departing Dempsey. "Should I detain her now, sir, for threatening the life of the mayor?"

"Give me a five-minute head start to strangle her first," he growled, pounding out after her. She was moving quickly as though concerned for her safety.

She should be.

"Think you've scored some points here, I suppose," he said to her back.

Spinning about, she ripped off her cap, setting free that revolution of untamable curls. "I answered honestly, Mr. Mayor. I didn't know what they were going to ask, and let's face it, you made clear your feelings about women in CFD. Though I suppose I should give you credit because you stuck to your guns with the same old chauvinistic bullshit. I don't have your respect, so you have no right to expect mine. Now, I've done my duty and I'm done with you."

Fury at her dismissal of him set his muscles seething beneath his skin. Hell if she didn't need a strict lesson about manners. While he pondered how this lesson should be dealt out, she pivoted and headed toward the elevator.

Dragging her to his office was out of the question—oh, the vultures would *love* that—and he needed to get her under control ASAP. Two long strides and he was on her like a hawk.

"We're not finished, Alexandra." He tucked a palm beneath her elbow, absorbed her whoosh of surprise, and pulled her through the nearest door.

# ◊ CHAPTER FIVE

Alex caught a glimpse of . . . *what the?* Family-sized boxes of tampons bathed in light from the corridor before the door was shut behind her.

Scratch that. Behind *them*. He had practically pushed her into . . . wherever he had pushed her.

"What the hell do you think you're doing?"

"Wait one damn second," he mumbled.

A yellow light flickered on and, rather than address the blistering shock that he had shanghaied her, they both chose to spend a moment surveying their surroundings. The glow from the bulb was weak but enough to semi-illuminate a supply closet. Paper towels, toilet rolls, and feminine hygiene products—more than could be found in the dedicated aisle at Walgreens—padded the walls.

Like a cell in an asylum.

A couple of tampons had dislodged from an open box and lay on a steel-wired shelf. Eli picked one up and studied it as if it might hold the answer to some great philosophical question.

"I've always wondered what was behind this door." He shook his head. "I must have someone check the inventory. Anyone could help themselves."

Indignation found its rightful place on her tongue

again. "Right, because the female city employees are probably rooking you left, right, and center out of tampons."

He pointed the tampon at her. "Listen, Dempsey, it's time you got off this Man vs. Woman kick you're on and start acting like a grown-up. Practical considerations are what drive the world, and practicalities dictate that you accept a man is physically stronger than a woman and stop making it into a battle that you have no hope of winning."

"Don't point that thing at me."

He placed it down carefully, like it was a loaded weapon. Which she supposed it was for a man who felt threatened by strong women. Unlike last night, he was completely put together—tall, imposing, a god in a blue dress shirt that molded perfectly to his impressive chest. With his sharp suit, perfectly coiffed hair, and cleanly shaven jaw, he was back to the slick machine she knew and despised.

"You crossed a line in there, Dempsey. Ran your mouth off when all I required was that you wear your dress uniform and a sweet-as-sugar smile."

"Like the good little woman. God, you're such a throwback I bet all your selfies are sepia toned."

"And it's a wonder *you* don't fall over with the weight of that chip on your shoulder."

She fisted her hips, trying to project a bravado she did not feel in such close quarters. "Don't think I don't know what's going on here. I'm just another PR strategy for the great Eli Cooper's campaign. Madison told me that this won't be the end of it, because apparently you can only get good ratings when a Dempsey props you up."

"And you thought you'd torpedo that by acting like a smart-ass and making me look like an idiot in front of the press?"

She shrugged, hopeful. "Did it work?"

"Yes, it did. You are a pain in my ass, but to be honest, Alexandra, it seems like you're going to an awful lot of trouble to avoid my company."

"I just don't like you."

He moved forward. She edged back, flustered by the worrisome notion she was trapped in a tampon-lined cell with a man who exuded such raw virility.

"Is that all?"

"Isn't that enough?"

The next few inches forced her into an acquaintance with the sanitary napkin section. The air she breathed was full of him—a masculine, clean scent that made her feel feminine and . . . dirty.

"Explain your concerns."

Where to start? "I don't want to be rolled out or whatever you've got planned as you wind up your campaign. I don't want people to think we're . . ." *Shut up, now.*

"We're what?"

"Involved in some way."

The bastard smirked. "Involved?"

Oh, God, she felt so stupid for even raising it as a possibility. Of course no one would think that. Look at him. Women dislocated their spines to get into cock-sucking position for this man.

Still, her mouth refused to stay shut. It had a point to make. "People, the press, tend to romanticize these things. They see stuff that isn't there."

"You think people will think we're a couple?"

"I know. It's ridiculous."

"It is?" he said at the same time she said, "As if I'd be interested in you."

The air between them, already fraught, shifted.

"Why wouldn't you be interested in me, Alexandra? I'm told I'm quite the catch."

She snorted. "If you're looking to reel in a great white shark."

"I think a hammerhead would be a more accurate description."

Whatever that meant, unless . . . did Eli Cooper just make a dick joke? Surely not, but now all she could think was *hammer* and *head* and how he would be hard enough to—oh, mercy, she'd gone far too long without satisfaction. True, space-filling, hammerhead-pounding satisfaction.

She called on all the reasons she disliked him. That too beautiful to be alive vibe where she wanted to smash his face in. How he came after Luke and fired Kinsey. And the disrespect, remember?

"I'm not some magpie, easily distracted by a Ken doll lookalike. I'm looking for something a bit more compelling."

"How many dates does it take to find compelling, I wonder?"

"What do you know about it?"

He waved off her question. "I make you uneasy, Alexandra. Why is that?"

"You don't. I'm just trying to understand why people are so bedazzled by all this." She gestured with her hand between them, knowing immediately she had made a mistake.

The closet shrank to terrifyingly tiny proportions as he loomed over her, appearing three times her size. There was no room to slip by, not that she felt an urge to run or anything.

"By all what?"

She crossed her arms over traitorous nipples, which only served to heighten her desire and further constrict the space between them. "You trade on your looks with the female voters, Mr. Mayor. All style, no substance."

"So women vote for me because of how I look, and not because of the issues? You're very dismissive of your gender, Alexandra."

Too right, she always had been. She was tougher and stronger than practically every woman she knew. It bothered her that the female sheep bought shares in the crap Eli Cooper shoveled by the bucketful.

"Not just women. The gays love you, too."

He laughed and said simply, "They do."

His good humor teased out her smile. It should have also deflated the pressure in the room, but it did not.

"After your behavior in that press conference, Alexandra, your utility to me is zero. Your high standards won't be compromised by spending time with a vacuous, cotton-brained dolt like me and you can get back to the Detective Martinezes and whoever else you think is worthy of your time."

It was all said with such easy self-deprecation that for a moment she was fooled . . . until he mentioned Martinez. From anyone else, she would think it sounded like jealousy. Those noxious fumes she'd inhaled last night had clearly damaged vital brain cells.

Determined to put this uncomfortable conversation behind her, she moved forward in the hopes it would prompt him to open the door. It brought her within inches of his massive tampon closet-filling body. And curse her ovaries, but they did a happy dance.

"Best not," he murmured.

"You need to let me by," she squeaked. For crying out loud, she had never squeaked in her life.

"Of course. If you don't mind feeding the beast."

"Feeding the what?"

"They're a slow-moving lot, reporters. Slothlike. Weighed down by all that righteous indignation about the freedom of the press and the public's right to know, not to mention the liquid lunches they see as their constant due. Go out now and you're playing right into their grasping, ink-stained hands." He cocked an ear to the door. "I'm doing my best to protect your reputation here. It wouldn't do to have a serving wench caught in a compromising position with the lord of the manor."

"You don't have the cleavage to make a good serving wench, Eli."

He chuckled, a low rumble of sex. "God, what I'd like to do with that mouth."

He didn't look at her when he said that, just kept his ear to the door like a safecracker checking for the click of the tumblers. Like he hadn't just upended her world with that casually provocative statement. Panic sloshed over her, buzzing her skin and loosening her tongue.

"It's your fault we're in here, hiding like—like

criminals!" When this met with zero response, she hissed, "And what's Detective Martinez got to do with it?"

He turned, eyes like fierce blue suns boring into her. "He was your last date."

"As far as you know."

"Have you heard from him?"

*Not a peep.* "None of your business."

He moved away from the door. "Has he called you?"

"I don't see how—"

The words stalled in her throat as his hand cupped her jaw and his thumb moved to the outer edge of her lip. The unbelievable sensuality of it sent her stomach into a loop-the-loop.

"Tell me."

"Why do you care?" The words felt like shards in her throat.

He paused, still holding, still staring into her eyes with that icy gaze. "About what?"

"Martinez." *Me.* Because with every new, bruising clash, something changed between them. Or maybe it was just her. Something built inside her that grew stronger in its urge to find him.

A sardonic smile lifted his mouth. "I might not be good enough for you, which crushes me. Truly, it does. But believe me when I say that Detective Martinez is not worth your time."

"Only I say who's worth my time."

He shook his head, a glitter of condescension in his eyes.

"You really disapprove of me, don't you?"

His answer was to move disapprovingly closer.

Close enough to sin, as the nuns at St. Jude's used to say, and oh, she wanted to sin with this man.

His mouth hovered so near she could smell the soap on his skin, the sweetness of his breath. The danger all around. A man as powerful, as controlling as Eli Cooper would know exactly what a woman needed. Would he demand total submission between the sheets? Would he make her call him "Mr. Mayor"? Would he trust a sassy firebrand like her with his cock in her mouth?

He shouldn't.

But she'd relish watching that flicker of uncertainty in his eyes while she unzipped him and unpacked his length. She bet he was as big as his ego. She bet he would fill every soaking part of her perfectly.

"You need to be taken in hand," he rasped, every word a provocative puff of air against her lips. "You are wayward and out of control and a danger to yourself, and if I wasn't your boss, if I wasn't worried about all the lines I've no doubt crossed every additional second I spend with you, I would be the one to tame you."

*Do it,* her lust-scrambled brain urged. *Take me in hand. Use those big, forceful hands to take me and tame me.*

"I'm not some animal to be domesticated, Eli," she goaded, knowing he would enjoy her spirit.

But not enough, apparently. Some inner battle raged on his face, and the winner, unfortunately, was common sense. The hand that would not tame her fell away. The body that would have no part in her domestication inched back, its masculine heat replaced by the cool chill of regret.

Sagging in her own skin, she tried to push her

shoulders higher to mask her disappointment. Which is when he stepped into what little personal space she had and lowered his lips to hers.

She should pull away, even though she had begged for it with her smart mouth. She should punish him for every crime he'd perpetrated. For being too good-looking, too sexy, too *everything*. But the kiss was like him—just too damn good. Warm and brutal, providing answers to questions she never knew she had. He teased with his tongue along the seam of her mouth, seeking that last nudge of acceptance as if it was his God-given right.

She parted her lips, and like a predator hinged on her threshold, he took.

The kiss turned wet and deep, velvety luxurious in its sweep across her mouth, its obliteration of her senses. He curled his hand around her neck and anchored it at her nape, as though he needed that to hold on. That strange notion thrilled her. He was taming her, but also fanning the flames of revolution. He was dominating her, but exhorting her to meet him beat for booming beat. She had never felt more . . . *equal* to another man.

She drew back, breathless. Changed.

"You make me so mad," he whispered, his voice incredibly raw, like a manifestation of the aching need thrumming between them..

She felt how mad he was against the fork of her thighs. The slippery warmth in her panties was testament to how mad she was at him.

"Then punish me, Eli." Who *was* this husky-voiced temptress?

One who was getting it done, because suddenly,

his mouth was on hers again, that wickedly talented mouth that he really should never, ever use for speech. Just pleasure. That's all that stupid, annoying, sexy mouth was good for.

She wanted to bite and suck and rub against him. Against all that man. Her body was not her own. It was this wanton thing, grinding against his flagrant erection. Somehow, he had pushed her against the back wall, wedging her in with paper towels and metal shelving and *him*. One hand tangled in her hair—she had no idea where her cap had gone—while the other cupped her generous ass and molded her flush to his cock. They were as close as two people could get with clothes on, like bold explorers, their bodies forbidden country.

One of her hands raked through his thick hair, the other traveled from his shoulder to his chest, needing to feel that steel under silk. Needing to rip his tie off, tear his tailored shirt open, expose his hot skin to her hotter tongue.

Expose herself.

She moaned, her desperation for more, for the pleasure she feared only he could give, echoing in the tiny space. But it broke the spell. Abruptly, he withdrew, the action sucking the air right out of her lungs.

He stared for painfully long seconds, looking marvelously disheveled. She had done that to him, mussed up his world for a few precious moments. Strong, rough fingers rubbed the skin at her nape, and she suppressed another moan.

"This thing between us, Alexandra . . . this thing," he grated, his voice so graveled it coated every nerve ending with his masculine essence. "It will pass."

Panic knifed through her, mixed with confusion at her body's overreaction to his bald statement. "It—it will?"

"God, I hope so, don't you?"

Before she could respond, the door was thrown open and he was gone.

# ❡ CHAPTER SIX

On the fifth floor of city hall, Eli stared at the snow falling sideways outside the window of the mayor's office, feeling not quite so much the lord of all he surveyed as a bit of a heel. Another glance at the iPad on the desk had him flexing his hand in readiness. He was known around city hall for flinging whatever slabs of tech displeased him against the closest wall, and he'd hate to ruin his hard-won rep.

"I told you we'd get good mileage out of this," Madison said from her perch on the edge of his antique mahogany desk.

"Exactly how is this good mileage?" He stared at the provocative headline again on the home page of the *Windy City Dispatch*:

### Sexy Lexi for Mayor!

Yet again, America's Favorite Firefighter was the toast of the town. The reporters loved her dry humor, her fresh take on politics, and her cavalier allusions to leaving the mayor to die in a smoke-filled corridor.

Madison was in full battle mode. "What we need now are a few public appearances to keep the good times rolling for the next month. A visit to Engine 6. Maybe a Bulls game with you and Dempsey sharing a hot dog—"

"How about a string of spaghetti while we gaze longingly into each other's eyes?"

She looked affectionately bored. "Eli, Alex Dempsey understands the game. She works for the city. She works for you. And even though you refused to play the angle like I advised, you did save her life."

"Hardly. I dragged her twenty feet down one flight of stairs. She's a loose cannon, Mads. She's not to be trusted."

And he couldn't trust himself around her. That whatever-the-hell-it-was in that supply closet just went to prove it. Kissing her was like falling into madness.

"Eli, I think you're underestimating the power of what happened yesterday."

"Nothing happened," he snapped.

Mads narrowed her eyes to curious slits. "You disappeared fairly quickly after the press conference."

"I had to take a leak. Or do I need to schedule that with you, too?"

"Okaaay, Oscar the Grouch. What I was talking about was the power of that exchange in the media room. The vultures weren't laughing at you. They were enjoying the"—she carved a hand through the air—"sizzle."

"The sizzle?"

"Eli, I'll let you into a little secret. Politics." She made a moue of distaste. "Not sexy." At his acerbic look, she continued. "Oh, you're sexy and you can usually make a statement about the city budget sound like a reading of Anaïs Nin, but there's only so far your charisma can carry us. You need a foil, someone to reflect your sexy back at you. People aren't just talking about Alex Dempsey, they're talking about *you* and Alex Dempsey. They like how she stood up to you and they like how the two of you sizzle."

The sizzle was the fucking problem. "I don't want to sizzle. I want to win."

She turned her own iPad around. "Up five points since the night of the fire. Two more than yesterday. That's all due to Dempsey."

Point taken. But the idea of trying to corral Alexandra was in a whole other suburb of Nutsville. "She won't work with us. Why do you think she tried to sabotage that press conference in the first place?"

"What happened to the guy who could talk anyone into doing anything?"

"He's been beaten down by corporate interests, union fights, and predatory women, including the one who got me drunk twelve years ago and took advantage of me. You were older and I was very impressionable."

She smiled serenely. These days, they had nothing but fond memories of their misguided drunken attempt at marital bliss, kick-started in the Chapel of Love, two blocks off the Vegas Strip.

"We have information on Caroline Jenkins, information that could bury her."

"Not going negative, Mads. I said it from the start."

They had run this argument many times, but no matter how desperate things got, ruining the personal life of his closest opponent was not the answer. Madison knew it was a long shot, but felt duty-bound to remind him on occasion that he was a scum-sucking politician.

"If you won't use our intel on Jenkins, then dating Alex Dempsey would answer all your problems."

His pulse quickened. "Dating? I thought we were talking about a few public appearances."

Madison stood and walked to the window, where she did her best thinking. He braced for the verbal PowerPoint.

"Dating the woman who, one, saved your life, and, two, represents the blue-collar vote that's been slipping away from you over the last year fulfills two purposes. You show that you have respect for the female firefighters who can do the job as well as any man, and you get an in with the unions. Her last name is an advantage. Combining two great familial legacies of heroism on one ticket is genius."

Discomfort nagged at his insides. "So, use a couple of dead firefighters to get votes."

She faced him. "It's not as if you don't have your own legacy, Eli. You're a war hero. Your father was a hero to this city in his fight against the mob. We're merely amplifying that with your connection to the Dempseys. The polls close on election night, we wait a week or two, then you and Alex part ways."

Apart from the fact that placing his father on the same heroic stratum as Sean Dempsey and Logan Keyes turned Eli's stomach, he felt the need to express the obvious hitch in this stellar plan. "I can't date a city employee."

Madison grinned. "I checked. There are rules

about fraternization between supervisors and subordinates within the same department, but not between you and one of your non–city hall minions. You could bang every schoolteacher and public librarian in Chicago and it would be completely aboveboard."

Completely. Aboveboard.

Why the fuck was he only learning this now?

Since that night six months ago when they had first clashed at Smith & Jones, he had assumed Alexandra Dempsey was out of bounds. Pussy non grata. Yesterday, he had worried about crossing a line with her, only to find now his behavior wasn't nearly as egregious as he'd originally thought. No longer taboo, but no less enticing for it.

Keeping the elation out of his voice took effort. "Even if I thought it was a good idea, there's still the matter of securing Dempsey's cooperation."

"You'll think of something."

Eli drummed his fingers on his desk as he played out different scenarios. He could threaten the whole damn brood with separation at Engine 6. It had worked before to bring Luke Almeida to heel. Technically, they shouldn't be allowed to work at the same house, but as they were foster rather than legal siblings, they managed to evade city regulations.

He could demand she play ball—she was a city employee, after all—but he'd rather not come down hard on her. Not when he wanted to do other things to her that involved the word *come* and *hard*.

*He could finally have her.*

No, he didn't want to bang a teacher or a librarian . . . just one sexy, curvaceous firefighter. But more than that, he wanted to dominate her in a way that made him practically vibrate with need. He could still feel her hot mouth on his, her eager hands scrubbing his hair and claiming his chest. Where the hell had Alexandra Dempsey learned to kiss like that?

Probably with all those dates she was constantly going on. Probably with fuckwads like Michael Martinez. The thought of her with a man like that—with *men* like that—spiked his pulse to dangerous levels. *Cool your jets, Cooper.* If he thought about her with someone else, that iPad on his desk wouldn't stand a chance.

Yesterday, he had told her this thing between them would pass. That he hoped it would. Eli dealt in realities. How to get a vote passed by the city council. Whom to slap down to "persuade" a decision to go his way. Craving a fantasy that was out of reach was a game he refused to play (except during long, steamy showers).

But now Alexandra Dempsey was no longer a fuzzy mirage. She was the woman who would win him the election—and who, until then, would warm up those cold, lonely nights on the campaign trail.

Now he just had to come up with an offer she couldn't refuse.

"Shitmotherfuckerprickfaceasswipe," Alex blurted.

If she were more like her brother Luke, she probably would have punched the locker door to punctuate that incredibly articulate outburst. Actually, she was just like Luke. Quick to anger, slow to forgive, but she was trying to be less of a raging hothead lately because it seemed to get her into nothing but trouble.

So, instead, she closed the door on the ketchup-covered T-shirt in her locker and drew a deep breath. As usual, someone was screwing with her. If it wasn't her rookie status, it was the fact she was one of only 140 women, just 3.4 percent of the total, in the testosterone-soaked CFD. If it wasn't her Dempsey-hood, it was her refusal to break down like a girly girl when faced with adversity. She deserved her spot on the crew. Her brothers supported her, but some of the other guys, not so much.

Murphy was the worst offender. She'd bet dollars to donuts the Jackson Pollack–inspired tee design was from him. He was always making cracks about her being on the rag if she looked at him crooked, like that could be the only possible reason his face offended her. He was sly about it, too, keeping his comments for when they were alone. A subtle invasion of her environment.

Complaining would make her look weak. Getting her brothers involved would draw accusations of whining. She didn't want to rock the boat. Lately, all she had done was rock the boat. Feeling glum, she headed to the lounge, where she was greeted by hoots and slow, insolent claps.

"Oh, shut up," she threw out to her crew. Getting razzed was not exactly unexpected. It wasn't every day a firefighter saved the life of the most powerful man in Chicago.

Or was kissed stupid by him. Her lips tingled in deliciously forbidden memory.

"Nice job yesterday, Dempsey." Derek Phelan, who was lower than her on the rookie pole but didn't seem to feel the effects. The penis benefit.

Heat scalded her cheeks. "Say what?"

"The press conference. You handled yourself well."

"Oh, thanks."

"Should have let him rot." Murphy squinted piggy eyes over a newspaper from his usual ass-dented spot on the lounge's sofa. "Guy wants to fuck with our pensions."

Before she could shape her fightin' words, Luke strode in. "Ladder drills in five, ladies. And I don't believe you were cleared for work, Candidate Dempsey."

She rolled her eyes. "I can't stick around at home, Luke. It's doing my head in." And no way did she want to look like she needed extra recovery time because she was a woman.

He jerked his chin toward the corridor outside the lounge and headed out. When they were alone, he put on his most intimidating expression, though his Arctic blue eyes filled with his irrepressible love for her dampened the usual Dempsey staredown. "You scared the bejesus out of me, you know that?"

"I did my job."

"Giving your air to a civilian is against every single precept we've taught you, Alex."

She glared at him, annoyed that her judgment was being questioned. "I made a call. It was the right thing in the moment."

Her brother looked unconvinced. None of them ever said it, but their overwhelming desire to protect her was etched in the grim lines of their mouths on every call. Especially Luke. She knew it came from a good place, and that sometimes she made dumb decisions (Survey says? Her love life), but she was good at this job. Damn good at it.

"You need to think, Alex. Less of this"—he clenched a fist over his heart, then touched a finger to her forehead—"and more of this. You only have to be stupid once to be dead permanently."

"It worked out."

"This time." He folded his arms, step one in what she knew was the Luke Speech of Parental Doom. "Dad didn't want you to go into CFD. When you applied, I should have put my foot down."

"Goddamn it, Luke. I already heard this shit from Cooper. I don't need my own brother telling me I can't do this job. Go bubble wrap a rookie who needs it."

Grunting, he changed the subject. "You read the gutter rags today?"

More crap about being saved by Captain Chicago, she supposed. Luke pulled out his phone and dialed up the front page of the *Windy City Dispatch* with its blaring headline: "*Sexy Lexi for Mayor!*"

Sexy *and* mayor? Boo yah! She'd take it.

"The press seems to think there's somethin' goin' on between you and Cooper."

"There's nothing going on. He just pissed me off, like he always does." So much so that the only relief was to rub her body against him like a cat in heat. Then fantasize later about taking him inside her, deep, to the root, until she'd come so hard her ears had popped. The finishing touch? She'd feed his sexed-out body to raccoons.

Alex Dempsey led a very vivid fantasy life.

Luke blew out a martyr's sigh. "I'm the resident hothead in this family, so don't even think about knocking me off my throne. Kinsey and I are closing on the new house next week and for once, everybody is operating on an even keel. Let's try to get through a few months drama-free, okay?"

"Sure thing, boss. The next time I have a chance to save citizen number one, I'll leave him to his own devices."

Kathy, the firehouse's admin, poked her head around the corner. "Alex, Captain Ventimiglia wants to see you in his office."

"Thanks, Kath," and then to her brother, "Am I going to be shouted at? Again?"

"Probably. I've prepared you well, young Padewan. Now go take your punishment."

She headed toward the cap's office, anticipating her almost daily walk by the Wall of the Fallen, where she usually liked to stop and send up a silent prayer. She had been fifteen when her adoptive mom, Mary, died from breast cancer. Two years later, Sean and Logan perished in a high-rise fire, but not before they saved three lives, including that of a ten-month-old baby. They went back in to grab an elderly man and never came out again.

Nine years ago, and it had almost destroyed the Dempseys.

But they had come back, strong, all of them now in CFD, doing it for their fallen. *Fire is stronger than blood,* Sean used to say, *and defend the people you love to the dying embers.* Sometimes it got her into trouble, but it was a mantra she lived by every day.

And speaking of trouble . . . As she took the corner, she pulled up short at an unexpected sight:

Mayor Eli Cooper.

Mountain tall, he stood immobile at the memory wall, his broad back bisected by those suspenders that were as much his trademark as his unrelenting stare and commanding voice. Who wore suspenders in this day and age other than firefighters and investment bankers? Perhaps the mayor was a firefighter wannabe. Perhaps he had spent his formative years playing with a plastic fire truck in his backyard, making *wee-wah* siren sounds.

The thought of Eli Cooper as a kid harboring hopes of growing up to haul hose made her smile, so when he turned, that's what he saw. She was smiling and it threw him. Something sparked in those ice-shard eyes, something that threw *her*.

She wiped the grin off her face before it could do any more damage.

"Firefighter Dempsey, how are you?"

"Fine. You?"

"Very well, thank you. No lasting effects from the incident?"

She swallowed. Lasting effects? *No, Mr. Mayor, as virile as you undoubtedly are, your shoving your tongue down my throat in a city hall storeroom has not left me carrying your devil spawn.*

"The fire?" he prompted when she didn't respond.

Oh, *that* incident. "Nope. All good." She cleared the awkwardness from her throat. "How's the cut?"

Eli touched the line of stitches above his brow. "Starting to itch, which I guess means it's healing."

A hush descended now that they were all caught up. She felt her blood vessels flushing open, heat rushing from inside out. Their previous encounters had always been charged, but never awkward, and Alex wasn't exactly sure how to act around this muted, distinctly less jerkish version of Mr. Mayor.

He turned back to the photo of a ruddy-faced Irishman in full CFD dress uniform, his lake-blue eyes sparkling, like he had a bawdy joke or long-winded tale on the tip of his tongue. Sean Dempsey, her adoptive father, the man she missed more each day instead of less.

"I was overseas on deployment when they died," Eli said quietly. "I wanted to come home, but getting leave for a nonrelative's funeral was too tough to swing."

"I hadn't realized you knew them." Sean, Weston Cooper, and Sam Cochrane had once been business partners and owned Dempsey's bar together a zillion years ago. Even so, Alex hadn't reckoned on Eli actually knowing her father or brother well enough to attend their burial.

"Not Logan, unfortunately, but I'd met your father. He was always good to me, checking in after my parents died." A slight shake of his head yanked him back to the present. "Captain Ventimiglia has kindly given us the use of his office. Come."

Ah, there was that tone she knew and despised. Command issued in his typical *dick*-tatorial fashion, he strode toward the cap's office leaving the sensitive area between her thighs to read far too much into that one clipped word: come.

*Yes, sir, please sir, anything you say, sir.*

Once inside and with the door shut behind them, he started, "About what happened yesterday—"

"In the tampon closet?"

He winced. She enjoyed that.

"It was incredibly inappropriate. In fact, you are more than welcome to register a complaint."

"Are you implying you were in control, Mr. Mayor, and that you abused your position when you abducted me in broad daylight on city property and took advantage of me?"

"I think it's clear I was not in control."

They both thought on that for a moment. Neither of them had been in control, not when his mouth claimed hers, not when her hands dug into his bull-like shoulders, and especially not when she had ground her aching core against his hammerhead of an erection.

*If wasn't your boss . . . I would be the one to tame you.*

"I appreciate your trying to do the right thing," Alex said, willing the hot blast ascending her chest to quell. "But while you might technically be my boss, what happened in that tampon closet had nothing to do with you abusing your position and everything to do with us letting off a little steam. Close quarters and the fact we don't much like each other will do that. Sure, if I had a dollar for every time I've been molested in a tampon closet—"

"Could you please stop calling it that?"

"I'd have a dollar." She tried to smile away her discomfort. "That was the first, and it will most definitely be the last."

He stared, perhaps wondering if she meant it would be the last time she allowed herself to be molested in a closet—tampon or otherwise—or if it was the last time she would allow him to do the molesting—closet or otherwise.

She wasn't quite sure herself. What she did know

was that she had enjoyed kissing Eli Cooper far too much, and that was *not* a good thing.

"You know why I'm here?"

"To make me aware of my rights to register a complaint."

"Yes, but now that you've assured me you were in complete possession of your senses and that I didn't abuse my position in any way, I'm here to make a proposition."

"Another proposition, Mr. Mayor?"

"Have a seat, Alexandra," he said, more softly than her jibe deserved.

Copping a squat allowed her a moment to collect her thoughts, and hell did they need collecting and parsing and assessing. On the desk sat a Starbucks cup with *Mayor* scrawled across it. Someone had Sharpie amended the hot-contents warning so it read like a seduction attempt: *Careful, the beverage you're about to enjoy is extremely hot.*

Poor Mr. Mayor, not even safe from predatory baristas.

"You want me to help you win the election," she said to get the ball rolling.

"Straight to the heart of the matter, as always."

"But you think I'll say no. You could make threats and bully me and throw your weight around, but you'd rather I came willingly."

*Came willingly.* She really needed to plan these sentences out better in her head.

"I would never force you to do something you were uncomfortable with, Alexandra."

The sizzle of sensual awareness aggravated her.

Needing to get this back to the good times they had enjoyed before, the ones that equaled "I hate you in spades," she stood and leaned against Venti's desk.

"Seeing as you're my boss"—*yep, preach it.* He was her boss. Her insanely attractive, built-like-a-tank, man-in-charge, don't-forget-he's-a-jackass boss—"you can order me to do anything."

"Order?" Sexy pause. "Yes, I suppose I can."

Oh-em-effing-gee, this got worse and worse. Every word out of her mouth sounded like an invitation for him to issue decadent, dirty, delicious demands. *Over the desk, Dempsey. Now. I'm the fucking mayor.*

She called on her indignation, buried as deep as the hole she'd like to crawl into. "Why should I help you? You've demeaned me, my job, women. And that's just in the last twenty-four hours."

"Merely a difference of opinion."

"I'm not going to be propped up as your puppet. You already did that with Luke and that *Men on Fire* calendar—"

He scoffed. "Hardly my idea."

True, it had been all Kinsey, but it had gone over like gangbusters, so Cooper scooped up the glory. "And then you used that whole shitstorm with Cochrane to make it look like you were the one doing everyone a favor by saving my job." She made her voice go all high and breathy. "Ooh, Eli Cooper listens to the voters. Eli Cooper sides with the underdog."

He looked unmoved. "Let's get a couple of things straight, Dempsey. I could have fired your brother when he went ballistic in your bar, punched out a CPD detective, and dragged CFD's reputation through the mud. I could have fired you when you lost your head over some name-calling and yet again dragged the fire department's reputation through the mud. Your family owes me. Besides, it'll just be a couple of dates."

She swallowed around the Sahara-dry lump in her throat. "Did you say dates?"

"Deaf as well as belligerent, are you?"

"I'm not dating you!"

"Correct, you're not. It's called a publicity stunt. God knows why, but people like us together. They like that sassy mouth of yours. They like the soap opera quality of our history. There's even a poll going on the names of our children. Sophie will be the first woman president of the United States, while Joshua will fight brush fires in California."

"That's . . . that's ridiculous. There'll be a woman president *long* before that."

He rolled his massive shoulders and rubbed at his neck like he was trying to work out a knot of stress. "You've entered my gray, gray world, Alexandra, or rather you've crashed into it like a Pamplona bull. We have a way of getting things done in Chicago. You scratch my back, I scratch yours. In fact, I think after I've told you a little bedtime story, you might have a different perspective."

That checked her. "It's mighty cold out there, Mr. Mayor, but hell has not yet frozen over."

"Wait until you've heard the story. There once was a green-eyed woman—"

"Was she a princess?"

"She certainly thought so."

She suppressed a smile, already highly entertained. "Go on."

He walked to the window, a pensive look on his face. She wondered what he had been like in court when he was in the state's attorney's office before his mayoral run. She'd lay odds he was magnificent, a real jury-charmer.

"This woman was loyal to a fault, quick tempered, and impetuous. Anyone who threatened her family had better watch out"—he raised a knowing eyebrow—"because she would go to the ends of the earth to protect them."

Alex studied her nails. "I like her already."

"She came up against an ogre and she let her temper get the better of her."

"I bet she felt better afterward."

"For a while. But then the ogre made threats to destroy her. The prince wanted to help."

Prince? *Oh, Cooper, methinks you oversell.* "My recollection is that the *evil humpbacked* prince and the ogre had a mutually beneficial relationship that prevented him from standing up for the princess."

His eyes whipped to hers and held her gaze unnervingly.

"Do you remember what I said to you when you came over to my house four hours after you cut up Cochrane's car, Alexandra?"

She jolted at the switch from fairy tale to reality. With startling clarity, she remembered the day Eli summoned her for an ass-chewing. There had been shouting and sniping, but once Wyatt and Kinsey had left, the atmosphere had turned dangerously intimate. She had tried to ignore that moment, place it in her brain's attic and refuse to examine it. Because when they were alone together, while she chattered inanely about his dog to fill the silence, he had said something she would never forget.

*I will do my best to protect you, Alexandra.*

He had meant her job, but also from the risk of being sued to hell and back by Sam Cochrane for criminal property damage. Later, after Kinsey unleashed the video of the incident into the world and saved Alex's job at the expense of her own, Cochrane had dropped his threat on the advice of his lawyers. But Alex had always believed there was more to it.

She had always suspected that Eli had persuaded his major donor, the man who funded his first campaign and whose endorsement Eli needed for his reelection, not to sue the city—and by extension, Alex personally. The thought of being in Eli's debt made her squirm, as did the notion that he had stood up to Cochrane on her behalf. What price had he paid for that? For her?

"I remember," she said, suddenly unable to meet his stark gaze directly. "How's Shadow?"

A brief spark lit up those forbidding eyes, showing his pleasure that she remembered. "Eating me out of house and home, as usual." The light dimmed, replaced by black ice. "What do you think happened back in August, Alexandra? True, that video kept you employed, because it was more politically expedient for me to play it that way. But Sam could have taken you to the cleaners in court. Do you really think he decided *not* to sue you merely out of the goodness of his heart?"

She tilted her chin up, all bravado. "His lawyers said it was pointless. That the video showing how drunk he was tainted his chances of winning."

"And you might recall that the CPD Breathalyzer test determined he was under the limit. The court of public opinion might have been on your side, Alexandra, but a court of law would have eaten you for breakfast. You destroyed a four-hundred-thousand-dollar car on purpose. Because a man called you a dyke and your brother a fag. On top of that, you rallied the city behind you, escaped with a rap on the wrist, and made Cochrane look like an idiot."

She smiled because she had made him look like an idiot. A big, fat, ranty idiot.

"I persuaded him not to sue you, Alexandra. I kept you and your family and this city solvent. And now you owe me."

In the ledger of who-owes-whom, Alex was fairly certain she would always come up trumps. "And I saved your life. I think that makes us even." She walked toward the door with the chorus of "We Are the Champions" swelling in her head. She would have done a jig, but no one liked a sore winner. "Good luck with that campaign, Mr. Mayor."

"Damn it, Alexandra, you don't get it, do you?"

With her hand on the doorknob, she turned to find him staring at her with nostrils flared and mouth set in an unyielding line.

"It's not over. Sam Cochrane is threatening to sue you."

# CHAPTER SEVEN

Her blood stopped moving beneath her skin. A dizzy mess of thoughts pinwheeled through her brain, and all she could utter was a barely articulate "He—he can't!"

"He can. The statute of limitations on civil suits is five years."

"But . . ." This could not be happening.

"Now that you're back in the news, Sam sees an opportunity to stick it to you. To make you sweat."

Which she was doing. Profusely. It was supposed to be in the past, not rearing its ugly bigoted head to bite her on the ass. "Is he suing the city as well?" she asked after a few silent moments passed, each one of them like an hour.

"No. He and I discussed it when this all went down last August. It's not in his interest to make an enemy of me, not while he has business deals that need city support."

"I thought it was done. I thought you sorted it out."

His expression turned even more brooding. "There was always a chance he would hold the threat of suit in abeyance to be brought out later. Without a written settlement, he can sue anytime within the statutory period."

"I'll be financially ruined." She felt like an inveterate gambler whose life had been thrown away in a card game, except she had been dealt the losing hand and, knowing it was toxic, played it all the same. But she hadn't weathered every insult, blow, or wave of opposition to come this far and fail.

"He's your primary donor, an old friend of your family. And I saved your life." She wasn't feeling nearly as cocky as she had a moment ago when she reminded him of that salient fact.

A brief smile quirked the do-me mouth that had opened her up and tortured her with his consummate skill. The man was an excellent kisser—and she suspected an excellent poker player.

"Yes, you did," he said coolly.

"You can make this go away, like before. He'll listen to you. And if you come down on CFD's side, it will benefit you on Election Day. Local 2 hasn't endorsed a candidate yet." The firefighters' union was about to declare, but was waiting for more concessions on the pension crisis.

"But he's not suing CFD, Alexandra. He's after you personally."

So that's how it was. "This is blackmail."

"It sounds to me like quid pro quo. I can keep Cochrane and his legal dogs off your back and you can win me this election." He placed a hand on the window frame and moved his gaze to the parking lot outside. The action drew his shirtsleeve taut against his biceps, mesmerizing her to a sensual dizziness. *Really,* hormones?

"And what about when the election is over?" Her heart twanged, the stupid lump already mourning the moment they were no longer a fake couple.

"When I win—which you'll help me to do—I'll be in a position to prevent him from moving forward with any suit because you'll still be under my protection. I'll demand he agree to a no-fault settlement that'll put you in the clear. You'll probably have to apologize, make a token donation to his favorite charity."

She paced the room, marveling that her jellied legs kept her upright. "Maybe I should talk to a lawyer." She frowned, remembering who was standing before her. "Another lawyer."

"Maybe." He crossed his arms. "And your family. Get their advice."

"No, I can't involve them." If her family knew about this threat they would move heaven and hell to help her, even Darcy, who was on the outs with her dad. And if Cochrane went through with the suit and she had to pay legal fees—or God forbid, damages—her brothers would give her the shirts off their backs. The house where they had grown up with Sean and Mary, where Alex and Gage still lived. Kinsey and Luke were about to buy their own place, plan a wedding, and now they would have to put everything on hold.

She refused to let it come to that.

He moved in closer, shrinking the room to the size of that city hall storeroom. "I'm a useful person to have on your side, Alexandra."

His words waved over her, seductive, dangerous, licking between her legs like a warm, probing tongue. She wished he hadn't kissed her, because it made her want things. Deep, secret things that involved him bending her over that desk and filling the wet, needy part of her.

"Can you take care of my parking tickets?" she joked, seeking relief from the blistering tension.

"Parking tickets, your legal issues." His gaze raked her, drawing her nipples into pleasurably painful buds. "I can take care of any number of your problems, Alexandra."

"What would I have to do?" And was he at the top of that to-do list?

"A few public appearances, photos in the paper. Nothing too compromising. We play up the connection, then amicably part ways after I've won."

There was that annoying heart twinge again at the mention of the end of their fake relationship. When she didn't even want the beginning.

It sounded so easy, a way to keep her family safe after all the hassles they'd endured these past six months. A way to be the one who contributed instead of the fuckup who needed constant bailing out of her unfortunate messes.

"It's only six weeks," he said, his voice with that husky tone that did wicked things to her insides. Six weeks of him talking like that to her? She wouldn't last six hours in his presence, and then she'd have to kill herself for her betrayal of her tribe.

"What about our problem?"

"Our problem?"

The bastard was going to make her say it. Well, she was fine with meeting it head-on. "This thing between us."

He sat on the windowsill and threaded his arms across his blockbuster chest. The fabric of his pinstripe pants molded his thigh muscles in a way that sent a flush on an all-stops tour of every erogenous zone in her body.

"It's chemistry, Alexandra. Merely a physical reaction that'll play well for the press and public." He cocked an eyebrow in challenge. "Worried you won't be able to keep your hands off me?"

"I think it's pretty clear who kissed who in that closet, Mr. Mayor."

"Perhaps, but actions speak louder than words. Your lips were very active. As were your hands." His gaze dropped to her traitorously active mouth. "We're adults. I think we can get through a few appearances without mauling each other. Unless you think you can't."

"I'm not one of your usual Trixies, Cooper. I can resist you."

"Excellent." He thrust out his hand. "Do we have a deal?"

She considered it. A handshake felt rather tame considering what was at stake: the financial future of her family, Eli's election chances, her soul. Maybe she should whip out her Swiss army knife and suggest they seal this in blood.

Abandoning the mental dramatics, she took his hand. Warm and filled with life, it conjured up wicked images of how good it would feel in a rough rub against her throbbing sex.

Oh. God.

She crashed through the in-for-a-penny gate and uttered the word that sealed her fate with Darth Cooper.

"Deal."

# CHAPTER EIGHT

The security guy at the VIP gate to the United Center executive suites was acting like Alex was a criminal. Or a Red Wings fan.

"Could you check again? My name is supposed to be on there."

With a grimace of infinite patience, he consulted his list for the third time. "Nope."

She was tempted to throw out a Hollywood-style *Do you know who I am?* but she refused to be one of those people. Feeling more anxious by the second, she checked her phone again.

Eli's assistant, Whitney, had promised Alex's name would be on the special list guaranteeing entry to where the beautiful ones hung out scarfing wings and pretending to watch the Chicago Blackhawks kill it on the ice. Executive suites were wasted on these people! Alex actually wanted to see the game— Hawks vs. Wings, who wouldn't?—and was now realizing that she'd have better luck seeing it on her phone.

It was her own fault she was running forty-five minutes late. Blue, her crotchety old Chevy pickup, had chosen today to exact vengeance for not having been taken in for a winter tune-up. The old girl refused to start, every turnover of the engine sounding like "Fuck you, Alex. Good luck finding a cab."

Then the cab she finally snagged after thirty minutes wasn't allowed to enter the VIP parking lot, so she had to walk. Usually not a problem; bipedal locomotion was one of her many skills. But it had started to snow. Blizzard levels with wind gusts that had her questioning why she lived in a place where the air hurt her face. Oh, to be Snuggie-wrapped on her sofa with a burrito, a Goose Island IPA, and a binge watch of *Homeland* ahead of her.

The security guy stared her down. "You're going to have to move aside, ma'am."

Whitney wasn't answering, which meant either Alex went home and looked like she'd blown it off or she'd have to call him. Except she no longer had his number because she had erased it before his eyes in protest. *Nice goin', dumbass.*

While she was pondering her options, her phone rang. "Hello?"

"Thought you were raised not to speak to strangers."

That lazy drawl coursed over her, shiver-shocking every cell. Since their "moment" in the closet, she had been far too aware of the sensual promise in that voice.

"You know me. I like to live dangerously."

"Something you're doing right now. Why the hell aren't you here?"

"I am. I'm at the security gate and they can't find my name—"

He swore in a manner that might lose the senior demographic.

"It's not my fault," she grated.

"It never is. Stay where you are." He hung up.

She gave a "just my pal, the mayor" shrug at the security guy, but he was already talking on his phone, and three minutes later she was in the elevator to the penthouse suite level. The first thing she'd do would be hit the restroom to thaw out and check the madness known as her hair and—

The elevator doors split apart to reveal a harried, pixie-featured blonde. Slacking-on-the-job Whitney, Alex assumed.

"*Where were you?*"

"I'm sorry." But Whitney was already manhandling her forward, and it took considerable muscle to manhandle Alex.

"The mayor's been asking for you," she said in a tone of disbelief.

*Well, you probably should have made sure my name was on the list, chicky.* Instead of griping, she cut the girl some slack. If she had to plan every minute of Dr. Evil's day, she'd probably drop the ball on occasion, too. "I need to head to the restroom first."

But her primping needs fell on deaf ears. This girl had a job to do: deliver lost firefighter to pissed-off mayor, and she was not stopping until the mission was accomplished.

The suite was The Tits: wall-to-wall flat screens, an amazing view of the ice, a full (open) bar, and . . . yes, food! Her stomach cheered. In an effort to lose a few pounds, she'd restricted today's calorie intake to three Babybel cheese rounds and half a mint chocolate Clif bar.

Though it looked like she'd have competition for

the nosh. There had to be at least fifty people here, a mix of Chicago celebrities and sports icons. She had walked into a Nike All-Stars commercial. Was that Billy Mendez, the pitcher for the Cubs, chatting with Bastian Durand, the Hawks' injured right wing forward? And Jeremy Castiglione, the Bulls' revered point guard? If these were the circles Eli moved in, then her dating options had just improved by a factor of ten thousand.

Except they would think she was already taken. *Taken by the mayor.*

Then all those dating options that were likely figments of her overoptimistic imagination vanished when she saw Eli.

*Whoa.* He wore black denim that hugged him in places she did not want to acknowledge but couldn't help herself because hells yeah, the man looked amazing in jeans. Up top he rocked a well-cut sports jacket and a white shirt open at the neck, just like the night of the fire. But this was an intentional skin reveal. Intentional sexiness.

She wanted to lick the hollow at the base of his throat and work on down like a ravenous kitten. The thought made her nipples harden. Then it made her mad.

*Dammit, nipples, stand down. It's just a publicity stunt.*

Beside him, inclining her head in a very intimate way, stood Madison Maitland, looking like she was fully recovered from her near brush with death a few days ago. As usual, she had it going on in a gorgeous emerald green wraparound dress that clung perfectly to her svelte body. Surprisingly the press had never made a big deal of her short-lived marriage to Eli, but then Alex supposed a PR guru like Madison Maitland was an expert at spinning a set of circumstances to her client's advantage.

Only right this minute, they didn't look like mere client-PR professional. Not one bit. Their cozy huddle set something dark and hungry clawing at Alex's chest.

She raised her eyes to meet Eli's penetrating gaze. He raked a thorough glance over Alex's body, taking vicious inventory and making her question, oh, everything. Unlike Madison and practically every other woman in the suite, Alex looked like a schlub in her bulky parka and her Joan of Arctic snow boots. The fifteen minutes she had spent squeezing into her Gap jeans were today's cardio.

Eli left his ex-wife/campaign manager/whatever and strode over. "You okay?" he asked, his voice intimate.

"Fine," Alex muttered, suddenly shy. Probably for the best, because shy girls didn't jump hot guys as if they stood between them and the buffet. Which, incidentally, he did.

"Give me your coat so Whitney can hang it."

"Oh—oh, sure." She made a move on the zipper of her parka, but her clumsy frozen fingers refused to cooperate.

He placed his hand over hers. Warmth zinged through her, snaking up her arm and radiating through her veins to the only destination that seemed to matter right now: the juncture of her thighs.

"Pretty chilly out there, huh?"

She nodded. Pretty warm in here, though. *In her*

*panties.* Moving her hand aside, he pulled on the zipper. More puckering of the nipples. Nothing but heated silence from him. It was excruciating and unbearably arousing.

*Say something, girl. Anything.*

"Sorry I'm late. My dumb truck broke down and I had trouble finding a cab—fucking Uber—and then it wouldn't drop me at the gate so I had to walk in the blizzard and . . . uh, I should shut up now."

His intense expression broke into a smile that short-circuited her brain. How lucky a woman would be to be regularly pinned on the end of that smile. If only he'd smile and never speak, he would be perfect.

With the zipper finally down, he shrugged her parka off her shoulders. The action brought his hard, muscular self within extra-sinning distance. His warm breath glanced across her cheek.

"Thanks for doing this," he said. "I promise I'll make it worth your while."

"You'd better," she whispered, enjoying this intimacy before she recalled the true reason for her presence among the gods. "Have you talked to Sam Cochrane?"

"Not yet. But after tomorrow with a few pictures online, it won't be necessary. It'll be clear that you're under my protection."

*My protection.* Falling under a man's shield was the one thing she had been fighting her whole life, but when Eli said it, she enjoyed an erotically forbidden thrill at the prospect.

"So how is this going to go down?"

"Go down?"

Did he have to repeat everything she said in a way that made it sound dirty? "The dating thing. Shouldn't we discuss that?"

He leaned in close. Well, closer. "I was thinking we'd just do what came naturally."

*N to the O.* If she did what "came naturally," she'd be licking the stubble off that jaw in ten seconds. Ground rules needed, stat.

"I don't think you should get too . . . handsy."

"Define handsy. Two hands? One? How many fingers are considered beyond the pale?"

*Two fingers would do nicely, thanks.*

"Just n-no kissing, okay?" she hissed, irked with herself for letting every word he said filter through her imagination and emerge as an intoxicating brew of top-shelf filth. The fully stocked bar was starting to look very inviting.

"No kissing," he murmured as he passed her parka off to Whitney, who had faded in like Ghost Assistant, doing her freakin' job at last. "Where?"

"Anywhere!"

"Just checking." He grinned, smug with getting a rise out of her. "You have to occasionally smile at what I say. That's why you're here, my sweet."

"Try to be charming instead of your usual moronic self, and the pearly whites might make an appearance. So what's happening tonight other than the game?"

"There's press here to capture our burgeoning affair." Said so casually that her pulse rate didn't even spike. Maybe there was hope she could become immune to his masculine wiles. "We'll take a few photos, visit with the players in the locker room after the game. Given where you work, I expect you can handle that."

"Believe me, I've seen enough naked men on the job that I could sue the city and make out like a bandit for a hostile work environment." At his look of concern, she clarified. "I can handle a little penis, Eli."

He let loose a full-throated laugh that made her feel like she was wearing a sweater on the inside. So much for that masculine wiles immunity. If only he would smile *and* laugh, but never speak. Then he would be perfect.

"Hopefully you won't have to handle a little penis, Alexandra."

Their gazes locked for a long beat, too protracted for the risqué comments to be passed off as anything but flirting. And not the fake kind, either. At least twenty seconds went by, which was a really long time when a man this powerful and attractive and damn him, *sexy*, was keeping you in place under his commanding touch.

"Drink?" He pressed a large hand to the small of her back, and her body lit up again. *This way, Alex, to a night of sensual torture.*

Make hers a double.

Eli was having second thoughts. And third, fourth, and fifth ones. Pity he couldn't say the same for Alexandra Dempsey, who seemed to be enjoying herself immensely with a man who was not him.

So he had temporarily abandoned her. He couldn't stay joined at the hip with her, not when everyone was vying for his attention, and not when he wanted to join other parts of his body to hers and growl, "Mine."

But she'd recovered from his absence with aplomb. She should have been bored stiff by Matt Cuddy, travel director for the Hawks. A former player, he liked to yammer on about how his knee blowout ruined his career five years ago. Not bad to look at, but otherwise the human equivalent of wet linguine. Like most hockey players.

Yet she was laughing at everything he said as though he were the funniest guy on the planet, in a way that she did not laugh with Eli. She had looked like a fiery vision when she'd exploded into the suite over an hour ago. Hair in a hullabaloo, gilded skin flushed like she'd fought a war to get here, her perfect breasts pulling fondly at the wool of her zipped sweater . . .

Those breasts were a menace. *She* was a menace.

This was what his life had devolved to: sneaking glances at a girl he liked from the back row of eighth-grade English while she flirted with the jock. Oh yeah, and he had lied to a woman to force her to spend time with him.

Two days ago at Engine Company 6, every argument he'd made to persuade her to cross over to the dark side had come up empty. He had not fired her brother. Nada. He had not fired her. Zilch. He had kept Cochrane off her back last summer. Who cares? Nothing made an impact, and as she waltzed out of that office, her body language singing an aria at having escaped his plans for her, he had panicked.

Eli never panicked. Not as a Marine. Not as an assistant state's attorney. Not as the mayor. But the idea of her walking out that door and *not* being his had sent his brain into lockdown. And apparently, the only way to reboot it was to blurt out that lie.

*Sam Cochrane is threatening to sue you,* instead of the less adversarial and much more romantic *Let me take you to dinner.*

Asking Alexandra on a real date should have been his first option, but too much had passed between them. Basically, the woman despised him—well, not his body, if that blistering kiss in the city hall storeroom was anything to go by—but the top note in their relationship was loathing. So the date option was bumped for the "you're about to be sued and made bankrupt" option. Because nothing spelled romance like the threat of legal proceedings.

*Eli Cooper, you are one sick son of a bitch.*

There was nothing for it now but to plow forward and make the best of it. All Alexandra needed to know was his imaginary protection from this imaginary lawsuit. And in the meantime, he would get to know *her* and watch the sparks between them ignite into a bonfire.

Time to get cracking on the kindling. Matt's questionable charms appeared to be wearing off—Alexandra's eyes kept wandering away from him to the buffet on the sideboard. Excellent. Eli had found his way in. After a moment loading up a plate for her, he approached just in time to overhear Matt bemoaning how hard it was to get 150 hotel rooms at short notice, especially in the postseason.

"No trouble this last year, though," came Alexandra's response.

Matt looked affronted.

"Because the Hawks sucked ass in the postseason," she explained.

"Yeah, I got it," Matt said.

Eli coughed to hide his laugh. No wonder she couldn't keep a man. Now for the next move in Operation Date-a-Firefighter.

*Honey, you must be starved. Have a bite to eat.*

*Oh, thanks, Mr. May—I mean, Eli.* Cue shy grin. *How thoughtful.*

He circled his prey, bared his metaphorical fangs (in the form of a selection of tasty finger foods), and . . . discovered to his chagrin he had been outflanked by Bastian Fucking Durand. Damn puck chaser.

"You looked like you could do with a little something," Durand was saying to Alexandra as he deposited a plateful of food into her hands.

Her mouth dropped open at the sight, either in surprise at his consideration or in full-on drool because she was hungry. "Probably should get my foot out of my mouth and fill it with something else, you mean?"

All three men stared at her.

"Uh, food, you guttersnipes." She popped a meatball into her mouth and turned to Eli with an eyebrow arch at the plate in his hands. "Is that for me, Mr. Mayor?"

"No. It's all mine and you can't have any."

She tried her best not to smile. Damn if he didn't enjoy this woman a little too much.

"Think I'll grab a beer." Matt moved away, then seemed to remember his manners. "Can I get you something?"

"I'm fine." Alexandra blew out a breath as Matt

loped off. "Another one bites the dust," she murmured to no one in particular.

"I'm Bastian," Durand said, as if Eli wasn't there and Durand's identity wasn't known by everyone in Chicago. "And you're Sexy Lexi. I saw you on the news."

"Yeah, well, it's all been overblown," she mumbled, then chowed down on another meatball.

"Nothing hotter than a woman with an ax," Durand said with a lascivious wink.

Eli balled his fists, inched closer to his soon-to-be-fake date, and brushed his knuckles at the base of her spine. Her surprised intake of breath was immensely gratifying. "Why, do you have a car that needs refinishing?" he asked Durand.

Ignoring him, the Meathead from Montreal went on. "Always wanted to be a fireman. I even applied back in Canada but then I was drafted by the NHL." He lifted one shoulder in that lazy French way. Saving lives or glory on the rink? So hard to decide, that shrug said.

"How's your groin?" Alexandra asked.

"*What?*" Eli blurted at the same time Durand said, "*Pardon?*"

"Your groin pull. I heard that's what put you on the bench. My brother Wy's a big fan. He's going to be stoked I met you."

"My groin"—Durand paused for effect—"is getting *strong-geh ev-very* day."

Alexandra laughed, a rather coquettish tinkle. Jesus H.

"Last summer," Durand continued in that annoyingly *French* tone, "the team got a tour of the firehouse academy, the Quinn. They said it was built on the site of the Great Chicago Fire."

"Where they think it originated."

"Started by a woman."

Both of them turned to Eli, who had felt a pressing need to interject at this point. Alexandra gifted him the stabby eyes of death. "*Excuuuse* me?"

"The legend goes that Mrs. O'Leary's cow was to blame. So we have a woman and her female livestock . . ."

Ever seen a cat arch its back and bristle? That's what his sexy firefighter did right then. "Are you blaming a fire that destroyed two-thirds of the city on a woman? *Because* she was a woman? Or her cow? *Because* it was female?"

"I'm probably being too hard on the dumb bovine," Eli explained in his most patronizing voice. "If the woman had tied up her cow properly, the city wouldn't have burnt to the ground."

Passion widened those melted shamrock eyes and sent her voice into a spike. "Burning to the ground was the best thing to ever happen to this city. Architects swarmed in, looking to rebuild, culminating in the World's Fair. This city is beautiful because of Mrs. O'Leary and her cow." She glared at him. "So you need to apologize."

"To Mrs. O'Leary or the cow?"

"To the entirety of womankind, you ass."

He grinned.

She sighed. "Why do I let you do this?"

"I don't know. But I should have waited until I had you alone so I could take advantage of all that passion of yours."

Blushing, she lowered her dark lashes tinged with copper so they spread like decorative fans on her cheeks. He loved getting her flustered. After fantasizing about her stretched out beneath him, or on her knees before him, or in every single lurid sexual position his filthy mind could conjure, getting Alexandra Dempsey flustered was his next favorite thing in the world.

"Anyway, it's been pretty much debunked," she went on, plucking an egg roll off the plate he had brought over. His chest warmed at this small victory. "The reporter who broke the story said he invented Mrs. O'Leary's involvement. Anti-Irish sentiment."

"Irish," he mused. "But, of course, it's all clear now, Firefighter *Dempsey*."

She broke into a husky, good-time-girl laugh that warmed other parts of his anatomy. "You're such a dick."

Bastian Durand was staring at them. In fact, they'd attracted quite an audience, including assorted members of the press. He'd have liked to say his intention in sparking Alexandra's emerald eyes and saucy mouth to life was purely political, to get those hacks gossiping, but it would have been a lie. His intentions were far more depraved than anything a politician could claim.

They held each other's gaze, the moment exquisite and strung on a wire. This time, she didn't duck or hide. This time, she accepted his appraisal as well she should. She was a frighteningly beautiful woman and she deserved his utmost attention.

"Did you always want to be a politician?" she asked with a wry twist to her mouth. "Because you haven't got a diplomatic bone in your body."

He wanted to laugh, because she was being a good sport when he didn't deserve it for teasing her and because no one harbors childhood fantasies of being a politician. "I wanted to be a lawyer."

Durand regarded him with undisguised disdain. So lawyers and politicians were lower on the glamour scale than firefighters and hockey players, it seemed.

"Like your father," Alexandra said, her big eyes watching him carefully. "You wanted to follow in his footsteps."

He nodded, relief coursing through his veins that she understood. They both recognized the importance of legacies.

"That's how it was for me, as well," she said. "Before I even knew what firefighting was, I had the itch for it. Dad would come home, smelling of smoke, and he'd . . ." A watercolor pink bloomed on her cheeks as she trailed off. "Well, I knew."

Evidently embarrassed at her admission, she slid her gaze to the rink. The Hawks were on the wrong end of a 4–1 score line with a minute left on the clock.

"Kane, get your stick out of your ass and hit the puck!" She shook her head. "If they keep playing like that, Matt's not going to have much to do come play-off season."

Eli heard a cough behind him.

With an oh-well shrug, Alexandra turned her head. "Sorry, Matty. Even with your gimpy knee and Durand's dodgy crotch, you could do better than that lot out there."

# CHAPTER NINE

Stepping into the back room of DeLuca's Ristorante in Wicker Park was like time traveling to medieval Tuscany. The scent of an indoor herb garden wafted lavender and thyme beneath Alex's nostrils. Hanging lanterns strung through indoor-planted trees painted it with the brushstrokes of a fairy tale.

They'd passed through a hallway next to the kitchen, and while the sweet tang of tomatoes and fragrant meats made her mouth water, it couldn't compete with the intoxicating male spice of her dining companion. What in the name of all that was holy was she doing partaking of a late-night supper with Eli Cooper in what looked like a very romantic locale?

*Strategy session*, Eli had called it. They'd visited the Hawks locker room, where Alex had indulged in a spot of unabashed ogling—really to piss off her "date"—and had more photos taken. Eli had insisted on a debriefing about how the night had gone.

He pulled out a chair, so natch she walked around to the other side.

"Sit here," he said, his fingers strumming the back of the chair.

Oh, he had been holding it for her. Surprise at his

behavior dampened the spark of annoyance at his bossy tone. She walked back, but before she could sit, he started tugging at the shoulders of her parka. "Let me."

She bit her lip, closed her eyes, and let him. With him standing so close, it was just as seductive as when he'd unzipped her jacket earlier on. More so. Because now he was behind her and there was something indelibly erotic about not being able to see him. Just feeling his breath hot on her neck, the ghost of his lips close enough to sin. If this was her reaction when he stripped off coats, how the hell would she not melt into a puddle if he moved to the next layer?

Which wasn't happening.

He pushed in the chair as she sat and moved around to seat himself. All very date-like behavior . . . except no date had ever done that for her. There was danger in being impressed by a little chivalry. Just because Eli Cooper was polite to a woman did not make him any less of an enemy. He probably thought women with their pea-sized brains needed assistance with things like sitting and coat-doffing and . . . orgasms.

She bet he was *really* good at assisting in that area.

The server, an Italian woman with big, scary hair that Alex immediately empathized with, stopped by to take their drink order: a Glenlivet for Eli and a double Macallan eighteen year for Alex because it was expensive and the city of Chicago was buying. Alone at last, Eli stared at Alex for a long, skin-heating moment.

"I was right to insist you sit there. The light hits you perfectly."

She swallowed around the lump the size of a bread

roll in her throat. "Makes my hair look less frightening, I imagine."

"Just highlights your natural beauty. You're a very striking woman, Alexandra."

She knew she wasn't an ogre, but damn, it sent her stomach into a wriggle to hear him compliment her that way.

"No one's listening, Mr. Mayor, so you can stow the sweet talk. Unless . . ." She looked over to the bar, where Eli's security detail was sitting with a club soda, his eyes trained on the room, seeking out potential assassins. "Is there press here?"

"I doubt it, except for our citizenry, who are all press of a sort. If someone takes a photo and tweets it, then the night is a success."

The pleasant wriggle in her gut turned uneasy. She was pretty sure she didn't want her family or friends to get the wrong idea, especially as the wrong idea was so, so appealing.

"What about Thing? Does he get to eat?"

"Thing?"

"Craggy Face over at the bar."

He smiled and *pop!* all hail the devastating dimple. "Hush, you'll hurt his feelings. He has to go where I go, but ravioli would dull his reflexes."

"Sounds like his presence might dull your love life."

He laughed, and the sound nearly gave her a mini-orgasm on the spot. "Most women like the idea. It makes them feel important to be with a man who needs that kind of protection. So, speaking of love lives . . ."

"Were we?" She plucked a piece of focaccia from the basket and dipped it into an herbed olive oil.

"Tell me more about these miserable dates you've been going on."

Miserable? Her cheeks flamed, remembering that Eli had been there a week ago when Michael Martinez dumped her in front of a roomful of watchful diners. Had the mayor been one of the rubbernecking observers? The memory of the detective flinching as she leaned in to brush her lips across his cheek still stung.

They say that what doesn't kill you makes you stronger. At this rate she should be able to bench-press a Buick.

"You do *not* want to hear about my dating adventures."

"What else are we going to talk about? Firefighters' underfunded pensions? Our diametrically opposed viewpoints on whether a man should pull a chair from the table for a woman? I'd like to enjoy my meal, thanks." He arched the mayoral eyebrow. "Tell me about your worst date."

Well, there was the orgasmless one-night stand against the jukebox in her family's bar a few months ago, but calling it a date was probably overstating it.

"Three words: spoken-word jazz."

He chuckled. "And the best?"

*This one.* A conclusion that was so sad she should just go home now and drown herself in the kitchen sink.

"Clearly none, because I'm still looking."

His eyes twinkled dangerously. The man was so handsome it tore at her lungs. "So how many men have you marauded your way through in the last year?"

Her swallow was audible. "Not seeing how that's relevant."

"Alexandra." Spoken in that commanding tone that made her . . . oh, God, she was starting to love how he said her name.

"I've only begun putting in the effort lately. Online dating. Tinder, that kind of thing."

"How many?"

"Thirty-four in ten months."

Sexy lip twitch. "How many were second dates?"

Her silence was thunderously embarrassing. "I know!" she finally said after three seconds that felt like three hours. "You think I'm a freak."

"Asked and answered long ago. Are you trying to win a bet?"

She tore the bread apart, needing to do something with her hands. "I'm just optimistic enough to believe that there's someone for everyone, even an undate-able weirdo like me. And if I cast my net wide enough, I'll find it."

It wasn't as if she'd never had a boyfriend. After college, she was all loved up with Justin, who thought her firefighter fantasy was "cute." During her three-year wait to get the call for CFD, she had worked as an EMT and racked up a shit ton of experience dealing with machete-wielding meth tweakers and bug-eyed violent winos. But Justin couldn't handle it, and she couldn't handle his suffocating concern. After she showed up for a date with a black eye sustained during a tricky run, it was adios, Justin.

She shoved a piece of bread into her mouth. "I even thought that this fake dating setup might put me in a different circle. Get me moving and shaking with better-quality talent."

He frowned. "Politicians, aldermen, lawyers."

"Baseball, basketball, hockey." Feeling playful, but mostly needing to assert some measure of control over this awkward conversation, she peeked at him from beneath the veil of her lashes. "I like the idea of my kids being bilingual."

The frown deepened. "For God's sake, Dempsey."

"What, is Bastian gay? Married? A nose picker?"

"He's Canadian. Now, don't get me wrong, some great things have come out of Canada. William Shatner, Leonard Cohen—"

"Bastian Durand."

"Poutine, Nathan Fillion," he continued as if she hadn't spoken.

"You like *Firefly*?" He probably knew Nathan Fillion from *Castle* instead of from the greatest science-fiction TV show ever created.

"Only idiots don't like *Firefly*, Alexandra. Canadians are also excellent at managing snow, but Durand is not your standard peace-and-ice-loving Canadian, he's French Canadian. The Maple Leaf Frenchies add an extra layer of snooty with their smug."

She rolled her eyes. "He wasn't snooty or smug, he was interesting. He's got a lovely smize."

"Smize?"

"Smiles with his eyes. Tough guy, but not afraid to show his vulnerable side."

Disgust crossed his disruptively handsome face. Eli Cooper wouldn't know a smize if it struck him with a puck. "Of course he's not afraid to show his vulnerable side. He plays hockey, which is for pussies."

She laughed. "This is so weird."

"What is?"

She gestured between them, unwilling or perhaps just unable to verbalize how much fun she was having. He was so charmingly sure, even when his assurance was invested in ridiculously incorrect opinions. And he liked *Firefly.*

"So what about you?" she asked. "The press never stops talking about your constant stream of marriage proposals. How many today?"

"Five. No, six. The fire has increased my stock." His long fingers strummed the table. "Dating's not so easy in my position. Fake dating is more my style."

"Tough with all those women chasing you on your morning jog."

He gave a self-deprecating smile. It undid her a little.

"When every moment is carved up and captured for public consumption, it can put a real crimp in your sex life. I have to be careful about how I approach that."

Hmm. She had never thought it might be difficult for him, but she'd had a little taste of life in the public eye in the last few months, and hand to God, she'd rather have a root canal with a rusty nail. She especially didn't enjoy how Finance Guy, aka Mr. Two-Pump-Chump, had set out for conquest *in her bar* so he could say he'd banged America's Favorite Firefighter. Multiplying that by a factor of ten thousand and extending it for years as the most eligible bachelor this side of the Mississippi? Well, she would not enjoy that at all.

"You took the plunge once."

"Never again."

"Madison or marriage?"

"Both. She's a wonderful woman, but it was a huge mistake, which we both recognized immediately. Your typical Vegas cliché. I was twenty-four, on leave from the Marines, and very drunk. We got it annulled a few weeks later."

The hitch of relief she felt in her chest that he didn't seem to have anything but a cordial relationship with his ex really bugged her. "You're disappointing women the world over. Having a nice, loving wife at your side, maybe even a couple of cherubic offspring, would play better for your image."

He considered this. "That's the problem. Marriage is all about image. People marry for money, power, family, society, or just so they can have someone to sit on the couch with and watch *Law & Order* reruns. It's for those who don't have the inner resources to be happy alone. If you have to rely on someone else to be content, then it doesn't say much about you."

She refused to take offense because this was Eli, who offended with every other word. "So the fact I'm looking for something meaningful makes me desperate and incapable of tapping into my poverty-stricken interior life?"

"Different strokes, Alexandra. I can't speak for you, but allowing someone that much control over my happiness sounds like a recipe for disaster. If I subscribe to that way of thinking . . ." He hesitated, as though seeking a way to reframe what he was saying. Not because he worried about insulting her, but because he wanted to get it right. "Putting all your trust into the hands of another person is dangerous. What if it's the wrong person?"

It was a chance she was willing to take. "Hopefully, you'll find out before any real damage is done."

His expression turned stark. "Years can go by before you find out a person's true colors. People always hide things, play parts."

That was a very bleak view. She leaned in because this smacked of a weird significance, the why of which she'd examine later. "Politicians, perhaps. But that's just an image you have to craft for your public, Eli. In your real life, you don't have to hide. With the right person, that is."

A flicker of what looked like pain in his eyes startled her. Maybe Madison had done more of a number on him than he let on, but her intuition told her there was more to it.

"Well, this has gotten very serious all of a sudden." With a slight shake of his head, he picked up the menu and skimmed it. "Let's start with the burrata, then the gnocchi with brown butter and sage, and—"

"You plan to order for me?"

He peeked up, and the light caught the blue-black of his hair and the shine in those shark's eyes. In that carnal gaze, she felt hooked by the sensual lure of a man who knew what he wanted—and it wasn't on the menu.

The mayor's eye-fucking game? A-plus.

"A lot of women like when a man orders for them."

"I think they like watching how your face lights up when you're acting all omnipotent."

"That's a big word."

"I'm a big girl." Damn, that sounded flirty, but the atmosphere was conspiring to tear down every inhibition she usually had around him. Which, of late, wasn't much. "Order away," she added dismissively. "I live to serve you, sire."

He looked pleased at her faux obeisance, and hell if she didn't actually like the flutter of pleasure in her stomach at the thought of gratifying him. At the notion of obeying every wicked command that tumbled from his sensuous mouth.

She needed to remember all the stunts he had pulled and how much she disliked him. That underneath the quips, flirting, and enough sexual tension to set off the restaurant's smoke alarms, they were actually at war.

"Two days later and I was still plucking bugs out of my bra!"

One bottle of Montalcino in, and Eli had learned three new things about Alexandra Dempsey. She was absolutely fearless: her tales of motorbiking solo around Vietnam after college (cue the bugs-in-her-bra story) had him alternately clutching his wineglass and suppressing concerned gasps. She despised the White Sox in a way he considered unhealthy. And she had collarbones that did strange things to his brain. He would never have considered himself a clavicle man, yet here he was.

This woman rocked the curves of Marilyn Monroe, the no-filter mouth of Chelsea Handler, and the spirit of Amelia Earhart. She was the real deal.

Aided by the wine and the stellar creations from

Tony DeLuca's kitchen, she had loosened up. Watching her eat had been one of the most pleasurable things to strike him in a very long time. She attacked her food with gusto, making *nom-nom* noises in the back of her throat that had him wondering how she would sound if she was to eat or lick or suck . . .

He hauled his mind out of the gutter. Long way to travel. "How did your family feel about you traipsing all over the world on your wild adventures?"

She made a face, suddenly someone's younger sister. "Luke shouted at me for a month before I left and then a month after I returned because I contracted a teensy bout of malaria. He's such an old woman sometimes. I thought it best not to mention that one time I was mugged in an alley behind my hostel in Hanoi."

He buried his face in his hands. "Jesus."

"Hey, the guy came out of that alley clutching the family jewels and wishing he'd never met me." She grinned, and he had no idea if she was teasing him or if she had truly kicked the ass of some Vietnamese mugger.

"Never thought I'd empathize with Luke. I should hire you for security."

The grin cooled. "Cute, Cooper, but you don't really believe that, do you? You think the differences between the sexes make my gender a liability in my job."

"You're strong, quick, and clever, Alexandra," he said honestly. "But I don't think all women are as resourceful or as competent as you. Ask most anyone, man or woman, who they'd prefer carry them out of a fire and they're not going to choose a female firefighter."

An indignant crimp furrowed the spot between her eyes. "Men will always be threatened by a strong woman, and as for women, apparently it's a female fantasy to have a big, burly fireman rescue them." Her sigh signaled her annoyance at such sisterly treachery.

"And it's my fantasy to have a sexy female firefighter give me the kiss of life." He gave a sorry head shake and murmured, "And you couldn't even get that right."

"Got it right later," she quipped, then blushed to the hairline of her crazy curls as she realized what she'd said.

He liked making her blush. Was she pinking up anywhere else right now? he wondered. Her breasts, her nipples, that heaven between her legs he dreamed of taking and holding him deep?

"It was a pretty hot kiss," he ventured.

"I've had better."

"No, you haven't." As he hadn't, he was 100 percent sure the feeling was mutual.

There was no missing the flare of remembered pleasure in those stormy eyes before she lowered them and picked at the bread basket. Clearly seeking a change of topic, she said, "So, our dads were in business together back in the day. You said you'd met Sean."

Feeling magnanimous, he allowed her to move on. "He used to come over to the house when I was a kid, long before he and Mary adopted you. I remember him as this mountain of a man, always laughing, a larger-than-life character. Later my father sold off his share in your bar to keep his financials aboveboard when he became state's attorney. He planned to go into politics eventually."

Her gaze softened. Not his intention, but a typical reaction. When your parents are murdered in your home while you hide away in an upstairs closet, it tended to unleash a woman's maternal instinct.

"Please don't."

She blinked. "Please don't what?"

"Give me that look, like I need a hug because of my tragic backstory. Poor little orphan Eli."

"I don't think you need a hug. I think you need a gag." She took a sip of her wine. "You've certainly managed to parlay your tragic backstory into an advantage for your political career."

*Well played, Miss Dempsey.* "A shockingly cynical viewpoint from one so young, but not wholly inaccurate."

She smiled her pleasure at being right. *Heart punch.*

A sudden, long-buried memory rose to kick him in the gut. Sun streaming on cherry wood. Black earth falling with a soft thud. A man in a Chicago Fire Department dress uniform with eyes as relentlessly blue as the lake in summer.

His parents' funeral was delayed because they needed to gather evidence and make sure nothing was missed before they were buried. For the case they would build later. But there would be no prosecution. Ronan Cutler, the mob boss behind the hit on his parents, was already dead in a raid on his estate two days after the murders, the triggerman with him.

The words of that uniformed man—Sean

Dempsey—sliced through him now with a painful clarity.

*Anything you need, son. We're here for you.*

A promise made to him the day of his parents' funeral. A life credit he had never cashed in, and even though he had not availed himself of Sean Dempsey's kindness, Eli knew it would have been given freely and without reservation.

Though he would have severed his left testicle before sharing that with anyone, Alexandra seemed to sense his discomfort as his memories claimed the quiet space between them. She reached for him and took his hand. He curled his fingers around her strong, elegant ones, and those words she spoke in that smoky hotel corridor came back in a gush.

*I'm here. I'm not leaving.*

If anyone from the press were watching, it would be a lovely moment to capture.

*A shockingly cynical viewpoint, Mr. Mayor.*

He withdrew his hand, packed away the maudlin in his mind. She seemed to recognize the awkwardness and instead of her usual bull-in-a-china-shop proclivity, she stayed quiet for a blessed moment.

"Who did you live with after your parents died?"

"My grandparents on my mother's side in Lake Forest. They were good people. Serious-minded, not given to great shows of emotion."

"And they kept the house for you?"

It wasn't the first time someone had mentioned it. Why would he want to stay there, sharing space with all those ghosts?

"I lived a blessed existence in that house until I was twelve and it was shattered." He looked her in the eye. "I'm not living there now to exorcise any demons. It's the site of my fondest memories, so I'd rather dwell on that than what came later." So it was quiet except for Shadow and he barely spent any time there, but returning to the house at the end of the day, if only for a few hours, was his touchstone. He didn't think it morbid, but others invariably did.

"We do what we must to hold on to them," she murmured, her finger tracing the lip of her wineglass. "Not a day goes by when I don't think of Dad and Logan. After they died, it was the ordinary, most mundane things that hurt the most. Seeing the dent in Sean's favorite armchair. The half-empty bottle of almond creamer. Logan was the only one who drank it, and I kept it until it was stiff and stunk up the fridge."

She looked up, her face open, no artifice in her expression. What must it be like to enjoy such freedom to say and do as you please? Some days, it was all Eli could do not to rattle and scream at the bounds of this cage he'd built to contain his emotions.

Under the twinkling lights, with her pandemonium of curls, she projected an aura of strength and goodness and beauty. He wanted to absorb it into his bones and blood. Possess it—and her with it.

He wanted to do very wicked things to this woman.

"The zabaglione here is an old family recipe and absolute perfection, Alexandra. Care to share?"

"You didn't have to take me home," she said from the backseat corner of the SUV as they drove through the North Side's icy streets. "I'm sure you're busy."

"Not really. The babies I need to kiss and the MILFs I like to ogle are all tucked away in their beds."

With Tom up front along with John, his driver, returning to the intimacy of before was a no-go. They both seemed to recognize it, so they let the drive go by in silence.

A damned uncomfortable silence on his end, though. The image he'd had of her as he put on her coat after dinner was on repeat in his brain like an irrepressible jack-in-the-box. She had a great ass, high, well rounded, and it looked amazing in jeans. His hand would look so fine shaping it, kneading it, maybe giving it a little slap. Moving his fingers to the cleft and stroking through to find lubricating moisture—

He shifted to accommodate his hard-on, an issue that had plagued him all evening. Filled his mind with budget numbers, precinct voting percentages. His problem with Cochrane, which always managed to put a damper on his mood. On reaching her house in Andersonville, he was tempted to let her go without comment so he wouldn't be tempted otherwise.

*Get ahold of yourself, Cooper.* He could see the woman he currently had nothing but a business deal with and who happened to hold a very low opinion of him to her door without molesting her. Not a store-room in sight.

"Thanks for dinner." Without looking at him, she exited. He got out, too, and walked behind her, ignoring Tom's threatening glare admonishing him not to even think about entering that house without a security scan being done first. She fiddled with her key and pushed her front door open. "All safe now."

Was it? He remained in place.

Her brow puckered. "You can rest assured your medal from the Order of Chivalry is in the mail."

"Must everything be framed as a battle, Alexandra? I was merely being polite and walking you to your door."

She huffed her annoyance. "You wouldn't do it for a man."

"I might. If he was puny or was carrying Super Bowl tickets and looked like he might be mugged at any moment." He placed a hand on the doorframe a few inches from her cheek. "Instead of taking everything I say and twisting it to suit your own ridiculous biases, how about accepting that tonight we ate some good food, actually conversed like human beings, and for once didn't want to gouge strips out of each other?"

She muttered something incomprehensible. Christ on the cross, this woman would be the death of him. It was like she was deliberately trying to pick a fight, get him riled, and—

A flash of recognition pinged him. "Are you embarrassed that we actually connected tonight on some other level than bickering?"

Even under the muted glow of a security light, he saw her redden. "Or maybe you're worried that this new phase in our relationship will supersede the old one?"

"Any chance you could speak English like a normal person, Cooper? What the hell does that mean?"

He edged forward another step, pleased when

she backed into the door. It fell open further, inviting them to privacy. To pleasure. "When we're going at it, there's an undeniable charge between us, wouldn't you say?"

"Don't be ridiculous," she said. Softly.

"Your attraction to me scares you, but what also scares you is that there might be . . ."

"What?" Her voice was barely a whisper.

"More."

He fisted his hand in that lush wealth of hair and let his mouth hover over hers. Ostensibly to give her time to back out, but in reality, there was no unringing this bell. The die had been cast. He had to kiss her.

Given his warning shot, she shouldn't have been shocked, but her lust-blown pupils broadcast her surprise. Her lips parted on a whimper and he took advantage because he was nothing if not a grasping opportunist. But he was fooling himself. The advantage was all on her side. She made a sound—half-purr, half-growl—and then threw herself into it. Her hands clutched his shoulders, her fingers dug in for leverage. Lost in her, utterly lost, he could only hold on, fighting the raging need inside him that was going to terminate with her back against the door while he drove deep into her wet, welcoming heat.

On a chilly North Side street.

While his security detail watched.

He drew back breathless.

Senseless.

Mindless.

"It's okay to like me, Alexandra."

"Not so sure it is," she breathed through kiss-swollen lips.

She had yet to release him, those big green eyes staring at him with a heady brew of pleading and desire. Tom would have a fit if he stepped inside her door. So would Eli's heart. But his cock would thank him.

He pushed her back.

"Eli!" she gasped.

"I'll just be a second," he barked at Tom. Eli closed the door. "Are we alone?"

"Yes, but . . . what do you think you're doing?"

"Ensuring this thing between us doesn't pass," and then his mouth met hers before either of them could reason their way out of the inevitable.


Alex had fantasized about Eli, not just because he had kissed her in that closet, but long before that. Even when he was a jerk, it fueled her fantasies, because it was deliciously sinful. Taboo. A man she despised who got her engine running unlike any man she had ever liked.

So the fact that she now liked him maybe 5 percent more than she had six hours ago should have ruined the forbidden fruit thrill, but it did not. Her feelings for him were a clash of discordant sounds: he was the jackass who disrespected her, but now he was also the boy who'd endured so much, the man whose life she saved, the god she needed between her thighs. Such complexity, and it only heightened every sensation, layering one on top of another until she could barely breathe for wanting him.

He was an evil fucking genius. And he was kissing her mouth, her jaw, her earlobes.

"Eli," she whispered as he fed hot kisses down her throat.

"Tell me to stop."

*Hell no.* She shaped her hands to his broad back and pulled him closer, giving him her answer. The reason behind his attentiveness to her parka-removal needs earlier was now clear—he'd been practicing to bring out his big game later. Rather efficiently, her coat was slipped off her shoulders, her scarf was unwrapped, and then the zipper of her hoodie was inched down.

*Skillz.* He had them.

He hesitated, and the moment terrified her with all its weighted uncertainty, but all he said was, "Pink."

Her favorite color—no, the irony didn't escape her—and the hue of her bra.

In record time, that pesky bra was unhooked with astonishing ease and her breasts were lacking in considerable support. Until they were cupped in Eli's very supportive hands. He pushed one strap off her shoulder, then the other, and exposed her completely to him. She felt his gaze, its sensuous weight on her skin.

"Beautiful," he murmured. "You're so damn beautiful, Alexandra."

*Alexandra.* Before she had chosen to see his use of her full name as a chauvinistic reminder that she was a woman doing a man's job. But she realized now how wrong she had been. Eli called her that because no one else did. Because he saw her like no one else could.

The out it provided felt liberating. She could be this new person with him, ceding control to his demanding desires. Let him tame her. Dominate her.

Own her.

He kissed the hollow of her throat, the line of her collarbone, and oh!—the pleasure that rocketed through her veins when his mouth latched on to her peaked nipple caught her off guard. Everywhere, she felt it. In her breasts and her belly. In her legs and her pussy. A tightening want that built with each soul-deep suckle. While his mouth drove her to the edge, his other hand palmed her ass, holding her core against his erection. Locking her into this prison of pleasure.

Throw away the damn key.

He unhinged his mouth long enough to rumble, "Get your other tit ready for me."

"Wh-what?"

"You heard me."

Moisture pooled between her thighs, his demand going straight to her clit. So bossy. So hot. Apparently satisfied he would be obeyed, he returned to lavishing attention on only one breast. It was crazily arousing that she could be so sensitive there, every nerve ending primed to ignite. That she could be this close—

*To coming.* Oh, God, she was going to come and he hadn't even moved below her waist. Lost in a fever dream of Eli's making, she cupped the breast not attached to his mouth and plumped it, stoking the fires of lust, loving how her fingers felt against her ruched nipples.

She was offering her aching breast to Eli Cooper like it was a rich, decadent dessert.

"You taste so fucking good," he panted, his breath hot against her damp, tender peak. "I knew you would. I knew."

"Please. Oh, God, Eli, please." And then he accepted the sensitive flesh she fed him on a heartfelt groan, as if it were water after forty days in the desert. Her orgasm hovered on that sweet edge, tottered, and as Eli changed up his hungry suckle with a scrape of his teeth across her abraded nipple, crashed over. She screamed her release while her body rocked against him in jerky throes, and then went completely still.

After several taut moments, he raised his head. "Did you just—?"

"Yes," she gasped, annoyed with him for asking, but mostly with herself for being a complete embarrassment. What the hell was wrong with her that she shattered with the slightest provocation? Gone in sixty seconds.

In the dim light filtering through the half-circle window of the front door, she watched his reaction, willing him to be a dick about it.

"Been awhile?"

*And we're back.* She called on the two brain cells she had left to form a few well-chosen words. "I've been fantasizing about the entire Hawks defense all night. You're just convenient."

"Well, I'd hate to inconvenience you," he drawled before he kissed her deep, and her lips clutched at him along with her hands at his shoulders. She hated herself for her weakness, but she'd hate herself more if she didn't turn it to her favor.

"I wonder what would happen if I kissed you somewhere else," he whispered thickly between brain-destroying kisses. "If I licked and sucked you where you need it most." He scraped his shadowed jaw against her cheek. "Tell me where you need it most, Alexandra."

Speech was impossible. Verbalizing her need was tantamount to begging, so instead she took his hand and placed it between her legs.

"That's my girl. Never be afraid to tell me what you need." After a few lascivious rubs against the seam, he unbuttoned her jeans and drew down her zipper. Agonizing in its slowness. With a testing finger, he pulled at the front of her panties.

"How many?"

"What?"

"When I asked you earlier how many fingers were considered too handsy, you thought of the ideal number to fill you. I know you did. How many?"

*Get out of my head, Eli Cooper.*

Not patient enough to wait for a response, he slipped one—not ideal—finger into her panties. Deeper. Oh God oh God. A hiss escaped his lips on finding her drenched and swollen in readiness for him. She tightened around his finger, an involuntary reflex.

He groaned. "Need an answer."

"Two," she gasped as his thumb pad brushed across her clit. The first orgasm was amazing, this second one was going to make that one look like— oh shit! She had no ready comparison because he plunged two fingers inside her, pumped her once, twice, three times, and sent her hurtling off the ledge. Again.

What the hell was he doing to her?

Control. She needed to grasp it now and wreck him like he'd done her. Panting her way back to an even draw, she reached for him. Jeans, unzipped. Shirttails, out. Hands, all over him. His eyes never left hers, steadier than her heartbeat, steadier than her hands.

How could he be so calm?

Time to muss this guy up. She palmed the hard glory she found between his muscular thighs. The fabric of his boxer briefs felt silky thin, too thin to contain the power bristling behind it.

"Alexandra," he grated as he rocked into her hand, eyelids falling to half-mast. Those two ideal fingers were still buried between her thighs like they had found home sweet home. Now they rubbed against her twanging flesh, mimicking the motion of her hand on his erection, earning their goddamn keep. It had never happened before, but it was starting to look like three times would be the charm—and this time, she wanted all his power inside her.

He grew huge under her touch, bigger than any of her furtive, filthy imaginings. All she could think of was the completion she would get from having this cock invade her, deep, as deep as she needed it. Two orgasms and her greedy inner slut demanded more. All of him.

An impossibility.

Because if this went any further, the wall between them would be destroyed—only to expose another one behind it. The one he insisted remain because he didn't much care for her profession and he likely didn't care for her. Using her for his campaign was his prime directive. She had joked that he was convenient, but it wasn't a joke, not entirely. There was nothing between them but panty-melting attraction.

The sex would be spectacular, but she wanted more than a mind-blowing lay. She deserved more.

And it would not—*it could not*—come at the hands of a man like Eli Cooper.

Her hand stilled. Dropped away. "We—we shouldn't do this."

He gave a low, pained laugh. "Worried I won't respect you in the morning?"

"I'm worried you don't respect me now."

"I respect you plenty, honey, but no one said there needed to be boatloads of respect for two people to have a good time."

"I'm not looking for a good time," said the girl who had just enjoyed two—*count 'em, two*—screaming orgasms. "I don't do one-night stands." Not anymore.

His laugh sent sensual shivers bone deep. Her still-sensitive pussy, that brazen tramp, clamped down on the pleasurable invasion of his fingers. She moaned, both wanting and dreading further completion.

"At least forty nights to the election, Alexandra."

Digging deep for the last crumbs of her self-respect, she splayed her hands on his chest and pushed. "Not. Happening."

Immediately he stepped back, and she mourned both the loss of his heat and the fingers he dragged through her plump folds on withdrawal. *Come back,* her sex screamed. The void he left was near intolerable.

"Seems I can't control myself when we get into tight spaces." His mouth was harsh with lust but his words were surprisingly conciliatory considering what she had just done. Left the most powerful man in the city with balls bluer than a Chicago summer sky.

"You think this is going to be enough, Alexandra? For either of us?"

"It—it has to be."

He opened his mouth to say more, but voices intruded, low and close. "I'm sure you've got it wrong," she could hear Gage saying. Someone muttered in response, probably Eli's security detail.

"Shit, that's my brother," she hissed, and then it was all systems go as Eli zipped up her hoodie—as if he'd done this many, many times before—leaving her bra just hanging there uselessly. Eager to be just as helpful, she pulled on his zipper, but it got stuck.

"You're too"—*hung, erect, hot for me*—"oh, God, fix it!"

He grunted in pain as the zipper jammed against his not-deflating-anytime-soon erection. She had no time to be flattered.

"Alexandra, I can handle my own fucking cock."

Stitch *that* on a pillow.

The door opened with Gage throwing out over his shoulder, "My sister and the mayor? Why, that's impossible. They absolutely hate each other."

Eli had tucked his shirttails into his now zipped-up jeans, though why he bothered she had no idea because it would be better to use it to cover his massive bulge. Meanwhile, Alex tried to telepathically direct her unhooked bra to travel several inches higher than where it sat now, *not* doing its job of keeping the girls in check. She shrink-wrapped herself against the wall as if removing her body from Eli's orbit could minimize the damage.

"See, hate each other," Gage announced, two steps away from laughing his head off.

Thing sniffed, seeking out evidence of hanky-panky. "Whole lot of hatin' goin' on, for sure."

"What are you doing here?" Alex snapped at her brother.

Gage grabbed his chest in mock surprise. "You mean, in my home, where I live?"

"I thought you were staying over at Brady's."

"So we hate each other now," murmured Eli, lazy and low.

"I'm far too evolved to hate anyone," she said defensively. "You annoy me and I hate your politics, but I can separate the sin from the sinner." Annoyance and hate were very different things, though neither seemed to be a barrier to her getting it on in the hallway of her home.

"Mr. Mayor," Thing said patiently.

Eli looked torn, so she helped him along by extending her hand.

"Thanks for dinner and for seeing me home."

He stared at her outstretched hand before lifting that stony gaze with a look of, *Really?* After a long beat, he clasped her in his strong grip. But if she expected that to be the end of it, she was a fool. He gathered her close to him and with his other hand, circled her waist possessively. Her knees melted.

His breath was hotly seductive against her ear. "Anytime you want to sin with this sinner, honey, you just let me know."

Then he released her and strode past Gage and Thing into the night.

# ◊ CHAPTER TEN

*Look who was spotted cozying up together at a late supper after the Hawks-Wings game last night. Our embattled mayor obviously needed a little time away from the campaign trail, and who better than Sexy Lexi, America's Favorite Firefighter. The two were clearly having fun discussing the menu at DeLuca's . . . and maybe more?*

*—Chicago Tattler*

Alex liked to spend the mornings of her days off easing into the world with coffee and a cinnamon-raisin English muffin. Checking in with Matt and Savannah on *Today*. Thinking about whether she should go for a run. Deciding that she should not.

She did not like to spend that time reading about herself online. Neither did she like to spend it getting the third degree from her brothers and their better halves. She just knew she shouldn't have opened the door when she heard that dull pounding. Nothing good ever followed a dull pounding.

"Where's the fire?" she snapped.

Thunderous rage stormed across Luke's brow. Before he could speak, Kinsey stepped out gingerly from behind him. "Please forgive him though he knows exactly what he's doing."

Oh, brother.

"What the hell were you doing at a Hawks game and an Italian restaurant with Eli fucking Cooper?"

"It's freakin' freezing. Would you like to come in or would you prefer to scream at me in the street like a fishwife?" She waved at Mrs. Gish, her nosy next-door neighbor with eyes currently on stalks, and strutted back to the kitchen, singing, "Oh, the weather outside can bite me."

"I just made coffee," she threw over her shoulder, "but it sounds like you might have had too much already."

"Alex, I want an explanation."

Kinsey walked over to the Mr. Coffee and helped herself. "He's just worried. We both are."

Her insides shriveled at being dishonest with her family, but none of them would take the threat of Sam Cochrane lying down. Kinsey would whip up some PR campaign and Luke would employ his usual MO—fists first, questions not necessary. They would back her to the hilt, physically, emotionally, and financially. She was tired of being the taker.

"It's a publicity thing." Best not to use the highly charged word *dating*. "I figure I'll get a couple of decent meals out of it. Might even meet a higher quality man."

Gage strolled in, wearing a tee with the excellent advice to "Save gas. Ride a firefighter." He was splitting his time between here and Brady's, so his entrances and exits were impossible to predict. Like last night.

"Hey, don't say you started picking on our girl without me." He winked at her and grabbed a coffee mug.

Luke was still rocking the death glare of doom. "Is he making you do this?"

"Nobody's making anyone do anything." Though the thought of Eli "making" her do things—to him, to herself—ignited a flame in her core at the raft of deliciously forbidden images that presented. "I'm just doing him a favor. After all, he saved my life."

Kinsey scoffed. "You were fine in that stairwell. That wily bastard dragged you out of there for the photo op. He was saving his campaign, and now you're playing right into his messed-up games."

Alex's phone rang and Darcy's smiling face lit up the screen. Needing a break from the visual dissection of the interfering family members present, she answered. "Good timing, D, the inquisition is here."

"Ooh, put me on speaker."

Alex rolled her eyes and obeyed.

"To get you all caught up," Gage said as he took a seat at the kitchen table, stirred his coffee, and grabbed one half of Alex's buttered English muffin, "Luke's jaw muscle tic is going loco, Kinsey thinks Eli's playing some messed-up reindeer games, and Alex claims she owes him for saving her life."

Darcy hummed. "Those pics of you laughing together at DeLuca's looked very, uh, intimate, I have to say."

"Exactly," gritted out Luke. He held up his phone, the screen showing a picture of Eli's head inclined toward her over their butter-and-sage gnocchi. Probably snapped while he was torturing her with his ridiculous views on cows or marriage or Canadians. Thank God no one had captured the moment she reached for his hand, comforting him as he silently recalled his parents. It was too private to be shared with the world.

"While your definition of romance, Luke, might be a bunch of scruffy-jawed, overpaid a-holes picking fights on an ice rink followed by you stuffing your face with ravioli, it's certainly not mine. We took in a game and grabbed some dinner. End of story."

"His poll numbers have been climbing since the fire," Kinsey said.

"Not just his poll numbers," Gage murmured with a pointed look at Alex.

Darcy chimed in. "It's okay to admit you want to spend time with him, babe. No one's going to hold it against you because you want him to hold it against you."

Gage chuckled. Luke did not.

"No fucking way," he snarled. "You'd better not be thinking about that, sis. I cut him some slack because I thought he took care of you the night of the fire, but now I see what his real game is. Guy's a gangster."

Wyatt walked into the kitchen, sporting a Hawks jersey and no trace of surprise at the impromptu family meeting. He opened the fridge, rooted around, and emerged with a box of moo shu pork leftovers that only someone with an iron constitution or a death wish would tackle. Their oldest brother lived in the duplex next door, and since Luke had moved out to set up house with Kinsey, he had been ambling in every morning doing the zombie-hunting-for-brains impression rather than heading to Mariano's and buying his own damn groceries.

"Come on in, Wy, and join the cavalcade of 'Let's blast Alex's very bad choices.' All we're missing is Beck."

"I'm here, *niña*," Beck said over the speakerphone. "Silently judging."

Mother of God, who the hell was putting out fires in Chicago?

"Not that I should have to explain this to anyone"—she arced a glare over the lot of them, including Wy *and* her phone—"but I am going to a couple of events with Eli Cooper because apparently the public loves living vicariously through the lives of other people. It's a publicity thing. He's my boss. I am not interested in him." Her voice had climbed a couple of octaves higher than usual, driven in part by the nuclear heat of Gage's knowing stare.

"Better not be," muttered Luke.

"He's such a tool that every time I see him I want to do serious violence to his body," she added unnecessarily.

"Uh-huh." Gage gave a wise nod. "Wouldn't have pegged him for the submissive type in the bedroom, but maybe he likes that. Gives him a chance to relax at the end of a long day playing at being king."

She shot her baby brother a look. "Violence that involves nut twisting and penis scrunching."

"God, Alex," Luke said. "There are sensitive men-children here."

Wy sniffed the moo shu pork. Satisfied it wouldn't

give him food poisoning, he dove in. "You meet Bastian Durand at the game?"

"Yeah, we got a tour of the locker room. He has a teeny-tiny dick."

"My next question," Wy commented drily.

Darcy cleared her throat. "Look, I know this family feels hard done by Eli because of certain events for which no one seems prepared to accept their share of blame. Luke *did* punch out a CPD detective on camera last summer. Alex *did* destroy my assholic father's car, also on camera. Kinsey *did* go behind her boss's back and release that video—"

"Your point, D?" Kinsey cut in.

"None of you are giving him a fair shake," Darcy finished.

Darcy's and Eli's families went back to the *Mayflower*, so she was clearly biased. Still, Alex felt herself inclining forward, waiting for something that might make her feel better about her mind-melting attraction to him. It couldn't be merely hormones running riot. Surely her subconscious detected something beneath the man's one-dimensional plastic surface.

Kinsey was wearing her most skeptical expression. "Oh, *puh*-lease enlighten us about St. Eli. Tell us about all those secret donations he's giving to the puppy shelter and his incognito soup kitchen shifts."

"I'm just saying that he's not the villain people make him out to be," Darcy went on. "He's a Medal of Honor recipient. Went through all that horror as a kid. He donated his inheritance and he doesn't even take a salary."

Kinsey snorted. "Spare us the Batman sob story. Madison worked that angle so well during the first election that the voting ballots were damp with tears." At Darcy's shocked gasp, she rolled her eyes. "Okay, it's sad. I get it. But we all have sad stuff. It doesn't give someone a pass on using it to manipulate people into dating them."

"No one is dating anyone. It's just a few public appearances," Alex insisted. "I think I'm enough of my own person to not feel pressured to"—*give him a blow job that would rearrange his brain circuitry*—"do something I wouldn't be comfortable with."

"I know how Madison's mind works," Kinsey said, still stuck on the publicity angle. "The poll numbers are finally going in the right direction and she thinks the two of you together are the golden egg. It gets him in good with the unions and detracts from the real issues." She stared at Alex in a way that made her want to confess all her sins, then offer up a decade of the Rosary. "I can see how he benefits. I just don't see why you'd agree to be a part of it."

"Like I said, I'm doing him a favor. And I know what I'm doing." Most of the time. As long as they ran, not walked, by all closets and avoided being alone together. Last night, she'd made herself clear: casual sex was out. Keeping the sizzle to subzero should be easy at public events where she'd be too nervous to even think about the things she'd like done to her by that talented devil-mouth. "If there's nothing else?"

Barely mollified, Luke turned to Kinsey. "Come on, sweetheart, we've got to meet the housing inspector. Last check before we close."

Kinsey looked positively giddy. "As long as you let me do all the talking. Not always your strong suit, babe."

"Cosigned," Alex said, steering them out the door. "Later, D and B," she called out to Darcy and Beck before hanging up.

On her return to the kitchen, she found Gage trashing the moo shu and shoving Wy to the table, all while muttering about how he'd cook breakfast. Again. Wy smiled slyly like that was his plan all along because let's face it, Gage made a mean Denver omelet.

Gage's mouth was grim with concern. "You are going to be careful, Alex? Luke might be going about this all wrong, but he has a point. Eli's sort of twisted."

"What makes you think that?"

"Just some stuff Brady said. He's got ice water in his veins and winning is all he cares about. We don't want to see you get hurt."

"I can handle Cooper."

"More like he wants to handle you," Wy muttered over the lip of his coffee mug. "Last summer, when you were over at his house getting your ass chewed out, it was as clear as fuckin' day. Guy likes you."

A delicious thrill ran through her. "He likes to piss me off."

Wy delivered his gunfighter squint. He looked tired, and not for the first time, she wondered what was so important it took him away once a week and kept his lips sealed tighter than a nun's knickers. Luke claimed it wasn't a woman, but speculation about their oldest brother's mysterious overnighters was rife.

"Fun night, brother mine?" she asked pointedly.

"Not as fun as yours," he quipped back in a very un-Wy-like manner.

She shot a glare at Gage, who must have been telling tales while she shoved Luke and Kinsey out into the street. "I wish you'd take that big blabbermouth of yours and move in with Brady for good."

"Damn, you're awful cranky for a gal who got some action last night," Gage said with that brazen grin that got him both into *and* out of trouble. "I had to tell someone how my poor innocent eyes were scandalized. And talking to Wy is like confessing to a priest. Without the judgment. Or the need to say penance."

Admittedly, Wy was pretty top notch in the "live and let live" department, unlike the rest of the Dempsey nosey parkers. Now he stared at her, concern in his usually unflappable expression. "If there was somethin' you needed, Alex, you'd tell us, right?"

Guilt pinched her chest. Lying did not come naturally to her, though if she spent more time with the mayor, the man's deflection and dishonesty might rub off her. *Or other things,* that craven voice in her head whispered.

"I've got this."

But she had the unsettling, yet oddly pleasurable feeling that Eli Cooper had her—exactly where he wanted her.

# ◊ CHAPTER ELEVEN

"Mr. Cochrane is already in your office, Mr. Mayor."

Eli barely managed to suppress his disgust with that news as he nodded absently at Kelly, his receptionist. Early again. Though Chicago's wealthiest businessman might prefer to assert his dominance by breezing in late, Eli was fairly sure Sam knew the mayor's schedule to a T, and planned his meetings so Eli wouldn't be in his office when Cochrane arrived.

Much better to make himself at home and make Eli look like the interloper when he walked in.

No matter how many times Eli strode into that office, if Sam Cochrane was already there, then the point was made. And today, as he entered and found that stone in his shoe sitting in Eli's chair behind Eli's desk, he felt singularly renewed in his plan to extricate his political life from Cochrane, come hell or high water.

"Sam."

"Mr. Mayor."

There was insolence in those two words. They both knew that Eli owed the office to Sam's backing.

Sam was powerfully built and trim for his age. His third wife, thirty years his junior, kept him physically active, and his brain found exercise planning corporate coups and how to screw over anyone who looked at him crooked. But the front lines of political power didn't interest him, not when so much could be gained by working behind the scenes.

Enter Eli.

At thirty, he was a year out of the Marines, working as an assistant state's attorney, when Sam Cochrane approached him with his kingmaker proposal. The then-mayor was a three-time incumbent who had allowed city hall to ossify during his reign of inertia. Eighteen months to the election, and everyone expected an unopposed run—like the previous two elections. Butting up against the status quo would take chutzpah and money in spades.

Eli had the chutzpah. Guess who had the money?

He was under no illusion about what he was getting himself into. Sam was a shark who tore through business enemies and allies alike with razor-sharp teeth, but Eli was sure he could temper that ferocity once he was in office.

Over the course of a year, Eli attended every community meeting in every rat-infested South Side death trap of a school. He met with grassroots leaders and listened to their needs. He wrote opinion pieces calling out the current administration's inadequacies and—*wait for it*—proposing solutions. By the time he declared eight months before the election, everyone knew who he was and what he stood for. He would be tough on crime, he would curb spending, he wouldn't stand for bullshit. (He even swore on TV during a debate, and that clip was played over and over. Street cred for the win.)

That's not to say the election wasn't hard fought.

It was. Precinct by precinct, ward by ward, Chicago's own Battle of Stalingrad. But what threw him over the top was not his looks or charm or passion. It was not even his service in Afghanistan, where he had been captured by the Taliban, making him a bona fide American fucking hero.

It was the human-interest element. They were voting for that little boy who had crouched terrified in that closet all those years ago. They were voting for the son of a great man.

"Glad to see you're none the worse for wear after the fire."

Eli walked to the window and looked out over the busy Loop streets of his kingdom. Another snowstorm was forecast, promising a dangerous evening commute. Treacherous roads ahead.

"I was fortunate."

"Damn fool for going back in, but it made you look good." He laughed quietly. "Pity it had to be Dempsey who saved you."

"She did a good job."

"And now you're rewarding her for it. People are loving the two of you together."

*Not just people,* Eli thought. He rather liked the idea of the two of them together himself, clearly a little too much, because he'd been in a foul mood since her rejection. Two weeks since he'd made Alexandra Dempsey scream with his mouth sucking on her gorgeous breasts and his fingers slicking through her tight pussy, and he was feverish with want. She had accompanied him to a few events since—the opening of a charter school for gifted children on Chicago's North Side, the Women's Business Development Center's annual luncheon. All calculated moves by Madison that kept the press in a frenzy about the budding romance between the mayor and the firefighter.

He was trying to respect her boundaries, but he also recognized that their chemistry was so potent that it was uncontainable by those walls she had built. Now he'd had a taste, and satisfaction wouldn't come until he'd claimed every inch of her.

"We're all about pleasing the people," Eli said in response to Sam's comment.

"You can control her?"

God no. "That's what people like. The fact that I can't. The fact that she has a mind of her own and she's not afraid to speak it."

"You taking her to the gala?"

Eli gave a noncommittal grunt. Tomorrow night he would have to poker up even more than usual. His father, the greatest and most beloved state's attorney Chicago had ever seen, would have an award named after him at a glitzy gala. Called the Weston Cooper Justice Award, in the future it would be given to someone who represented the late public servant's principles of truth, justice, and the American way.

What a joke.

Eli turned in time to catch Sam staring at that photo of Weston Cooper shaking hands with Mayor Daley. He was so young then, just appointed as state's attorney, a life of promise spread out before him. That Sam dared to look at it enraged Eli to the point he had to grab the windowsill to prevent him from pummeling the older man.

"Just watch she doesn't get too mouthy," he said with a derisive sniff. "You screwing her yet?"

The roar in his blood at Sam's disrespectful tone made Eli's hands itch to commit murder, but he'd learned long ago the virtue of keeping his emotions in check. Show them—the other candidates, Sam Cochrane, even the good people of Chicago—weakness, he might as well withdraw from the race now.

But with her . . . losing his shit with her, whether it was fighting or fucking, that would be downright liberating.

"I happen to admire her greatly." It came out sounding pompous.

"After all that shit with my car, how you tried to protect her, insulate her . . ." Sam shook his head. "I should have sued her into the grave. But I could see you had a soft spot for her."

Not soft, all hard. He wanted her and it was making him insane. Other women repelled him because they weren't her.

"Firefighter Dempsey is good for my numbers, that's all."

"She's never been one for impulse control. Her father was the same."

"You used to be Sean Dempsey's closest friend," Eli said casually. The reasons why Sean and Sam fell out were a mystery, and Eli would never ask him about it outright. One day, Sam would tell him.

But not today.

He pivoted in the mayoral throne, facing Eli. "The city council is still bitching about the sign. Are they going to give me trouble?"

Eli sighed. Sam wanted to mount his name in twenty-foot-tall letters on one of his skyscrapers along the river walk. It would be a blot on the downtown landscape and the city council was not impressed. "There'll be a vote on the ordinance next week."

"Trump got away with it a couple of years back."

"And that's what you're aspiring to?"

Sam parted his lips to form a shark's smile. "Every Gotham needs a villain, Eli. Just be glad it's me and not you." Unsubtly, his eyes flicked to the photo of Eli's father. The one that spelled all that soon-to-be-crushed promise.

"Make sure it happens." He stood with an exaggerated brush of his lapels. "It's a small thing to do in the grand scheme of things, don't you think?"

With Sam's departure, Eli was left to think about those small things. Death of his soul by a thousand cuts.

*En Cachette.*

Alex blinked at the antique silver-framed nameplate by the door and studied the email on her phone again.

**En Cachette, 69 E. Schiller, 2 p.m.**
**Please don't be late! —W**

She might be within spitting distance of the tony boutiques of Oak Street, but she had never heard of an exclusive clothing store on the top floor of a five-million-dollar brownstone in the middle of Chicago's wealthy Gold Coast. Perhaps it was some sort of kinky sex club—and why did that idea in the same headspace as Eli Cooper excite her so much?—but that seemed less likely when she remembered that

Eli's assistant, Whitney, had sent her the address for her sartorial makeover.

Apparently, the mayor didn't trust her to dress herself. Alex was inclined to agree, but she would have been much happier to spend a few mind-numbing hours at Macy's with her posse rather than be prodded by whatever lay behind this door. Tomorrow night, there was an award gala dedicated to Eli's father, and guess who was going as his date?

Alex Dempsey was about to kick it Cinderella-style.

The last two weeks had been torture, leaving her as horny as a three-balled tomcat. At the events she attended with the mayor, they were never alone, a state of affairs she suspected he had manufactured. His polite, respectful distance confirmed it, the "fake dating" scenario he had promised. But when a girl's had a sex ninja like Eli Cooper yielding orgasms with the lick of a nipple, she was bound to be feeling a touch dissatisfied . . . with her own hand in particular. The empty spot inside her craved fulfillment she suspected only he could give.

She knew what the bastard was doing. If she wanted to get off, she needed to get on board the Eli Cooper Sexpress. Come sin with the sinner.

She pushed the buzzer, and after a few seconds heard, "*Bonjour?*"

*Bonjour?* Holy croissan'wich, this shit was for real.

"It's Alex Dempsey. I was sent here by—"

"*Oui, oui.*" The door clicked, making the barest of moneyed hums to signify she was invited in. She climbed up a narrow stairway until she reached the top floor, made up to look like a French brothel circa 1859. The décor consisted of grosgrain ribbon wallpaper, lavish drapes, and furniture that looked like it'd collapse if your eyes rested on it longer than ten seconds. Onyx black mannequins dotted the space languidly, wearing a lace bra here, skimpy panties there, as if someone had started dressing them and lost interest midway through.

A petite brunette emerged from behind a screen in a cloud of perfume that stung Alex's nostrils from ten feet out.

"Meez Dempsee? It eez a pleasure!" She gave Alex the wet fish handshake, all while assessing her with a cool, judgmental gaze. "I am Odile. We are going to have a lot of fun, you and I."

"Sure." Alex would be the judge of the fun levels. "I'm here for a dress. There's this gala thing . . ."

"*Oui, oui*, I know all about it. Come with me."

Alex was ushered into a dressing room with a rack of prom-like dresses, a triptych mirror, and plush carpeting. Without so much as a by-your-leave, Odile whipped off Alex's parka, scarf, and hoodie with a skill that rivaled the mayor's.

"You are . . ." She fluttered a perfectly manicured claw over Alex's outfit of jeans and a tee emblazoned with the slogan "Silly boys. Girls want fire trucks, too." ". . . More full-figured than Monsieur Mayor led me to believe."

"He said I was skinny?"

"*Mon Dieu, non!* He said you looked to be a size ten, but men can never judge these things, and they will always undersize." Her smile was arch. "It plays better for them later in the bedroom."

Alex rolled her eyes.

"I viewed some pictures of you online. There are plenty to choose from." An unfortunate truth. Her fifteen minutes after the Cochrane incident had lasted about three months. For a while there, she couldn't raise a beer to her lips in a bar without someone snapping it. And now here she was at the center of another media typhoon.

"You are more like a sixteen, *non*?"

"Fourteen." On a good day.

Odile walked to the rack of dresses and pulled off something horrendous: lavender taffeta that Alex wouldn't wish on her worst enemy. Well, maybe Murphy.

"Sorry, that's just hideous."

"Hmm. Monsieur Mayor chose something else for you, but he did not tell me about the tattoos. He was adamant that you wear this." From the rail, she plucked a garnet red cocktail dress with a plunging neckline, a dipping backline, and a fluttery hem.

It was absolutely gorgeous.

"But it will reveal your tattoos, and at such an important event, I do not think it would be suitable."

A wild and insistent pulse started up in Alex's veins. She wanted to wear the dress Eli had chosen. "Can I at least try it on?"

Odile shrugged in a very Continental way. "Why not? But I will find something else that covers you up in the meantime. Perhaps a wrap." She smirked. "Or a burka. There is *le lingerie*, as well."

"Underwear?"

"*Oui*," she said with a sharp look, likely because Alex had translated *le lingerie* into unsexy English.

"Monsieur Mayor picked it out himself. He was most certain about what he wanted."

Alex's heart rate sped to danger levels. A heated blush crept across her body as it remembered its reaction to Eli's mouth sucking on her breast and making her come so fast she should consider submitting to Guinness World Records.

Odile was saying something and Alex fought to pay attention.

"What's that?"

"Your bra size, *mademoiselle*?"

"Thirty-six-D."

Another French smirk. "Oh, he pinpointed that exactly."

# CHAPTER TWELVE

Her hair was all wrong. Straight and sleek and scraped back so severely her temples stung.

"It looks perfect!" Darcy and Kinsey both squealed like tweens at a One Direction show as K applied another spritz of hairspray. Getting ready for her big date had turned her friends into the kind of people Alex had avoided in high school. Peppy people.

"Now, just to make those eyes a little smokier." Darcy tipped Alex's chin up and started applying, smudging, and reapplying, though Alex questioned the necessity, given that the minute she saw Eli, her eyes would turn all smoky with lust anyway. Cosmetic enhancements so not necessary.

"Wow, you clean up good, girl," Kinsey murmured, now sounding like a proud mama.

Alex blinked at her reflection in the mirror, marveling at how a little makeup could go a long way. The dress, understated yet sexy, fit her perfectly. Darcy had lent her a pair of red Christian Lacroix shoes that managed the miraculous feat of making her ankles thin and her appearance statuesque. The overall effect was startling. She hadn't gone to her high school prom because no one had been interested (or brave) enough to ask her, and now she felt like she was getting another chance with the star quarterback. She'd be the envy of all the other bitches. Go Wildcats!

"It's just a gala thing," she said, more to herself than to the others. "They're naming some award after his father."

"Yes, but it's an important event honoring his father's legacy," Darcy reasoned, a knowing smile playing on her lips. "And he bought you a dress."

And underwear. Underwear she was dampening right now just thinking about him.

"What's wrong?" Kinsey asked. "You've gone red."

She'd never had girlfriends to confide in, or anything worth confiding, but now she was bursting at the seams and had to get it out.

"I don't know what I'm doing here. I'm fake dating the mayor but we've already groped each other in a tampon closet and I've had two amazing orgasms and he's had none. He's choosing what I wear, including my underwear, he doesn't respect my job or me, so why is it that all I can think about is having him so deep inside me I can't walk straight for a week?"

"Whoa." Darcy's eyes flew wide. "He's had none of the orgasms? No, don't tell me. He's sort of like a big brother to me and that's totally TMI."

"I told him I didn't want a one-night stand."

Kinsey squinted. "Before or after the orgasms?"

"After."

"Dang, that's cold, girl."

Darcy looked puzzled. "Tampon closet?"

"Long story. Yesterday, I'm at this private boutique, which looked like a French whorehouse, and it was clear he'd been there before with other women because he has a fucking tab." Other lithe, smooth-haired, nontattooed women. "It's where he buys them lingerie and dresses."

Darcy peeled back the scrap of red silk covering Alex's dusky pink balconette bra. A low whistle followed. "Looks expensive."

"Three bills. And a C-note for the panties."

"Which he picked out," said Kinsey. "Poor no-salary Eli. Those investments of his must be doing terribly."

"*And* he paid for dinner that night at DeLuca's, after the hockey game. Pulled out my chair, ordered my food, took off my coat." Along with her bra. *Get your other tit ready for me.* Oh, God. "He's so damn dominant. I don't think I should be sleeping with a guy who dresses chauvinism up with chivalry."

Darcy put her hands on Alex's shoulders. "You don't need to be simpatico on everything. He's hot, he gets your engine running, and he's into you. Just enjoy it."

Kinsey touched a finger to her lips, considering. "Are you worried that you're just a prop for his campaign?"

It was impossible to ignore the media's fascination with the heroism of their respective families. Viewed in that light, their hookup made a compelling narrative—and made her uneasy about his ulterior motives. The man had a ballot box where his heart should be.

"I don't doubt his attraction to me, but neither can I ignore the fact we're somebody's PR wet dream. I suppose the idea of being used, for whatever reason, doesn't sit well." The girls looked sympathetic, knowing that the memory of her last sexual experience with Mr. Two-Pump-Chump still pinched. How she'd felt like a man's conquest. A joke. It was why she was carefully combing through the choices.

"Look, we know that Team Get Alex Laid has been sort of falling down on the job," Darcy said, "but it's largely down to the fact that our charge has changed. You want more than a good time, we get it, but sometimes asserting yourself sexually can be just as empowering as holding out. You have more control than you think."

Deep down, Alex knew that she and Eli were on an equal footing as far as the sexual chemistry went. She trusted that her pleasure would be paramount with him—uh, two orgasms in less than three minutes! Odder still, she liked him despite his caveman tendencies.

"Unless you're falling for him . . ." Kinsey had apparently missed her calling with the CIA.

Darcy's face lit up. "Awesome! I've been rooting for you guys from the start."

"No," Alex said a touch too vehemently. "I'm attracted to him, but that's all there is. Besides, he doesn't believe in the sappy-ever-after."

Darcy's face fell.

"I just don't want to be with someone who doesn't respect me and what I do. Or who's using me to get ahead."

Kinsey hummed. "Not even for the amazing orgasms, orgasm hog?"

Alex opened her mouth. Closed it. Maybe she'd been looking at this all wrong. What did it matter what she thought of his worldview, his total lack of political correctness, or even his sketchy motives as long as he was delivering the goods in the bedroom, the hallway, or maybe a fire truck? Since when had she become so fussy? If she let things continue as is, she'd be donating her very intact body to medical science with hardly any wear and tear. If this man did it for her like no one else, if he could bring her to orgasm with a couple of blazing looks and a hot mouth sucking her nipples, then why not take advantage?

Darcy spoke to her in the mirror. "While I'd love to see the two of you ride off into the sunset, if it's going to end in a few weeks anyway, you may as well enjoy it. Hit it and quit it."

"He *has* had the hots for you from day one," Kinsey said over Alex's other shoulder. "I was with him in that restaurant, the night he spotted you. It was like his world stopped spinning. Even after you almost tanked his mayoralty when you destroyed Cochrane's car. Even after you made him look like an idiot in that press conference, which he deserved. He's still here. Wanting in your very expensive panties."

"You're the one who's been down on him all along. Now you're telling me to jump on board?"

"Orgasms, babe. If you can separate it out, then a little joyride of the cock variety won't kill you."

Alex stared at her reflection, relishing the feeling of having slipped into a new skin. *You have more control than you think.* With a last-minute plump of her breasts, she made sure those puppies were displayed to their best advantage.

Hit it and quit it. What could possibly go wrong?

• • •

Eli should have stayed in his armored car.

But it would have looked off if he didn't meet his date for the evening at her door. It had been so long since he was on a real date, and he had never been on a fake date, but even he knew that shuffling awkwardly from foot to foot while her family buried you with their glares was part and parcel of the experience.

Alexandra lived with Gage, and Wyatt lived next door, so Eli was at a loss to explain why every single one of the Firefightin' fucking Dempseys, including Beck and Luke, who did *not* live nearby, was standing in the hallway of her home. Had they taken personal time from work so they could posture and give him the Gypsy stink eye? Were fires raging and drunks going thirsty? From upstairs, he heard shrieking that sounded like Darcy. He assumed Kinsey was up there, as well, because, why the hell not?

Luke looked around and in some unspoken communication, seemed to get the go-ahead to represent the group.

"So, Cooper, we understand there's some sort of arrangement between you and our sister, this publicity stunt where you vampire-suck her life force and use her for your campaign. We figure she's a big girl and that's between the two of you."

So the "vampire-suck her life force" statement was a bit over the top, but he appreciated that Luke was approaching this with a certain level of maturity. This was no one else's business, and Alexandra was a grown woman who could handle anything he threw at her. As she had so ably demonstrated when he'd sucked on her heavenly breasts and she came like a rocket.

Against the wall where Luke now stood.

*Terminate that line of thinking now, Cooper.*

Luke was still droning on. "But that doesn't mean we can't give you a little friendly advice. You might be using my sister, but if I hear that you hurt her in any way, shape, or form, then this truce we have going on will be over so quick you won't even see us comin' at you. Got it?"

"Luke, stop bullying him," Eli heard from somewhere above. "That ego of his is exceptionally fragile."

All eyes fired upward to find a goddess about to descend among mortals.

*Christ Jesus.*

Eli had seen the dress on a hanger. He'd spent all day imagining her both in and out of the dress. Now the whole package—hair, makeup, that drop-dead-gorgeous body—stole his breath clean away.

The bra he'd chosen had lifted and shaped her stunning breasts into weapons of cock destruction. Her spectacular legs tapered to fuck-me heels; her shapely hips swayed in a manner that could topple governments. Those tattoos on her arms, the brands of her tribe, riled him something royally. She was like the bad girl his mom would have advised him to avoid if she'd lived long enough to see him date. As for the panties . . . ah, the panties. He couldn't see them except in his mind's eye. They were pink and lacy, barely a scrap covering the cleft of her perfect ass with frilly wings on either side. Later he would blow on them, watch them flutter under his breath. Watch the gooseflesh he'd raise on her skin as his mouth drew close to where they needed each other most.

He was in danger of getting a not-so-fake hard-on for his fake date in front of her whole damn family. Perhaps if he stared longer at the tattoos, he'd remember that she was the sister and daughter of fallen Dempseys, true Chicago heroes. Unlike the man they were honoring tonight.

Her regal descent complete, she raised expectant eyes to his.

"Hi," she said, and dragged her bottom lip between her teeth.

Woman, have mercy.

"Alexandra, you look beautiful. I should have no problem palming you off on some quality talent tonight."

She tipped her nose up. That pleased her. "But let's go higher than beat cop. Is the police commissioner spoken for?"

"He is, but the deputy commissioner is a free agent. Bad breakup last year, so he should be very susceptible to your particular charms."

He held out his hand, inviting her under his protection, and his heart cranked out a dangerous beat when she took it and squeezed.

"Have fun," Darcy said in a singsong voice from the top of the stairs.

Alexandra rolled her eyes and muttered, "Is that likely?"

"Fun is one of my platforms," Eli said, enjoying the smooth skin of her palm. "After crime prevention and job growth."

She let loose a husky laugh, then clammed up with a guilty look at her broody brothers.

"Let's go." To the rest of them, but especially to a steely eyed Luke Almeida, he said, "Don't wait up."

The last time Alex was in the backseat of a car with Eli was two weeks ago after dinner at DeLuca's, and about two minutes before she came in her hallway. Twice.

Good times.

Sneaking a glance, she found him staring at her with not a small amount of breath-robbing heat. Perhaps he was remembering, too.

She swallowed. "Are you nervous about tonight?"

He hit her with that look, the one that turned her lady parts soft and her nipples hard. "Cops love me. Or I should say, they loved my father." The resignation in his voice clashed with the hot smolder.

"He was a great man. The city doesn't forget that kind of thing."

His lips moved imperceptibly, and she got the impression that he checked a curse.

Maybe he was tired of it coming up. During the last election, it was *the* talking point above everything else: the issues, his movie star looks, even his military heroics. Barbara Walters had made herself and everyone dewy-eyed when she interviewed him just before Election Day. Eli's pride in his father had reminded Alex of her love for Sean, invoking a weird commonality with him before they had met. It was why she had voted for him.

Yes, she, Alex Dempsey, had voted for Eli Cooper.

Now, that light in his eyes, the one that shone his

pride in his father's accomplishments and how one man went up against the mob in Chicago and lost, had gone out. It was weird to see him in a bad mood. He seemed to make a living out of presenting a certain face to the world.

"Sit closer," he murmured.

"So you can look down my dress?"

He laughed that whiskey-rough rasp she loved. "Yes."

She scooted in, leaving a foot of space beside them. Can't make it *too* easy. With a dutiful glance at her abundant cleavage, he gave a wolfish smile. "Do you like what you're wearing?"

"It's beautiful."

"The woman makes it beautiful." He dwarfed her hand in his and traced lazy, erotic circles on her wrist. "Is your family giving you a hard time about me?"

"They're just protective. They tend to take their lead from Luke, and he's not your biggest fan."

"What about the men you work with?"

"It's not a problem." So a few guys had made snide comments about her "wartime collaboration." She'd lived with nasty innuendo her whole career in CFD; a few extras she could handle. If it kept her family safe . . .

Only now she was beginning to think she didn't mind being here with him, getting all dressed up in clothes he had chosen for her. There was a lot to like about how Eli wooed.

She felt her butt scoot over a smidgen. The intimate interior of the car pressed in on her.

"If anyone gives you a problem, you'll come to me about it." Not a question, but a command.

"I can take care of it, Eli."

"Let me enjoy this rare moment of looking out for someone other than myself, Alexandra."

She wondered who took care of him. When he went home to the house where his parents were murdered, did he sit alone in the dark with his expensive scotch and his dog at his feet imagining a world where men didn't break into your home and execute the people you loved more than anything?

This was not what where her mind should be wandering. Back to the orgasms.

The car stopped and Eli curled a hand around her neck. "Just one thing." He unclasped the French knot Darcy had spent an hour crafting.

"Eli! That took forever."

"I like your hair down. Uncivilized, rebellious. Like you." His fingers tangled in her locks, mussing them out of downtown sleekness and into the wild boonies. All the while, he stared at her with those ice-blue eyes. "I don't think you should change for anyone, and especially not for me." His thumb trailed to her bottom lip and hovered there.

"Don't you dare smudge my makeup," she hissed through quivering lips. "It's perfect."

Lights of challenge brightened his eyes. "Shouldn't have said that, honey." And then he was kissing her, making a mess of her makeup, of her panties, *of everything*. His fingers, those dominant instruments of pleasure, burrowed in her hair, while his tongue tangled with hers expertly.

Drawing back, he touched his lips, as though savoring his sensual assault. "I'm glad you're here, Alexandra. Tonight, I really need . . ." He placed a hand on the door handle and drew a breath. "I'm just glad you're here."

Stunned by that admission, she tried to haul herself back to the reality she knew existed outside this car. "Eli, wait, I need a mirror. I can't go out like this." She had no idea what *this* was, but she was damn sure it was not worthy of the mayor's arm candy.

"Yes, you can. You look like how every woman should when getting out of a limo."

"Like a bedraggled hobo?"

"Like you've just gotten some action." With his hand still wrapped around hers, he dragged her out of the car into the street.

# CHAPTER THIRTEEN

The Crystal Ballroom at the Knickerbocker Hotel exuded all the grandeur and glamour of 1920s Chicago. A gilded domed ceiling shone above crystal chandeliers, each one dripping with opulence the likes of which Alex had only seen in magazines or on TV. This was not her scene at all.

But it was most definitely Eli's. The room was filled with arrogant lawyers, top cops, city dignitaries, and Chicago's glitterati. These were his people, he was their god made flesh, and while everyone looked great in a tux, no one looked as born to this dazzling world as the man at her side.

Thankfully, she didn't have to move too much in her heels—everyone came to pay homage to the mayor. He made a point to include her in every introduction, and if someone barely acknowledged her or dismissed her with a cutting glance, that someone very quickly fell out of favor with Chicago's most powerful man. The conversation would sputter and die, and the offender would shrink away in confusion, unsure of what he'd done to merit the mayor's silent censure. Through all the bowing and scraping, Eli kept his hand glued to her waist, the heat of his palm a brand on her sensitized skin through the barely there silk. All these people vying for his attention, and Eli's focus was singularly on Alex.

The woo was strong with this one.

After another forty-five minutes of "Mr. Mayor, I need thirty seconds of your time," Alex's eyes wandered to the beautifully set tables, willing the dinner gong to sound (or however these people announced the arrival of the real food). The tiny, albeit delicious, hors d'oeuvres of crab and avocado were not cutting it, and if she grabbed the third glass of champagne calling her name, she might start to get sloppy.

And then her stomach growled, because she was all class.

Eli turned away from a bouffanted woman who was complaining about dog poop problems in the Streeterville and squeezed Alex's waist. "Hungry?"

"Oh, God, no, my stomach is always this chatty."

The killer dimple popped in to say howdy. "Let's get you something decent to eat." With a polite smile, he abandoned the dog poop lady and headed toward the tables.

Everyone followed. Now *that* was power right there.

The seating was boy-girl-boy, so she found herself with Eli on her right and the police commissioner on her left. Over the appetizers of one measly prawn and an oyster mushroom sculpted to look like a flower—*uh, really?*—the commissioner's wife voiced her fascination that Alex was "showing those men how it was done." On her other side, the commish made conversation with Alex's breasts before switching his attentions to the almost comparable rack of the woman to his left. Eli was busy schmoozing, so

Alex took a moment to enjoy the relative peace of not having to make stilted conversation with anyone.

Her clutch, sitting on the table, started to dance. With a quick glance to ensure no one was looking, she pulled it to her lap and extracted her phone.

It was from TSN. Or The Sex Ninja, as she had rechristened Eli in her contacts.

*Are we boring you?*

She texted back: *More like starving me.*

He leaned in, his breath hot against her cheek, his scent like a drug. "You ate your first course too fast. I prefer when you linger over each juicy morsel."

"As it was barely enough to satisfy a chicklet, lingering was never an option. And since when am I here for your entertainment?"

"Since I entertained you awhile back." He smirked. "Twice, if I recall correctly."

Heated remembrance flushed her body. "Nobody likes smug, Mr. Mayor."

"I think you like me any way you can have me. You're just too damn stubborn to admit it." His words whispered across her skin and then his knuckles followed suit, glancing over Darcy's tattoo of Logan's name. Alex had noticed he took every opportunity to touch her since he'd picked her up at her house. Know what else she noticed? That she loved every second of it. The last few weeks without his attention had left her craving those magic digits of his in a seriously bad way.

"Fairly sure that *like* is a word I will never use when thinking about you, Eli."

His wicked mouth moved closer to her ear. He breathed her in, and just that inhale, like he needed her scent to keep him sane through the madness of his life, was enough to set her body vibrating with need. "I've been subsisting on memories these last two weeks, Alexandra. The sounds you made when you came, the grip of your soft, wet flesh around my fingers. I'd say *like* is a rather tame word for what's happening between us, don't you think?"

Holy. Wow.

She was saved from having to answer—as if she had any possible coherent response to those erotically charged words—when the entrées arrived. As the mayor's plus one, she was served first, and she was glad of the chance to quell her thundering pulse and enjoy some sorely needed relief from his unrelenting potency.

"Now, savor every bite, Alexandra. I want to feel your enjoyment."

Mmm. Time for a little payback in the tease department. Once assured that everyone else was occupied *oohing* and *aahing* over the beautiful presentation of the entrées—lamb, which Alex adored—she dipped her finger into the rich sauce drizzled over it and sucked. Slowly.

A touch obscene, she suspected.

A graveled growl sounded to her right. Definitely a touch obscene.

She faced him and bit down on her lip, all innocence. "Did you *feel* my enjoyment, Eli?"

"Acutely, you witch." He placed his phone on the table, and her gaze was drawn to the bright screen's message thread. Another smile gathered pace inside her.

"Thorn? What happened to Splinter?"

"You got an upgrade." That devil mouth curved in faux resignation. "I suppose I'm still an anonymous string of digits in yours."

"A girl's gotta keep her secrets." She popped her phone back into her clutch, ensuring she powered it off first so he wouldn't see the nickname she'd given him. That gorgeous head was already big enough. "Now hush with the barely adequate flirting, and let me eat in peace."

His laugh drew the stares of their dining companions, and her ovaries went *kaboom*. He tangled a finger in her curls, held it there for a beat, and let go on a sigh.

During the dessert course—a milk chocolate torte with hazelnut and violet (delish, but so tiny)—the police commissioner rapped a mic to begin his speech. Behind him, a large photograph of Weston Cooper faded in as if projected from the heavens. His image had been a prominent fixture during every news story about Eli at the last election. Now Cooper Senior—or Coop as the commissioner referred to him—stared out at the audience from beyond the grave, the spitting image of the man beside her.

"Coop was one of the finest men I knew," the commissioner was saying. "Would give you the shirt off his back, the dime in his pocket, his last cigar."

As he droned on about the sainted Coop, Alex's gaze slid to Eli, or more accurately Eli's right hand. As the commissioner's speech ramped up, Eli's grip on the steak knife handle he'd been holding tightened. To the point that she worried he might squeeze it into matchsticks.

She leaned in. "We okay?"

He turned, and what she saw pinned her back: undiluted disgust. His irises had darkened so much they swallowed all the blue. Blinking, he dropped the knife, its clatter against the plate enough to pull him back to being the charmer the world knew.

"Just fine."

"And now to accept the first Weston Cooper Justice Award, Mayor Eli Cooper."

Amid thunderous applause, Eli turned to Alex and gave her a brief wink before heading toward the podium, his progress slowed by the claps on his back and outstretched hands he shook on his way up. He was right—cops loved him. Once on the dais, he clasped hands with the commissioner and turned the glass trophy, shaped like a scale (for justice, Alex assumed) over in his hand. Clearly, a speech was expected, yet Eli merely stared at the award for several uncomfortable moments.

"A few words, perhaps, Mr. Mayor?" It took this interjection from the commish and nervous titters from the audience to drag Eli back from wherever he had gone. He let out a good-natured chuckle and seemed to compose himself as he began to speak.

"Ladies and gentlemen, it's a privilege and a pleasure to be here with you this evening. The Chicago Police Department is a stellar example of men and women protecting and serving our great city, and sacrificing their safety for the better good of our citizens." He looked at the award again. "Unlike the brave Chicago police officers, as well as the other remarkable first responders who put their lives on the line every day . . ." His gaze sought out Alex when he said that. "My father didn't go to work expecting that any particular day might be his last. Wearing a suit and making speeches for a living isn't the noblest or most dangerous of professions, as I'm sure every lawyer— or politician—in this room will tell you." The crowd laughed at the jibe. Eli's smile was patient. Phony.

Something felt really off about this.

"But he got caught up in something beyond his control and he paid the price for it. He would be very pleased that his name is being carried on with this award. He was a great believer in justice."

He arced his gaze over the room. "Thank you."

The commissioner's wife was a lovely woman, but if she didn't stop talking very soon, Eli was going to fly into a murderous rage.

". . . Your father was so generous with his time. It always amazed me considering the long hours he worked, but come Thanksgiving, he was the first to sign up for the homeless shelter lunch . . ."

His father had never been one to resist a photo opportunity, all credits he was storing away for that mayoral run he planned to make. Eli's gaze wandered to the award on the table. Its glass glinted, the little sparks of light like shards in his eye.

". . . Sara would have made a wonderful mayor's wife. She was Bill and Elizabeth Cantor's daughter, wasn't she? Of the Lake Forest Cantors?"

His mother had been North Shore royalty who married down when she fell in love with an idealistic young law student at the University of Chicago. The tone was clear. Alexandra Dempsey was no Sara Cantor Cooper. With her unkempt curls, vibrant tattoos, and exotic skin tone (*Is she Middle Eastern?* Eli had overheard at the next table), his date was not mayoral wife material. She wasn't even mayoral date material. But he wasn't looking for anything beyond a mutually beneficial arrangement. Both in and out of bed.

She had left a few moments ago to visit the restroom and he was already antsy, his fingers itching to stroke her golden skin and twine her unruly hair. Just keep her near. It made no sense, but having this firecracker of a woman by his side tonight was about the only thing getting him through. During the speech, he had come close to smashing that award to the floor and screaming the truth about Weston Cooper. Letting the world know that his father wasn't the hero everyone thought he was. Just the opposite, in fact.

A fraud. A criminal.

Seeing her out there, watching him with those big green eyes, had calmed him. Alexandra Dempsey as therapy. Go figure.

And he needed his next fix. Scanning the room, he found her standing over at the bar, talking to—Christ, that motherfucker Michael Martinez. Protectiveness lashed over Eli with such violence it shocked him to his core. He could tell from the change in her body language that she and the good detective weren't merely shooting the breeze about the Hawks' latest debacle on the ice.

Just as Eli was about to walk over and make a damn fool of himself, Alexandra left Martinez and headed his way. That she was pissed to all hell was as clear as the crystal chandeliers above their heads, and her ire added an extra tilt to the sexy switch of her hips.

She came to a stop, fists clenched, her entire body an ode to barely tethered control. Predictably, his cock jumped to attention. She refused to make it easy and he loved it.

"I'm leaving now."

"We haven't danced yet." He stood and covered her fist with his hand.

"I don't want to dance," she grated.

"Just one, honey, then I'll take you home."

He led her to the dance floor and gathered her in his arms. Already a warship of a woman, in heels she stood almost as tall as him, yet her body slotted in perfectly with his. She rested her palm lightly on his shoulder, barely touching him, just the minimum necessary to get her through the next three minutes. She couldn't avoid his chest, though. The heat of those breasts, the ones he had sucked deep and dreamed about for months, lit a fire inside him.

*Come fly with me . . .*

Couples swayed quietly on the dance floor to Tony Bennett's croon. It was all so polite, the last word he'd use to describe the woman in his arms.

"So what did Detective Martinez have to say for himself?"

"You know very well. You threatened to fire him if he didn't end our date."

He affected a bored sigh. "Actually, I told him if he laid a finger on you I'd beat him down to traffic cop." He drew back to look at her. "I can do that, you know."

Those green eyes flashed. "How can you be so high-handed about it? How. . . why would you even do that?"

"Because he wasn't right for you."

"Who are you to say who's right for me?" She palmed his shoulder, pushing, but he retained his hold at the small of her back. "How dare you use your power like that?"

"You're happy for me to use my power to solve your Cochrane problem."

"Oh, you mean the blackmail-me-into-fake-dating-you scheme? You can forget about it. I'd hate to think what else you'd demand of me in return. How you'd use it to get some advantage. Because that's all I am to you—a means to an end."

The timer on the bomb in his brain did what it had been resisting for three weeks: it finally hit zero.

"Goddamn it, Alexandra, I've been clamping down on every muscle in my body trying *not* to take advantage of you. I only have to think of you and I'm as hard as steel. I only have to see you and my mouth waters, remembering what you tasted like and how wet I made you." He squeezed her hand and pressed her body against his subtly, showing her exactly how he felt. "I only have to stand inches away from you to imagine the sheer ecstasy of burying my cock deep inside you."

Remembering where he was, he lowered his voice to a strained whisper. "You want to know why I told Martinez to dump you? Because I overheard him talking to someone about how you were falling out of that dress, how great your tits were, and how he couldn't wait to get you on your knees. He was so damn disrespectful he's lucky I didn't break his nose on a urinal and flush his head down the toilet."

Her mouth wobbled. "I—I can take care of myself. I didn't ask for your defense."

"I know. I know you'd never ask for it. In this case, I had information you weren't privy to, so I made the call to remove him from play."

"Oh, for my own good, I suppose." Her growl traveled a straight line to his harder-by-the-second dick. "So you can talk about what you want to do to me, but—but he can't?"

"My mind might be a cesspool when it comes to the things I'd like to do to you, Alexandra, but it's a private cesspool. I'm not sharing it with my buddies. I'm not broadcasting it to the world, though anyone in this room could look at the two of us and understand exactly what we want from each other. The only person who needs to hear my plans is the woman who'll be on the receiving end of every filthy, depraved thing I plan to do to her. Maybe you're looking for a bad boy or a good guy. Well, you won't find him in me. What you will find is a man who knows how to treat his woman."

"You're not playing fair," she said. Moaned.

"Fuck fair. I'm a no-good, dirty, rotten bastard who knows what he wants and will fight like hell to get it. I'll destroy anyone who says a word against you, who lays a hand upon you, who gets in my fucking way. But I won't accept compromise. I won't make the choice for you or allow you to use the circumstances—me looking handsome in my tux, you feeling gorgeous in that dress—to put any kind of gloss on this. I'm not promising you the fairy tale. I don't believe in it. But if you come to me of your own free will and spend a night in my bed, I promise you won't regret it. I will show you what it means to be worshipped."

She was breathing heavily, the beautiful swells of her breasts lifting with her discomfort. He planned to make her a whole lot more uncomfortable.

He buried his nose in her neck, breathed her in. "You know that buzz you get through your skin when we're together. Talking, bickering. Just being. I know this crazy chemistry between us spins your insides like it does mine. But I won't push you anymore. You know what I want."

"Tell me."

Christ, she was killing him.

Killing. Him.

"You, in my bed, begging me to take you somewhere you've never been. Screaming my name. Coming all over my cock. That's what I want. If you decide that you don't want to explore this, it will wound my pride, but I promise that I'll absolve you of all duty to my campaign. I won't talk to you, text you, interact with you in any way except for what's necessary to protect you from Sam Cochrane. This decision is yours, Alexandra. It will always be yours. You don't have to say a word now. In fact, I like the idea of you being stunned speechless because you're going to use these moments of quiet to think about it."

She looked at him as if he had just escaped an asylum for the criminally insane.

"Th-think about it?"

"C'mon." He steered her back to the table to pick up her purse and wrap, then through the ballroom to the exit. People tried to stop him and talk, but he ignored them. He had their vote, and even if he didn't, it wouldn't matter.

"Eli, what are you doing?"

He didn't answer, just kept an eye on the straight line to the door. There were probably a million places he could take her—a hotel suite, a conference room, a damn closet—but that's not how it would go down. Not tonight.

Outside, he found Tom, who had signaled for the cars to be pulled around. Eli shucked his jacket, caped Alexandra's shoulders, and steered her toward the town car.

She stared at him, astonished. Any other time, he'd be enjoying it, but he was too wound up.

He opened the back door. "The driver will take you anywhere you want."

"That's it?"

"I'm taking the SUV home with my security detail. The drive's about twenty minutes and I'll wait another half hour. If you arrive before that time is up, I won't get drunk and I won't try to manage my hard-on by myself."

Her brow knitted. "What the hell are you playing at, Eli?"

"If I get in the back of that car with you now, I will fuck you, Alexandra. Have no doubt. I'll kiss your breasts and suck your nipples and lick between your insanely gorgeous thighs. You're so damn responsive that I'll have you coming in seconds and begging me for more."

"Now wait a—"

He brushed his mouth across hers, needing a little something to tide him over. Her indignation tasted so damn sweet and he prayed it wasn't the last time he would have it on his lips. "I need you to sit in the car for a while. Inhale a breath. Call a friend. Take the time I'm giving you."

"And if I'm not there?"

He could feel a pained smile shaping his lips. Lake swimming was lovely this time of year, but he doubted even those icy depths would have any impact on his raging boner.

"Then I'll be hungover tomorrow and hoping to God my serious case of blue balls doesn't make me murderous during whatever campaign shit I have to deal with."

He stepped back in the knowledge that if he didn't leave now, the town car would soon be a-rockin'. As he turned, his last image was of his furious hellcat toeing her sexy heel and looking like a swift kick to the groin was in his future.

"You are a grade-A dick in the highest order of dicks, Eli Cooper."

He battled a smile and called out over his shoulder, "Tell me something I don't know."

# CHAPTER FOURTEEN

Some days the supply of curse words was insufficient for her needs.

Alex peeled off the heels she was crap at wearing and set them beside her in the seat well of the town car. *Wiggle, wiggle.* Exposing her feet to the heated interior provided not nearly enough of a distraction from her tumble of thoughts, especially as the jacket she wore smelled of Eli. Another one of his nefarious moves, that knuckle dragging shyster.

He might as well have raised his leg and peed all over her. She did not need his protection. She had overbearing brothers for that.

But for all his bossiness, for all his interfering know-it-allness, the connection between them was irrefutable. Like fire, it had no choice but to seek out oxygen. It needed it to exist. She wasn't sure what point she was trying to make to her muddled mind, but she knew that his mouth on hers might help her catch her breath. His hands on her breasts and his fingers stroking between her thighs might help inflate her lungs. This man would be her personal self-contained breathing apparatus.

The things he had said to her on the dance floor, his laundry list of wicked wants: if that was the seduction, what the hell would the sex be like? On the other side was the stick: *I won't talk to you, text you, interact with you in any way.* Could she stand to sever their connection and deny herself this pleasure? The very idea that her body—not her heart!—refused to let her walk away from this was troubling in itself. A woman in control should be able to toss off a *ta-ta, loser* and never look back, right?

She thought back to Kinsey's words about separating out the orgasms and just enjoying the (cock) ride. Easier said than done. Could she make it as easily done as said? Time to see if she was as kick-ass as she claimed to be.

Finally, Eli's SUV pulled up outside his house. (So she'd headed straight to Lincoln Park and beaten him by five minutes—he was not the boss of her.) Slipping her feet back into their high-heeled prisons, Alex opened the town car door and, less than gracefully, clambered out into the biting January chill. No going back now. The windows of Eli's car were dark tinted, so she couldn't see him, but it only enhanced the cloak-and-dagger nature of it all. Not that she needed extra thrills with Eli—on the anticipation scale of one to ten, everything was turned up to eleven with him. He excited her like no man she had ever met.

The passenger-side door opened, and a long, suited leg stepped out followed by the body of the hottest guy on the planet. He saw. He froze. His lips moved and then *he* moved, stalking toward her with terrifying purpose. She backed up one step but he was on her in a flash, his hands curving around her face, his mouth hot and needy.

"You're here," he whispered between all-consuming kisses.

"Of course I'm here," she said. He tasted of fire and longing. It intoxicated, overwhelmed, and affirmed she had made the right call. "Did you really think you could scare me off with your daytime Emmy reel submission of ridiculous ultimatums?"

He quirked a relieved grin, and that he had actually entertained doubts that she might come touched her deeply. "I thought you'd do what you were told and take the time to think it through. Be sure."

She splayed her hands on his broad chest. His tie was undone, as was the top button of his shirt. She had plans for the rest of those buttons.

"I want you, Eli." She swallowed down the lump of vulnerability threatening to ruin her 'tude. "And thirty minutes or whatever buffer you thought was necessary was just another thirty minutes I couldn't spend naked with you."

He closed his eyes at that, like she had said the most perfect thing.

A cough sliced through the dark. "Mr. Mayor."

Eli touched his forehead to hers, almost in apology. "There are some things that need to happen first, honey. Security things."

"Oh." Over his shoulder, Thing hovered, his face like a rusted-over lock. Eli pulled her aside to let the man pass.

"He needs to check the house first." Enthusiastic my-master's-home barks echoed from the house as Thing opened the door. "And then Shadow needs to be walked." Eli looked annoyed, and while she wasn't annoyed, it made her nervous. Any delay and she might pull a typical Alex Dempsey fuck-my-filter move and say something blatantly unsexy.

"Would it be better if we just got busy in the car?"

"Not a chance. We're going to be classy and do it in a bed."

*Do it.* She wanted to giggle like a schoolgirl. Eli steered her up the stoop and through the big oak door. Predictably, Shadow went nuts, but not on Eli. He jumped right on Alex like he was greeting an old friend.

"Whoa, boy!" She laughed, glad of the distraction and a chance to bury her trembling hands in something warm and soft—before she wrapped them around something hot and hard. Oh, God, she was as excited as this big old puppy.

"I've been replaced," Eli said indulgently. "So fickle."

"He's just a fan of the new and shiny. Like all men."

Thing descended the stairs. "All clear."

Eli nodded and handed him Shadow's leash.

This was not well received. "You know I can't do that, Mr. Mayor. I can't leave my post outside." Embarrassment bracketed his mouth as his glance flicked over Alex with a look that said, "Not even so you can get laid."

"Just up and down the block. Your partner is still outside and you'll never have to take your eye off the house."

"Mr. Mayor, this ain't up for negotiation."

"Tom," Eli said in that authoritative tone Alex loved. "Have you met Miss Dempsey?"

Thing turned suspicious eyes on her. Grunted.

"Not only is this woman capable of hauling thirty pounds of equipment—"

"Forty."

"Forty pounds of equipment up a gazillion flights of stairs. Not only can she save the lives of men twice her size before she's had breakfast, but I would happily put my safety in her hands and trust that she could crush the nuts of anyone who tried to harm me."

She pressed her lips together against a smile. That had to be the sexiest thing she had ever heard.

Eli laid a hand on the security guy's arm. "Dog. Walk. Now. I'll set the alarm and you can drop him off in ten minutes."

Thing's lips were set in a mulish line, but apparently there was a threshold to his insubordination, and he let Eli muscle him out the door.

"Eli," Alex murmured, gesturing at what he'd forgotten.

He opened the door again, put the leash (now attached to dog) and a poop-bag in the hands of a stone-faced Thing, and sent Shadow out for his nightly walk. On shutting the door again, he breathed out a sigh of relief.

"It's not easy being king." Before she could respond, he had locked both of his hands in hers, dragged them up above her head, and covered her body with his hard, muscular one. "But I do so enjoy it very, very much."

Then he ravaged her mouth royally. Holy *mamacita*, his kisses could cure world hunger. He could win gold at the Olympic Games of kissing. He—

A gentle rap on the door interrupted her crazy internal commentary. "I don't hear the beep," Thing muttered like a grumpy ghost from the other side.

Eli smiled against her mouth, released her, and entered some numbers on the panel to the left of her cheek. *Beep.*

He stood back and scrubbed a hand over his chin. "As tempting as it is to take you against this wall, I've been dreaming about this moment for some time and I want to do it right." He held out a hand. "Come to bed with me, Alexandra."

She took his hand, thinking *hell yes,* and something else far more terrifying.

If he kept asking nicely, she might just be willing to follow him anywhere.

The mayoral lair was cool grays and dark greens, very masculine, and oh so Eli. A full-length mirror stood sentry against the far wall. She giggled, unable to contain her nerves.

"What's so funny?"

"Is that where you spend hours asking who's the fairest of them all?"

"I like to do a daily check-in. Thirty minutes max," he said good-humoredly. With a couple of clicks, the fire in the hearth sprang to life, the heat quickly spreading needed warmth over her goosefleshed skin.

He shaped his chest to her back and stood her in front of him facing the mirror. Eyes glued to hers, he slipped his tuxedo jacket off her shoulders and threw it over a nearby chair.

As usual, his intensity made her nervous, so she

started babbling. "I still have the one you gave me the night of the fire."

"Lucky jacket, draped all over this beautiful body." He brushed his hands over her tattoos with something like reverence. She shivered. "Your ink does things to me, Alexandra."

*And you do things to me, Eli Cooper. Dangerous, yearning things.* She blinked those treacherous thoughts away, scattering them to the four corners of the room. The clothes might be coming off, but the Kevlar would remain firmly in place around her heart.

He unzipped her dress, shrugged it from her shoulders, and peeled it down. She stepped out of it and he threw it over a chair. The fact that the last time they'd been in such close quarters he'd teased two orgasms from her within the span of three minutes should have created some semblance of self-confidence as she stood before him, yet she felt more exposed than ever in his towering presence.

"Not fair that I'm half naked and you're fully dressed," she pouted.

"It's fair. It's perfectly fair."

He moved her hair aside and kissed her neck, tenderly, *unfairly*. His eyes never wavered from watching her in the mirror.

"Not fair," she whispered.

Velvet kisses of worship trailed the top of her spine and followed a slow, sensual descent. With the back of his knuckled hand, he skimmed her flame-lit skin, leaving dancing sparks in the wake of every touch. The curve of her stomach, the side of her breast, the flare of her hip. The sensations were incredible.

"Not . . . fair." She closed her desire-heavy eyelids and absorbed the unbearable eroticism of a man taking his time. The men she had been with before seemed so immature now compared to Eli.

But really, she didn't want to miss a thing, so she dragged her eyes open. Avidly, she watched as he pulled his tie off and let it fall to the floor. Next his cuff links, which he placed on the dresser.

"May I?" She wanted to be the one to unbutton his shirt. Expose him like he had done to her. For a moment, she imagined they had just come home from a dinner party with friends. In her domestic fantasy, they'd had a good time with convivial company, but all night they had stolen needful glances at each other. Knowing that this moment would come, when they would strip each other slowly.

She kicked that ridiculousness to the curb. One-night stands didn't do couples dinner parties.

He cupped her hips as she undid each shirt button. *One, two, three* . . . All the time, he burned her alive with an intense regard, while she kept her eyes at chest level. Meeting his stare felt too raw. Too real.

She got to the last button, spread his shirt, and *pause for the national anthem because, daaamn,* the man was heart-stopping in his perfection. The scars on what had to be painted-on abs, wounds he must have picked up during his time in the Marines, only added to his animal magnetism.

With greedy fingers, she traced the geography of his hero-ravaged skin, remembering his military accomplishments and what he must have faced over there, remembering his parents, and what had happened in this house. A sobering thought, but that was his pain, and it would be presumptuous of her to take it on. Shucking his shirt entirely, she ran riot over his chest with her hands. Touching, shaping, planning a course of attack for her hungry mouth. His beauty had shocked her into an awed silence.

"I've wanted you from the first moment I laid eyes on you," he said quietly.

Her heart missed a beat. Then another. She swallowed and it started up again.

"You had a funny way of showing it. You were rude. Chauvinistic."

"I was," he conceded. "I saw you standing with Gage at the bar in Smith & Jones, wearing that Gandalf Hates the Yankees T-shirt, all hair and fire and attitude, and it stunned me that someone could crash through me like that."

"Gage has that effect."

He didn't smile at her poor attempt at diminishing the moment. Because it felt like a moment. Too large for her to comprehend.

"You were rude," she repeated, her voice unsteady, her hands shaky from the force of her feelings as she unsnapped his tuxedo pants.

"Pigtail pulling, honey. Inside every man struck clueless by a woman is a snotty little schoolboy on the playground."

She battled a smile. Lost the fight. "You liked me."

"To my horror."

"And when I carved up Sam Cochrane's car, did you still like me?"

"It was a stupid move, wild and crazy, but damn it if a part of me didn't love that you stood up for your people and your comrades. For yourself. Not enough people do that." He kissed her, long and sweet. "But officially I was pissed. Baby, I had to be."

She drew down his zipper, taking note of a very impressive bulge. "I've been nothing but trouble for you, haven't I?"

"Yes, you have, and now I'm going to make you pay. You're going to find out what happens when you poke the beast." He pushed her onto the bed, and she watched with her mouth watering as he stripped to his boxer briefs. Magnificent, powerful, and tonight he was all hers.

"Now, turn over."

The words were a low-voiced command, issued with Eli's typical certainty that they would be obeyed. Still, she hesitated, partly to prolong the moment, but more so he wouldn't think he was getting his own way.

He gentled her jaw. "Do you trust me to make you feel good?"

"You've always made me feel good. Even when you make me mad, piss me off, and drive me to distraction. Everything you do turns me on."

"Just goes to prove orneriness is a natural part of your makeup."

She hooked a finger in the band of his boxers. "I want to give you pleasure, Eli. It's been much too one-sided."

"There's nothing I want more than to see those beautiful lips of yours wrapped around my cock, sucking me hard before I drive in deep. But first, I'll be taking care of you. Making you come several times is my only goal tonight, Alexandra."

"Is this the Chicago way? Come early and come often?"

His smile could end wars. "Knowing how responsive you are to my touch, that would be a yes. Now, turn over. Won't tell you again."

*Yes, sir.*

She rolled to her front and crawled about halfway up the bed. She knew her ass looked *pret*-ty fine in these panties, and his full-throated growl confirmed her confidence.

"Lie flat."

He lay down beside her, propped on an elbow, and she turned her head so she could admire the view. Then it started.

At first, just the softest touch of his finger pads along the ladder of her spine. Teasing, igniting her skin to sun and flame. The sensory onslaught built and took hold as he trailed fingers down to the border of her panties.

"Eli, please."

"What?" He sounded leisurely, unbothered by it all.

"Please don't wait. I need you so badly."

Her legs had started to shake with the anticipation, even before he parted them with those large, blunt hands. As though he worked for a living instead of sitting in his ivory tower, making decisions that affected millions. It was like this secret part of him that only she knew. How rough and brutish and filthy-minded he was under that golden facade.

He dragged on her panties, a slow, erotic rake down to her thighs.

"God, you are perfect. I could spend forever exploring this patch of skin right here." With hot kisses, he christened the spot where the crease of her thigh met the round of her ass. Exquisite—and exquisitely frustrating.

"It's been so long, Eli. If you don't—ah!" He slipped a finger between her thighs. She bit back the scream of pleasure on her lips, refusing to give it to him.

He rubbed through her folds. "How do you want to come, honey?" Continuing to saw his fingers back and forth, he kissed every inch of her booty. Her body undulated, chasing the motion of his clever digits.

"How about sometime soon?" she gasped.

In a split second, he had flipped her on her back, and had those panties off and her thighs spread wide. Totally exposed, all she could do was get wetter and wetter while he stared at her like the mysteries of the universe lay between her legs.

"Wider."

Was that even possible? She moved her thighs apart until her knees practically touched the edges of the bed. The glow from the fire lit up the hard planes of his cheek, the rigid line of his jaw.

She rolled her hips in blatant appeal, craving the grind, some small measure of relief. Her hands grasped at the bed cover. "I hate you right now."

That earned her an evil chuckle followed by a stroke of a solitary finger along her outer lips. Any second now and she would fly apart, lose herself in the oblivion she was hurtling toward. He heeled his hand against her entire sex and gave a lascivious rub.

"I—I don't think I can hold on, Eli."

"You don't have to. Let go and then let me do it all over again."

She exploded, and the fact that it had been pre-cipitated by his giving her permission to come was something she would store and unpack later. That wasn't her. Was it?

He sucked on the finger he had bathed in her juices. "You taste so damn good. Need more. Need you."

She squeezed her core, holding on to the sparkling quivers, determined not to allow a single whispering touch unravel her again so soon. But this time, he went even slower. Maddeningly so, as if he knew her job would be to resist. He placed a feathery kiss on the inside of her thigh, then one on the other.

Then in between.

She clamped down on her bottom lip until it hurt enough to overpower the glittering sensation below. She'd always thought Eli Cooper was a smooth talker, but now she realized that slick mouth was wasted on politics. It was made to bring bordering-on-painful physical pleasure.

His tongue traced the outer lips, dipped inside, but never hit the hot spot of her clit. Every lick slickened and teased, maddened and aroused. Another skill to add to his sex ninja résumé: Eli Cooper, Tongue-Fucking Master.

"Touch those gorgeous breasts, honey," he or-dered. The rumble of his voice, husky with desire, all boss against her throbbing pussy, nearly sent her over.

She undid the front clasp and let her aching breasts spill free, but not for long. Soon, she had cupped them in her hands, massaging them until her nipples peaked to hard tips. She heard his groan of appreci-ation against her sensitized sex.

His dark head bobbed between her thighs as he sought untrodden paths of ecstasy. She'd had no idea it could feel like this, that the long, obscene licks through her sex could ignite something more than a coming orgasm. Seeing this powerful man tending to her with such absolute absorption wrapped her up in a crazy kind of joy.

She felt beautiful under his tongue. She felt loved in this moment. She felt . . . on the brink of something terrifyingly real.

He applied an unbearably arousing suction to—at last!—her sizzling clit and she erupted.

"Eli!" Her hands grabbed his hair and held him fast in a glorious grind through her greedy, wracking orgasm. He stayed with her, lapping up her feminine satisfaction, pinning her with hands on hips until it was nothing but twittery aftershocks and his hot breath keeping the embers stoked below.

Watching—and feeling—Alexandra come almost did Eli in. He was granite hard, so close to going off, but it was important that he treat her right. After her rotten year in the man-trenches, he wanted to worship her.

He knew he'd have to sate his need soon, but first he took a moment to absorb this woman in all her postorgasmic glory. Her skin was flushed, her eyes as bright as jewels. Freed from the restraint of the demi bra, her perfect breasts begged for his greedy touch. She was like a spirited thoroughbred straining at her harness, but this woman could never be mastered and he would be a fool to try. Much better to enjoy her earthy life force and let her glow rub off on his darkness.

"Is that it?" she asked, her voice thick with need.

He laughed. "Two orgasms not enough?"

Her gaze did a slow meander down his body and fixed on his tented boxers. "I need all of you inside me, Eli, and I know you need it, too. Please don't make either of us wait any longer."

Her honesty unraveled some tangle of emotion inside him and he responded the only way he knew how: he stamped his mouth over hers and took what was his right. This slow-burn plan he'd had died a quick and necessary death. Primal urgency ruled their movements. Fueled by desperate hands and frenzied mouths, they kissed their way to total nakedness.

Her mouth dropped open.

"What's wrong?"

"We're gonna need a bigger condom. If the female voters could see you now, that election would be a slam dunk." She circled his swollen cock and with slow, rhythmic strokes, moved her hand up and down, the slide progressively easier because of the pre-cum slicking the head.

He had trouble getting the words out. "Only one voter gets to see this, honey."

"I knew this was all a scheme to get me to check that box on Election Day."

"We do what we must."

Her hands explored, caressed, pumped him until he just about lost the power of speech. He wanted to do a million filthy-gorgeous things to her: fuck her saucy mouth, drag his cock between her beautiful tits, sink into that sweet pussy he could still taste on his lips.

"You can do it all, Eli. Tonight, I'm yours."

So much for losing the power of speech. Apparently, he was so far gone he didn't even realize when he was verbalizing his wildest fantasies.

She continued to palm him, her green eyes sparkling jewels of temptation, her olive skin lustrous in the firelight. "Tell me what you need. And be specific."

*Be specific.* He had hit the fucking mother lode—the woman of his fantasies craving his demands. And he had so many.

"Suck me off. Start slow."

A slight hitch at the corner of her mouth disappeared as she scooted down the bed and parted her lips to take him in. Tentative inches at first, then a methodical suckle, each return taking in more. Needing an anchor, he tunneled his fingers through her wild hair and held her in place, as if that one motion could convince him who was in control. Around her, control was a slippery thing, likely to elude him with each passing second in her presence.

He might be giving the orders here, but she was the one in charge.

Just as he felt that sizzle of impending orgasm, she released him with a pop. God, he'd been so close, but she had other plans, and hell, he didn't mind. Taking his cock in her hand, she rubbed the swollen head around the dark nipple of one gorgeous tit. Like she was using his dick as an instrument, writing a story on her body. Pre-cum leaked on her olive skin, and she—oh, good fuck—massaged it into her puckered nipple.

"Jesus, Alexandra." Hands down, that was the most erotic thing he had ever seen. Her eyes, heavy lidded with a mix of dark desire and strange innocence, held his captive.

"Eli, I need you to fuck me. Now."

He lost it. Just lost his mind. He pulled her up level and lay over her, settling into the welcoming embrace of her thighs. Their mouths met in a crush of want and heat, unlike any kiss he'd ever given or received. He captured her moans. She caught his right back. Against his rigid cock, she felt so wet and accepting, the only place he wanted to be, and she rolled her hips, begging, willing him to thrust all his tension inside this woman who made him feel like a god. Or more of a god than he usually felt, which was saying a lot.

"Please," she moaned. "Oh, God. Condom. We need—"

Fuck. He had been about to slip in unholstered. This was what she had reduced him to.

"On it."

Two seconds later and he had a condom out of its packaging, but his hands were . . . shit, his hands were shaking like he was a randy teen his first time out, and it took him three tries to get everything secured.

"Been awhile, huh?" she asked with that smart-assed grin, a nice call back to that first time he'd made her come in the hallway of her home. After sixty seconds, he was about to shoot back at her, but then all coherent thought fled as he gripped her sweet ass and drove in balls-deep.

She arched into him, screaming her pleasure at taking all of him.

"Yeah, it's been a while," he gritted out as he withdrew, "and you're going to benefit, honey. I'm going to fuck you so hard you'll see stars." He plunged again, loving how her lusty moans set off vibrations throughout his body.

"Hockey stars, perhaps?"

Jesus, this woman's mouth. "I will fuck the ever-loving smart-assery out of you, Alexandra." He got started on that, pumping in and out, in and out. Deeper, harder. "I'm going to fuck you so good the only word on your lips will be my name. The only answer to every question will be my name. Now say it."

He claimed her mouth, kissing her fiercely to let her think on it awhile. The coil in his gut tightened with every thrust into her slick channel. Her hands were everywhere—his shoulders, raking his back, squeezing his ass to seal their connection.

When he released her mouth, she murmured on a blissful sigh, "Asshole."

"My other name, honey."

She squeezed him like a satin fist, dug her heel into his ass. "Prick."

He stalled. Dawdled. Started again. More languorous this time because he suspected that might piss her off.

"Don't slow down!"

*Bingo.* "My name."

He kissed her again, loving the tangle of their tongues, pouring every ounce of feeling he could into it. Emotion he hadn't realized he had, or had to spare.

"Eli," she screamed as she crested toward that peak of pleasure.

He started up that driving rhythm again, long, possessive strokes designed to pleasure her for making him feel and punish her for making him fall. And when her pussy fluttered, gripped, and locked him through the onslaught of her orgasm, she said his name again.

Softly now, and that word had never sounded sweeter or more freely given. He didn't want to think about why he needed that or why being buried inside her was his personal heaven. He didn't want to think.

So he let the sensations claim him and trigger a climax that knocked out the power grid that used to be his brain. And his last thought as he emptied all he had inside her was that he knew what he was doing here.

Mostly.

# CHAPTER FIFTEEN

Alex unhinged one uncooperative eyelid, then the other, and her hand moved instinctively to find him. Gone, the sheets cool. He'd been up for a while.

The clock said 6:08 and her fuzzy head agreed. The Cheshire cat grin that stole across her face was inevitable. She was in Eli Cooper's bed.

Last night, Eli's dominance of her body had been like something shifting into place. It was as though he knew something about her that she didn't—a disturbing thought indeed. She had always assumed she should be the aggressor, and given her sassy mouth and Amazonian frame, men expected it of her. Tough, strong women like Firefighter Alex Dempsey were supposed to be getting it done between the sheets, yet it had never seemed as satisfying as it should have.

With Eli, she loved obeying his filthy, inventive demands. Did that make her submissive? She didn't know and she didn't care. She just knew that this dynamic worked for her and she wanted to explore it.

If only he was here so she could explore it without leaving these warm, sex-rumpled sheets. She'd read somewhere that he was an early riser because he had so much to do and didn't want to waste a single minute. She guessed it was time to go waste some of those mayoral minutes. But first, a little poking around was in order.

The bathroom was big, bemarbled, and filled with—yep—beauty products. He probably got crates of L'Oréal hair gel sent to him with Amazon Subscribe & Save. She squinted in the bathroom mirror to minimize the horror. Makeup smudged, hair as big as Wisconsin, body feeling appropriately used after multiple orgasms.

In the bedroom, she shuddered at the idea of redressing in her evening wear, so she rooted around for something more comfortable. Ransacking a dresser, she found and threw on a U of C T-shirt, inhaling it to tide her over until she encountered coffee or man (either would suffice). Last night, she hadn't had time to absorb her surroundings because she was too busy being walk-ravished into the bedroom. Now she took a moment. Assorted artwork and photos dotted the walls on this floor, but there were conspicuous blanks, perfectly spaced-out squares that were slightly discolored, as though they'd once housed frames that had since been removed. She counted five of them on the landing.

What remained were pictures of Eli as a kid with family members: his mom, grandparents, what looked like cousins.

But, Alex couldn't help but notice, none of his father, the revered Weston Cooper.

Were those the photos that were missing? He hadn't spoken much of his dad, though in interviews, whenever his name came up—and inevitably the manner of his death—Eli was always respectful. Distantly respectful, if she thought about it. His face only seemed to light up when he talked about his mother. At that Women in Business luncheon last week, he had told a voter-baiting story about how his mom put his dad through law school. That personalized insight into the sacrifice of a modern marriage had gone down a treat with the crowd, but she suspected there was more to it.

She thought back to his odd reaction on getting that award and his ambivalence about Weston Cooper's heroism. His hand gripping that steak knife.

Slowly, she moved downstairs, noting that the first-floor walls still had all the pictures intact, including several with his father. The public area of the house. Finished with her nose-dawdle, she padded into the living room and just about doubled over with lust.

Eli sat on a paperwork-strewn sofa, laptop open, Shadow at his bare feet, the epitome of "Ralph Lauren invades the Hamptons." A faded blue Henley did a terrible job of hiding his stunning musculature. Soft, touchable jeans had clearly been washed far too many times if the rips revealing peeks of his tree-trunk thighs were any indication. And the coup de grâce—he was wearing glasses.

She didn't think it was possible the man could get any sexier, but here he was, yet again making a mockery of her ridiculous preconceptions. He looked up, and his glass-rimmed eyes traveled over her body, foretelling a wicked plan to take her before she'd had her coffee. Yes, please!

"Morning, Alexandra." All raspy and sexy. God, she couldn't stand it.

She held up a finger. "Just a sec."

Three steps back the way she came took her out of his sight. In the hallway, she did a little dance, thanking the sex gods for blessing Alex Dempsey, a mere mortal, with a night in the bed of one of their own. *Oh, great ones, I will use him well.*

Done with her homage, she looked down to find Shadow gazing up at her with eyes aglow and tail a-wagging. Bending to doggy level, she whispered in his ear, "Not a word to your master about what you just witnessed here, buddy. His ego is already as big as his dick."

She swore the dog winked at her.

Back in the living room, she was on him faster than double-struck lightning. Between blistering lip locks, she said, "Your morning-after care sucks, Cooper. I wake up and there's no hard peen nudging my butt demanding attention."

He laughed. "I meant to come back before you opened your eyes but I got distracted. Paperwork."

"So flattering. But I forgive you because I now get to do the deed with nerdy eyeglass-wearing Eli." She drew back. "I can't believe I've never seen you in glasses before. Why don't you wear them all the time?"

"Because I'm already hot enough. I put these on and I'd be lucky to walk ten feet without losing all my clothes to Eli-mania." And while on the lovely subject of losing clothes . . . He peeled off her shirt, raising his glasses to get a better look. Then he made a colossal error.

He pushed them up to the top of his head!

"Don't even think about it, buster," she ordered as

she replaced them on the bridge of his nose. "I don't care how blurry, *or clear*, I look to you. I demand my early morning sex nerd-style."

Sighing his acquiescence, he moved a folder aside, and her gaze was drawn to the cover with the seal of Veterans' Affairs. "That doesn't look like campaign stuff."

"It's not. I'm working on a new program with the Veterans' Court."

She'd heard of this, a court system designed to administer cases of military vets. Momentarily distracted from the Cooper glory, she said, "I don't really get why there has to be a separate system. Isn't crime the same regardless of who commits it?"

"Yes and no. One in ten prison inmates in the U.S. has a military background, and a lot of the behavior that gets them in trouble can be traced to inadequate services for PTSD and long wait times for counseling. Many self-medicate with alcohol, drugs, have poor employment rates. It's a perfect storm for sending vets into the criminal justice system. The veterans' court looks at ways to keep vets out of prison for nonviolent offenses and help them get their lives back on track—before they derail completely." He picked up the folder. "I've been reading some of the cases because I plan to give it more funding for mental health and mentoring services."

Her memory strayed to the scars on his body, the stamps of his heroism and his duty to country. With two brothers who were ex-military, she understood the difficulties with reacclimation stateside. Luke, especially, had been a terror. "How did you get through it, Eli?"

"I kept busy," he said, not misunderstanding her. "I went to work in the state's attorney's office and I powered through." He pushed her unruly hair behind her ear. "I may have drunk too much, but that could just as easily be attributed to being a lawyer. I probably should have talked to someone, but my grandparents didn't believe in therapy and I guess I internalized that."

"You've had to work through a lot of stuff."

His smile was grimly beautiful. "The human condition. If it ain't painful, it ain't interesting."

True, that. "So, when your parents died you didn't see a shrink?"

He shook his head. "Shrinks were for crazy people. In Lake Forest, traumatic events are overcome with stiff upper lips, a double scotch, and a round of golf. I'm a black belt in all three." He skimmed his hands down her sides, seeking and finding all her curves. "I think I turned out okay, but I recognize that's not the solution for everyone."

"Like Brady? Gage said it's been slow going, but getting better."

A shadow crossed his face but quickly brightened to a smile. "I don't worry about him as much anymore. Your brother's been really good for him."

Brady had been just as good for Gage, who went through a tough time with his biological mom in the fall. "That's why you introduced them. You hoped Gage would heal Brady." And this man didn't believe in the fairy tale? She dropped a kiss on his lips. "Sounds like you've been a good friend."

"To be honest, I was sick of all his doom and

gloom. Someone had to take charge and make something happen."

Eli's grip on the reins, even when it wasn't his horse to ride, always had to be absolute. Great for her in the bedroom, but she could see that it might be troublesome in other rooms in the house. Fortunately, she wouldn't have to worry about that. Soon she wouldn't have to worry about any of it.

*Just enjoy the cock ride, Dempsey.*

Needing the distraction that she knew only his hands could give, she squirmed in his lap, loving the bite of the denim through her erotically thin panties. His thumbs veed over her mound, then trailed farther south and under until they encountered soft, soaking flesh.

"You a little sore, honey? I worked you good."

She wished she didn't blush around him so much. "I like it. I like the reminder of how good you feel inside me."

"You did say it had been a while," he said with a sly bent to his tone.

"Fishing for tales of my past misdeeds?"

"If I was to believe you, you're as untouched as the driven snow because no man can see past your startling honesty and tough-girl attitude to the real woman underneath."

She felt her bones go stiff. He felt it, too.

"I see. Just give me a name. I can have him taken care of within the hour."

She smiled, though she really shouldn't enjoy that Eli had that kind of power and was unafraid to use it in her defense. "I believe you, which reminds me. You are not to retaliate against Michael Martinez because he informed me of your Neanderthal behavior."

Glowering ensued. "He was supposed to keep that information to himself."

"I mean it, Eli. No payback. You got what you wanted."

He rubbed his thumb over her nipple, inducing delicious shivers. "Yes, I did. I suppose I can be magnanimous in victory."

"Ass," she muttered.

Smug grin. "Tell me about the last guy. Maybe I can transfer my wrath to someone who's more deserving."

She should never have opened this can of wormage. "Only my pride was the casualty here, Eli. I'd been dating, once a week, all duds, and then after one encounter with a dickhead in a four-hundred-thousand-dollar luxury vehicle, suddenly I was interesting."

"Ah."

"Yeah. Ah." She squirmed, not a sexy writhe this time. "I let myself get picked up in my own bar by some stockbroker type. Just sex while under the influence."

He stared at her with that immovable gaze. "So, he didn't call you?"

Typical man, assuming that a woman's ultimate goal was to get that follow-up call. She fixed him with a disapproving glare, letting him know what she thought of his stereotyping. "No, he didn't. Instead two nights later he came back into the bar with a bunch of rowdy friends and I overheard them taking bets about who would be next to tap America's Favorite Firefighter."

His fingers gripped her waist. "How rude." He

said it with a lethal quiet, as if this type of rudeness deserved the death penalty. At his hands.

"I knew what I was doing. But I did feel foolish, and then I felt . . . careful." She needed him to understand that she had no expectations here. Eyes open, fun times ahead. Next topic. "So what about you?"

"I told you, I don't date."

"Well, no one said you had to date to get some." She made a flourish with her hands over her very naked breasts, a gesture of acknowledgment that not dating could be very rewarding indeed.

His gaze turned molten. "Honey, you had your chance to extract my secrets last night in the postcoital afterglow, but instead you chose more sex."

She raised a fist to the ceiling in triumph. "I will always choose more sex. But now I want to know how long it's been for you. Who was it? Lemme guess. Some campaign intern whose panties get wet whenever you walk in the room?" *Ugh,* she hated this skank already. She needed to stop talking, but a part of her had to know what the competition was like.

Not that it would make a difference to Eli. He'd made it abundantly clear that she should keep her expectations as low as dirt.

"No interns." A sharp look said the suggestion was beneath him.

"Who, then? Do I know her? It's that Whitney chick, isn't it?"

"I would never sleep with an employee." At her arch smile, he added, "A direct report."

"So that leaves Madison," she joked.

And . . . there it was. The air heaved with the weight of his nondenial.

"You mean the last time you had sex was twelve years ago with your ex-wife?" Rather wishful, but laughing it off seemed like the only way to play this and not look like a lovesick, jealous harpy.

"When neither of us is seeing anyone, we have an arrangement." Those all-knowing eyes measured her reaction. "Just to scratch an itch. Like divorced-with-benefits."

Her stomach whirled in a slow, sick spin. This was . . . oh, God, this was awful. *You wanted to know, dummy.*

Maybe she was overreacting and it was truly ancient history. Seeking clarification was on the tip of her tongue when he said the one thing she might have been able to survive this conversation without hearing. "It's just sex. It doesn't mean anything."

Anger rose swift and sharp. "She's your ex-wife and you have an arrangement to have sex with her when the need arises." When he had an itch to scratch. "I would say it means a great deal."

Feeling exposed in every possible way, she drew back and reached for the shirt he had peeled off five minutes ago during a much simpler time.

"Alexandra, it's purely fulfilling a biological need. Don't tell me you don't know the difference between sex that means something and sex that doesn't."

"Of course I do." She shrugged his shirt on with jerky movements that made her breasts wobble. He didn't even look, just kept those relentlessly blue eyes trained on hers. "Sex with your ex-wife means nothing." The ex-wife he worked with day in, day out. The ex-wife he shared that cozy huddle with at the hockey game. The ex-wife he ran back into that hotel to save.

Oh yeah. Sure sounded like nothing.

His brow darkened. "Lawyers are trained to never ask a question they don't already know the answer to. A corollary is to never ask a question if you can't handle the answer. You asked, and I told you. There are enough lies in my life but for this, with you, I want it to be honest."

On ramshackle legs, she scrambled to a stand, amazed she had the power. Was he actually congratulating himself for being so upfront? Was she supposed to be blown away because he acted less like a sleazy politician and more like a human being? Of course, the problem with that reasoning is that all truths had to carry the same weight.

Well, this truth was too heavy for her.

"You're right, I did ask. I guess I wasn't thinking of the law degree I needed to navigate a conversation with you. Well, you've scratched *this* itch, counselor, so feel free to get back to what's familiar." She stormed out of the room, pulling his T-shirt down as she marched.

Why the hell was she so put out by this? Eli had barely blinked an eye when she told him about Mr. Two-Pump-Chump . . . was that why she was upset? Because Eli couldn't manage even a hint of jealousy over the last man she slept with?

No. That was not what this was about. Alex just did not agree that a man could have a casual sexual relationship with his ex-wife and expect the woman he was currently knocking boots with to be copacetic with it.

In his bedroom, she squeezed into her sexy underwear (bought by Eli) and her gorgeous dress (bought by Eli). Did he still buy gifts for Madison? She resisted going there, but her mind was already hurtling down the track. He clearly had a tab at the House of French Whoreish Lingerie, so if he wasn't buying bustiers to keep his staffers quiet, then he must be stocking up on crotchless panties for his ex.

Madison was beautiful, thin, sophisticated, the perfect partner for a glib, smooth-talking politico. Ah, hell, Alex was jealous, through and through, and she knew it was crazy and unreasonable given the fact Eli had promised nothing. But neither could she help the negative energy pumping through her veins.

Heading down the stairs, Alex practiced her reasonable face, but at the bottom was the man himself, looking so handsome it hurt.

"Could we talk about this like two adults?"

"Nope, I'm feeling pretty childish right now."

"Jealousy suits those beautiful eyes of yours, Alexandra."

It came out cool, condescending. If he hadn't sounded so goddamn amused and above it all, she might not have exploded—or blurted something she couldn't take back.

"I'm done with you and your campaign. You're a thug in a suit and I don't trust you."

The air, previously chilly, dropped to Lake Michigan in January levels. It was a rotten thing to say. She had basically accused him of abusing his position, but the bottom line was that he was using her for the campaign, and by election night, it would be over. Not that she wanted more, but getting involved with him—or getting *more* involved with him—would be disastrous to her mental well-being. The walls around her heart had to be reinforced.

She knew what she was to him. A diversion, comic and sexual, on the campaign trail. She was barely girlfriend material for a regular joe, never mind a double-talking, fine-wine-drinking, cuff-link-wearing man like Eli. He was the hottest guy she had ever seen, so out of her league they hadn't invented his league yet. It was like Future League of Hot Guys We Can't Place Because They're Too Fucking Hot.

He scared her. This weak, needy side of herself scared her.

He picked up her shoes from where she had slipped them off in his hallway last night. It seemed like weeks ago. "I'll take you home."

"I can cab it."

"Don't test me, Alexandra." She heard no give in his tone.

Schlepping it in a taxi Cinderella-style, wearing her fancy gown and too-high heels, was probably not the greatest idea. While she wrestled with that decision, he pulled a parka from a closet and wrapped it around her. It felt like ten times her size, and in it, she knew she must look as small and defenseless as she felt. Shadow looked on, probably thinking he was going for a walk, and she wanted to throw her arms around him. Absorb his comfort in this new world order.

Her walk of shame came courtesy of the mayor's motorcade because, hey y'all, let's slap a big X-marks-the-spot on the dummy's fabulous night of hot sex with Chicago's smokin' mayor! On the journey home, they sat miles apart, Madison the invisible chaperone between them. Neither of them spoke—not a single attempt to soothe or appease from him—and by the time they arrived at her house, she was spitting nails. Of course he walked her to her door, because even when he was an asshat he was a gentleman first.

As she fumbled with the key to her front door, Gage opened up and gave her the elevator look, down, then up.

"You ok—?"

"Stow it, Gage." With one foot on the last step of the hallway stairs, she heard what could have been a clearing of the throat but was more likely a sexy growl.

"I had a great time last night, Alexandra."

She shrugged his coat off and let it slide to the floor. Infusing a whole lot of sway into her hips as she climbed the stairs, she gifted him the perfect view of the ass he had worshipped last night, and would not be getting further access to in this lifetime or the next.

"I had a great time, too," she snapped over her shoulder. "Now take your damn coat and head east until your big, fat head floats!"

# CHAPTER SIXTEEN

*Trouble in paradise for Mayor Cooper and his feisty firefighter? After they made headlines for their tempestuous turn around the dance floor at the Weston Cooper Justice Award gala last week, the two have not been seen in public together. The mayor refuses to tango and tell, preferring to keep mum when questioned in the morning press conferences. Attempts to reach Firefighter Dempsey have been unsuccessful.*
*—Chicago Tattler*

Five days. Five days without a word.

Oh, she saw him on the news. It was impossible not to. The man *was* the news. He was followed everywhere he went, from a visit to an after-school program where he played basketball with the kids to a meeting of concerned parents for the Chicago Public Schools system. With each new sighting, she strained to see if he'd replaced her, but he appeared to be riding solo. Alex imagined she saw Madison in the background, doing her job, and every glimpse sent a hot snake of jealousy crawling through her insides. Then she felt embarrassed and petty.

Damn Eli Cooper.

He had made no promises to her, so his admission about his unfinished relationship with his ex-wife should not have affected Alex in this way. A free agent, he was welcome to conduct his sex life any way he chose, but sleeping with an ex seemed like a whole other level—a whole other meaningful level. How could they do the deed and divorce—ha!—it from all the feelings they once had for each other?

Her posse was split down the middle: Gage and Darcy thought *So what? All that matters is who he wants now.* Kinsey had taken Alex's side, though there'd been a hint of disappointment in her tone that Alex was letting this get under her skin. Such girly weaknesses were not permitted in the enjoy-the-cock-ride code.

What the hell did it matter? Alex and Eli were not in a relationship. The man didn't even believe in love. The fairy tale was for suckers, and she was another lamb waiting in line for the love'll kill you slaughterhouse. Instead, Eli Cooper was getting his sexual appetites satisfied without the inconvenience of a connection. His ex-wife one week, the woman who saved his life the next.

Yet . . .

When he'd stripped her bare with his eyes and his hands, she had seen something there. Some link between them that grew stronger with each encounter, whether it was a sexy banterfest, a sixty-second orgasm, or a night of hunger awakened and barely sated. He was looking for something—and why did it feel like she was the one person who could give it to him?

*It's good to be king,* he had said. Pretty fucking lonely, too.

Seated in the back of the truck on her way to a

traffic accident scene, she tightened the strap on her helmet and mulled over the maudlin turn her thoughts had taken. What a sap. Strangely, she missed him. Not just his muscular, scarred body and those clever, clever hands. She missed his voice, his snark, his quick mind, his cocksure opinions. And she missed how special he had made her feel, transitory though it was. With Eli Cooper, she felt like the only woman in his world.

*Wise up, dummy.* Hallmarks of a good politician.

Determined to shove him from her mind, she shook her muddled head and focused on her job. Venti was calling out updates from the computer in the cab of the truck as they barreled toward Lake Shore Drive and Addison, mere steps from Cubbies territory. A semi had collided with three cars on the Drive during morning rush hour, and they needed all hands on deck.

CPD was already on site, working to move cars aside so the first responders could cut a path through, but Engine 6's truck still met the immovable force of stopped traffic at least two hundred feet from the pileup. Up ahead, they could see the truck bed of the semi embedded in the roof of an SUV. Shit, that was not good. There was a reason why trucks were not allowed on the Drive.

"Fox, Dempsey, with me," Venti barked. "The rest of you work with CPD on getting these cars cleared for the EMTs."

Why the cap had chosen her wasn't clear. Other members of the crew had a ton more experience with this kind of incident.

"What've we got?" Wyatt asked before she had a chance to.

"One dead on the scene, at least eight injured ranging from critical to a broken ankle . . ." A pair of EMTs were doing CPR on a guy laid out on the ground. So much blood . . .

They picked up the pace, heading toward the SUV wedged beneath the truck's flatbed. The vehicle had lost a quarter of its height, dangerously compressed in a way that prevented the doors from being opened without cutting equipment—and even that would be difficult given the angle. A uniformed cop stood hunched over at the smashed window, alternating between speaking into a radio and assuring the driver that help was on the way.

Alex assumed they were the cavalry.

Venti called out the details. A heavily pregnant woman was trapped in the SUV, her leg pinned, but conscious enough to speak. The LT in charge from Engine 69 was Alex's former lieutenant at Engine 6, Tony "Big Mac" McElroy, a rock-solid guy who was also a good friend. On seeing them, he nodded them over.

"Her leg's stuck under the dash and we need to collar her before we can cut her out . . ."

"But you can't fit anyone through that back window," Wy finished, assessing the crushed roof of the SUV below the forced shelter of the flatbed.

"Yeah, she's at thirty-nine weeks. Not in labor, but if we don't move her right, it could turn to shit real quick."

Alex went to unsnap her jacket, knowing now why Venti had chosen her. Sure she was bigger boned than the average woman, but in this case her slimmer female frame was a benefit.

"Keep it on," Wy said about her jacket. "You're going to need protecting from the glass." Within sixty seconds, he had boosted her up and passed her through the back window opening. Landing butt first on a lovely collection of shards, she smiled grimly at the crunchy sound they made. Good call, bro.

"Ma'am, can you hear me?" Alex asked the driver while Wy passed in the collar they'd use to keep the woman's neck in place during the extraction.

"I—I can't move my leg and . . ." Splintering panic made her voice high pitched. "It feels wet! I can't tell if it's blood or my water's breaking."

Alex ripped off her glove, reached around, and checked the woman's pulse. Strong, thank God, but she had an ugly gash on her temple, and she was clearly in some distress. Her hand cradled her swollen belly protectively.

"What's your name, ma'am?"

"Wh—what?"

"Your name? I'm Alex."

"M-Mia." She gasped through her pain. "Mia. And . . . oh, shit. This baby's coming."

Of course it was. Babies, both the unborn and the untethered kinds, were not known for their timing.

"You hear that?" Alex called out over her shoulder to the crew, careful to keep her voice modulated so as not to spook Mia. "Get the paramedics in here. This lady would like to have her baby." With one hand supporting the back of the driver's-side seat, she adjusted it until it reclined to a forty-five-degree angle.

"I'm going to put this collar around your neck, Mia. Try to remain as still as you can." The access was awkward, but Alex managed to get the collar in place. Where the hell were the EMTs?

With the sound of Mia's obviously increasing pain ringing in her ears, Alex turned back to Wy, who was leaning in. "She needs to be pulled out now."

Venti said something she couldn't hear, but Wy was on hand to translate.

"All EMT crews are busy with other vics, and the next round of support is five minutes away. Now she's collared, you need to get out so we can take the Hurst tool to the back and rip this bad boy open."

Mia screamed. "This is fucking happening! Believe me when I say I know. It's my fifth."

Alex shared a worried look with Wy. In her days as an EMT, she had come across all sorts, but dragging a kid out of Hotel Utero in a glass-ridden, torn-to-shit sport-utility vehicle was most definitely not in her repertoire. One thing she did know: if a mother of four said her baby was coming, then the baby was definitely coming.

"I'll get the supplies," Wy said.

The next ten minutes passed in a messy blur. Mia's contractions were coming less than a minute apart and starting to blend into one another. During one of the downtimes, Alex went to work releasing her trapped leg—another nasty cut but not life-threatening—and pushing the seat back as far as it could go. She would have preferred to move Mia into the back, but maneuvering a woman at close to full term—and in labor—around a crushed SUV was not so easy. The best she could do was slide her across to the passenger seat so she'd be in a better position to deliver her baby. A pillow behind her head to make her somewhat comfortable against the side window, and they had themselves a less-than-ideal, but cozy birthing space.

"Okay, Mia, you're the expert at this. I'm just here to make the catch." Alex hauled in the deepest breath she could, drawing on all her experience to quell her jangling nerves. The baby was already crowning, Mia was panting up a storm, and everything was happening much too fast.

"We okay?" Wy called in, and only because Alex knew him well could she tell there was the slightest worry threaded through his voice.

"Just fine," Alex returned, then to Mia, "So do you know if we're meeting a boy or girl today?"

"A girl," she panted. "I have four boys already and—and I'm ready for a girl. Or thought I was." Her face, shiny with exertion, scrunched in concern. "Have you done this before?"

Made the catch? Alex was only the best catcher on the Engine 6 crew. She'd even been chosen to represent CFD during the annual charity ball game against CPD last September. So maybe she hadn't caught *a baby* hurtling down the chute, but she had great hands. She could do this.

"Tons of times," Alex said with the easy assurance Mia needed to hear in these fraught moments. "Now, on the next contraction, you're going to—"

That sentence died a quick death because *scream-push-pop* and suddenly Alex's hands were full with a slippery bundle of action. Wow, this baby wasn't fooling around. Only instinct kept the package in the secure hold of Alex's hands.

"Is she okay?" Mia gushed out after a few seconds, catching her breath. Woman was a total pro.

Alex swiped a finger across the baby's nose and mouth, removing the amniotic fluid, and waited one, two, three . . . she gasped her first breath, hauling a breath of chilly January air into her little lungs. Praise the Cubbies.

Did Alex think *little* lungs? Seconds later, Chicago's newest citizen bellowed a shieldmaiden's cry, letting Mom and anyone within a five-mile radius know she had arrived. Look out, world!

"Oh yeah, she's more than okay." After wrapping her in a towel Wy had supplied, Alex placed the fresh-born babe against her mom's chest, keeping her own hands in reserve in case Mia was too weak to hold her. But she hadn't reckoned with a mother's innate strength. Mia's arms locked naturally around her own flesh and blood as her lips brushed the crown of her dark-haired head.

"Just wait till your papi sees you, *niña*," she murmured, adding sweet baby talk that only moms and babies understood.

"How we doin' in there?" Wy called out, cutting into the female power cocoon. There was work to be done getting Mia and her baby to ultimate safety, but for now, all was right with the world. Another kick-ass girl had joined the ranks.

Alex met Mia's blissed-out mama smile. "Fucking awesome."


Tired, but still riding the high of this morning's run, Alex let herself into her home. She had showered back at the firehouse and all she could think of was catching a few Zs before she headed into the bar for a shift.

Well, that wasn't all she could think of. There was *him*, but she was doing a pretty good job of cramming the asshole into a dank spot in her mind. Which left room for little baby Alex, who was doing just fine at the hospital with her very grateful mom and dad. Okay, so they hadn't named her Alex at all—just a spot of wishful thinking on her part—but she felt a humbling connection to this kid who'd fought her way into the wintry world under such tricky conditions. What Alex did every day was important, and every moment on the job affirmed her decision to join the CFD tribe. And she didn't need a bossy-as-all-get-out throwback Neanderthal who was still hung up on his ex to complete her. Get back to your cobwebbed corner, lizard dick!

A warm bed and clean sheets beckoned, but just as she was heading upstairs, the doorbell rang. Shit. Her next-door neighbor Mrs. Gish probably wanted Alex to shovel her sidewalk again.

"Delivery," said the bright-eyed FedEx guy as he moved from foot to foot to stave off the positively balmy twenty-degree cold. At his feet was a medium-sized box with no visible markings, which she signed for and pulled inside. Not heavy, just a little awkward. Unpocketing her Swiss Army knife, she sliced through the box and unveiled the contents.

Her pulse rate shot into the stratosphere.

That tricky bastard.

# CHAPTER SEVENTEEN

"Mr. Mayor, you're proposing a hybrid plan to manage the underfunded fire and police pension plans and bring— Eli, are you even listening?"

Eli looked up from his phone to find his chief of staff, Kenneth, Madison, and the rest of the campaign team staring at him in the fifth-floor conference room at city hall.

"Sure, I'm listening. 'The hybrid solution will include self-managed plans along with a social security–like element,' etcetera, etcetera." He waved off the recitation.

"Say it like you mean it, Eli," Kenneth chimed in.

Madison cocked a hip. "The debate is in less than two weeks and your lack of engagement worries me, Eli. When Jenkins comes after you on the math, you have to be able to shut her down."

"I know the math inside out. My original platform was pension reform, and if the fucking unions weren't still so in love with Dick Daley, who left it in this putrid mess, I wouldn't even have to answer questions about it." For three years, he had struggled with the municipal unions to get them to understand that pension reform was a necessity. They were living in la-la land, where they thought twenty years of service guaranteed a gold watch and a cottage in Lake Geneva.

His gaze dipped to his phone again. She should have gotten it by now.

This week had almost killed him. Begging a woman's forgiveness was not his style, and frankly, he had done nothing that needed forgiving, except tell the truth. Which Alexandra apparently was incapable of handling.

Did he go apeshit when she told him about that prick who callously used her, then bragged to his friends about nailing America's Favorite Firefighter? So *maybe* his brain had done a 360 in his skull and *maybe* his lungs and heart had fought a cage match at the thought that anyone would dare to hurt her. But he kept his reaction on the DL, because he didn't want to be that guy. Jealous guy. Who technically had no reason to be jealous because this thing between them was supposed to be casual.

Casual. What a stupid fucking word. These past five interminable days without her had crystallized what was obvious to him from day one, though he was too stubborn to admit it: nothing about his feelings toward Alexandra Dempsey were even in the same zip code as casual. His blood boiled in her presence. His body became a cauldron of want and need. Every nerve ending shrieked to rawness when he was denied the chance to touch her. And when he did lay his hands on her silky skin, his IQ dropped to single digits and he devolved to a cock on two legs.

How did that qualify as casual?

It would fade soon. It had to. This depth of attraction never lasted, though he couldn't recall a single woman who had turned him inside out like this, not even Madison. Their relationship had been—and still was—civilized compared to what he had with Alexandra. Civilized conversations, civilized arguments, civilized sex.

With Alexandra, he felt dangerously unmoored. Out on a narrow ledge with the wind battering him, the only anchor the plunge of his cock into her body. He wanted to fuck her into oblivion—and to not have to pick through the rubble of a romantic entanglement afterward. This should not be so hard. *He* should not be so hard. All the time.

His phone buzzed with an incoming text message.

*You manipulative cocksucker.*

Ah, the poetry of an angel.

He texted back: *Morning to you, too, my sweet.*

Madison frowned at the interruption and moved on to property taxes, which after weather, potholes, and the Cubs' lovable loser status was Chicago's favorite topic of conversation.

*You think this gets you off the hook?*

*I think you're talking to me right now.* Standing, he gestured to the team that he needed to take this outside. He dialed Stake as he walked. She'd gotten another upgrade in his contacts list.

"Dempsey's Porn Shack."

"Honey, let's not fight."

She growled. "Buying out the entire stock of undies at your French whorehouse is not going to sway me."

"Still, you texted. To tell me you're not swayed." He paused. "Do you like them?"

"Of course I like them, you asshole! They're beautiful. Sexy. Pink." She laughed a breathless giggle. "Very pink."

"I noticed it's your secret favorite color."

"I refuse to accept them or the account you opened at En Cachette in my name. I can't believe you did that." There was the appropriate mixture of awe and disgust in her voice.

"I want you to have all the sexy unmentionables you need. Whatever makes you feel good while you're out kicking a mugger's ass or saving some drunk dickhead's life."

"You must think that's such a cliché. The tough-as-nails tomboy with the girly pink panties fetish."

"I think it's just one more layer to the intriguing woman I'm enjoying spending time with."

Her surprised silence was like a third person who had conference-called in. He needed her to know that he liked her—not just her gorgeous body and untamable hair, but *her*, this woman with soft curves and fierce edges. This woman he had tricked into spending time with him.

He batted that errant thought away and directed his mind to something more pleasurable. And absolutely necessary.

"I'll see you tonight." Not a request. Almost a week without her had been impossible.

She huffed, "I'm working. At the bar."

"After." Nothing but deafening silence, which he took for acquiescence. "I need to get back to a meeting."

"I'm wearing one of the bras now."

His breath trapped in his lungs and it took a moment to make those suckers work again. "Which one?" He had chosen a half dozen, but his favorite was. . .

"The rose-colored satin with the bow detailing at the edges."

*That one.*

His feet moved forward in a lust-driven daze toward his office.

"It has a front closure."

He knew that. "The best kind," he managed in a strangled whisper.

He picked up the pace. Whitney tried to say something to him as he walked through the suite, but he held up the hand of no. Closing the door behind him, he leaned against it heavily.

"Where are you now, Alexandra?"

"In my bedroom. Surrounded by sexy unmentionables my *lovah* bought for me."

He could see her clearly in his depraved mind's eye. The swells of her breasts plumping over the satin edges, her hourglass figure begging for his hands to explore. And that sweet, shapely ass . . . He rubbed a hand over his cock, now punching the zipper of his pants.

"Lie down on the bed. Now."

She laughed that husky sound that invariably sent a shot of blood to his groin. "Yes, Mr. Mayor."

He grimaced. He didn't want to be Mr. Mayor to her. He wanted to be Eli, just Eli. He wanted to hear his name on her lips when she came. He wanted her to need what only he could give her, and to beg for it until she was hoarse.

"I'm lying down, just like you demanded." There was a pertinence mixed with obeisance in her tone that made his balls tighten.

He remained silent, listening to her breathing, trying to control his own. He had painted a scene, set it in motion, but he wouldn't call "Action." That would be down to her.

"You still there?" she asked after a few long beats.

"I am."

She muttered a curse. "Why did you buy these things for me, Eli? And the clothes last week?"

"Because I wanted you to look beautiful. Feel beautiful."

"For the papers."

"Screw the papers. When you look and feel gorgeous, that makes me feel good." He drew a deep breath. "It's just you and me, Alexandra. Here. Now."

He meant in this moment, on the phone. But with the words out there, feeding off the energy between them, he realized that he might mean more.

He might want more.

After a terrifying pause, she spoke again. "I like the bows on the side of the matching panties." She sounded embarrassed to be admitting a weakness for these feminine touches. He wanted to know all her weaknesses, which he suspected would fit well with his strengths. "They're pretty. And they untie."

His lips shaped a smile. "They sound very convenient."

"I don't want to untie them," she murmured. "It would ruin the pretty."

Holy ribbons and bows. "Then find another way."

"Already there, Eli."

The groan he let loose was probably heard in the basement of city hall.

"You're fucking killing me, Alexandra."

"I like when you call me that. It makes me feel . . ." She trailed off.

"Makes you feel what?"

Another pause that kept him on the edge of his seat, and then she finally breathed, "Sexy."

That wasn't what she had wanted to say. She'd checked the truth at the last second because however her name on his lips made her feel would have revealed too much. He should be glad that she was making the effort. Keeping what was happening between them in the realm of mutually rewarding pleasure.

Should be.

"Tell me how your breasts look, honey."

Her nervous laugh spoke her gratitude that he didn't push the issue.

"I look pretty fucking hot in this underwear, Eli. And I feel very, very wet."

*Brain, I hope you're enjoying this visit to my pants.* He gripped the armrest of his chair, anything to prevent his hand from seeking gratification. He couldn't . . . not in the mayor's office. There were lines that even he refused to cross.

But there was no good reason his woman should suffer.

"Touch yourself, Alexandra. Imagine my mouth on you, sucking and licking. Imagine how good that makes you feel. How hard it makes me feel."

"Eli," she gasped, the sound shockwaving down his spine and terminating in a sizzle of desire in his groin. This was madness, but that's what she had driven him to. Close to jacking off with the political greats of Chicago watching.

*Click.* "There's my call waiting," she murmured.

"Alexandra—"

After an interminable moment, she came back on the line. "Gotta go."

"Who is it?"

"Just Bastian. Later, Mr. Mayor." She hung up.

Bastian Durand? That maple-sucking puck chaser.

Dempseys on Damen was busy, fairly standard for Hawks game night, which happened to coincide with two-for-one Rolling Rocks. Unfortunately, the boys were getting their asses handed to them by the Blues, and probably could have done with a little help from a certain NHL right forward.

Bastian Durand's call had been rather timely, though Eli likely thought she was lying. Well, that wasn't a lie, but . . . Intuitive and smart as Eli was, he had caught her loaded pause when she told him how his use of her full name made her feel. Saying she felt sexy on hearing "Alexandra" uttered with that commanding voice was the truth, but not the whole truth. Cards on the table here? When he called her that, she felt like his woman.

After the stunts he had pulled, he did *not* deserve to hear that.

Caught between the desire to punish him and her desire *for* him, she'd chosen the former. Immature? Perhaps. Cutting off her orgasm to spite her sex life? Definitely! But she'd never claimed to be grown-up about these things. Eli Cooper thought he could throw some pretty, and pretty expensive, lingerie in her direction and she'd forget that in moments of boredom he got his jollies with a bout in his ex-wife's bed.

At least, she hoped it was in her bed. Christ on a cracker, had she and Eli had sex in the same bed where he found comfort with his ex? Had he stripped Madison before that mirror, warmed her skin in the heat of that fire? Had he—

"Phone," Gage said, cutting into her fiftieth mental breakdown this week. "The liquor distributor. Something about tomorrow's delivery."

Last time, they'd been a day late and five cases of Grey Goose short. It never ceased to amaze her how much top-shelf vodka cops and firemen could down. She headed to the back office.

The phone was in its cradle.

Eli Cooper was in her chair.

And Gage was going to get an earful for his damn interfering. Her brother must have let the rat sneak in through the alley door.

"What are you doing here?" she demanded, when really she wanted to say, *My, you look hotter than the hinges of hell in that tux* with a chaser of, *Why are you wearing a tux and not taking me somewhere as your date, you prick?*

He cocked a pissy eyebrow. "We have unfinished business."

"There's a box of tissues behind you, so have at it. As for me, I'm quite finished." She gave him a smile so sweet it could cause diabetes. Perhaps implying completion *might* have occurred after she had taken Bastian Durand's call.

His eyes flashed, a crack of lightning across a sca-blue lake. "Show me."

Her breath caught at the intensity in his tone and expression. "Show you what?"

"My gift."

Of course she was wearing it. He was a man of impeccable taste and insatiable appetites, and wearing something he had touched and chosen next to her skin turned her on.

"I don't have time for this."

"Neither do I. The League of Chicago—"

"Superheroes?"

His lips twitched. "*Businessmen* are holding their annual get-sloshed-and-smoke-cigars event tonight. I'm going stag. In case you were wondering if I had a date stashed in the car."

"I wasn't," she lied.

"I'm known for my fiscal responsibility. And it wouldn't do to take one date while the woman I'm sleeping with is at home warming my bed."

This man's nerve. "No one would ever call you wasteful, Eli."

He smiled, just a flash. "So don't waste my time now. Show me how the bra I chose for you shapes your breasts perfectly."

She remained still. It killed her a little, but surrender was impossible. He gripped the armrest of the swivel chair at the desk, his knuckles like snowy peaks in a desert landscape. She watched, mesmerized, how he held his body, quietly, dangerously, all coiled-up energy, ready to strike.

*Do your worst, Mr. Mayor.*

His brows slammed together, dark slashes over eyes flat with anger. "Are you going to make me apologize for something that happened years before I met you? I can't take back my marriage to Madison and I can't ignore the years we've known each other."

"That's not it and you know it. People have previous relationships, baggage, I get that. But people don't usually continue to sleep with their ex-wife whenever the mood takes them."

He threw up the hand of drama. "Goddamn it, woman, who else am I going to sleep with? In my position, I can't do casual relationships discreetly, not without it biting me on the ass later. If I need—"

"Sex."

"Yes, sex, then going with someone I know and trust and who won't blab about it to the press is eminently preferable."

She felt a brief stab—oh, who was she kidding? A deep plunge of the knife—at his mention of trust. He had this special relationship with Madison, years of knowledge and nuances and *trust*, and Alex was the Jenny-come-lately.

"It's none of my business."

"Coy doesn't suit you, Alexandra. I haven't been with her in months. Not since June of last year."

"What happened?" she shot out, unable to disguise her bitter jealousy, though this news of how long they'd been apart should have made her feel better. "Did she wise up?"

"I met someone."

The words punched her in the gut, made her legs weak and her mind foggy. *I met someone.* Who the hell had drawn Eli away from the spiderweb charms of his ex-wife? Who the hell else did Alex need to create a voodoo doll for?

He continued to stare, those eyes like supernova suns, telling her something. Telling her . . . that she was a complete and utter dumbass.

"Oh." There wasn't enough air in the room to fill her lungs. ·

He had met someone. In June.

"You stopped sleeping with Madison because of this other person."

"The idea of sleeping with anyone while I was obsessed with another didn't sit well. This woman has been all I can think about for months now, and I'd rather blue ball my way through it than fuck a placeholder."

So much to unpack in all that, but she focused on the one word that blazed brighter than every other. "You're obsessed with her."

"She's difficult, foul-mouthed, a pain in my ass. I can't put her in a dress or give her a compliment without her squawking about it. Her family hates me and I don't think so highly of them. She's also funny, gorgeous, and the sexiest woman I've ever met."

Relief spread in a lush wave through her body. "Just to be clear, we *are* talking about me, right?"

His exasperation was downright adorable. "Yes."

*Nicely done, Mr. Mayor.* With shaky fingers, she opened the top two buttons of her shirt. Paused.

He shifted in his seat. "More."

"Bossy." She continued with the buttons, each one revealing more satin, more skin, more heart. Which was really, really inconvenient. But he'd come here and said all the right things. All of them. He didn't apologize for his past behavior—and she would have hated him if he had—and he didn't try to dress up what he had with Madison. Instead, he tore her world apart with the simplest of sentences.

*I met someone.*

She drew her shirt back to reveal her rack, beautifully encased in rose pink satin, and was rewarded with a hissed intake of breath.

"Like what you see?"

His nostrils flared with desire. "Hold your breasts."

As if in a trance, she moved her hands to cup the weight of her breasts. The bra showcased them perfectly, but her hands placed them in a spotlight of their own. Slowly, she trailed one hand down her stomach, absorbing every shiver, every heated sensation, until she reached the snap of her jeans.

Which she undid.

His eyes exploded with interest, devouring her as she drew the zipper down and tucked her fingers inside her new panties. Her moan on coming into contact with her wet, sensitive flesh filled the room. All the pent-up frustration at not finishing what she'd started earlier with Eli turned her need crystal sharp. Her eyelids felt heavy, but she resisted closing them. Better to keep them open so she could watch him watching her. The biggest turn-on of all.

*I met someone.*

Sparks of joy lit her body and the movement of her hands sent her body undulating, her arms compressing her breasts so that they squeezed together, giving her stellar cleavage.

"Eli," she moaned, and it triggered his strike. In a split second, he was on his feet, then down on his knees, dragging her jeans south in one efficient motion.

"I'm here, honey." He gently pried her fingers away from her center and gave them a lascivious lick. "I've got you." His breath felt hot over the skimpy pink triangle shielding her core. His fingers brushed fire against her skin. He undid one bow at her hip, then the other, pulling the fabric down before inhaling her like she was a fine wine. Wearing these things he bought her made her feel sexy, but under his lustful gaze and possessive attentions, she felt irresistible.

As soon as his tongue touched her, the throb at her core picked up triple time. But this wasn't a gentle lapping between her thighs. This was sexual hunger at its rawest as his tongue licked, speared, and owned her. Why was it always better with him?

"Oh, God. Eli, *oh*—oh, that's so—"

Just *so*.

Five seconds was all it took for her orgasm to slam through her with the force of a 400 psi hose. It pinned her to the door, to the floor, to the spot, sending her rigid with the shock of its pleasure, then boneless on the ride down.

On Eli's ride up, he kissed her belly, her breasts, then her mouth, his lips still wet from her. "No one else will satisfy you, Alexandra, not even your own fingers. If I'm in the room, in this city, on this god-*damn* planet, I will be the one who takes care of you. We clear?"

She moaned her agreement.

"We clear?"

God, he expected her to speak after that? "Yes."

He would take care of her until he dumped her, come Election Day. Brave, kick-ass Alex Dempsey wasn't afraid of a thing, but this terrified her. She'd have to be cool about it when their stunt had come to an end, but inside she would be crushed because she was falling for him. Sinking into this big hole where she couldn't get purchase on the slippery sides. He might have met someone, but it was just a sexual fixation for him. The old screw-her-out-of-his-system ploy that happened to have the added benefit of winning him the greatest prize of all. When he got what he wanted—the mayoral throne—she would be out on her ear.

But for now, he was hers.

She kissed him urgently. It was the best way she could think of to apologize for being a crazy-assed, jealous bitch. Then she pulled on the band of his tuxedo pants, thinking that maybe she had another way to apologize.

"Can't. I'm running late."

"I need you. Inside me. Now."

He closed his eyes, clearly marshaling his strength. How she loved testing his control.

"I'm going to be suffering for the next few hours while I listen to a bunch of old, gray dudes recount tales of sticking it to the little people and bemoaning the city's move to raise the minimum wage. It's only fair you suffer a little, too."

Her gaze fell to the space between their bodies. His erection tented his tuxedo pants, straining to reach her. *Here, boy.* "Well, the cock-inside-me plan would have enormous benefits for you, Eli."

He laughed, a low and pained sound. "I'm not above a little suffering for you, Alexandra. You wouldn't believe my scotch bill for the last six months."

"I drove you to drink."

"Many times."

What every girl wanted to hear.

But *this* girl wanted to hear more—his grunts and

moans, her name on his lips when he shot off inside her. She unsnapped his tuxedo pants and sprang free his impressive erection. "It's not safe to walk around like this, Eli. You could do yourself an injury."

His hooded gaze did little to hide his banked desire. "Well," he gritted out, "if it's for my health."

She loved the feel of him in her hands, the soft skin over that rod of steel. All that power. He smoothed a condom on and with no preamble—unless you counted his ass grab lift off the floor—drilled between her thighs.

"Oh my God!" The sensations were unreal: the fullness, the reach, the constricted nature of her passage, knee-cuffed by her jeans. Every thrust dragged against her swollen clit on the return, the perfect friction to bring her to climax.

In his eyes, she saw the same molten hunger she'd felt when he feasted between her thighs. The same drive to possess her, body and soul. She came, and he followed her over, so gorgeous in his abandon, her name an awed whisper on his lips.

*Alexandra.*

And she answered silently, *I am yours.*

Knowing what she did to him made her feel powerful, just as knowing what he did to her made her feel weak.

He disposed of the condom and rearranged his clothing, while she watched in a fuck-drunk daze. He covered her with the protection of his body once more. "I'll be back home around midnight and I want you there in my bed. Security will know to expect you. Yes?"

"Yes."

He drew back, pulled up her jeans, and buttoned her shirt slowly, never breaking eye contact.

"What did Durand want?"

"A tour of the firehouse and . . . a date."

"Doesn't he read the papers?" He unleashed a very unkind diatribe about Bastian's language skills, concluding that he was as dumb as a puck and likely didn't understand anything not written in French.

"And you told him what, exactly?"

"Tours of the firehouse are every other Wednesday."

"And?"

"That I barely have time to fake date, never mind the real thing."

They shot goofy smiles at each other, both ridiculously pleased with themselves. And on that he left her, disheveled, half satisfied, and more than a little lost.

# ☙ CHAPTER EIGHTEEN

The library in the Mid-America Club might seem like a strange place for the annual League of Chicago Businessmen soiree, seeing as how most of the men here only read stock reports, the *FT*, and *Crain's*, but its leather tomes and air of erudition set the tone of privilege nicely.

Eli should have felt right at home.

He had been groomed for this. His childhood was filled with events in places like this. Family parties, birthday celebrations, graduations. Determined to continue the golden upbringing his parents had planned for him, his grandparents had ensured he mixed with the right people in the right venues. *Your parents wanted you to carry on the family traditions of service to your community and country.* He had the wealth and education to initialize, the will and fire to make it happen.

Four years ago, when he found out his father's true nature, Eli donated his entire inheritance—two million and change—to the Wounded Warrior Project. Everything but the house in Lincoln Park, which had belonged to his mother outright. He had wanted the gift to be anonymous, but his financials were an open book, so even that put him in good graces with the voters. These days, he lived comfortably on the trust fund his grandparents had set up for him and a few solid investments, untainted by his father's legacy of lies. Financially, anyway.

"Mr. Mayor," he heard with an apologetic cough behind him.

He turned to find Caroline Jenkins, his closest rival in the upcoming election. Unprepossessing in appearance, she wore boxy suits and an unfashionable hairstyle that did her no favors, but she made up for her mousiness by being as sharp as a tack. In another lifetime, Eli would have liked her a great deal.

"Caroline, we're not on show now. Call me Eli."

"We're always on show, Mr. Mayor." She flicked a glance around the room, an acknowledgment that the rest of the league watched in longing expectation that a spot of late-campaign drama might enliven the stuffy atmosphere.

"I have to admire your tactics," she said with a brittle smile. "If I were the suspicious type, I'd say you and Madison Maitland set up that rescue stunt to boost your flagging numbers."

He tutted. "Next you'll be saying that I started the fire myself."

"Or that you're dating Alexandra Dempsey to grab a few extra votes."

He laughed warmly. "We do what we can. Better that than something else."

She narrowed her eyes at him, comprehension dawning, and a shadow of resignation crossed her face. Christ, if she was going to give up without a fight, then she most certainly did not deserve to rule his city.

"You're as clean as a whistle, Caroline. One arrest

for an animal rights protest back in college, but otherwise you're above reproach."

She didn't look hopeful that he hadn't dug deeper. He took a sip of his Pinot, an excellent vintage from 2007 the club kept on hand for Eli alone.

"Your husband, on the other hand . . . well, his fondness for Swedish nannies seems to have evaporated only to be replaced by his cozying up with nubile campaign staffers."

"The kids grew up. My husband didn't."

He shrugged. "My drunken Vegas marriage wasn't enough to keep people from voting for me. You'd be surprised what people will put up with in their elected representatives."

"So you've kept my husband's indiscretions to yourself because it's not salacious or damning enough?"

He poured a second glass of wine. "When I started in this business, Caroline, I was idealistic. The notion of serving my city and contributing to my community and the greater good of its citizenry was a very powerful inducement. It's hard to hold on to that after almost four years in the dirt." He gestured at the glass. "Try the Pinot. You'll like it."

She took a cautious sip as if concerned it might choke her.

"And now you're jaded," she said.

"Aren't we all? But not enough to think that destroying a woman and her family is worth a few extra votes. Depending on the timing, I think your campaign would recover, but your children would be hurt." Two girls and a boy, the youngest barely in her teens.

She raised a surprised eyebrow. "I got into this business expecting mud flinging, Eli."

"So what do you have on me?"

A discontented huff escaped her lips. "You're untouchable. So you haven't come through on all your promises, but then it's not as if you could. Running a city like Chicago is a losing proposition from the start. Too many competing interests, not enough resources. The only reason your numbers dropped was because of incumbent fatigue, but allying yourself with the daughter of a Chicago hero has paid dividends across the board. As far as your personal life or your financials"—she shook her head—"my people couldn't find a thing."

"You're not looking hard enough, Ms. Jenkins." A stentorian voice cut in to the intimate conversation.

Sam Cochrane.

Caroline smiled thinly. "I don't have the resources of one of the nation's greatest newspapers behind me, Mr. Cochrane. I'm sure you know everyone's secrets."

"I do," he said simply, not looking at Eli. But the implication hung in the air with menace all the same. The atmosphere chilled enough to encourage Caroline to make her excuses and join another group.

"Aw, now you've gone and scared her off, Sam. Just as she was about to reveal all her secrets ahead of the debate."

"Who needs that when you've got dirt on her and a six-point lead because you're banging America's Favorite Firefighter?"

Eli moved the glass of Pinot a few inches away,

knowing that he might go Hulk-Smash any moment. Getting red wine out of his dress shirt was an absolute chore for his dry cleaner.

Sam clipped the end of his Cuban and made a five-course meal of lighting it before he spoke through the puff of smoke. "You've had your fun, but it's time to cut her loose."

Eli balled a fist against his thigh. "Are you telling me who I can fake date now?"

"You know Dempsey's only good for the short term, a curiosity for the public to fetishize. She's not the kind of woman who can take you to the top, Eli. Can you imagine her greeting the wife of the French president for a state dinner or leading tours of the Lincoln Room? Jackie O she ain't."

Eli barked out a laugh because, one, he thought Alexandra Dempsey would be a breath of fresh air across the White House lawn and, two, Sam Cochrane really thought he could bankroll his puppet to the most important office in the land.

"Sam, even if I had presidential ambitions"—which he did, but hell would freeze over before he'd admit it to this assclown—"you would be the last person I'd choose to make that journey with me."

Sam's face turned livid. "I haven't invested millions of dollars to have you screw it up now. I made you, Eli, and I can just as easily unmake you."

All true, but lately Eli had realized something startling. Sam Cochrane might have the goods to tank Eli's campaign, but he wouldn't, not as long as there was the slightest hope that Eli would let the mogul continue to kiss the mayoral ring. In the past few weeks with Alexandra, he had learned that hope was a very powerful thing—and it overrode practically every other negative emotion.

"A month ago, I almost died, Sam. That kind of jolt to the senses makes a man think about how he's been living his life. The decisions he's made. The decisions he should be making." Eli nodded in Caroline's direction. "Maybe it's time you switched horses. All she needs is a new hairstyle and a designer suit. Red would look good on her. And if you get in on the ground floor, you could say you backed the first woman president of the United States. Hillary's just so polarizing, don't you think?" He inclined his head, and enunciated each word to ensure there was no misunderstanding. "I'm forecasting significant changes for my next administration, Sam. Fewer tax incentives to real estate development. Less kowtowing to business interests. Gotta fund that firefighter pension shortfall somehow."

That whirring noise was the sound of Sam Cochrane's brain working itself into an apoplectic fit. God, that felt almost as good as sinking his tension into Alexandra, something he would be doing very soon.

Unfortunately his enjoyment of Sam's sputtering discomfort was short-lived. Out of the corner of his eye, he spotted Tom coming toward him, his face as grim as the reaper's.

"What's wrong?"

"Mr. Mayor, there's been an accident."

Alex pounded through the door to the clinic, frantically searching, not that there was much to comb through. Empty chairs, a receptionist's window, and pictures of gamboling puppies. Was that supposed to be comforting?

He sat in the corner, alone, slumped forward, his dark head bent over his knees like he might hurl at any minute.

"Eli," she whispered, hunkering down before him. "How is he?"

He looked up, and the pain she saw on his handsome face tore through her.

"He's still in surgery. At least a broken leg, an eye injury, probably liver damage."

"Oh, God, that sucks." When she'd gotten the message from Thing that Shadow had been hit by a car after he escaped the mayor's security detail and that Eli asked her not to come over tonight, she'd debated staying away. Leaving midway through her shift at the bar and hopping in a cab when the man you were sleeping with had specifically *not* requested your presence seemed like crossing a line. But now that she was here, she knew she'd made the right decision.

"Shouldn't you be working?"

"As soon as I heard . . . well, I didn't want to leave you alone."

He gusted a sigh. "I'm never alone."

Ah, gotcha. She straightened to a stand. "I'll just—"

He pulled her down into his lap and pressed her close to his chest. The faintest trace of cigars and privilege mingled with his usual spicy, masculine scent. "I mean that I'm always surrounded by security and staff and people who want a piece from me. I'm glad you're here. I need you here."

"You need my Amazon strength. He's going to be a bear to lift into the car."

His wry smile was a kick to her ribs. "Talk to me. About anything."

"Hawks lost tonight. Probably could have done with Durand."

He arched an eyebrow of move-it-along. Stifling her smile, she considered the less controversial conversation options. "I delivered a baby this morning."

"You did?"

"Yeah, a girl in the middle of a pile-up on Lake Shore. We couldn't get her mom out of the car in time, so I went in, and ten minutes later, out comes baby. My first."

He looked suitably impressed. "Wow."

She grinned. "Wow, indeed. This kid had a set of lungs on her, I'll tell you. And she was so fierce, like this wrinkly little alien who crash-landed on the Drive and was here to shake things up."

"Typical woman. Barely seconds old and already causing trouble."

She mock punched his shoulder. "We do like to make our mark."

"Yes, you do." He took her hand, measured it against his huge one. She loved how feminine he made her feel with the smallest of gestures. Chair pulling, coat doffing, enveloping her in the embrace of his big body. They stayed like that for a while, okay with being quiet.

After a few moments, he spoke again. "It's going

to kill me if Shadow doesn't make it, Alexandra. Coming home to him is the best part of my day."

She nodded, while inside her heart squeezed at his pain.

"Best part of his day, too, I bet. He gets so excited when he sees you." He wasn't the only one. Alex's heart beat like that of an eager puppy faced with its owner every time she saw Eli Cooper. It had been like that from the first moment she met him in Smith & Jones all those months ago, and every encounter since just increased the pounding until she wondered if her stupid love muscle might give out from the exertion. Just up and collapse.

She traced his jaw with her finger, loving how strong it felt under her touch. Along the seam of his sensuous lips, she ran her thumb. How could those lips be so soft? All the time, he watched her with that heart-wrenching Eli Cooper intensity.

"Tonight, when Tom came to tell me about Shadow, I thought—" He broke off, and in his eyes, she saw stormy emotion that seeded dangerous hope in her chest. "I thought you were hurt, Alexandra. I knew you weren't on shift at Engine 6, but when Tom told me something had happened, I feared the worst. I did not enjoy the feeling."

Her heart flip-flopped at his concern for her, but she needed to nip this in the bud. "Eli, I can't promise nothing will ever happen to me, but you're looking at a well-trained firefighting machine who works with the best platoon in CFD. Good firefighters feel the fire, understand the limits, and know when to pull back. And I'm a damn good firefighter."

Color flagged his cheeks. "Almost a month ago,

you put your life in danger to save mine. I've since learned that giving a civilian your air is not SOP."

"Paperwork for a dead mayor is a bitch."

"Honey—"

She touched her fingers to his lips. "I like pink, but I worry that it's too feminine, so I keep it to my underwear. I cry at Super Bowl Budweiser commercials, but I make sure I've watched them online first so no one can poke at me on game day. All my life I've been living on a knife's edge between what it means to be a woman and what's expected of me. In my job, with the guys I've dated, from my brothers. They want to protect me and all I can see is their love, which crushes me because I worry it diminishes their respect for the part of me that's a professional first responder." She took a breath. "I guess what I'm asking is: what am I to you, Eli? Am I a woman or a firefighter?"

She was difficult and unruly, and she needed the man who could handle her. Her guts and her glory, because damn it, she was worth that. Eli's attentions to her so far were distinctly of the me-Tarzan-you-Jane variety, and while she adored the hormone overdose in her body whenever he was near, she craved his respect equally.

Those steely eyes took her measure. "Just two choices, Alexandra? Why limit yourself?"

She pressed her lips against a smile. Hell and damn, this guy did it for her like no one else. "Well, there's also 'bitch.' If someone doesn't call me that at least once every twenty-four hours, I figure the day for a failure." At his frown, she rushed on over the emotion clotting her throat. "There are worse things, don't you think? They're just names, and sometimes

I relish them because men who call me names are scared. Scared little boys who feel threatened by my all-round awesomeness."

"Woman, firefighter, or bitch? However do I choose?" He twisted his fingers in her hair and pulled her close enough to share his breath. "What you are to me is . . . Alexandra. And *she* defies categorization."

Something melted inside her. Her heart, perhaps, or her lungs, given the sudden breathing difficulty. It was a moment before she could speak.

"Eli, the night of the fire I assessed the situation and made the call based on the risk-reward. You were worth the risk and now I'm reaping my reward."

That threw him. Was the idea of having someone in his corner that unexpected? She supposed the constant attacks on his character had to be wearisome.

"Not so sure I'm worth the risk. I'm not a very nice person."

"Yet I'm here."

"Should I be jealous of my dog?"

She buried her joy in his dark, wavy hair. "You might have Hollywood looks, dubious charm, great hair, and a giant penis, Eli Cooper, but that puppy of yours is the real selling point."

He laughed, long and hard, the deep bass tone drawing the attention of the receptionist, and Alex joined in, thrilled to have taken his mind off his troubles, if only for a moment. Hugging her close, he sank his weary head into the curve of her neck.

She had no problem being his anchor. People rarely understood that she was actually as strong as she looked.

# CHAPTER NINETEEN

For the first time since he had become the mayor of Chicago, Eli was contemplating something he had never, ever done:

Sleeping in.

Of course, this shocking turn of events was only made possible because he had found someone worth sleeping in with. She was here. Snoring softly. Drooling a touch. The incomparable Alexandra Dempsey.

Likely sensing that he was sleep-stalking her, she turned over, blissfully naked, and snuggled all those warm, womanly curves in close.

"You're here," she muttered in a rusty voice, eyes still shuttered.

"I am."

One eye crept open cautiously. "But it's—what time is it?"

"Just before seven."

She bolted upright, breasts in an erotic sway, hair in that rumpus he adored. "It's happened, then."

"What?"

"Insert your preferred apocalypse here. Because that could be the only reason why Eli Cooper is not on his laptop or phone, scheming, planning, or shouting at somebody."

He pulled her down into his arms and kissed her. "Yes, the apocalypse has happened. And it's called Alexandra Dempsey."

She thumped his shoulder. *Ouch*. His sexy fire-woman could pack a punch. "So if the city falls apart, I'm to blame?"

"Politicians always pass the buck. You know that."

She growled and burrowed further. "Did you call the vet?"

"Yep. He slept okay, vitals are good, even had something to eat. I'll go pick him up at nine and bring him home." To think how close he had come to losing the one constant in his life—well, the one after the woman in his bed. Finding your heart lying outside your chest and in the form of a curvy, thrill-seeking firefighter was disturbing, to say the least.

"So, nine you say," she murmured, carnal slyness in her tone.

"I did, you minx. Turn over."

"That's more like it." When she twisted away from him, her eyes widened in surprise, reflected in the full-length mirror he had moved opposite about ten minutes ago.

"No, that's more like it," he murmured against the delicate shell of her ear.

"You've been busy," she said on a breathy sigh. "Rearranging the furniture."

Those moss-green eyes darkened with desire. He moved back the sheet just enough to reveal her curvaceous nakedness but still retain the heat of the blanketed cocoon. His hand ghosted over her hip, danced along her ribs, before landing where it belonged on her full, soft breast.

"You've accused me of lacking substance"—he molded her warm flesh—"and of being vain"—he feathered his fingers down the curve of her belly—"and of spending hours looking at my own reflection. Figure I may as well play to this image you have of me."

She cuddled her ass against his erection, the motion undulating her body and showing her breasts to their best advantage. Smiling that cat's grin, she recited as fact, "You *are* incredibly shallow."

His answer was to splay his hand over her sex and nudge her legs apart. She shifted her thigh up and back so she was completely exposed in the mirror. Her pink, succulent flesh pulsed under his fingertips, and he stroked, his satisfaction and hers increasing apace with her wetness.

She moved her arm back to curl a hand around his neck. The motion did incredible things to her already perfect tits. Unable to resist the temptation, he stroked his cock along the inviting cleft of her ass. The insanely pleasurable friction had him panting against her neck. Would it always be zero to *fuck, yeah* in two seconds with this woman?

With his fingers, he parted her while she sawed against his hand, seeking the best angle to get herself fully juiced.

"Baby, I need to get a condom." He hated to break the connection, but if he didn't suit up soon, there was only one way this could end: skin-to-skin nirvana.

"I trust you," she whispered.

He stilled. "What?"

She held his gaze in the mirror, steady and resolute. "I'm on the Pill and I've always used condoms. I want you inside me and I want to feel everything. I want it raw, Eli."

Sweet Jesus. That she would trust him with something so precious knocked his world off its axis.

"Honey, you sure?"

"I'm clean, Eli, and I know you'd never hurt me."

Not physically. But there were other ways to hurt. If she ever found out about the lies he'd told to make her his, they would be finished. *He* would be finished. Liars and cheats only prevail in politics, not in real life.

"Please, Eli. I need to feel every inch of you."

She ground her ass to his stiff cock and shifted to give him the access he needed. Fullness ruled his chest; everything in him was brimming over. Her acceptance with her heart and her body was a priceless gift, one he didn't deserve. But he would take it anyway because he was black-hearted and selfish to the core.

And obsessed. Don't forget obsessed.

He slipped inside her, the slickness of her arousal easing his hot entry. He buried his worry with a deeper thrust into her soft heat, letting the welcome he found there muffle the negative. It was his first time in years without protection. It would have felt good with, but without the barrier, it leapfrogged the good and transcended the great to become frightening in its intensity.

"Eli, that's—oh, God," she moaned. Her hooded gaze held him prisoner in the mirror and he tore his eyes from hers for fear of revealing too much. Instead he focused on where they joined, this banter between their bodies, this safer place. His naked cock gleamed, every pumping drive picking up more of her wetness.

"Touch your clit, Alexandra," he urged in her ear while he hooked his arm under her knee. The move forced her thighs wider and exposed her sex to their jointly riveted gaze. Seeing his dark-fleshed cock pistoning her pink, pliant heat turned him into a raging beast.

"Look, baby. Look at how you wreck me," he husked out as her fingers fondled her clit and drew her orgasm to the surface. In the wave of her scream, he went off, lashing hot, uncontrollable jets inside her.

Branding her as his. Only his.

" *Star* Wars or *Star Trek*?"

"I sincerely doubt that will come up during the debate."

Alex sat on Eli's comfy sofa with her feet in his lap, the fire warming the room and her toes while another snowpocalypse raged outside. Eli had taken his first day off in five years to tend to Shadow, who lay on his doggy bed in a postsurgical, druggy daze. The poor puppy's right paw was bandaged; his eye was covered in a pirate's patch; and his head had stitches to match the gash where the vet had knifed through to fix the liver damage. In other words, one hot doggy mess.

"I'm easing you in," she said. "You're the one who has to prove yourself in the debate next week. I'm only trying to help."

"Trying to help me mess up, more like. You're not even going to vote for me!"

She laughed, loving that indignation in his tone.

Apparently creaming her panties over everything else he did wasn't enough, he had to have her vote as well. "Okay. Convince this undecided voter that Cooper deserves four more years. *Star Wars* or *Star Trek*?"

"There's a Millennium Falcon, still in its original packaging, in the attic."

"Impressive." Said in her most awesome Darth Vader voice. "But it's a trick question. The answer is 'Can't these two great universes just get along?' Also, if you hear any noises from the attic later, ignore it. Probably squirrels."

His phone beeped on the kitchen counter for the fiftieth time and he ignored it as he had done all morning. It made her feel special to know that the world could be falling apart around them, but Eli's focus right now was just her and Shadow. This happy little triumvirate of her imagination.

She eyed him shrewdly over her coffee cup and took a bite of a Bavarian Kreme donut. So long, T-ball, time for the bigs. "Cubs or White Sox?"

Brow in a sexy crumple, he switched on his patented soulful look, the one that induced a choir of orgasms across Chicagoland. "Both teams are excellent representatives of the sporting traditions of this great city—"

She threw her half-eaten donut at him. It glanced off his head and hit the floor. Shadow lifted his jaw, recognized that it was a losing proposition, and laid it down again.

"Panderer."

"I can't pick one. I'd alienate an entire demographic."

"It's the Cubs, right?" No self-respecting North Sider could have kept a White Sox fandom undercover.

"I plead the Fifth." He squinted at her outfit. "Is that my tie?"

She pulled up his U of C sweatshirt to show how she had used his blue-and-silver striped tie to keep his black silk PJ bottoms from falling down. She was hippy, but not so pear-shaped she could keep those babies on without a little belted support.

"Why, did you need it?" she asked coyly.

"I was thinking of wearing it to the debate." His gaze shifted to a dark hunger. "C'mere, honey. I need to try on my lucky tie."

She crawled over and into his arms. Snuggling with Eli in this world away from it all, she allowed herself the luxury of happiness. Never had another person's embrace felt so right.

Her contented gaze arced over the room. Bright and cozy, it was filled with books and art, mementoes and trophies commemorating Eli's storied life. On a shelf opposite, his law school graduation photo sat beside a picture of his team in the Marines. Next to that was a portrait of his parents with a ten- or eleven-year-old Eli, not long before they died. This morning, she had found the award named for Eli's father on the kitchen counter, just thrown there, and had taken the liberty of giving it a prominent place on the shelf.

He massaged the nape of her neck, tangling his fingers in her curls. Eli was rather obsessed with her hair. *Handfuls of sin,* he called it.

"They'd be so proud of you, Eli."

"That I lie for a living."

She turned in his arms, met his veiled gaze. So guarded, not like this morning as he faced her in that mirror and pounded his essence into her, body and soul.

"Not everything is a lie." Was it?

After a taut moment, he said, "You once told me that you always knew you wanted to be a firefighter. Every time Sean came home, smelling of smoke."

She nodded, unsure where this was going but happy to give him time to make his point. "I had no idea what he did but there was something about it. About him. He made me feel safe and I knew that his job made others feel safe. People slept better at night, people made it another day because he was there for them."

"He was a hero to you."

"Before and after. He was an instructor at the Quinn and when I was a kid, I used to worry that when I signed up for CFD, he'd treat me like shit. Or worse, take it easy on me. But by the time I made it there, he was gone and he never got to see me in bunker gear." Luke said he wouldn't have let her join if he'd lived. It crushed her to think she might never have been good enough in her father's eyes.

"Eli, heroes don't all wear capes or fire helmets or badges. They also wear dog tags." Sometimes she forgot how much this man had given already, between his service to his country and the loss of his parents. "Some of them even wear suits. In fact, I'm going to tell you something I swore I would take to my grave."

She bit down on her lip, and pushed out quickly, "I voted for you in the last election. Partly because you're hot enough to melt butter and I'm shallow like that. Partly because you had good ideas and I wanted to see things change. But mostly because of Sean and Logan."

Something unnameable melted the ice in those eyes, but all he said was, "Alexandra."

Emotion reigned in her chest. "Whenever I saw you on TV talking about your parents, I recognized someone who understood what I had been through. Losing people we loved in the line of duty. I had never met you and I never expected to, but we had this terrible, beautiful thing in common." She took his hand and placed it over her breast, trying to tell him with her hammering heartbeat what words seemed inadequate to convey. "My heart stopped beating the day they died, and my family kick-started it again. I know you're this amazing problem solver and that for the longest time, you've managed alone, but if you ever need to talk about it, any of it, I'm here."

Even when they were no longer *they*.

Thoughts chased each other across his face before finally settling on a pain that scared her. How had it come to this, where the idea of hurting this man made her chest ache like fire?

"You think you can save me, Alexandra?"

She rubbed her nose against his. "I *know* I already did."

He merely smiled at that, the heartbreakingly sexy grin that didn't just short-circuit her brain but also jerked her heart around her chest like a pinball. Yesterday, she had helped to bring a new life into the world. Witnessing the child's first breath, a warm puff against the frigid winter air, had filled Alex with a thundering sense of wonder. She felt it again now, the possibilities of life and love.

Eli Cooper might not have her vote this time around, but he had something far more valuable. Her heart.

The wily, manipulative bastard.

# CHAPTER TWENTY

Alex walked into the firehouse, tripping like a schoolgirl through a field of daisies. Feeling that swoop in her stomach that could mean only one thing.

She was in love.

Desperately, hopelessly, draw-hearts-in-dusty-surfaces in love. And boy, did she know how to pick 'em.

Eli Cooper was not the kind of man a girl should fall in love with. Oh, she acknowledged he was exactly the type of hunk women the world over would give their left tit for a chance to kneel at his feet. Which she had, many times. And she didn't have to surrender any body parts.

But he was bad news for her because he could not be tamed. Put a woman who believed fiercely in the power of love at loggerheads with a man who thinks love exposes him to potential betrayal and the math was always going to be fuzzy. He might have done a smash-and-grab of her heart, but he didn't love her, maybe never could. *Yet* . . . She wanted to believe that beneath that jaded exterior there existed a heart that wanted to beat again. She felt these deep pockets of sadness in him, voids she knew she could fill if he'd let her.

At the Wall of the Fallen, she darted a quick glance

up and down the corridor and assured herself she was alone. With fingertips to her lips, she transferred a kiss first to the framed photo of her oldest brother, Logan, and then to Sean.

Smiling to herself, she headed to the locker room, passing a couple of the A shift on their way out. They smirked, and one of them muttered something that sounded like, "Gets around."

"What's that?"

They exchanged smartass glances and kept walking. Weird. In the locker room, all eyes shot to hers: Derek, Murphy, and Wy.

"Good work, Dempsey," Murphy said with a sneer. "The union's endorsed your boyfriend, so I guess you'll be getting some extraspecial attention tonight. Looks like you'll need it after that newspaper article."

"Shut it," Wy said to Murphy before waylaying Alex with a strong hand cupping her elbow. "With me. Now."

"What's wrong? What newspaper article?" She let him steer her to the shower room.

"Been tryin' to call you."

Her phone was . . . shit, on Eli's nightstand. This morning, she'd gone to grab it and he'd gone to grab her and now, no phone. "My battery's dead. What's up?"

Was he pissed about Local 2 coming down on Eli's side? She wasn't even sure how she felt about it, except that it was one more stepping-stone to victory for Eli and one step closer to when she'd be no use to him. So yeah, it sucked donkey balls.

"There's somethin' online about you," Wy said. "About your dating."

"My dating?"

He grimaced. "Online gossip shit. But I just wanted to warn you because it's not nice."

"Show me."

He pulled up his phone to the *Red Eye* site, a division of the *Chicago Tribune*, Sam Cochrane's paper. Uh-oh. She froze as he tapped a few links out. "No matter what happens, we're behind you, Alex."

She was a visual person so she went for the pics first. So many of them, some better quality than others, but all of them weaving a sordid tapestry with one damning conclusion.

Alex Dempsey went on *a lot* of dates. It seemed like every instance of her talking with a guy in a bar or breaking bread with a man had been captured and collaged. Hands shaking, she swiped through photos with captions like: *A cozy pizza night—what are his favorite toppings?* In that one, her date was caught ogling her breasts (they *were* spectacular!). Another memorialized that super awesome time she'd spilled a drink on her T-shirt. If you squinted, you might see some damp nipple action, which apparently was enough to earn the provocative caption: *Find 'em hot, leave 'em wet—an old firefighter maxim.*

She'd seen some of them before in the wake of her brief spell as a D-list celeb last summer. Haters gonna hate and all that. She shrugged off her embarrassment. The gutter rags had forgotten that she had sat through every one of those miserable dates, and as itchy as this made her feel, it would take more than a few boob jokes to derail her.

"So what? I had to expect I'd get a few hits since I've been dating Eli."

"Dating. Eli." Said with all the portent of doom those words inspired in a Dempsey.

"Doing this publicity thing," she amended quickly. "Maybe you should read it."

She readjusted her focus and scrolled back up to the top. A chill stole across her skin at the headline.

### America's Favorite Firefighter Earns Her Title

Quickly she swiped down to the text.

*Look who's been seen out on the town with a variety of suitors over the last year. A regular on the Chicago singles scene and dating websites, Firefighter Alex Dempsey plays hard and dates harder. Whether she works hard, who knows, but CFD's 24-on/48-off schedule gives her plenty of time to meet and flirt with customers at her family's bar, Dempsey's on Damen. Seems she's found the perfect way to relax—with as many men as possible. Is she offering to clean their hoses or does she reserve those talents for Mr. Mayor?*

"They can't say that. It's—oh, God, this is terrible." She looked up to find Wy watching her, his mouth a forbidding seal. "Everyone here has seen it, haven't they?"

"Yep."

She didn't dwell on her misfires on the dating battlefield overmuch. If she did, she wouldn't have been out there on the front lines, week in, week out. But this . . . how the hell was she supposed to get any respect in CFD if she was the focus of such tawdriness?

Wy's phone rang and Luke's name popped up on the screen. "Yeah, I'm with her now." He listened, frowned, hung up. "Let's go." Never a wasted word with their Wy.

"Where? I have to work."

"Luke's found coverage for you and Kinsey wants us to meet her at M Squared. When we're through with that fucker Cochrane, he's gonna wish he'd never heard the name Dempsey."

The last place Alex expected to be spending a morning was in a conference room with views overlooking the icy Chicago River at M Squared, Madison Maitland's PR firm on North Wacker. Practically everyone she cared about was here: Luke, Wy, Kinsey, who with Madison was assessing the article on her iPad.

Everyone, that is, except the one person she needed to see most.

Alex stood at a sideboard near a trio of cut crystal decanters—this entire setup had a real *Mad Men* vibe—because she was too hopped up to sit down. She so needed to talk to him, but without her phone, she didn't know his number, and the last thing she wanted was to navigate the city hall switchboard. Or ask Madison to call him. Pride, and concern about how they would react, kept her from letting her family see who she truly needed at this moment.

"Any chance we can get this started?" Luke grated. He'd hugged her when she'd come in, a wall of muscle-seething anger, and even though she knew it wasn't directed at her, she felt responsible all the same. Here she was, at the eye of the storm yet again.

Kinsey smiled thinly at Luke. "Babe, give us a sec. We're getting there."

The door crashed open and all eyes shot to the new arrival. Eli.

*Thank God.* Alex had never wanted to see anyone so badly, had never wanted so much to run to someone and have him hold her close, but maybe this wasn't the best time for the lovers-in-the-meadow embrace.

Eli, however, had not received the memo.

He stalked toward her, his intent apparent: flay her alive with his gaze, comfort her with his touch.

She tried to motion with her eyes, *No, not in front of my family.*

The prick still came.

Those strong hands made to dominate and pleasure her rose to cup her jaw. "Are you okay?"

*Yes, because you're here.*

*No . . . because you're here.*

"I've been better."

"I tried to call you but—"

"I didn't have my phone," she said before he could say it was left on his nightstand. Stable door? *Locked.*

He rubbed his thumb along her jaw, as if craving one last connection with her skin, then dropped his hands. "I was going to say it's in my pocket," he murmured, "but I'm getting the impression you'd prefer I threw it in the river than give it to you here."

In unison, they turned to the conference table. Alex knew what she'd see there, but knowing it didn't quite prepare her for the truth bomb that was about to explode.

"What *the fuck* is going on here?" Luke yelled, verbalizing succinctly the views captured in the room's surprised expressions. "Alex, are you telling me that you . . . and him?"

"Luke, babe," said Kinsey.

"Don't 'Luke babe' me," her brother snapped at his fiancée before turning to Alex, his lips curved in a sneer. "I thought this was some publicity stunt. Are you fucking mad getting involved with him? For real?"

Eli bristled, a whirl of raw energy beside her. "Talk to her like that again, Almeida, and you and I will have words."

Luke stood, and but for the fact the large conference table separated them, Alex knew he would have lunged at Eli. "You've made her a target for every shit head with a cell phone. Are we really going to pretend that this is a good thing?"

"I will protect her."

Luke scoffed. "Right. Well, mission accomplished, Cooper, you've got my union's endorsement. How long before we see the statement distancing the mayor from the woman who's bad news for his campaign?"

"Luke," Alex cut in, her body moving in front of Eli's as if she could protect him. As if the most powerful man in Chicago needed protecting. Of course he didn't. But she wanted to shield him. His skin might be as thick as the ice pack out on the lake, but sometimes it felt as though no one was in his corner.

"This isn't the time to discuss my sex life."

Wyatt and Kinsey winced at her choice of phrase. Wincing didn't quite accurately describe Luke's expression.

"Really? Because it seems like everyone else wants to talk about it. I don't care that you've dated half of Chicago, but have you forgotten what he did to Kinsey? The hoops he made me jump through to get my job back last summer?"

"Luke," Kinsey said, her hand on his arm. "It all worked out. Let's try to focus on the problem at hand."

"He's the problem! Cut him out and she's okay."

Alex had heard quite enough. "Luke, I know that since Dad died, you've always felt responsible for us. You've made sacrifices, and the idea of me being hurt on the job or in any other way makes that muscle in your jaw"—she pointed—"yeah, that one . . . It makes it twitch like the clappers. Yes, you kicked Kevin O'Shaughnessy's ass when he called me 'sturdy' in the eighth grade and yes, you wiped my tears when Jimmy Carter stood me up at junior prom—"

"Jimmy Carter stood you up at junior prom?" Eli muttered behind her.

She elbowed him sharply and absorbed his "oomph." So not the time.

"I'll never forget every single thing you've done for me, Luke. I love you, but you have to let me handle this. And you have to accept my decisions."

With an expression dueling between fury and love—a typical Dempsey mash-up—Luke sent a piercing glare over her shoulder at Eli. "You're choosing him."

"Yes."

It shocked even her to hear it said with such conviction. One word, clear and unmistakable in its intent. Luke blinked once, twice, and apparently lost the use of his legs, because he collapsed into his seat. Behind her, Eli cupped her arms, squeezed, and pulled her back against his solid chest.

Something Alex couldn't put her finger on clouded Madison's eyes before she cleared her throat. "Now that the pissing match is on hold, gentlemen, let's discuss what needs to happen."

"The *Red Eye* is one of Cochrane's papers," Alex said. "Has he been following me?" She turned to Eli and spoke with her eyes what she couldn't say in front of her family. *Was Cochrane gathering evidence against me to use in a lawsuit?*

His brow darkened in understanding. "I doubt it. All those images were easy enough to gather. Facebook, Instagram, whatever. People have been snapping you forever because of your fifteen minutes last summer, so it was all out there on the Web waiting for someone to put it together—"

"And make me look like a triple-skank ho."

"This is a shot at me." Fury re-formed Eli's features to a statue, his granite jaw looking like it would shatter if she touched it. "Things have been strained between Sam and me lately, so this is the standard saber rattling while he figures out how much he can push me around. It was bound to happen eventually, but he's broken the rules of engagement and involved a civilian. Not cool."

*Not cool.* From the look on Eli's face, things were about to get very hot for Sam Cochrane.

The sun was beating in Eli's chest where his cold, black heart should be.

Alexandra Dempsey loved him.

She hadn't said it aloud, but the moment she placed her body between his and her brother's, absorbing every one of Luke's blows like bullets, he suspected.

The moment she said yes, she chose *him*, he knew. This incredible woman loved him.

He wanted to touch her, hold her, take her home, get her naked, and spend all day and night adoring every inch of her. Loving her the way she deserved.

*Better get someone else on board, buddy.* The way she deserved was with honesty and openness, not with a manipulative charlatan who had lied to her, just to get his own way.

And that was just the tip. Every day, Eli felt his arteries clogging with despair, his veins choking up with not just plain old politicking dishonesty, but with something deeper and soul-deadening: he was more like the old man than he'd thought. Now he wanted to taint Alexandra Dempsey with her family legacy of heroism and make her as dirty as his blackened soul.

However, this grasping opportunist also knew a good thing when he saw it. A month ago, he had almost died, and now the woman who had saved him in more ways than one was defending him to her whack-job family. He would take this gift he had intercepted and run with it to the end zone, because he couldn't very well screw himself over now, could he? Better to use all that unhealthy self-loathing and line up a more suitable target.

"I want him buried."

"My advice," said Madison, "is to do nothing. It's gutter rag gossip and our response needs to be proportionate. Getting into a public feud with Sam

Cochrane right now is a bad idea, especially as we have bigger problems." She flicked a glance over the room. "It might be better to talk about this in private."

"Is it about Alexandra?"

A reluctant "Yes."

"Have a seat, honey." Ignoring the hairy-eyeballed glare from Luke, he led Alexandra to the conference table and sat down beside her, his arm resting on the back of her chair. He resisted the urge to twine his fingers in her hair. "If it's about her, then just say it."

"Eli, I really don't think—"

"Spit it out, Madison."

She crossed her arms, seeming more pissed than the average Mads. "Did you threaten a CPD detective with the sack if he didn't end a date with Firefighter Dempsey?"

"No, I did not."

"Thank God," Madison said.

"I threatened him with demotion to traffic cop."

Eli was rather pleased at how the air crackled with the energy of this new information. After a couple of electrified beats, Kinsey broke the stunned silence with a laugh, then caught the eye of a fuming Madison. "Sorry, but that's . . ." She shook her head, still smiling. "Unexpected. Nicely done, Eli."

He returned his former assistant press secretary's smile. He'd always liked her, and firing her for disloyalty was one of the hardest things he'd ever had to do. *It's not easy being king.*

"Who did the good detective blab to?"

"NBC," Madison said. "My usual contact called to get a comment."

"I'm happy to give one."

She shot him a look that would have had a lesser man clutching his balls. "You will shut your mouth, Eli Cooper, until we work out a plan. Now the police union will be all over your ass, and just when we thought we had this sewn up. What the hell were you thinking?"

He shrugged. "I wasn't. It happened in a fury-fueled daze. The man made disrespectful comments to someone else about Alexandra. I overheard and told him it would be necessary to curtail his date or I would be forced to curtail his career."

"Wait one second," Luke cut in. "Who was the cop?"

"He talks like this all the time," Alexandra said to Kinsey. "It's like Shakespeare and Iron Man had a love child."

"I need a name, Alex." Luke again.

"Michael Martinez," Alexandra muttered. "Gage set us up. They play hockey together."

"Right wing," Wyatt said. "A bit slow on the breakaway."

Luke's brow knitted furiously. "Martinez from the Fifth District? That guy's an asshole! What the hell were you doing on a date with him?"

"Luke," Kinsey said. "Not really the time."

"Well, it's a damn good thing someone was around to put this guy straight. Jesus, Alex, you really know how to pick 'em."

Alexandra stood and placed her hands on the table. "A minute ago, Eli was the anti-Christ, but now you're okay with him because he acted like a cave-man and protected your poor, clueless sister from a guy you don't approve of? What the fuck, Luke? Do you suddenly recognize him as one of your Cro-Mag tribe?"

"'Okay with him' might be pushin' it, but, Alex, sometimes you need someone to reel you in."

"Why? Because you can't be there twenty-four-seven—"

"After what happened last summer with Cochrane and that car, yes. You never think of the consequences. Kinsey lost her job and I almost lost her!"

Alexandra blanched, and the room followed suit with the awkwardness of Luke's declaration. For the first time, Eli saw how hard she had it. He'd thought it was limited to institutional misogyny, but she was getting it from every angle. The press, her coworkers, and even the brother who was like a father figure to her. He also saw why she had refused to confide in her family about the renewed threat of Cochrane. The threat Eli had invented to manipulate her into his campaign—and his bed.

She loved them all so much. The thought of putting them through any pain, setting a test of their loyalty to her, which he knew they would pass with flying colors, killed her. She was protecting everyone by bottling it up.

"I think we're getting off topic here," Eli said, reaching for Alexandra's hand. "I'll deal with any blowback about Martinez from CPD in due course."

Luke's eyes gravitated to Alexandra, who had retaken her seat and refused to meet her brother's gaze. Evidently hurt by his sister's reaction, he turned to Eli, his face as hard as the table between them. "If you had a chance to do it over with Martinez, would you play it differently?"

"No."

Alexandra cursed under her breath.

Eli and Luke squared off, a silent conversation running between them.

*You might not like me, Luke, but I am her choice. You need to respect that. Respect her.*

*You're a fucking dick, Cooper.*

*I'll stipulate to that, but it doesn't change what's happening here.*

*If you hurt her in any way . . .*

*Understood. Good talk.*

"Now," Eli said, turning back to Madison. Do nothing? No way in hell was he going to let this attack on his woman go unanswered. "I have an idea on how to hit Sam Cochrane where he'll hurt."

# ❖ CHAPTER TWENTY-ONE

As a girl, Alex had spent a lot of time sitting outside the principal's office at St. Jude's for any number of infractions, smoking in the bathrooms and setting off minor explosive devices, to name a few. But she'd never felt so full of dread as she did right this minute, waiting in the reception area of the penthouse office suite of the tallest building in Chicago (forget Willis, it would always be the Sears Tower to her).

That Luke harbored ill will over how close he came to losing Kinsey had sliced through her. But she didn't blame him. Her poor choices had set in motion a chain of events that almost put the kibosh on his happy-ever-after. All this time she had been blaming Sam Cochrane, Eli, anyone but the real culprit—Alex Dempsey and her blazing temper.

She refused to be the one who took from everyone else any longer. Those self-help books and lifestyle sites were always saying that a woman should be the heroine of her own life. Well, screw that. She was going to be the *hero*, even if it meant doing the one thing she thought she would never be forced to do.

"Mr. Cochrane will see you now, Miss Dempsey," the smooth assistant said before she stood and threw open the door, presenting Alex like a magician's trick.

Sam Cochrane raised the gray-green eyes he had in common with his daughter, Darcy. His desk was huge, the largest she had ever seen. Ten megamoguls could have sat behind it, yet Cochrane still managed to infuse the space with his outsize presence. Alex stepped into the room, feeling like she was dragging through a waterlogged cornfield.

"Have a seat, Miss Dempsey. This is unexpected, to say the least." He gestured at the chair before her, and she sat and sank into the butt-sucking leather, guaranteeing she was lower than him. Classic mogul move.

"Have you come for an apology?"

"I have, but not to get one. To give one."

That startled him. *Humility from a Dempsey,* his curious expression said.

"I never apologized for what I did to your car last summer. I was provoked, but it was inexcusable." She almost choked on the words, but they needed to be said.

A few moments ticked over before he spoke. "You know, Miss Dempsey, your father was a friend of mine. A business partner, but a friend first. We used to box together at that CFD gym where your brother trains."

Beck trained at a dingy rat hole on the south side— it was where he'd met Darcy's brother, Jack, and later, Darcy. The start of their teenage love affair. Alex hadn't given much thought to why the son of a billionaire would be punching leather at that kind of place, but if it held some sort of nostalgia for Cochrane, then she guessed it made a weird sort of sense.

"You and Sean fell out. Why?"

He looked at her sharply, as if no one had dared have the temerity to ask that question. "He stole something from me." He tapped the table with his knuckles. "But never mind that. I'm curious about why you're here subjugating yourself after so many months. It's not as if I can change anything about the story *Red Eye* ran on you yesterday. My staff has complete editorial independence, and then there's that whole First Amendment thing."

"I think you could change it if you wanted to. Run another story, print a retraction, but I don't care about that. I don't care what you say because my family will stand by me. They care about me, Mr. Cochrane." *Not like yours,* she didn't need to add.

He smiled thinly, understanding her implication. She could handle the reporters' barbs, and though she hated that her dating was now a part of the public record, she would weather it with her family by her side. With Eli.

She loved him, but the jury was still out on how he felt about her. He probably liked her, maybe cared a little. But the big L? And even if his feelings could match the depth of hers for him, could the slick politician and the sharp-tongued firefighter make this work?

In an uncanny spot of mind reading, Sam Cochrane said, "You'll just drag him down, Miss Dempsey. He could go all the way, but not with a woman like you at his side. And even if you thought it would work, do you really think the mayor of Chicago, a man who needs a twenty-four-hour security detail, will let you keep your dangerous job?"

His well-aimed barb struck home. In a million

ways, she was not the woman for Eli Cooper, but damned if she'd let Sam Cochrane think he'd won any points here.

"Don't worry about Eli and me. What you should worry about is that Eli won't be your puppet any longer, so you've decided to try and punish him through me. Well, do your worst, Mr. Cochrane. Sue me, take me for everything I have. It won't stop what's important; the people who are in my life will still be in my life. Loving me, faults and all."

"I don't doubt it, Miss Dempsey. But I must take issue with one thing you just said." His eyebrows rose in consternation and, Alex was startled to see, surprise.

"Sue you?"

Eli heard her before he saw her, but then that was so often the case with Alexandra. She was a potent presence in his life before the rest of his mangled senses could catch up.

"I don't need an appointment," she snapped at Kelly before the door was thrown open and she crashed into his office.

"What's happened?" If one of the papers had said something else . . .

Those green eyes flashed her temper. "I talked to Cochrane."

His heart sank like a bowling ball in his gut. Of course. Did he really think his sins wouldn't come back to wallop him upside the head? The only question now was which sin Cochrane had chosen to divulge: the sin of the father or the sin of the son.

He stood and came around the other side of the desk. "Have a seat."

"I'm through following orders from you. I was about to say I can't believe you did it, but actually I can. Because it's precisely the kind of behavior I'd expect from you." Hurt clouded those green pools. "Why, Eli? Why did you pretend he was suing me? So you could use me for your stupid campaign? Milk me for all I was worth?"

Relief flooded his chest. This wasn't good, but it was the lesser of two evils, for sure. How could he convince her that this scheme was seeded in a moment of madness? A nanosecond of fear that his chance to be with her would vanish into the ether if he didn't do something fast? He cycled through a number of possibilities.

*I'd already saved you from being sued. It was merely . . . a fudging of the timelines.*

Too Clintonesque.

*You owed me, so I made up that story before you bounced me out of the room.*

Too victim blaming.

*I wanted . . .*

He wanted.

"I wanted you."

She stared as if he were speaking another language. And in a way, the words were perfect nonsense because of their absolute simplicity. Plainspoken and so not Eli Cooper.

"I wanted to date you, Alexandra," he clarified.

Those emerald eyes flew wild. "You wanted me for your campaign, you mean, and you knew I wouldn't cooperate, so you used lies and blackmail."

"No, Alexandra, listen to me. I wanted you. Just you. In a selfish, ruinous, soul-destroying way. From the minute I saw you in Smith & Jones seven months ago, I've wanted you with a ferocity I can't even fathom. I saw a chance to bring you into my orbit and I took it."

"Bullshit! If you wanted me, why didn't you just ask me out on a date? Like a normal fucking person?"

He scoffed. "Are you kidding? You would have shot me out of the water."

"You don't know that!"

Anger flared at her refusal to take some responsibility here. "I know this. I used a trick, but you wanted the trick. It gave you the perfect psychological out. You could pretend you were spending time with me under duress, when really it was what you wanted all along. We needed the catalyst to start this thing between us. Convincing you was so easy. You caved—"

"Because I thought my family was under threat! I thought they'd be ruined."

He shook his head. "You could have found a way, talked to Darcy, rallied the clan, but you didn't. I held out my hand and invited you to climb aboard to pleasure and hell, and honey, you grabbed at it. You liked how I made you feel just as I liked how you made me feel. So I lied then, but I'm being honest now. How about being honest with yourself, Alexandra, and admit that you wanted me, too?"

So he'd bamboozled her and now he was talking about honesty. Demanding it from her. Twisted, maybe, but there was logic in what he was saying.

Unfortunately, the logic was going unappreciated. "You tricked me, you bastard."

"Alexandra, asking you out on a date would have resulted in the slapdown of the century, and you know it. So I thought I'd encourage you to come on board by reminding you of all I'd done to save your ass, professionally *and* financially, and when you still weren't convinced, I—"

"Lied?"

"Panicked."

This admission of vulnerability didn't have quite the impact he hoped for. She started to pace, hands on hips, fire in every step. "Let me get this straight, Counselor Jerkface. You wanted to date me, so you asked me to fake date you for a publicity stunt, because you didn't think I'd say yes to a genuine request for a date. And your means of persuasion was to threaten to sue me?"

"*Protect* you from a threatened lawsuit."

"Which you invented." An uncanny awareness came over her face. "Have we . . . have we actually been dating this entire time? *For real?*"

"Would that bother you?"

"Yes! Usually both parties are in on the dating decision, Eli."

"You've probably figured out by now that I usually get my way. Sometimes, it requires me to detour to X, Y, and Z on my travels from A to B, but the end point is inevitable. You weren't going to make it easy, it's just not in you. There's never been a moment I haven't wanted you. I thought as mayor I couldn't date you but I was wrong, and if I'd done my research I'd have figured out that I could have had you sooner."

That set her off again. "*Could have had me?* Your

arrogance, Cooper. You've got it all worked out, haven't you? That smooth patter, the legalese, the assurance that you're always right, and hey, no one really got hurt because there was no actual threat. I'm hearing everything but the one thing I need." She marched to the door, muttering what sounded like "pus for brains," "scrotum cheese," and other FCC-fineable nuggets.

*Shit.* Full-fledged panic flapped in his chest. In two long strides, he had sandwiched her against the door, his chest against her back, his mouth in her hair. "Honey, please."

Breathing heavily, with fists clenched, she spoke to the wood rather than address him directly. "I thought my family was going to be ruined. I've been worried, you asshole!"

"It was never going to come to that."

"Because this lawsuit never existed. But the problem is only one person had this crucial piece of information. Like only one person knew that we were dating."

"That wasn't cool. I get that," he said against her ear. "I made a mistake, dug a deep, dark hole, and suddenly my dreams are coming true and I can't believe how lucky I am to be spending time with this gorgeous woman. Now why the hell would I go against my self-interest and crush my dreams, honey?"

She tapped the door with her balled fists. "Stop. Oh, God. Please stop talking. I hate you so much right now."

"That's okay, because I'm crazy enough about you for both of us. But you're right. I've hurt you and I'm sorry."

Twisting to face him, she placed her hands on his

chest, her fingertips digging in as if she might pluck out his heart at any moment. He was shocked to realize that he might be okay with that. It was hers to love or destroy.

"I'm furious with you."

"You've every right to be. I've lied and cheated to make you mine, but I never promised to play fair. How I feel about you isn't noble or pure, it just is. In this crazy, fucked-up life I lead, you are my one constant. And I need you, Alexandra. So fucking bad."

"God, you . . ." Fury fired her beautiful features, stealing her speech, and the moment balanced on a razor-sharp edge. Losing her now after they'd come so far would be unbearable. He loved her so damn much.

Holy fuck. He loved this incredible woman.

Seconds ticked by, as long as hours, the only sounds the beat of their thunderous hearts, the shallow intake of her breaths, and his dumb brain praying that he hadn't messed up this one perfect thing in his miserable life.

Then he heard a new sound, one that sent hope soaring in his chest: the click of the door she'd just locked.

"I despise you right now, Cooper."

"Coming through loud and clear."

She pushed him back to the desk, poking his chest. "I may punch you, bite you, crush your nuts between my thighs. It's going to be the best hate sex *I've* ever had. And *your* survival is not my first concern."

Jesus. All those months he'd wasted thinking they could never be together. What a fucking tragedy.

Her hands pulled at his belt, undid the buckle. He flipped their positions, lifted her on the desk, tore her parka off, and ripped her sweater over her head. It was frenzied and hot and life-affirming.

Thankfully there was nothing sharp or heavy in her grasp radius.

She jerked him forward by his tie. "Is there anything else I should know?"

The chance at redemption sat up between them. He could tell her everything. How his mayoral win four years ago was predicated on the lies of his father, on his own lies as he traded on Weston Cooper's sterling reputation as a man of the people who was cut down for waging a war on organized crime. He could blurt the truth and watch her love for him wither and die. Feel his blood turn to ice in his veins. His heart shriveling to a husk.

None of those options appealed. He refused to give her up.

Instead he kissed her with his dirty, lying lips. "You know everything."

"Lie. Better." His woman was no fool, but she seemed prepared to overlook the rest. For the moment, anyway. She pulled his pants and boxers down and palmed his erection roughly. And he'd take it like her man because he deserved it. "Cubs or White Sox?"

"Taking that one to the grave, honey."

On a sexy growl, she kissed him with a sharp nip of his lower lip. "No blow jobs for a while, Eli. You do *not* want my mouth near your cock right now."

"Wait . . . *on* the desk?"

Disapproval pinched Kinsey's mouth, which Alex found particularly amusing considering no one had so much as blinked about Eli lying his ass off over Sam Cochrane's "lawsuit." A guy could be a deceiving toe rag as long as it came from "a good place," according to Darcy. But God forbid anyone get some action on an antique mahogany desk in the mayor's office.

She had been so mad at him, she still was—which made for amazing sex—but on reflection, she knew he was right about her likely reaction if he'd asked her on a date. She had convinced herself that she was dating him to save her financial hide from that lawsuit. For her family's well-being. But deep down, she knew that she had wanted him all along, and that the supposed threat from Cochrane gave her permission to indulge the taboo of becoming Eli Cooper's woman.

It disturbed her that he knew that before she knew it herself.

From their corner table near the jukebox in Dempsey's bar, Alex knocked back her Goose Island Winter Ale and skittered a look over the busy crowd of cops, firefighters, and badge bunnies. Lowering her voice, she said, "We did it with the greats of Chicago watching from the hallowed walls. Ditka, Jordan, both Daleys, and"—she gave a shifty look—"the 2005 World Series winning White Sox."

Darcy did the dutiful fake spit move on the hardwood floor at the mention of the Great Enemy. Kinsey just arched an eyebrow. It was a Chicago thing, and Cali girl hadn't completely acclimatized to their ways.

"I used to have meetings in that office." She shuddered. "I might have even sat on that desk."

Beck took a seat, set his beer down, and threw an arm around Darcy. "What'd I miss, *princesa*?"

Darcy smiled sweetly at her fiancé. "Your sister playing doctor with the mayor on his desk at city hall."

Beck shot to a stand and grabbed his bottle. "Time to poke darts in my eyeballs."

"Aw, Becky, don't go," Alex called after her brother with the girly nickname they had tortured him with as a kid. "I haven't even told you about my fantasy to do the mayor in a fire truck!"

"I can't hear you," he sang back.

Ignoring the judgy expressions of the bar's patrons, Alex sighed and turned back to the girls, who were laughing their heads off. "I used to make him buy me tampons at the drugstore even when I didn't need them. Poor guy was seventeen years old before he found out a woman's cycle wasn't every two weeks."

"Probably best you scared him off, as this conversation is now for lady ears only," Darcy said around sips of her Cosmo. They'd been trying to get her into less chicky drinks, but it was slow going. "So you still think Eli doesn't believe in the sappy ever after? Because this desperate, panicked lie of his does not sound like the action of a man who merely wants to get laid. Threatening the cop, sex in the mayor's office, the scheme to get him to date you. All evidence points to the guy being nuts about you."

Alex reached for her stock answer. "Step back, D. You're looking at the temp piece of ass, not perma-partner material for a politico. I'm the kind of girl who yells in a crowded blue bar about her dream to do the mayor of Chicago in a fire truck. It's all fun and games, but he's gonna wise up real soon and figure out I am bad news."

"He seems to be liking unfiltered Alex just fine," Kinsey said with a perceptive squint over her dirty martini. "And he'd have to be an idiot not to know how you feel after your throwdown with Luke at M Squared."

Alex groaned. "Oh, God, was it that obvious?"

"That you're in love and scared to death?" Kinsey reached across and squeezed her hand. "All you're missing is the big scarlet EC carved in your forehead pronouncing you Eli Cooper's woman."

They didn't know the half of it. How he held her so tight while they waited for Shadow to get out of surgery, those sweet moments of bliss just talking, debating, and *being* on his sofa—every single second pulled her so deep she could barely breathe for wanting him. No need for soft, dateable Alex Dempsey 2.0 with Eli. She could finally be herself.

Darcy looked like a squirrel who'd just discovered a fuckload of nuts that none of the other squirrels knew about. Before she could go off on one of her happy tangents and design an *Eli Forever* tat, Alex cut her off at the pass.

"It's just the way it's all come about. The campaign, how he needed me for the union endorsement. I wish he'd asked me out on a date before it all happened so I'd know that he wants me for me and not all the blue-collar votes I'm bringing in." Eli might claim to have been obsessed with her for months, and he might have employed a few underhanded tricks to woo her, but how could she separate it out from her contribution to his campaign? "Besides, I'm not sure he has it in him to give like that. That openness I need. There's this part of himself he keeps closed off and it's so opposite to how I do things."

"Here's something novel. You could ask him how he feels," Kinsey said, all wise and shit. "Otherwise you're waiting for the guillotine to drop on election night."

Darcy rubbed her shoulder. "He loves you, babe. I know it."

Alex wished she could share her friends' confidence. Ten days to the election, and every hour felt like a countdown to D-Day, where D stood for Dumped. When the ballots returned in his favor, would her utility to him be exhausted? Would he be looking ahead to his next career challenge? Four more years as mayor of Chicago, and then he'd turn his focus to governor or senator or . . . the White House.

Fuck-a-duck. President Eli Cooper.

She didn't need Sam Cochrane to tell her she was not the pearls-and-Anne-Klein-shoes type.

It was going to blow chunks when it was over. But she refused to have any regrets about her decision to get involved with Eli, or at minimum, she would have the right regrets. Mercifully, Alex's phone rang just in time to forestall a bout of sucks-to-be-her. Another number she didn't recognize.

Kinsey looked sympathetic. "More press?"

"Yeah. When I'm bored or drunk, I answer and pretend they've gotten the wrong number. Usually I'm a doddering old dear who thinks the caller is trying to sell jumbo-sized condoms. It confuses the hell out of them." She let the call go to voice mail, but of course, they never left a message. Once someone had phoned to tell her Eli was at that moment in *her* bed and Alex needed to lay off her man. Actually, Eli was in a live interview on the news, and as talented as the guy was, bi-location wasn't one of his skills.

The number rang again. "Oh, screw it. Ready for some fun?" She winked at the girls and hit the answer button. "*Yeeeees*," she said in her best old-lady.

"Alex, I'm Callie Benson with the *Springfield Recorder*. We're calling to get a comment on the rumors about Weston Cooper."

She started. This was a new one. "What rumors?"

"That the U.S. Attorney's Office was investigating him on criminal conspiracy charges before he died."

Eli loved the city in the morning, even in winter, and nowhere was it more beautiful than along the river walk on Lower Wacker. They had done wonders with this area in the last few years, turning it from a dank, soulless strip of land that even drug dealers would have reservations about visiting into a bright, safe walkway with access to restaurants and the numerous starting points for the river and lake tours during the summer. On either side, gleaming glass monoliths stretched to the sky, a gauntlet to anyone willing to take them on.

And it was about time someone did just that.

Sam Cochrane had messed with him for the last time. It was one thing to allow the tycoon to throw his weight around like an overgrown child to ensure certain decisions fell his way. If he wanted to ruin Eli, drag his father's name through the mud at the bottom of the Chicago River, then that was his prerogative. But no one messed with Eli Cooper's woman.

From a bench on the south side of the river, Eli looked up at the tower of steel and glass, feeling the city come alive around him. Just past seven and commuters were pounding their feet along the bridges and streets above his head as they headed for offices and the daily grind. And on the north side of the river, a bevy of construction workers were preparing to mount the last five letters of that humongous sign announcing Sam Cochrane's ownership of a piece of prime real estate overlooking Eli Cooper's Chicago.

Eli dialed a number on his phone. When the recipient answered, he spoke a single word. "Now."

Unfortunately, it wasn't quite on par with the stuff of Hollywood. As gratifyingly dramatic as that word sounded to his ears, it still took a few moments before the order went into effect. From his chilly vantage point, Eli watched as two City of Chicago employees served an injunction on the foreman to halt further construction on Sam Cochrane's skyscraper.

He stood and turned toward the stairs that would take him to the street. No rest for the wicked, especially someone as wicked as Eli Cooper. Cochrane's salvo had been returned.

*It was on.*

Three hours later, Eli strode into a city hall media room unusually packed to the rafters.

"Ladies and gentlemen, whatever could be of such interest to the fourth estate this frigid February morning?" A few chuckles greeted that. The vultures had been bored lately because his significant election lead in the home stretch left little to report on. He did so enjoy throwing them a few crumbs every now and again. "I'll just open it up to questions. Mac."

Mac Devlin waggled a pen between his thumb and forefinger. "People are questioning the city's timing of this injunction, Mr. Mayor, coming so soon after a rather negative article about Alex Dempsey was published in one of Sam Cochrane's papers. You didn't seem overly concerned about that sign before."

"I'm always concerned about anything that's an eyesore in our beautiful city. I have an excellent relationship with Sam, and it's no secret that he's been very generous to my campaign and with his endorsement of my administration. I'd hoped we could come to an agreement. Seems that can't happen, so it'll be up to the courts to decide."

"And in the meantime, the first three letters"— Mac held up his notepad and delivered an exaggerated squint—"that's C-O-C, of Sam Cochrane's last name are left, uh, dangling on the side of his building."

"Signage interruptus," someone offered, causing the vultures to chortle malevolently.

A brief smile lifted his lips. Madison had wagged her finger at him and said, "You couldn't wait for the H and the R, could you?" And no, he could not. He wanted everyone to know what he thought of Sam, and if it was spelled out in letters of his own making, all the better.

"He's welcome to remove those starting letters at any time—at his own expense of course—but if he never gets to finish that sign it will be as clear as a

Chicago morning in spring who owns the building anyway. Pretty damn appropriate for such an expression of ostentatious manhood, I think."

That sent the vultures into peals of laughter.

"Hey, Mr. Mayor, how many proposals today?" Kenny Fiedler again. He must be running a book on it.

"No idea, Kenny. Been otherwise occupied." He was already moving toward the door, with a renewed spring in his step. "That's all I've got for today, ladies and gentlemen. See you tonight at the debate."

# ◊ CHAPTER TWENTY-TWO

Fifteen hours later, a considerably less spry version of Eli finally made it home. His muscles protested every move, blunted from what felt like years on the campaign trail. The alarm didn't beep to tell him it was armed, but he knew John, one of his security detail, was here with Shadow.

He walked into the living room and his heart lifted clear through the roof.

Alexandra.

She lay sleeping, sprawled on his sofa, not in the least bit ladylike. *Jackie O she ain't.* The dog bed had been pulled up to the end cushion and Shadow was curled up with the eye not covered by a patch trained on his sofa mate. Watching her, keeping her safe.

Shadow loved Alexandra Dempsey, and Eli knew exactly what that felt like. He sat down beside her, and the motion was enough to turn her in to him. She nuzzled into his neck.

"You're back," she whispered, sleep-husky. "How did the debate go?"

For fuck's sake. "You didn't even watch it?"

She smoothed away his indignation with a kiss. "Politics bores me. Wiped the floor with the opposition, I assume."

"Sure did. I thought one of the security guys would still be here. Didn't you have a shift at the bar?"

She breathed deep from his skin, like she was storing his scent for another day. It made him think about a time when he might not have her—some horrible, apocalyptic future ruled by love-destroying zombies when he would have to live on memory fumes.

"Beck covered for me. I couldn't bear to leave my brave little guy." She rubbed behind Shadow's ears. "I think he likes me a little."

"He's crazy about you."

The TV was on, but muted. A very tanned, very naked man sporting a spare tire that wouldn't have looked out of place on a Mack truck was walking around a nice house with a clipboard in his hands. "What are we watching?"

"*Buying Naked.* Nudists trying to find real estate and society's acceptance. It's stop, drop, and watch television."

"It is?"

"Everything on TLC is. They have the best shows. *I Didn't Know I Was Pregnant!*, *Sister Wives*, *Alaskan Women Looking for Love*, *Sex Sent Me to the ER*—"

"That's not a real show."

"It is, and it's as awesome as it sounds. Skydiving accidents midcoitus. Ball gags used in a manner that's off label. You know, the usual." She stroked his jaw. "Poor Eli, look at all you've been missing while achieving world domination. I didn't make banana bread, by the way."

"Okaaay."

"I wanted to take care of you when you came home," she explained. "I was going to make banana bread. That's what my mom used to make as a special treat, especially when something big was happening for one of us."

His heart left his body right then and wandered around in a state of confusion. "Honey, that's so sweet. But if you think that the way to a man's heart is through his stomach you're aiming too high."

She laughed. "I fell asleep, which is probably for the best because I can't cook anyway. In case you haven't figured it out yet, I'm not the homemaker type. "

Perhaps not, but she made his house a home, just by her presence here. He kissed her eyelids, her nose, each of her cheeks, her lips. Shadow turned on those sad brown eyes, seeking attention, so Eli stroked the rough patchwork of fur on his head and spent a moment soothing him. Soon his heavy head dropped and his drug daze sent him to doggy dreamland, where Eli hoped there were cats to chase and bacon to eat.

If this were any more perfect, he would think it was a setup. He had been a beast in the debate, answering on his strongest areas with authority, deflecting on the issues where he was weak. At home, Shadow was on the mend and Alexandra was here in his arms where she belonged. Eli Cooper was winning at fucking everything, and it couldn't get better.

But it could get a whole lot worse. He was a liar and a master manipulator. She knew some of it and seemed to accept it as the day-in, day-out of politics. Part of the game and his need to dominate every aspect of his life. But the things she didn't know—what his father had done, what Eli had done—would send her packing, for sure. No more cozying up on the sofa to watch dumb TV shows. No more coming home to this.

To his heart.

"I had this weird call last night," she mumbled sleepily.

"Hmm," he hummed in her hair. Sleep was overtaking him at a rapid pace.

"From a film production company. Molly Cade wants to play me in a movie."

"Who?"

"Molly Cade? Oscar-nominated actress? America's sweetheart? Well, she used to be before her husband dumped her and took her to the cleaners. Apparently she's making a firefighter movie this summer in Chicago and they want to rework the script to include episodes from the life of yours truly."

He chuckled. "There'll be no living with you once your life is immortalized on the silver screen."

A shadow flitted like a dark-winged bird across her face, perhaps because his words implied a future together. After all they'd been through, surely she saw the inevitable. Jackie O she ain't, but Alexandra Dempsey would very soon be Chicago's First Lady.

The brass ring was within his grasp, the victory so sweet he could taste it.

"I actually had two odd calls."

"Let me guess, you're to be awarded the Presidential Medal of Freedom."

She giggled. "Not this year. But that's okay because a girl needs something to strive for." Concern replaced playfulness in those sink-into-me green eyes. "A reporter called asking about your father. Something about an investigation into him by the U.S. Attorney's Office before he died."

Every muscle in Eli's body locked up as if superglue was hardening in his veins. Madison had mentioned a call to her office earlier and he had dismissed it as a desperate dig by the opposition.

"They wanted a comment and I told them to call the mayor's office. You must get so sick of all these hits against you. They'll try anything to bring you down now that you're so close."

Unavoidably, his gaze attached to the bookshelf display, the one with his University of Chicago graduation photo, the shot of his team in the Marines, Eli shaking hands with the president of the United States a month after he took office at city hall. His proudest moments. And beside them was the Weston Cooper Justice Award.

He'd left it behind at the gala, his only concern that night convincing this woman to let him worship her in his bed. One of his security team had retrieved it. On discovering it thrown haphazardly on his kitchen counter, Alexandra had marveled that it wasn't taking pride of place in his home, so she'd put it there. And now it shone malevolently, those scales of justice mocking every single one of Eli's achievements.

"Eli, what's wrong?

A line separating his old life from his new was about to be drawn. The past was another country, and if they had a chance of making it, he had to leave it behind. Eli the liar. Eli the manipulator.

Eli, the son of a Chicago hero.

He stroked her thigh, taking strength from her

heat and goodness, and said the one thing he'd prayed would never need saying.

"We need to talk."

*We need to talk*. The four most terrifying words in the English language.

She sat up straight and looked into the eyes of this man she had foolishly and irrevocably fallen in love with. "Should I not have spoken to that reporter? I don't know how she got my number and . . ." Heart thudding, she trailed off at his stark expression and painted on a wobbly smile.

"No, it's not that." He scrubbed a hand through his hair. "Weston Cooper wasn't the saint everyone made him out to be, Alexandra. He was just a man."

She blinked, not understanding how this was the lead-in to getting dumped. Maybe she was going to hear that his dad wouldn't have approved or . . . She thought back to the missing photos, the thousand-mile stares, the clues her brain refused to compute. Had Weston Cooper been a different man behind closed doors?

"They're all just men, Eli. But some men do great things, even if they're not the best in other areas." A flutter in her chest started up, thinking about what areas Eli's father had failed in. As sister to foster brothers who had all endured fucked-up parental situations before finding a safe harbor with the Dempseys, she understood that the roses often came sporting big-ass thorns.

"When I was a kid, I adored him." His gaze traveled to the family portrait hung up in the living room for the public to see. "I didn't even realize that what he was doing was all that special until later. After. He was just Dad. He put on a suit and went to work at seven every morning and came home and played with the dog and me every night at six. I thought he was perfect, but he wasn't."

Those last three words were grated out.

"No one is," she whispered.

"Sean was. His legacy is forged in fire. No one can take that away from you. What he did, laying his life on the line for his job, his city, his family, for total strangers—that made him a true hero. Logan, too."

Confusion tore at her brain. "Your father was a hero of a different kind."

"Stop calling him that." He spat out the words, his eyes flat discs of fury. "Because he wasn't. He was a liar and a fraud and he's the reason my mother is dead."

"Eli, what are you talking about?"

What she saw in the harsh cut of his mouth terrified her. "A week after I was elected four years ago, Sam Cochrane came to see me. He wanted to make sure I was ready to scratch his back now that he'd bankrolled me to the top. I was happy to ease up on him for a few things, minor shit—it's quid pro quo, after all—but I wasn't going to give him any significant preferential treatment. That's when he played his ace."

"What, Eli? What did he tell you?"

"My father was a crook. He was actually working with Ronan Cutler, the mob boss who killed him. "

The chill in her heart spread to every part of her. "Th-that can't be right. How would Cochrane know that?" Perhaps not the right question, but there were so many and she had to start somewhere. What he had said was mind-boggling.

"Cochrane and my father might have been friends, but that never stopped the bastard from investigating people. If he thinks he can get an edge, he'll put people on it. Go to any length to find it. He got a tip, found out something, who knows? He was probably blackmailing my father with it. After my parents died, Sam held on to it because he suspected it would be more useful to him if he bided his time. He would use it to catch me."

"You make it sound like he's been planning to back you for office for years."

He didn't respond, which was an answer in itself. And his eyes . . . those eyes were filled with something she had never seen: hopelessness.

"Two days after my parents died, the cops raided Cutler's compound, killed him and his top people. There were only low-level peons left, none of whom knew about my father's involvement with the mob. He had been giving Cutler a heads-up on raids, advance moves of law enforcement. According to Sam, my father wanted out. The guy Cutler sent was only supposed to threaten our family, a message to my father to continue to play ball. But the assassin overstepped his bounds. Killed them both."

"And no one else knows?"

"There were suspicions. After Sam told me, I contacted someone I knew who had worked in the U.S. Attorney's Office at the time. They'd been investigating my father, but he was killed before they could indict him. With all the major players out of the way, it seemed fruitless and a waste of taxpayer money to bring it out in the open. My father's legacy would have been destroyed. Every case he ever prosecuted would come under scrutiny."

"And you," she said slowly, the full impact of what he was saying creeping up on her like an icy wave. "You would come under scrutiny."

"This city loves him, Alexandra," he said, passing over her observation. "It needs heroes, men who stand tall, and even if he made this mistake, he was still a decent man in other ways. A good husband. The best father."

And a criminal. She thought back to all those interviews Eli had given before the last election on local and national TV. His obvious pride in his father and his accomplishments—it had all been genuine, she knew that. Now he had to poker up whenever the sainted Coop was mentioned and pretend that he was still the great man, not responsible for his wife's death or for orphaning a twelve-year-old boy.

All terrible, but still her mind kept circling back to the present.

"But it helped you get into office. What he did, what people think he did."

Standing up to a mobster. That heroic act. *That lie.* She drew back, needing the space to comb through and untangle what she was hearing. The only sure ground was quicksand.

He noticed her withdrawal, frowned. "My father's legacy might be the reason I got into office, but I've proved myself. I know I have. I love this city."

She didn't doubt that. She'd seen it in the hours he put in, the dedication, but. . .

"People voted for you because of what your father did, because of what he stood for. I—I voted for you." Because she saw her own pain reflected in his. Because of Sean and Logan.

On his face was frustration that she was choosing to see it in this way. But he'd had years to parse this; she was still reeling.

"I didn't know then what he had done."

"But when you found out, you kept quiet. You let people think he was this great man. A hero."

His look condemned her naïveté. "What was I supposed to say? 'Thanks for your vote and oh, by the way, my father wasn't quite the hero after all'? How would that help? Who would that serve?"

Eli's raised voice drew Shadow out of his drug-induced slumber. He looked up, concerned that Mommy and Daddy were fighting.

"*My* father was a hero, Eli," she gritted out. "*My* brother was a hero. They died doing their jobs for this city. How can you not see that supporting this false image of your father compromises *their* memories, people who truly died honorably?"

The pain that wracked his expression cut her to the marrow, but it had nothing on the hurt in the space around her heart.

"I know that," he said quietly. "Do you think I don't know that?"

But Eli's father hadn't died honorably. His father had worked with a killer to ensure his continued freedom to terrorize. His father had pretended bravery when he had no right to do so. People still talked about him with reverence and awe.

In the same conversation as her father and brother.

Gaze blurred with tears, Alex walked over to the bookshelf where she had placed the Weston Cooper Justice Award a week ago. With a quivering hand, she picked up the piece of glass, shaped like a scale, and walked into the kitchen, where she dropped it into the trash.

Eli followed, but didn't acknowledge what she had done with a word or glance. "Alexandra, I am not my father."

Yes, but right now it was so hard to separate them. "I know you're not. I know I can't hold you responsible for the sins of your father, Eli, but you're responsible for your sins. Your actions. You've used this to win votes." *Her vote.* "You're still using it to win votes."

She'd known what he was like from the beginning. Eli Cooper had more moves than a roach in a bowl of cereal. Every decision was calculated to the infinitesimal detail. Nothing was left to chance. He wanted to win the election.

He wanted to win her.

But now those niggling doubts about her usefulness to him and his campaign nipped at the edges of her querulous mind. Knowing all those things he was capable of, the lengths he'd go to ensure victory—it was all mixed up in her head and her heart that hurt so much.

"I trusted you—" Her voice broke, and what came out next was a rusty whisper. "I—I defended you to my family. Took hits for you. I let you inside my body with no protection because I trusted *you* would protect me. We all trust you to protect this city, Eli."

He cupped her face with those weapons of pleasure that had taken her to heaven so many times. "I have protected you, Alexandra. From day one, from moment fucking zero when I saw you in Smith & Jones last summer, that's all I've wanted to do. That's why I'm telling you everything now, so there are no lies between us. This . . . this thing with my father. It's not pleasant, but I've been trying to distance myself from it. From him. Forge my own path."

She jerked from his grasp. "How can you ever do that? You've lived with secrets and lies for so long that you don't know what it's like to be open. Would you have even told me if that reporter hadn't called?"

"I . . . I don't know."

Well, at least he was honest about *that*.

"Alexandra, listen to me—"

"So you can needle and debate and convince me with that smooth patter of yours? When can you tell a politician is lying? When his lips are moving. And your lips are always moving, Eli. You're always talking and kissing and making me feel amazing, but those lips of yours are just broadcasting your lies."

"I love you," he husked out. Strong hands pushed her back against the kitchen island. Pinned by his hard body, hearing those desperately uttered words, she felt herself sinking under his thrall again. "That's not a lie. That's the God's honest truth. And I know you feel the same way."

She shut her eyes against what should have been a dream come true. This man she loved telling her exactly what she wanted to hear. But that was the problem—he was playing her again. It was like Cubbies fans thinking this year would be different when they'd been screwed over time and again. Still, they returned to Wrigley, bought more shitty hot dogs and overpriced beer, because they were at the ball game. They were on hallowed ground and getting screwed was part of the experience.

Well, screwing wasn't enough to rose-color *this* experience. The Eli goggles had to come off.

"The truth, Eli? Since when have you been on even the barest speaking terms with the truth? Everything out of your mouth is said with one goal in mind: how will this help me win? Whether it's sabotaging a rival during a date or inventing a lawsuit when you don't get your way."

She had almost been fooled, sensually bludgeoned by these plays of a man used to getting everything he wanted. To have someone want her badly enough to employ such black-ops tactics—how flattered she had been. Her friends thought the stunts he had pulled were romantic. For God's sake, Kinsey had fallen for it. Even if Alex could get past this deception, how could she continue looking into those eyes and not see the gaze of the consummate liar?

He held her face, leaned his forehead to hers. "Honey, we can get through this. Look how far we've come already. All the obstacles we've smashed to get here."

"You mean the rivals you've crushed and the pieces you've moved around the board?" She pushed him away. Her heart felt like it was shredding inside her, layers stripping off one at a time. "You got the firefighters' union endorsement because I made you look good. But not just me. My family of heroes made you look good. You appropriated the legacy of my dead father and brother because your own is corrupted. Soiled."

She struck her breast where the memory of Sean and Logan lived. The men she honored every day. All along, she'd worried that Eli was using her to win over her tribe of fire, but it was worse than she could ever have suspected.

"You haven't just used me, Eli. You've used *them*. And I'll never forgive you for that."

She had no idea what impact her words made because she was already running toward the door, swiping at her leaking emotion, pushing away her pain with every step.

He didn't try to stop her.

Eli Cooper had finally given up.

# ❂ CHAPTER TWENTY-THREE

It wasn't every day that someone managed to get a jump on the mayor of Chicago's security team, or the mayor himself, but then Eli supposed that after the last few weeks, nothing should surprise him.

That Eli had been sucker punched by a Dempsey? Not shocking in the least.

What did surprise him was that (a) this particular Dempsey *made an appointment* to hit the mayor soundly on the jaw and (b) the strike did not come at the hands of Luke or Beck, who were generally acknowledged as the ones with homicidal tendencies.

Eli rubbed his sore jaw and marveled at how his ten o'clock—one Wyatt Fox—could stand before him with such calm. He would have loved to have this man in his Marine unit.

"Huh. So, would you like to sit?" Eli asked his attacker, one hand still holding his jaw as the other gestured to the chairs in his office on the fifth floor of city hall.

Firefighter Fox flexed his punching hand, tweaked a knife-straight eyebrow, and took a seat in one of the comfortable leather chairs across from Eli's desk. Endeavoring to keep it friendly, Eli sat in the other armchair a few feet away from Wyatt.

Who then crossed his arms and stared as if it was Eli's job to make conversation with the man who had just committed a Class 2 felony. One would think he punched out public officials every day.

Eli's jaw hurt, but better to feel something, anything, than this numbness in his chest, this lump of ice where his heart should be. The last two days without her had been a living nightmare. He had damned any chance of a future with her by going against type and making honesty the best policy.

There was irony in there, somewhere.

"How is she?"

"She's a Dempsey," came the gruff reply. In other words, she had her family and all their strength running through her veins. She would survive this. She would survive Eli.

Eli wasn't entirely sure that he would survive her. Or that he wanted to. Without this woman in his life, he felt like a big fat heap of zero.

"What has she told you?"

"Nothin'. But I found her cryin' in her cornflakes yesterday morning. Would have come sooner but this was the earliest I could get on your calendar." He shrugged as though that was enough of an explanation, and Eli supposed it was. He'd made the woman he loved cry and she would never trust him again.

"Have you ever wanted something so badly that you'd sell your soul to have it?"

Wyatt clenched his fist, perhaps contemplating whether another punch might prevent Eli's imminent devolution into melodrama. "Something or someone?"

"Either."

He considered this in the manner of a man who had never thought about it before. But Eli knew better. A man like Wyatt Fox thought about things a great deal.

"I have."

"And don't say you've never lied or kept a secret," Eli said, "because all your mysterious trips downstate say different."

Wyatt's eyes widened in gratifying surprise. *Gotcha, Mr. Fox.* "What do you know about it?"

"Enough. When I first started this thing with Alexandra, I had background checks run on the whole family. I needed to be sure there weren't any skeletons rattling around in the Dempsey closets. I have enough of my own without taking on anyone else's."

What he'd found out about Wyatt Fox wasn't exactly damning, but the fact that he was holding back from the rest of them spoke volumes. Those weekly trips to Bloomington were no doubt tied to the monthly transfers out of his bank account. So strange. It wasn't as if the Dempseys wouldn't welcome more strays into the fold. Neither did Wyatt seem like the kind of guy who would be ashamed of a past indiscretion, which made his motives for the subterfuge all the more puzzling.

Wyatt appeared only mildly affected by this revelation. "Are you threatening me?"

Eli waved that off. "God, no. I just think that a man in your position, a man hiding something from his family for whatever reason, might understand that sometimes people lie. With the best of intentions. I wanted your sister. I've wanted her from the moment I met her. That's not to say my motives were a hundred percent pure, but there's never been a second when she hasn't been on my mind."

"So you pretended Sam Cochrane was going to sue her to force her to date you."

"Put like that it does sound . . . Shit, okay, that sounds bad. Really, I saw an opportunity to spend time with her. Get to know her—"

"But the lawsuit stunt isn't what's upset her. It's something worse."

Worse, and possibly unforgiveable. "It is and, for once in my life, it's a situation I can't talk my way out of. It's a done deal and there's nothing I can do to fix it."

A moment of not uncomfortable silence—and, perhaps, understanding—passed. "Are you expecting me to pull for you now, Cooper?"

"Just thought you might feel a tiny bit remorseful about hitting me."

"You deserved it." Wyatt gave a cursory glance over his shoulder. "How long before I'm cuffed and sent to lockup?"

"Think nothing of it. I'm going to win her back, you know." Those words came from some deep place where a fool's hope lived. Hell, he'd been a fool for this woman from the start, and if he was going to take a header, he would make sure it was spectacular.

"And I'm gonna enjoy watching you make a complete fuckin' idiot of yourself. Because that's what you'll have to do to be within a snowball's chance of gettin' with my sister again." He stood, zipping up his CFD fleece as he rose. "What did you do in the corps, Cooper?"

"Ground intelligence. You?"

Wyatt's smile was a slow burn. "Sniper." He held out the hand he had just used to almost rearrange the mayor's face. Eli clasped it and shook firmly enough to make the man wince.

"But then I expect you already knew that, Mr. Mayor."

Alex landed a kick to the bag in the gym at Engine Company 6 and imagined it was Eli Cooper's head.

No, his balls. Though according to the latest on-line gossip she'd definitely not read, because she was definitely not obsessing over Eli's every move since their bust-up, she could leave the personal injury stuff to the mayor's inability to put one foot in front of the other. Per the reports, he had tripped and bruised his jaw when stepping out of the shower. Like she believed that for a second.

Someone had hit him. Hard. She only wished she'd thought of it first.

Compounding her misery was the fact it was the worst day of the year for a singleton: Valentine's Day. Whatever. She preferred to see it as The Day Before the 50% Off Truffles Sale at Fannie May.

Sweat rolled off her, drenching her tank. She aimed a foot at the bag. Its resounding thump should have felt good, but nothing did.

How could he use her like that?

She got it now. All that distrust he carried, the looking over his shoulder waiting for the knife in his back. *Years can go by before you find out a person's true colors,* he'd said that night at DeLuca's. *People always hide things, play parts . . .*

He was talking about Weston Cooper, but he could just as easily have been describing himself. His father had betrayed him and his mother in the worst possible way. He'd committed a crime, brought death on his family, then left Eli with this legacy he couldn't abandon.

*Refused* to abandon.

Of course, it wasn't Eli's fault his father was a criminal—she knew that—but he had benefited nonetheless. He could give away his inheritance. He could refuse to take a salary. But he continued to profit where it counted. Politically. The unions had endorsed him, and no way could he pretend that the legacy of Weston Cooper didn't play a part.

To her soul-sickening shame, Alex herself had played a part. Local 2, her own union, had come out for the mayor. Her "romance" with Eli had prompted that endorsement, and now all those old insecurities about being a traitor to her tribe—to the people of her heart—came back to haunt her.

*All. Wrong.* She kicked the bag again.

"Alex, you need to see this," she heard Wy calling behind her.

"Busy." Marinating in her disgust for a certain smooth-talking dickweasel.

"No, you're not. Get in here now."

So he hadn't raised his voice, but that was about as heated a tone as she'd ever heard from her stoic brother. She followed his voice to the lounge, where the B shift was watching TV. The ten o'clock news, and from the clock on the screen, they were only a minute in.

Marissa Clark was on deck, by the looks of it on Michigan Avenue. Which was sort of strange because she was the six and ten anchor on NBC 5 and never did the field reporting.

*"We're used to seeing Chicago's great architecture being lauded the world over, but this week it's getting more attention than ever. First with the city council's move to halt the installation of an 'architecturally tasteless' sign on Sam Cochrane's riverfront building. Now, on this Valentine's Day, it would seem a certain someone would like to remind a certain someone else that our city's skyscrapers can send more visually impactful messages."*

The camera pulled back to show the skyline behind Marissa, and more particularly the Crain Communications Building, though most people called it the Diamond (or more crudely, the Vagina building). Traditionally used to get the city amped at the start of Bears or Hawks season, tonight its window lights had been manipulated to showcase a different dispatch.

Alex gasped.

Up high, for all the world to see, was a message for one person:

*Eli*

*Alexandra*

With a big, red, flamboyant heart.

That no-good, unscrupulous pigfucker!

Her phone rang in the pocket of her sweats and she pulled it out, expecting more of the media calls she had been ignoring all afternoon. Thankfully, it was only Kinsey. "Did you see the news?"

"I'm watching it now."

Marissa was jabbering on about how the mayor's office had released a statement assuring citizens that no taxpayer dollars or campaign contributions had been used for the current lighting scheme.

"*Neither the mayor nor Alex Dempsey could be reached for comment, though we have to wonder what woman could fail to be moved by such a romantic gesture.*" Marissa's eyes shone glossy and it wasn't from the cold.

"I wish you'd tell us what he did," Kinsey said, "because last we talked you were going to ask him how he felt. Now we have this gag-inducing hearts-on-buildings business, so what's the problem here?"

"It's not so simple." Alex had shared with her friends and family that she and Eli were kaput because she elected to pull out before she was pushed out. She longed to confide in them, but it wasn't her story to tell. "This is just another stunt. Like everything with him."

"Well, it's a pretty good stunt!"

Sighing, Alex turned away from the crew, which was watching her avidly, waiting for her to break down in a girly puddle of mush, she supposed.

"He can light up every building from here to Bangkok. Maybe he'll electrocute himself and do us all a favor. Gotta bounce." She hung up with Kinsey and faced her crew. "Something to say, gentlemen?"

"Wouldn't want to risk it," Derek said. "Like my balls where they are. Outside my body."

"I can*not* believe you're all on his side now. You're supposed to hate his guts!"

"My union has spoken," said Murphy, that fickle idiot.

Wy met her gaze. "He's doin' the best he can with what he's got."

God, where was Luke when she needed him? "You make it sound like he's some emotionally stunted geek who doesn't know how to speak to a woman. The guy is a professional bamboozler and that's what he's doing to you and everyone in this city. He's not playing fair."

"Who said love was fair?"

*Ack!* Her phone rang with a number she didn't recognize. More media. She silenced it.

"I need it to be fair." That's all she had ever wanted. To be treated on the job not as a woman, but as an equal. To be treated on her dates not as a job, but as a woman. It wasn't fair of Eli to throw his power around like a spoiled child because he didn't like a particular outcome. He had so much at his disposal—money, charm, now the support of an entire city—and she had nothing but her titanium spine and justifiable sense of outrage.

"He's an ass."

"Sure is," Wy agreed, rubbing his chin.

Her gaze zeroed in on the reddened knuckles of his right hand. "It was *you*," she hissed. "You hit him."

He pulled her aside into the corridor. "Of course I did. Did you think I was going to let him get away with what he pulled here? How he hurt you?"

"You don't even know what he did."

He gentled her jaw and forced her eyes up to meet his blue-gray ones. They sparkled with an intensity and passion she rarely saw because he was always so guarded. As a child, she had been closer to her other brothers, especially Gage. While Wy's love and loyalty were never in doubt, he was the one who seemed to need them the least.

"He made my beautiful baby sister cry. That's all I need to know."

Here come the fucking waterworks again. "Oh, Wy," and before she knew it he had enveloped her in his unyielding strength.

"I know how hard it is for you here," he whispered against her hair, "and how you never once complain. Murphy rakin' you over the coals, implyin' you're not tough enough for this job. I know what he's been doin' to you, but I also know that you can handle it. Because that's how you've always been. So fuckin' strong. And not once have I seen you lose it until this shit with Cooper."

"I tend to eat my emotions," she said on a sniff. "Burritos and ice cream get me through."

He huffed a low laugh and she cheered a minor victory because Wy was so hard to crack.

She bit her lip. "Was it just one punch?"

"Yeah, I kept it fair. He didn't fall over or anythin', but it surprised him."

"Good," she whispered.

"He's not going to give up, Alex. He enjoys the challenge, and now he's got the touchdown of the election, you're the conversion. That lawsuit he invented? Only a politician would come up with a scheme that twisted."

She drew back, swiped at her eyes. "Right. And no matter how romantic Darcy thinks his shenanigans are or how swoonworthy Kinsey thinks that building love letter is, it comes down to this: I can't trust him. Keeping me in the dark, trickery and lies, that's his default setting. He doesn't know any better, Wy. It's ingrained in him because of his job."

His genetics.

She would never betray his confidence, but knowing what she did about Weston Cooper put a gloss on the situation that no one else could see. Eli was upholding the legacy of a criminal to prolong his stay in the mayor's office. It was a slap in the face to every true hero.

Eli Cooper and Sam Cochrane deserved each other.

# ◊ CHAPTER TWENTY-FOUR

"Shouldn't you be getting home to your empty mausoleum and crippled dog?"

Eli looked up from his desk to find Madison leaning against the doorjamb, briefcase in hand, coat draped over her arm.

"Even Shadow can't bear my company." Last night, Eli's sad sack vibes had driven Shadow to turn his back on his master in disgust and lie across the hearth. His banged-up puppy missed Alexandra. "Anyway, I have all I need here."

Madison stepped inside. "You'd better be talking about scotch."

Sighing, Eli pulled out a bottle of Glenfiddich from the bottom drawer along with a couple of cut-crystal old-fashioneds. The city of Chicago had a zero-tolerance policy for alcohol on city property, but screw the rules. Tonight he planned to get well and truly smashed.

He poured a couple of fingers apiece and slid one over to Madison, who had taken a seat opposite. "What news of the campaign?"

"Numbers are perfect with a practically unassailable lead two days out. Operation Date-a-Firefighter was a stunning success. You terminated a little earlier than we had planned, but the overall benefit was the same." She raised her glass. "To four more years."

He stared her down. "Why didn't we work out?"

She mouthed an "ah" and took a moment to consider. "You were too young and too drunk. I was too jaded and not drunk enough." It left her lips sounding well rehearsed.

"No, later. In the last few years, we've had more dinners and spent more time together than most married couples, maybe had more sex than most married couples, yet we've never wanted to take it further. It's not as if we don't get along."

"You have an aversion to commitment and I have an aversion to dirty socks on my bedroom floor."

"I feel as though we could have overcome these obstacles."

She knocked back her drink in one gulp and placed the glass down. Ever graceful, she stood and moved toward the window. It was where she did her best thinking.

"Remember that day you came to M Squared after Alex Dempsey had been maligned in the news for her dating escapades?"

He nodded, though she couldn't see him. All her focus was outward over the city streets.

"You crashed through the door of the conference room, all fury and passion and vengeance, and bee-lined straight for her. Nothing else existed for you in that moment, only her."

Not just in that moment. Since the first moment. In Smith & Jones, he had recognized something in her that he didn't just crave. It was the part of himself he was missing. This good, pure thing he needed to wash away his sins and make him whole.

Brave, beautiful Alexandra, following in the footsteps of heroic giants. She'd accused him of appropriating her family's legacy because his own was corrupted. Soiled. All true—God, what a dick he was—but as always, there was more gray than black-and-white in this sordid tale. Every decision Eli made before the age of thirty was to honor the father he had idolized since before he could walk. Law school, the Marines, Chicago's mayor. Finding out what Weston Cooper had done, the monster he had become, had killed something inside of him.

This astonishing woman had shone light on his darkness, love on his blackened soul. Not her dead father and brother, not her CFD connection. Just Alexandra. And his heart ached for her.

He looked up to find Madison facing him, sadness haunting her eyes. "If I marry again, I'd like my future husband to look at me how you looked at Alex Dempsey. It's what every woman deserves."

*Shit.* So self-absorbed in his own problems, Eli had taken an age to realize how truly high up the scales of idiocy he had climbed. He was the worst friend ever.

"I'm sorry, Mads. I've been an insensitive ass."

Lowering her gaze, she smoothed her skirt, picked some lint off it. "You're a man, Eli. Insensitive ass is *the* job description. It's my own fault. I thought if I pushed you toward her, we'd be killing two birds. A benefit for the campaign and you'd get her out of your system. Then you and I could go back to . . ." She palmed her brow, her distress palpable. With a mental hitch of her bootstraps, she morphed into tough broad Mads. "Don't fret your giant, arrogant head. My feelings, my problem. I'll get over you."

There was nothing he could say that would make this situation better, so he kept his mouth shut. She walked to the door, pride in her stride, and turned when she got there.

"These oh-so-romantic gestures with the buildings are all well and good, and they certainly don't hurt your campaign, but you're not going to win her with flash. You can't just Eli Cooper this problem into submission."

"Then, what?" He felt like a cad asking the woman who still loved him, the woman whom he had never loved enough, how he could win the heart of the one he loved more than anything. But Mads had always given him the best advice. He doubted that would ever change.

"She needs what every woman wants, Eli. For you to walk into a room and see only her."

Alex pulled on the tap for a pint of Guinness and let it settle for the requisite couple of minutes. Dempsey's was half full. Not bad for a Monday night in February with no Hawks or Bulls game, ten below outside, and the general malaise of a city knee-deep in the armpit of winter. Tomorrow was Election Day, and the mayor was poised at a healthy 58 percent in citizen flash polling. As he only needed 50 percent plus one vote to get an absolute majority, the lead was considered virtually insurmountable.

"Not out celebrating with your boyfriend?"

Alex let go of a sigh, which turned into a growl

because this was the kind of night, month, and year she had been having. "Murphy, my man, what can I get you?"

He climbed onto a stool, that dumb Irish potato head of his eyeing the draft beers like he didn't already know what he was going to order.

*Guinness*, she mouthed just as he said, "Sam Adams."

Huh, maybe an old dog could be taught a few new tricks.

A couple more of the Engine 6 crew trickled in. Derek Phelan took a seat beside Murphy and ordered a Bud. Gage brought a crate of Blue Moons up from the cellar and unloaded them into the bar fridge.

All around her, life kept calm and carried on, and she was supposed to be okay with it. She had her job. She had her family. Soon, she hoped, people would forget her part in the silly season entertainment.

She would not forget.

He would be a permanent fixture on the news for the next four years. He would be mentioned with disgust whenever a pay contract or the firefighters' pensions were on the bargaining table. She would need to quit listening for his laugh. She would need to stop searching for his smile.

God, how she hated him, but mostly she hated this side of her he had unveiled. This weak, needy woman who wanted those long fingers plundering her body and the safe embrace of his made-for-her arms. All attached to the body of a Norse god with the mind of a sewer rat. She had let the domineering parts of his personality slide—his relentless pursuit of her, his crushing of the competition, his control of her in the bedroom—because it was sexy to be wanted that way. But she couldn't be with a man who traded on the so-called heroism of the man who fooled the world. If he couldn't see that, then Eli Cooper was not the man she thought he was.

*The weather outside can bite me . . .* The misery index inside was twenty below.

She looked around, craving a distraction. Derek to tell a dumb joke, Murphy to poke at her so she could whip out the bitch-slap, Kinsey and Darcy . . . to come rushing in like there was a flash sale on Victoria's Secret undies?

"Did you see it?" Darcy shrieked, her eyes alive with excitement.

"Of course she hasn't seen it," Kinsey said. "Would she be standing here as calm as a Hindu cow if she had seen it?"

Everyone stared at her.

"Hindu cows are revered and safe from danger," Kinsey clarified. "Hence, their calm."

Okay. "What am I supposed to have seen?" If Eli Cooper had sent her another text-by-building, she was going to be furious, then thrilled, then furious again.

"Eli called an impromptu press conference."

Alex rolled her eyes. "Was I the subject of this press conference?"

"No," her girls chorused.

*Oh.* Well.

"Didn't mention you once," Kinsey said, rubbing it in, a devilish gleam in her hazel eyes.

Disappointment chilled the space around Alex's hammering heart. Eli giving up on the woo so soon was more disheartening than she expected.

Darcy handed over her phone. "Watch."

Murphy and Phelan leaned in, Gage laid a chin on her shoulder, and she angled the phone so they could all see it better, then pressed the play button on the screen. The video started with Eli striding into the media room at city hall, a god among mortals, dressed impeccably, except his tie was askew and his hair looked like it did after a vigorous bout of debate. The horizontal kind.

Had he already sought out familiar female comfort? There was no sign of Madison. Maybe she was rearranging her clothing back in the mayor's office.

"*I have a prepared statement. I won't be taking questions.*"

His voice was low, dangerous, and as always, demanding of the fullest attention. A shiver of dread passed through her, like someone had danced on her grave.

"*Almost four years ago, a few weeks after I took office as mayor, I came into possession of certain information about my father, Weston Cooper. This information, after I'd verified its accuracy, confirmed that my father had been engaged in a criminal conspiracy with Ronan Cutler, who was being investigated by the state's attorney's office at the time. The conspiracy involved my father revealing the moves of law enforcement and ensuring decisions by the state's attorney's office would be settled or manipulated in favor of Mr. Cutler and his associates. When my father decided to end this relationship, he was murdered by Mr. Cutler along with my mother.*"

The hitch in his throat at the mention of his mom ripped Alex's heart out of her chest.

*"Although I had this information, I chose to keep it to myself for largely selfish reasons. I had just been elected and I convinced myself that it would have no bearing on my ability to do the job. I was my father's son, but I did not emerge from the Chicago political machine, and in my hubris, I believed that I was above politics. I could separate myself from the past. From my father's misdeeds."*

He paused at that moment. Looked out at the media vultures, but it was as if he didn't see them. It might have been her imagination in thinking his eyes tilted toward the camera.

Toward her.

*"I was wrong. My father's false legacy as a great man gunned down for doing his job has gained me considerable political capital, even to this day. My use of it is an insult to the brave men and women who have and continue to put their lives on the line in the exercise of their duty every day. I have not engaged in any illegal activity, though I recognize that this claim might be suspect considering the source. But I have lied to people I cared"*—he paused—*"care about and manipulated the public trust. So yes, in that sense, I am my father's son."*

"Knew he was a crook," Murphy muttered, only to be hushed loudly by everyone else huddled around the phone.

*"I am not withdrawing from the race. At this point I would rather let the Chicago citizens decide how this information might affect their vote. I recognize that this puts a different spin on things. In fact, I hope to God it does."* He stared at the camera again, those ice-pick blues challenging anyone who was listening.

*"I've been in a number of tricky situations, both personally and professionally, but none of them compare to the fight I am in now. The fight of my life."*

Alex clamped her hand to her mouth. *The fight of my life.*

Did he mean her?

The media room at city hall erupted, but Eli was already a ghost, the video's end as abrupt as his exit. Shaking, Alex set the phone down on the bar and glared at it.

"That . . . that . . . idiot!" Not as colorful as her usual, but the best she could manage under the circumstances.

Five sets of eyes stared at her in shock.

"He's only gone and demolished his chances."

Kinsey narrowed her gaze. "Did you know about this? About his father? Is this why . . . ?" She waved a hand.

Alex rubbed her forehead. "Yes, he told—" She clammed up as Murphy and Derek were watching avidly. She'd been about to blab about Cochrane's involvement, with his daughter and the gossips of Engine 6 in earshot.

"Let's take this somewhere else," Kinsey said, moving toward the other end of the bar.

"The public has a right to know," Murphy whined.

"Read a newspaper," Gage muttered.

Alex grabbed the Macallan and poured four extra-large doubles.

"You, too." She pushed the glass toward Darcy. After Alex had downed her whiskey, she placed both palms on the bar.

"I think . . . I think he did that for me."

Darcy's expression was so animated that it was almost a shame to see the joy wiped off her face when she sipped the scotch. She stared at the glass like it had slapped her, then regrouped. "Certainly looks like it. He does something manipulative and dishonest, and now he's wiping the slate clean with the one thing that will likely destroy his political future. It's so romantic."

Kinsey pursed her lips. "This from the girl who had a hissy fit when her man told her seven years later that he'd dumped her for her own good when they were teenagers."

Darcy shrugged. "But I recognized that Beck's decision was good for us in the long run. Eli's had this information and he could have continued to hold on to it. He could have waited until after tomorrow when he would have been assured of the win. It's not as if he could be driven out later—he's not the criminal here. But telling people now, that's . . ." She trailed off, apparently overcome with awe at Eli's seemingly selfless actions.

Alex knew the feeling.

Yet the hurt and suspicious part of her wouldn't let go. "But all these years he kept this secret, used it to prop himself up. How can I give him a pass on that?"

"You loved Sean, didn't you?" Darcy shot back.

Alex jolted at the snappish tone in her friend's voice and slid a glance at Gage and Kinsey. They merely shrugged, clearly as clueless as Alex.

"Of course."

"Well, Eli loved his dad, too. He looked up to him, patterned his own life after the blueprint Weston Cooper created. He even went further and joined the

Marines, and I bet his father's memory was first and foremost that day he enlisted. Just like your heroes drove your decision to join CFD. What if you found out that Sean had been setting fires to make himself look like a hero, maybe even the blaze that killed him and Logan?"

"I'd be crushed," Alex said quietly.

Darcy's eyes flashed. "Eli found out that the man he had worshipped as a father and a hero was a fraud. Not only that, but this same man is the reason his mom is dead. Maybe he's made some kind of sketchy peace with that over the last few years, but think how hard it must have been for him. How it must have destroyed him. I don't pretend to know his motives for keeping it to himself. Political, self-serving, whatever. But maybe part of it was this need to hold on to the man who had defined his life. Keep the Weston Cooper he remembered alive." She knocked back the whiskey, grimaced— bless her heart—and slammed her glass down with a *so there*.

Alex's lungs had gone on hiatus. She knew Eli had adored his father before his world had been turned upside down, inside out. First with his parents' deaths, then with the revelation about his father. Hearing that must have been like Weston Cooper dying all over again. And here she was judging him for his actions when she had no idea what pain he'd endured to make those calls. Instead of comforting him, she'd made it all about her.

*Walk a mile, Alex.*

If she ever needed the wisdom of her posse, it was now.

"Gage, what do you think?"

"I think he's a piece of work, sis." He threw an arm around her shoulders and squeezed. "And I hate that he hurt you, but throwing himself on the grenade like that? It's just wild. And Christ knows he's probably the only guy who can handle how difficult you get." He added a cheeky grin.

Next, she met Kinsey's gaze, needing the guidance of this woman who was as much big sister as she was friend.

The ice-cool blonde looked disgusted as she thumbed in Darcy's direction. "Hallmark Movie here might have a point."

Darcy fist pumped the air. "You need to go down to city hall now! Like Hugh Grant in *Notting Hill*."

Kinsey's brows drew together. "Press conference is over, D," and then to Alex, "Babe, you're going to have to decide if this is a true leaf-turning moment—"

"Or just another move on the board," Alex finished.

"What I know for sure," Kinsey said as she extracted her phone and scanned the screen with an imperious eye, "is that right now, my boss is freaking the fuck out."


"So Madison must be having kittens." Brady passed a double scotch over to Eli, then took a sip of his own.

"Siberian tiger–sized ones." He'd switched off his phone and holed up at Brady's to get away from the press, but mostly from his campaign manager. She was pissed to all hell at him, and not quite so appreciative of the fact that he had merely followed her advice:

He'd walked into that media room, and all he saw was Alexandra.

Going deep cover also meant that Alexandra couldn't get ahold of him—if she wanted to. He longed to go to her, fall on his knees, and tell her in private what he had already said in public. Had she understood what he was doing? *This is how much I love you. I will destroy every barrier that separates us even if I end up destroying myself.*

But who knew if it had any impact on her? Maybe she saw it as just another desperate stunt. The last play of a play-ah.

Best to let her sleep on it. She was the queen of the knee-jerk reaction, and any decision on her part should come from a well-thought-out place. He would ride out the next twenty-four hours alone. Or with a bottle of scotch as shotgun.

"Gage on shift tonight?" he asked Brady, silently praying he wouldn't be here turning the scene into *The Penis Monologues*.

"At the bar."

Maybe that's where she was. His feet itched to charge over there and—what, exactly? Reap his reward for telling the truth at last?

"You want to see her," Brady affirmed.

"So fucking bad." Eli leaned back in the armchair and surveyed Brady's loft. In the last couple of months, he'd added some comfortable furniture so it was less East Berlin industrial and more Chicago chic livable. Feathering his nest with Gage, he supposed.

"But I've done a lot of the running in this relationship and I need a sign from her that she wants this as much as I do. Wants us."

Brady nodded his understanding. "It was the same with Gage—except he was chasin' me down and I couldn't figure out why." A big smile lit up his face. "Of course, *I'm* not the most eligible bachelor this side of the Mississippi—"

"Fuck you."

"And I ain't been featured in *People*'s Sexiest Man Alive issue."

"Jesus."

"Twice," Brady tacked on with smug grin.

Throwing the scotch would be a waste of good liquor, so Eli lobbed a cushion, which Brady caught with ease.

Eli sipped again, relishing the burn down his throat, taking a moment to find his way in the conversation. "That's what I'm worried about. That I'm all shiny surfaces, too glib and shallow for a woman like that. Or that it's all she'll see. I fessed up not just so that I could make this black cloud that's followed me around forever disappear, but also so I could be worthy of her. Look at her people, what they did, what they do." He had never had to fight to impress— or win—a woman before. Low-down, in the dirt, bare-knuckled combat. The notion that looks, charm, or sheer willpower might not be enough was sobering.

Brady squinted at him, looking as thoughtful as Eli had ever seen him. "Has she seen you at your worst?"

From the cavalcade of stunts he had pulled to make her his to confessing how he had covered up his father's crimes, Eli would say Alexandra had seen a side of him that was not exactly exemplary.

He nodded.

Brady dropped his gaze to the tumbler of amber liquid in his hand. "What you've done for me and your country, what you've done for this city, and what you did in that press conference . . ." He met Eli's gaze head-on. "I'd say that she's also seen you at your best. And if she can't put all those parts together and understand the whole messy, fucked-up, human picture, then she hasn't seen you."

# CHAPTER TWENTY-FIVE

The Drake, headquarters of the Cooper campaign, was a madhouse. City hall staffers, grasping hangers-on, sharp-clawed media, political wonks—you name it, everyone who wanted to either bask in Eli's victory or wave him on to the gates of hell was here. His revelation had thrown the race wide open as the city grappled with what it meant for their vote. Was he a charlatan like his father or merely a good man trying to make the best of the bad hand dealt to him? Since the polls had shut an hour ago, the decision was balanced on a knife's edge, too close to call.

No one who could help was answering Alex's calls. Kinsey couldn't get ahold of Madison, and Alex had tried to call Eli but he wasn't picking up. Just hearing his voice on the message sent her stomach into a lurch. So cool, so dominant. So Eli.

After her shift at the bar, she had tangled up the sheets and lain awake all night thinking. Thinking was not something she did well. Snap decisions? She was a pro, but a clear analysis of what was good for her? Not her strong suit. A visit to Sean and Logan's snowy graves in Roseland had helped some to unravel the knotted ball of thoughts. What Eli had done, the blow he had dealt to his campaign and his political future . . . she had to believe he did it for her. Coming clean was his way of showing her he had changed. That she had changed him.

He had taken a risk when the reward was unknowable. Possibly negligible. She needed to risk it all right back.

He was likely holed up with a team in a hotel room, ready to descend to pump his fist in victory or hang his head in defeat. Trying to look like she had every right to be here, she approached the elevators with a vague plan to get off at each floor above fifteen and drop-kick anyone standing sentry in a suit and dark glasses.

"Are you a guest at the hotel, miss?" A suit, likely CPD, halted her progress at the elevator bank.

"No, I'm . . ."—*America's Favorite Firefighter, the mayor's savior, Eli Cooper's woman*—"I'm not." Doubts furrowed soul-deep ruts in her mind. She was nothing. She had no right to be here, no reason to expect Eli would see her. Surely he would have answered her calls if he wanted her here? Come see her if that media room confession was his way of saying he truly loved her?

She gave what she hoped was a winning smile. "I need to see the mayor."

Dark Suit twitched his nose. "Only people with clearance can see the mayor." Pronounced *da mayor*.

"Have we got a problem here?"

Alex turned to the sultry voice to find Madison Maitland, looking less like the cool, sophisticated campaign manager and more like a woman on the edge. At least three hairs were out of place. Alex's day had started off as a crapfest, and now it had just gotten ten times worse.

"I need to see Eli," she said, trying to infuse Dempsey bravado into that statement.

Madison stared at her, her lips sealed, her perfectly plucked eyebrows veed in thought.

"Okay."

Alex flinched. "What?"

Madison flicked a glance at Suit 'n' Glasses. "She's clear to go up."

He opened his mouth to protest but shut it at whatever he saw on Madison's face. The woman had the crush-your-balls look down.

They stepped into the elevator together. There was no Muzak, no talking, just staring at their fun-house mirror reflections in the brushed stainless steel. Anything to avoid the shit ton of awkward that was stinking up the space.

"How are the numbers?" Alex finally asked, because the elevator was making the slowest ascent ever.

"It'll come down to the last precinct, the last vote." Madison sounded strangely energized. The elevator reached the eighteenth floor. The doors fell open. Another security guard checked and nodded at Madison while coolly assessing Alex.

Madison walked into the corridor, with Alex following.

The elegant brunette stopped and faced her. "He made a deal with Cochrane last summer so you wouldn't be sued. Kinsey's handling of the video and that petition kept your job, but it was Eli who fixed it with Sam on the lawsuit. Let himself get pulled deeper into that fucker's web. I knew Cochrane had something on Eli but he never told me what it was. What his father had done." She chuckled mirthlessly. "You wouldn't believe how impressed he was when he saw that video of you cutting up Cochrane's car. He thought you were so brave."

Alex snorted, her eyes filling with tears. "Not so brave when someone else has to clean up your mess." Kinsey and Eli had done that for her, and she had spent months blaming other people for her crazy behavior. As if her loyalty to her family excused everything. And then she had castigated Eli for his loyalty to his own family.

Now this. He had thrown himself on his sword because he loved her more than he loved being king. And she loved him. So much. No trick, no manipulation. Her imperfect hero.

"That's what we do for the people we love," Madison said, a genuine smile now lighting up her sharp-boned face. "We make sacrifices, clean up messes, lie, cheat, steal to win them. He didn't know it at the time, but the moment he met you, he was a goner."

Alex's heart threatened to bust out of her chest. How wrong to feel this much joy when Eli's election chances were still teetering on the brink. But her heart had always been her biggest liability—and her largest asset. It got her into trouble and steered her to this man.

"I've cost him the election."

Madison shrugged, put her hand on the doorknob to a room at the end of the corridor. "Possibly. But he'll be the first person to say he won the true campaign anyway."

• • •

Eli was glued to the TV in the hotel suite, waiting for the last few ward results to trickle in. What the hell were the counters doing down there? Eating fucking pizza instead of tallying the damn ballots, he'd lay odds.

It was much too close. But when you threw a wrench in the works like he had, then it was always going to be a Sisyphean task. For every voter who admired his honesty there were two who thought the apple didn't fall far from the tree. For every woman who swooned at his romantic gestures there were three who hated that his heart belonged to another.

The local NBC news affiliate was busy detailing his demise with their typical glee. Last week, he'd been the most romantic man in America. This week, he was a conniving monster. Can't win for losing.

"Quiet," Kenneth called out to the chatty staffers, "the fifteenth ward is in."

*"Results from the fifteenth ward and it goes to . . . Caroline Jenkins. That places her at 49.2 percent of the vote against Mayor Cooper's 48.8 with six wards left to report."*

Low curses blanketed the room, but then his team got back to work making calls and checking in with polling stations. Anything to avoid looking at him. More than once, he found a staffer, usually female, gazing at him with a mix of wonder and pity before dropping her eyes in embarrassment. Only a fool would shoot himself in the ass like he had, that look said.

"Eli," he heard behind him. Madison.

"Any news from the forty-eighth?" he asked without turning.

"Howdy, Mr. Mayor."

He shuttered his eyes against the possibility he might be imagining her presence. She had come to him at last. Slowly, he turned as if that could ensure she wouldn't bolt, but Alexandra Dempsey was not a runner. She was the bravest person he knew.

"Sucks to be you right now," she murmured.

He coughed out a laugh. Not at all. It was great to be him.

She was wearing jeans and those favorite boots of hers and that parka he had peeled off her at the Hawks–Red Wings game, then later that night when he made her come. Twice.

*Get your mind out of the gutter, Cooper.*

But he couldn't. Thinking of the woman before him inevitably led to lust, as well as admiration, respect, fury, and love. Every part of her appealed to every part of him, and his heart howled to be completed by her touch.

"Let's talk, Alexandra."

He walked toward the bedroom of the suite and pushed through the door. She followed and shut the door behind her.

"Eli, what you did—"

"Do you mind if I speak first? I need to get it off my chest before you say something nice." She was here, so that had to be a good sign, but he refused to take anything for granted.

She bit down on that fleshy pillow of her lower lip.

"Seeing as I don't do nice, that's rather optimistic on your part, but okay."

Still busting his balls. Perfect.

He inhaled what felt like the deepest breath of his life. "This is probably not news to you, but I'm a dick. I'm a complete asshole. I'm everything you've ever called me and probably a few things that hillbilly trucker mouth of yours hasn't thought of yet. From the beginning, I've been trying to control everything. It's how I've always powered through all the shit I've endured. Through every situation. Hell, I sabotaged a date because I didn't want someone else to have you."

She smiled, a ray of sun cracking the clouds. "It was a lousy date anyway."

"I used an extremely underhanded method to force you to spend time with me."

"Well, I probably would have shot you down." Her brow furrowed. "Maybe instead of focusing on all your nefarious shenanigans, you should start selling me on awesome Eli."

He scrubbed his mouth. "I'm only realizing now that winning the election was secondary, Alexandra. Winning you was always my evil plan. You were right to despise me, to call me out on my shit. You were right to do everything in your power to resist me because I wasn't the man for you. I wasn't worthy. Maybe you sensed that."

She touched his lips with two cool fingers. "I'm going to stop you there. I have no right to demand you make yourself worthy to win me. To change for me."

He took her hand, kissed her palm. Just being able

to touch her like this made him wild with joy. "Honey, you do. You've every right to demand that you get the man you deserve and, hell, if I can't change for you, then I can't change. Before I met you, I was pretty numb. Since you've entered my life, I feel everything to the max. The food I eat with you is the best I've ever tasted. The orgasms I have with you are the best I've ever experienced. The breaths I take with you are the fullest I've ever drawn."

The corner of her lush mouth quirked. "Food, orgasms, breathing. Very important."

"They are! They're all worth fighting for. We're worth fighting for. You said I never saw you as an equal and you were right, but not the way you think. You're a goddess and I'm not worthy to worship at your feet, but I'm happy to spend the rest of my life trying to be good enough for you."

"Eli." Uttering his name in a throaty whisper, she placed her palm on his chest. So soft, and yet she completely undid him. His heart leaped, reacting to his woman's strength wrapped around it. The cage of her hand, the mistress of his soul.

"Oh, God, Eli, I said you could confide in me. That I would be there for you if you ever needed to talk, and the first time you opened your heart, I fucking blew it."

"It was a lot to take in. I don't blame you for how you reacted. Not a bit."

She looked forlorn. "And then what you did in that press conference . . . I know I goaded you, but it was never meant to destroy your campaign, you moron!"

"Yet there would have been no other way to prove

to you how much I love you." He gathered her close. "You held up a mirror and showed me what I'd become. How I'd risked turning into him with every gray decision and every turn of the card. I needed to break his legacy, annihilate it, because I could no longer let it remain tied to mine. I'm my own man. Not Weston Cooper's son, not Sam Cochrane's puppet. But with that said, I'll still happily admit to being a slave to another."

Her smile was shy, not like his Alexandra at all. "Is this person difficult, mouthy, liable to say the wrong thing, and a general all-around pain in your ass?"

"Yep. And my heart belongs to her completely."

She squeezed his hand. "And her heart belongs to you, too. Unfortunately for you and your political future, her mouth and family come with it."

He grinned and pulled her into his arms. Never letting go.

"Many years ago at my parents' funeral, Alexandra, your father told me to call on him if I ever needed anything. I never did make that call, but I knew he was there for me, and that if the occasion had arisen, he would have welcomed me with open arms."

"He would have. He did." Tears sparkled like glossy jewels on her lower lashes. "Eli, I think Sean's spirit was with me the night of the fire, looking out for both of us. Making sure I'd be strong enough to save you. That we'd be strong enough to save each other."

A connection forged in fire. Mutual life debts, mutual responsibility. "The universe is telling us something. Or someone up there thinks we should stop screwing around and make a go of this."

She sniffed. "Thought you didn't believe in the fairy tale."

"Who needs the fairy tale when crazy, messy, sexy reality with the woman I adore is a million times better?"

"Eli, I love you so much." The tears that had been threatening for the last five minutes finally spilled down her cheeks. "And now you've made me cry. Again. You—you prick!"

"Aw, honey, let me kiss it better." He claimed her mouth, swallowing her laugh-sob, savoring her emotion. They stayed that way for a few blissful moments, until their pulse rates calmed to manageable levels.

"I know what's going on here," she whispered against his mouth, a breathy hitch in her voice.

"You do?"

She smiled through her tears. "All these years, you've been an honorary Dempsey under that sexy skin."

"God, I can't *wait* to tell Luke."

Her husky laugh rocked his world. "If they love you a tenth as much as I do, then you should be in good shape."

"I know. I've witnessed it and I've got so much to learn."

He knew she would teach him, carry him the rest of the way. Just like that night in the hotel when she infused his body with air. With new and wondrous life. Eli Cooper was one lucky son of a bitch to have been rescued by Firefighter Alexandra Dempsey.

There was a tentative knock.

"Yes," they both said together, then grinned inane smiles.

"Sorry to disturb," Madison spoke through the door, "but the forty-eighth ward results are in and it looks like a couple more are about to call it."

"Be right out." He gathered his love close and lowered his lips to hers in a kiss that joined their souls and forged that fiery connection anew. Win or lose, he could handle anything, because he had the prize in his hands right now. This inimitable woman.

"You ready for whatever comes next?"

Her radiant smile was filled with love and desire. With hope for their future together, come what may. He still couldn't believe his luck.

"Whatever happens, Eli Cooper, you'll always be the tricky, complicated, sexy, devious bastard I love." She stepped toward the door and held out her hand. *I'm here*, he heard in his head. *I'm not leaving*.

"Let's go give 'em hell."

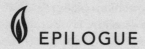 EPILOGUE

*E*TA *10 mins. Order a Glenlivet in 5.*

Alex frowned at the text message from her date. Where had she heard that one before? So damn bossy, but then that was why she loved him.

It was probably foolish to expect that Eli's first day on the job would end at a reasonable hour, but she still held out hope that he could get here for a celebratory dinner at Smith & Jones before she took to eating the napkins.

Losing the election to Caroline Jenkins—twice, if you included the recount after the vote was so close—had been a considerable blow. But nothing kept a man like Eli Cooper down. Within four months, he had put in place everything necessary to open a private law practice dedicated to the needs of returning veterans. His calling would always be service oriented. He was an honorary Dempsey, after all.

*You're already a round behind,* she texted back.

*My evil plan. Get you drunk and horny.*

Warmth spread through her, and it wasn't down to

her second Macallan. A server arrived at the booth, their regular table at S & J, with a platter covered in one of those fancy silver domes. This place got more and more pretentious by the second.

"Compliments of the chef." She whipped off the dome and walked away.

Alex stared. Blinked. Stared some more.

At a blue velvet ring box. Just sitting there, at the center of the platter, ostensibly minding its own business, but really demanding every shred of her attention. Furtively, she looked around to see if anyone else was watching, but the hipsters were too self-involved tonight. America's Favorite Firefighter had finally become a footnote in the city's history.

Beside the box lay a scroll of paper, like one of those ancient legal documents, tied with a pretty pink bow. Her secret favorite color, which matched exactly the new lingerie she had charged to her account that afternoon at En Cachette. Sexy unmentionables she could feel in a silky, sensuous slide against her skin.

Every girly girl instinct screamed, *Go for the bling!* but she elected to keep it classy. First time for everything. She untied the bow and unrolled the paper to reveal a letter in Eli's sprawling, masculine hand.

*Alexandra,*

She shivered her pleasure. Even in print, his use of her full name curled her toes.

*You can see the box, so you know what it means. But it also means so much more. You've put me through the wringer already and I like to think*

*I've repaid you in kind. I hope you're ready for a life of adventure with a guy who hasn't always said it right but has always known what he wanted.*

*I told you once that I met someone. I also told you that this woman was a pain in my ass, sexy as hell, foul-mouthed, absolutely gorgeous, and that I was obsessed with her. What I didn't say then was that I had fallen in love with her, probably that first moment I saw her in this restaurant. Likely the moment she told me I was a patriarchal, woman-hating asshole. Definitely the moment she destroyed the four-hundred-thousand-dollar car of one of the city's most prominent citizens. Because that was the moment she destroyed my heart and any hope I had of resisting her.*

*You know I don't believe in fairy tales, but I believe in writing my own story. It wouldn't be much of a yarn without you in it, chewing the scenery, providing cliff-hangers in every chapter, and ensuring that each precious day of our lives together is a page-turner. I want to travel with you to wild and untamed places, in the world and in my heart, scale jaw-dropping cliff faces, and descend into dark alleys where no doubt you'll rescue me like you've done from the start.*

*So, my beautiful Alexandra, will you take my hand and be my love from here on out?*

*Eli Cooper, Esquire*

*P.S. Go Cubbies! (You now know everything about me.)*

Hot tears filled her eyes and fell in fat drops onto Eli's note. His proposal to love her despite the fact she was difficult, foul-mouthed, and a pain in his ass seized her heart with a cutting joy. And she still hadn't seen the ring.

Instinctively, her hand moved toward it, but a big, dominant paw got there first. She raised her gaze to the face of the man she adored. My, he looked handsome in a charcoal gray suit with a blue-and-silver chevroned tie. She couldn't wait to rip that tie off and let him use it as a blindfold or restraint or . . . hmm, one thing at a time. There was another kind of proposal on the table.

He slid into the booth and curled his strong arm around her shoulder. His assessing glance at her cleavage confirmed she'd made the right purchase that afternoon.

"Did you order my scotch?"

"I got distracted," she said, laughing as she swiped at her tears. She wanted to kill him for getting her all worked up like this. "And you're late."

"Traffic from the bar to the table was a bitch."

"You were here all along."

He grazed his lips against her earlobe and nipped gently. "You know I like to watch."

Heated pleasure bloomed across her chest and up her neck. They'd gotten a lot of use out of that floor-length mirror over the last few months.

"Weirdo, stalker, jagoff—"

"You planning to kiss my cock later with that mouth?" He stopped her litany of insults with a searing kiss that rearranged her gray matter. She would never get enough of him.

Cupping his lantern jaw, she broke the connection and inhaled a fortifying breath. "Tell me about your day."

"Alexandra—"

"I need to know." Guilt over her man's incredible sacrifice still gnawed at her. She had to know he'd be happy with this new life. With the woman who'd upended all his plans.

Understanding dawned on his Hollywood-handsome face. "My client roster is full. I'll be helping a lot of people who need it. Believe me when I say I have not one single regret, and that you are the hottest, scariest, and best thing to ever happen to me." He picked up the scroll of paper. "Goddamn it, I'm a lawyer who just put my heart's desire in writing. Now, say yes, honey, and make an honest man of me."

Honest? Impossible.

"Is that an order, Mr. Cooper?"

"I think we know you've always been the one in charge, Firefighter Dempsey," adding with a wolfish grin, "Outside the bedroom, anyway."

She smiled through her threatening tears, pleased with that. Now that she had passed her one-year anniversary in CFD and was a full-fledged firefighter, she was planning her next career move: to become the first woman in Chicago to join squad, the unit that covered dive, collapse, and all manner of tricky rescues. She hadn't told Eli yet, but she knew he'd have her back. On the mornings she came home from her shift at Engine 6, he hugged her so tight to his body he almost squeezed the life out of her. He might never fully come to terms with the dangers she faced in the job she loved, but he didn't nag. Just gave her the support and respect she needed.

Alex Dempsey 2.0 could retreat back to her hidey-hole. Kick-ass Alexandra was here to stay.

"Go on. Show me this ring, then."

He flipped up the lid to reveal a pink—of course—diamond ring set in a bed of clear jewels. She knew nothing about cuts or carats, but she knew enough to recognize the box as Tiffany and the size as planetary. Those investments must be doing very well indeed.

He plucked the ring from its velvet bed and slipped in onto her finger so fast her head spun.

"I haven't said yes."

"Just see how it looks," he murmured.

The master manipulator struck again. And it did look wonderful on her hand, just as the man felt wonderful wrapped around her body, heart, and soul.

Dragging her blurred gaze away from the ring, she looked into those ice-blue eyes, softer now with his love for her, and came to two inevitable conclusions.

This man was incredibly blessed to have met her, and . . .

"Yes, Eli Cooper, I'll marry you." She kissed his smiling and oh-so-wicked mouth. "Consider yourself saved."

Keep reading for a sneak peek of

# SPARKING

## THE

# FIRE

## By KATE MEADER

The third sizzling installment in the
Hot in Chicago series

Available in 2016 from Pocket Books!

# CHAPTER ONE

"You can go right in, Firefighter Fox. He's waiting for you."

Wyatt Fox nodded at Kathy, the firehouse's perky admin as he stood outside the cap's office, contemplating his next move. The *going in* part was a foregone conclusion—he had been summoned after all—but how he would handle what lay behind that door was still up in the air. Normally, Wyatt would have knocked. Raised his right hand, curled his fingers into a fist, and rapped the door. But he had a pass to just waltz in, so mercifully he didn't have to complete even that simplest of motions. He didn't have to be reminded that the tendons in his shoulder were shredded like Mini-Wheats after he'd wrenched it during a tricky rescue two weeks back. Either that or let that shithead—sorry, *citizen*—take a header off the LaSalle Street Bridge.

Suicide attempt averted. Three months off squad his reward.

Unless he could somehow persuade the cap that it wasn't as bad as all that.

He gripped the doorknob with purpose, ignored the wince even that small action produced, and strode in like a man without a care in the world.

Captain Matt "Venti" Ventimiglia lifted his gaze from a file on his desk.

"Fox."

Venti was a pretty cool cat, not one for small talk, which Wyatt appreciated, especially as his own family could talk the hind legs off a herd of mules. Sitting at the dinner table with the Dempseys—his cobbled together foster family—was like an episode of the *Brady Bunch* on steroids. And now that they all had hearts-and-flowers happy-ever-afters to call their own, it approached Disney to the nth degree at every gathering.

Wyatt took the seat Venti gestured at.

"At least three months, according to the doc," the cap said.

Good, straight to it. "Docs can be wrong."

"If you push it and make it worse"—he knifed a look with that—"then you could be looking at six months or more."

"I'm not good at sitting around," Wyatt said, as if that was a valid enough reason to put him back on active duty. It was a family trait, both Dempsey and the original. His biological dad was never one for letting the grass grow under his feet, always keeping Wyatt and his brother, Logan, on the move. Needs must, when you're trying to stay one step ahead of the law.

The cap sniffed. "You hear about Dave Kowalski?"

The change-up gave Wyatt pause, but as he wasn't having any luck going against the tide, he figured he'd swim with it for a while.

"Hollywood Dave? Word's out that he's looking

at six weeks in traction." Kowalski was the CFD's designated consult for that TV show about Chicago firefighters, the one where fires broke out every ten seconds (nope) and everyone was screwing their co-workers (if only). Years with his nose permanently wedged in the asses of his actor pals had apparently dulled Dave's reflexes to mush. The idiot had neglected to step out of the way when a roof caved in on him. If Venti was trying to compare their situations . . .

The cap smiled that crooked grin of his to put him at ease, knowing that Wyatt's mind had crashed the gate and was hurtling down that track.

"They need someone to take his place."

Wyatt shifted in his seat, thinking on that.

"Before you shut it down," Venti continued when Wyatt remained silent, "let me tell you it's not for the TV show. It's a ten week movie shoot from now through August. You know how the city is always looking for revenue, and to up its appeal for production companies. Cade Productions asked for someone from Engine 6 to be the consult."

Something pinged in his chest. As a firefighter—a rescue squad firefighter—Wyatt had learned long ago that his instincts were, if not exactly a friend, that guardian angel on his shoulder keeping his ass in one piece. But the reason for *this* hitch in his lungs was escaping him right this second.

"Why Engine 6?"

Venti grinned and waited a beat until Wyatt got it.

"Because of Alex. They think they'll get more play if they have an in with America's Favorite Firefighter."

Last year, his baby sister, Alexandra Dempsey, had

made a name for herself slicing up the Lamborghini of some rich douchebag who insulted the family during a road traffic accident run. And if that wasn't enough, she got herself involved with Eli Cooper, Chicago's mayor, who proceeded to tank his campaign, and subsequently lost his reelection bid to prove he loved her. The whole mess had Hollywood written all over it. But he knew his sister had turned down offers to have her romantic shenanigans immortalized on-screen. Looked like the vultures were looking for another way to skin that kitty cat.

"Might be better to keep these movie people on a short leash, don't you think?" Venti asked with a cocked eyebrow, reading Wyatt's mind. Or at the very least recognizing that "don't mess with the Dempseys" was as ingrained in Wyatt as it was in the rest of his crazy motherfuckin' family.

Wyatt sighed. There was logic there, but hanging with Hollywood types and artistes was not how he wanted to spend his rehab. It was the kind of thing his brother Gage would be better at, he of the billboards and firefighter calendars and all-around exhibitionist tendencies. Kid had never met a camera he didn't want to bang.

He was just about to offer Gage's services when something Venti had said poked his brain matter like a Halligan through termite-ridden drywall.

"Back up a sec. What's that about production companies?"

"The city wants to encourage more production companies to come here—"

"No, the other thing. The name of the production company that asked for the consult from 6."

Venti squinted. "Cade Productions. Headed up by that actress who had all that trouble last year. The big-ass divorce from Ryan Michaels, the 'I'm so exhausted' rehab, the hacked photos." The cap was well known for spending more time reading *People* than *Fire Engineering* magazine. Anyone who dared touch the latest issue before Venti laid his eyeballs on it better find latrine duty enjoyable. "This is supposed to be her big comeback—"

"And is she in the movie? Molly Cade?"

That garnered more than a squint from Venti; it earned Wyatt a skin-penetrating stare because Wyatt had sounded . . . animated. He didn't do animated for anything or anyone.

Except for Sean and Logan, his foster father and biological brother, both long gone. For Roni, as well, very much alive and vexing.

And once, for Molly Cade.

A smile spread slowly across Venti's face. Fucker. "Fan of Ms. Cade's work, are you?"

Big fan. Of how hard her tongue worked when wrapped around his cock. How good her tight, lithe body worked his until every one of his atoms had exploded in the kind of pleasure he'd never experienced before or since. They had crossed paths at a strange time in Wyatt's life. In the intervening five years, whenever her saw her on the screen, a cavalcade of what-might-have-beens marched through his brain. Ridiculous, for true. Oscar-nominated actresses who commanded multimillion dollar paydays weren't exactly his usual diet.

Not that his sex life had improved much. Definitely more watch-your-weight than three square meals.

Molly Cade was currently in his zip code. Or soon would be. Dubbed America's sweetheart in all those dumb romantic comedies when she wasn't playing some macho loser's helpless love interest in the latest summer popcorn movie, her one step outside her wheelhouse had yielded that Oscar nod for some indie film. And then it all turned to shit for her in the last year.

But before she was all that, before she was *the* Molly Cade, she was the one woman who had snuck under his skin. It would be mighty interesting to see if she had the means to make him itch like before. Come alive like before. Keeping her and her production company out of his sister's orbit would be a bonus.

He met Venti's gaze squarely, not caring what the cap might think about his sudden about-face.

"When do I start?"

"You have to admit he has a great ass."

Molly Cade turned to the speaker of that bald statement and gave her the slitty eyes. Calysta Johnson—bestie, Gal Friday, and fellow ass connoisseur—remained oblivious to Molly's glare, too busy ogling the *ass*-ets of Gideon Carter, costar on Molly's latest movie venture, *Into the Blaze*. Molly followed Cal's gaze to where Gideon the Idiot stood just as . . . yep, he rang the old-timey firehouse bell affixed to the wall of the Robert J. Quinn Fire Academy on Chicago's West Side. At the clanking din, he whooped like a frat pledge and nudged the ribs of his right-hand dickhead, Jeremy.

Molly couldn't help her sigh. "Sure, great ass. Pity it's on his shoulders."

Cal chortled. "If I was ten years younger—"

"Or had a brain injury."

"I'd be all over those perfect globes." Quirking a grin, Cal aimed a glance past the hulking steam-powered engine in the lobby and checked her phone again. "Our contact is late."

"You make it sound like a special military op. We're just meeting the Pabst Blue Ribbon–drinking, potbellied hose hauler who's going to make sure that this movie is more authentic than a Ken Burns documentary."

Cal squeezed Molly's arm. She could always tell when Molly was nervous. "Hon, this is going to be a huge success. Your way back onto the A-list, into the fickle public's hearts, and their big fat wallets."

"I don't care about being A-list or making bank on the first weekend. I just want"—she balled her fists and placed them on her hips, growling her determination—"I just want people to hear my name and not think 'Ryan Michaels's pathetic ex' or 'her tits look bigger on the silver screen than they do in those hacked photos.'"

"Well, they do look bigger. That's the magic of Hollywood."

Molly barked a reluctant laugh. Thank God for Cal, who always managed to tell it like it was and shut down those invites to the pity party.

"Speaking of photos, did you see them?" Cal jerked her chin to the west wall, where a battery of frames hung in a grid. They both moved toward them.

The Wall of the Fallen.

Molly studied the pictures, her hands behind her back, feeling a touch ghoulish. Like she was invading this sacred space. Faces shone back at her, some smiling, most not, all dressed in their CFD uniforms. Each of them someone's father, brother, son, friend. Their courage and sacrifice blanketed Molly to the point that the problems she had endured this past year paled in comparison.

Slowly, she walked past the memorial until she came to the two she recognized: Sean Dempsey and his foster son, Logan Keyes.

Sean was that stereotypical hale and ruddy-faced Irishman with the twinkle that not even his grim official photo could dull. Beside him, Logan stared out from beyond his fiery grave, a hint of a smile teasing the corner of his mouth. Nine years ago, they had given their lives, spawned a legion of bar tales, and inspired a family of foster kids to follow in their footsteps. One of them, Alexandra Dempsey, was as well-known for her on-camera and romantic exploits as she was for her bravery. Her story of fierce familial loyalty, headline-grabbing heroics, and a love for the ages—the movie poster was already designed in Molly's mind—would add the human interest element to *Into the Blaze*'s pulse-pounding action sequences. Unfortunately Alex and the CFD had stonewalled Molly's efforts to tell it. Months of no calls returned and then a sternly worded letter from former Chicago mayor, now hotshot lawyer Eli Cooper informing Cade Productions that Firefighter Dempsey's story was not for sale.

Six months of fighting tooth and nail with Ryan's lawyers for her rights and dignity had soured

Molly on smooth-talking lawyers. Where there was a will . . .

The Dempseys, as the foster siblings were collectively known, worked at Engine 6—which is why she had requested one of the company to be the consult when the usual CFD-designated tech was injured. It was a long shot, but if she could learn more about the Dempseys, find a way to connect with them, maybe they'd open up and let her tell their story. Time was nipping at her heels, though. Shooting started in two weeks, the adapted script was ready to go; it just needed the imprimatur of America's Favorite Firefighter to varnish it with the sheen of success.

This was to be Molly's comeback and it would be spectacular.

"God, they are positively smokin'." Cal held up her phone to showcase the cut body of Gage Simpson, one of the Dempseys, posing in the charity firefighter calendar that had taken the city—and country—by storm last year. "Two of them in those beefcake calendars, one of them a ripped boxer, the hot tamale sister. Wonder what the mystery brother looks like."

So did Molly. Four of the Dempseys were unafraid of the public eye, but the fifth—Wyatt Fox—remained a shadowy figure who shunned the limelight. She hadn't looked all that hard, but not a single, clear photo of Mr. Fox had come to light. Not even on Facebook.

"Probably got thrashed by the ugly stick. But the rest of 'em"—Cal gave a low whistle—"must be something in the Chicago water."

Have a care, Cal; they were standing before a monument to the city's finest and bravest. Molly turned her head, ready to admonish her friend for her crassness, only to find that Cal's mouth had fallen open and her gaze had redirected to some point over Molly's shoulder. "Or maybe it's what they're feeding them down at the firehouse," she murmured.

A curious shiver thrummed through Molly's body before she heard, "Miss Cade?"

The shiver magnified in intensity, though that wasn't right. It rocket-fuel-boosted every cell in her body to the level of a quake. She turned.

*The Marine.*

Her brain tried to compute the image before her. The same rugged features, but more weathered. The same fit body, but more space filling. The same uncompromising blue-gray eyes, but more distant.

It was also in the wrong place at the wrong time wearing the wrong . . . *nah-ah*, Chicago Fire Department T-shirt that stretched taut against chiseled pectorals, the sleeve hems pushed north by biceps she remembered gripping as he pistoned those trim hips into her over and over.

Five years ago.

Five years of climbing a pinnacle of fame to that coveted spot on the A-list. Well, four years. The last year wiped out all that had gone before. Every high, every joyful moment.

But before it all began, back in a simpler time, there had been a week—six glorious, sex-filled nights, actually—with the Marine. Who was not a Marine at all, it seemed, or no longer was.

Cal, seeing that Molly had been struck stupid, donned her personal assistant hat and stepped forward.

"Hi, I'm Calysta Johnson. I've been emailing CFD Media Affairs about today's meeting, and this is . . ."

"Miss Cade," he grated. Or perhaps Molly only imagined that husky tone, wanted to think he was affected by this reunion as much as she.

Molly felt like her legs would give out. A thundering sound started in her head. Her blood. The Marine-firefighter said something to Cal, maybe his name, but she missed it.

She had never known that name, had never wanted to. That was their unspoken agreement. No names, no history, no future. Just six nights of scorching passion and inhibitions annihilated. He had done things to her no other man had ever done. Plumbed the depths of her pleasure and scaled her to orgasmic heights she had forgotten existed during the icy wasteland of her marriage. She used to like sex. She used to like the person she was during sex, but Ryan had drilled it out of her—literally—with his all-consuming focus on himself.

"Mol?"

She turned to find Cal, eyes wide with concern.

"You okay?"

Molly swallowed. "Yes! I'm fine!" Squeaky voiced, about to fall over, but otherwise okeydokey.

She met the cool gaze of the Marine. "Mr. . . . ?"

"Fox. Wyatt Fox."

Oh. My. "God."

He stared.

She stared back. It was *him*. Not just him from all those years ago, but *him*, the elusive Dempsey. How was it possible that the man who had lit her on fire, body and soul, was also the same man who could get her closer to her heart's desire—a way in with his sister?

Wyatt Fox. It suited him. Clean, masculine, not a syllable wasted. Like James Bond, if 007 had added cowboy-Marine-firefighter to his stable of personae.

*Fox. Wyatt Fox. License to thrill—and send your panties plummeting.*

A manic giggle bubbled up from somewhere deep, the same place where illicit laughter in church originated. The wicked, don't-you-dare-Molly kind of giggle she had never been able to smother whenever Pastor Morrison delivered his sermon with a booger hanging from his nose. Every Sunday, without fail, at St. Peter's Episcopal Church in New Haven, Missouri.

She held out her hand. To distract from her tremble, she parted with that giggle. Wily move, she thought.

Wyatt Fox stared at her as if she had lost her mind. *Don't worry, Marine, that train left the station long ago.* Only now was she starting to put the splintered mess back together again.

She cleared her throat, drawing on Serious Molly. Though she was quite enjoying this giddy version. It had been awhile.

"Thanks so much for meeting with us today."

No reaction. Whatsoever.

God, this was priceless. The one guy on the planet who could probably map all her freckles and he clearly didn't remember a single one—or her! But that had been their game, hadn't it? Each night, they would circle each other in that hotel bar as though they were strangers, as though they hadn't already memorized every inch of each other's bodies, the pulse points, the weak spots, every breathy sound.

Could he be reverting to their previous dynamic? Is that why he was looking at her as though she was nothing to him? Or had she truly made so little impact?

He dwarfed her hand in his giant one, squeezed once, and let go. As if her touch offended him. No, she was reading far too much into this.

"Miss Cade."

"Molly. Call me Molly."

The prickle of heat on the back of her neck could only mean one thing.

Cal was staring at her and compiling a list of questions in her head to be brought out later over a bottle of Pinot.

"Hey, do you guys, uh . . . know each other?"

Or why wait? Just get it out there and clear the air. *Thanks, babe.*

Not a muscle moved in the Marine's—*Wyatt's*—face, not even an eyelash, but then . . . then . . . *yes!* A slight rise of his eyebrow, like the ghost of a breeze fluttering practically invisible molecules. He *did* remember. The enormity of his reaction, and what it meant, smashed her to the ground.

He was feigning ignorance, allowing her the freedom to admit or deny.

For the past five years, her life had not been her own. A Faustian bargain she had made knowingly, of course. Hello fame, good-bye privacy. But those hacked photos infecting the Internet, that *violation,* had not been her choice.

Her heart clenched at Wyatt's small gesture of discretion. Gallantry. So perhaps banging Molly fifteen ways from Sunday before she was famous might not be worth bragging about, but any other guy would be salivating at the chance to compose a headline of *Hot Nights in the Sack with Molly Cade!* Instead Wyatt was giving her the choice whether to reveal their past affair.

Tears pricked her eyelids at the unexpected kindness. *Get it together, Mol.*

This prior connection could *not* get out. She was trying to rehabilitate her sorry rep, not create more gossip for the gutter rags. Which is why she really should not have said in answer to Cal's question about whether they knew each other, "Depends on your definition of 'know.'"

One razor-straight eyebrow shot up, hovered near the cocoa brown hairline, and lowered slowly. How gratifying to be able to throw him like that. He had always been so unshockable.

"We had some mutual interests once," Wyatt said, a devilish gleam in those blue-gray eyes. "Bars. Shakespeare." Sexy pause. "Elevators."

Heat rose to her cheeks.

*Point to you, Mr. Fox.*